The
House
Between
Tides

The House Between Tides

Sarah Maine

**FREIGHT
BOOKS**

First published in the UK as Bhalla Strand 2014
This edition revised and updated and published in the UK as
The House Between Tides 2016

Freight Books
49–53 Virginia Street
Glasgow, G1 1TS
www.freightbooks.co.uk

A CIP catalogue reference for this book is available from the British
Library.

ISBN 978-1-910449-78-3

Typeset by Freight in Plantin
Printed and bound by Bell and Bain, Glasgow

the publisher acknowledges investment from
Creative Scotland toward the publication of this book

For Richard

Prologue

∼ *1945* ∼

The woman stood a moment on the old drive and stared up at the boarded windows, a dark silhouette against the grey walls, then she turned her back on the house and went down to the blaze on the foreshore.

Figures moved in the smoky shadows, small awed groups, lingering after the drama of the auction. They drew back as she approached, a gaunt stranger in a black coat, and a whisper rustled amongst them. *Piuthar Blake!* She drew nearer to the flames. *Bho Lunnainn…* Gusts of wind formed small tornadoes of sparks, and the woman's eyes followed them until they faded over the drained stretches of sand. *Blake's sister. From London.* An outsider now. More of the house's contents crashed onto the pyre—a broken display cabinet from the study, an easel riddled with woodworm. The flames were suppressed for a moment, then leapt to consume the offering—and a way of life.

Earlier in the day there had been a macabre episode when the moth-eaten birds and animals had been brought out, their glassy eyes catching the flames, flashing a sharp reproach. A hotel owner had bought the stag's head from the landing and the rarities had been sent to Edinburgh, while anyone who fancied a tatty guillemot as a souvenir had bid a few pennies. The rest, dusty and faded, had gone onto the bonfire, and she had watched them burn. But she had turned away when the once prized black-and-white diver from the dining room was brought out. It had been found in the back of an old boot cupboard, ravaged by mice, together with more paintings, wrapped in old hessian, too late for the auctioneer's hammer. The paintings had shocked her: the tormented scenes and heavy brushstrokes exposed too painfully the anguish of her brother's broken mind, and she had ordered that they too be destroyed. All except one, a watercolour which she remembered well, painted when his talent had been at its outstanding best, and she lingered over it while the others burned, then put it carefully to one side.

A figure approached her. 'That's the last of it, Mrs. Armstrong.' It was Donald. She turned and nodded, smiling slightly, and they stood together, the flames casting flickering shadows across their faces.

'Do you remember the last fire you and I sat beside?' she said, wistful now for other times, and watched his face until the memory found him.

'The day we all went to see the seal pups? Cooked fish on the beach?'

She gave an echo of her puckish smile, grateful that he remembered. 'A perfect day.' And she turned back to the fire. 'I often think of it.' A smile brightened her face and was gone, and a gull circled them, gave a cry, and flew off across the machair. 'And now there's only you and me.' The flaming easel fell noisily into a void beneath it, sending up a spray of sparks. 'I thought that day marked the beginning of everything, but the world tore itself apart instead—' And hell came to earth on Flanders fields.

She looked towards the foreshore, where they had pulled up the boats that day, empty now, then she glanced back at Donald, seeing in the middle-aged man the child who had once run shouting beside her as they splashed barefoot through sparkling pools left by the retreating tide, drenched in sunshine, the divisions of class overruled by the compact of childhood. But there had been other children too. Her brother, and his.

She strained her eyes across the strand, shedding the pain as she had taught herself to do, and looked instead at the vibrant Hebridean sky. Midsummer half-light. But when the last colour had drained from the west, she knew there would be a pale light in the east, and she clung to that thought, keeping her back turned resolutely on the house.

All day the men had worked to fix boarding across the windows, entombing the house, blinding it. The thud of their hammers still pounded in her head, but at least the job was done, and in the morning she would leave. 'What will become of it, Donald?' The man beside her stayed silent. 'At least the land is in good hands, and the farmhouse is now your own.' She brushed aside his renewed thanks. 'A few papers to sign and then the matter is completed.'

The fire was almost sated now; it had burned quickly, fanned by gusts which blew unhindered across the two miles of open land. 'I don't suppose I'll ever come here again.' Her voice was barely above a whisper, and her cheeks shone wet in the firelight. Donald moved quickly to hold her, turning her face into his shoulder as he might a child, not a woman who was almost old—and she smelt woodsmoke in the tweed and was comforted. A sharp crack, and a spark shot from the fire, igniting the dry grass, burning brightly for a while, then it died, leaving a charred and blackened patch. 'I've been visiting ghosts, Donald.' He tightened the arm which held her, saying nothing. 'And thank God it was *you* who found poor Theo, and brought him home.'

The spectators were dropping away, back across the strand or over the machair to their homes. 'Leave the ghosts where they belong, Emily.' He released her and took her arm instead. 'Come home with us now.'

They left the embers shimmering low on the foreshore, a beacon in the encroaching darkness, and made their way down the well-worn track which linked the two houses. The woman paused just once and looked over her shoulder to where Muirlan House stood immense, dark, and sombre against the streaked lead and crimson of the western sky. He gave her a moment and then urged her forward, towards the glow which beamed a welcome from the windows of the factor's farmhouse.

Chapter 1

The first bone he had dismissed as dead sheep. There'd been others— ribs decaying amidst rabbit droppings and debris from the collapsing ceilings, or bleached vertebrae. But the next one was a long bone, and he held it, considering a moment, then rocked back on his heels.

This was no sheep.

He leant forward, interest sharpening, and scraped at the sandy soil, revealing more stained bones and recognising a tangle of threads from decaying textile. A rotting plank half-covered the remains. He tried to move it aside, but it stuck fast, then he straightened, aghast, as certainty came. The plank was an old floorboard, nailed down, and the bones were underneath it.

He stared down at the remains, thrown off balance, then bent again, his mouth dry, and explored further until he came to the pale orb of the skull. Then he stopped.

The body had been placed on its side with the head hard up against a boulder in the foundations, the chin dropped to the chest, exposing the side of the skull. Exposing not a smooth roundness but a fissured depression, choked with sand. His mind roared as he reached forward to clear crumbs of mortar from the half-buried jaw, flicking an indifferent wood louse from the bared teeth, his hand trembling as he uncovered more of the crushed temple and the dark orbit of an eye. Then he straightened again and stood looking down, the trowel hanging loose in his hand. It was the snapping of fast wing beats that broke the spell, and he ducked instinctively as a rock dove bolted from its roost in an alcove—*bloody bird!*—and he glanced at his watch, twisting it on his wrist. Out of time. The tide had turned, and the wind was strong. Storm coming. He quickly bent to cover the bones again, then grabbed his jacket and ran to the Land Rover.

The empty stretch of sand, which, for a few short hours twice a day joined Muirlan Island to the main island, was disappearing fast. Had he cut it too fine? He revved the engine hard as the vehicle descended the track and he reached the point where track met sand. Then the battered vehicle sped across, through the shallow water, spray arching from its wheels as it rounded the rocky outcrop at the midway point, following the vanishing tracks which had marked his route across that afternoon. Swooping terns accompanied the incoming tide as it flooded the sandy stretches between the headlands, closing in behind him. He glanced in his rear-view mirror at the grey bulk of the house silhouetted on the ridge, and gripped the steering wheel. A body, for Christ's sake!

Then, as he tore across the wet sand, he glimpsed a figure in a long dark coat standing on a little headland, staring out towards the house. A woman? He looked more keenly. A stranger—The Land Rover plunged drunkenly into the last deep channel and he revved the engine again to pull up the other side, releasing his breath as he felt firm ground beneath the tyres. Then he swung the vehicle to the right, wiping damp palms on worn jeans, and headed down the single-track road, skirting the edge of the bay, to find Ruairidh.

Chapter 2

As the last of next morning's tide retreated across Muirlan
Strand, seabirds swooped over the sand ripples, and the low
morning sun turned the remaining pools to glittering silver.

Hetty had risen early and now followed the ebbing tide across
the sand towards the island. At the halfway point, she stopped
for a moment and looked around at the vast, empty bay, then
continued on her way. The start of her route across had been
marked by tyre tracks, but these had soon disappeared, washed
away by last night's tide. It didn't matter, of course, because
Muirlan House was clearly visible, outlined against the sky
on a ridge ahead of her. Presumably it was safe just to head
straight for it now that the tide had pulled back. The tyre marks
reappeared as she drew closer to the island, and they rose from
the beach to become a track, which she followed, stepping along
the grassy strip between deep wheel ruts. Birdsong floated down
on the soft air, freshened after last night's storm, and she lifted
her head to listen. Skylarks! When had she last heard skylarks?

Ahead lay the house, and she stopped where the track passed
between two crumbling gateposts and stared at it. It was huge!
Much bigger than she had imagined, somewhere between an
oversized country vicarage and small baronial seat. And beyond
it, lower down the ridge, she saw another house, a rambling two-
storey farmhouse with outbuildings, which was, in fact, much
more the sort of place she had been expecting.

She continued through the gateway up the old drive towards
Muirlan House. A low wall encircled it, defining an apron of
garden, the top stones laid to form a crenulation, but the wall had
been breached in several places and stones lay tumbled in the

long grasses. A side gate, which once gave access to pastureland, lay rusting away amongst the stones in a patch of nettles. As she neared the house, she saw the windows were boarded up, which gave the house a closed, unwelcoming air, as if refuting her right to be there. She breathed deep, summoning up her courage, and the breeze carried to her a sweet scent from a patch of blown wild roses which spread, abandoned, across a heap of broken trelliswork. Cheered by this, she lifted her chin and walked up to the front door to find, as expected, that it was locked, secured by an iron bar and a businesslike padlock, recently oiled. The work of Mr. Forbes, no doubt.

But as she turned away, she saw that his precautions had not deterred determined intruders, who had simply ripped away the boarding from one of the ground-floor windows, ignoring the daubed warnings: DANGER! UNSAFE! KEEP OUT! YES, YOU! Fragments of shattered chimney pots and roof slates lay strewn amongst the clover and underlined the message.

But a sign on the adjacent window gave her a mighty pulse of excitement, spiked by disbelief.

PRIVATE PROPERTY.

And she felt a sudden need to get inside, to see for herself, now, at once—before excitement curdled to stark terror at the responsibility of ownership. Her eye fell on an old fish crate lying on a clump of thistles, and she glanced back at the broken boarding. Why not? She looked both ways, an urban instinct, but there was no one about, nothing to stop her. Besides—incredibly—the place was hers. She went quickly, before she could change her mind, fetched the crate and positioned it under the window, and then she was up, through, and over. Like Alice, she thought, as she landed with a crunch on broken glass and splintered wood, and dusted the grit from her hands. And how ridiculous, when the keys were with Mr. Forbes and she had only to ask.

And then, in the stillness of the abandoned house, she became a trespasser, intruding where she had no business, and her courage faltered. She stood motionless as the feeling grew within her, resting her hand on the stained wall, and she listened to the great silence around her. Her palm absorbed a chill dampness from the wall, and she withdrew it, wiping it against her coat, and she looked around at the empty room.

Not just empty. Wrecked.

~

On her journey north, she had pressed her face to the train window, telling herself that this trip would mark a watershed, a new beginning. This was where she would take back control and focus her energies. But somehow it had felt more like a flight, or an escape from something… and as the train passed through the built-up midlands and the industrial north, doubts had crowded in. Whatever was she doing? It was madness! She knew nothing about restoring houses, or about running the hotel which she planned would follow. Perhaps, after all, she should listen to Giles and sell, and then invest the money. But as the train passed through the Borders and slowed to meet the demands of the West Highland line, she became lost in the scenery and her mind steadied. At least when she'd seen the place she would know what to do. And so she had sat up straighter, putting aside a thriller plucked from the bookshop at Euston, and listened to the unfamiliar cadence of the attendant's voice as he pushed the trolley through the swaying train, which now skirted the mountains, pressing northwards, offering glimpses of sea and far horizons.

After a night in Fort William, the self-proclaimed Gateway to the Highlands, she had picked up a hire car to drive the last hundred or so miles, crossing the bridge which now linked Skye to the mainland, and then boarded the ferry to the Western Isles. It had been a smooth crossing, and when they docked, most of the disembarking vehicles had turned towards the village, but her directions were to continue straight on, away from the small harbour community, where the road had soon dwindled to a single strip of potholed tarmac. It crossed a desolate landscape of moorland and peat bog, where low roofless ruins stood stark beside small grey lochs and streams. Returning to the village had begun to seem an attractive option until, from the top of the next rise, she had seen a fringe of coastline and a greener landscape of small fields with grazing cattle and sheep, and had felt a surge of delight.

The cottage she had rented for the week had been a bit further on, and when she got there she'd left the car and walked out onto a spur of land and stood looking across a vast expanse of drained sand. So there it was: Muirlan Strand. And there was the island, as her grandmother had described it, on the edge of the world, and there, standing tall on a ridge, she had seen the house itself, the painter's eyrie, silhouetted against the complex hues of the western sky.

The wind had gusted fitfully around her, snatching the cry of a gull. Six hundred miles she'd covered these last two days, but that moment had made it all worthwhile. And then the sound of an engine had shattered the silence, and she had seen a Land Rover racing across the strand towards her, sending up fans of spray on either side. It had rocked through a deep channel, climbed up the foreshore from the beach, then turned onto the road and was gone, leaving behind a deeper silence broken only by the bird's cry, and the wind.

But that was last night.

In that low evening glow, Muirlan House had had a mystical quality, but in the sharper light of morning, the illusion collapsed, and its true state was revealed. She took a step forward, placing her feet carefully, and looked up at falling ceilings and green damp-stained walls, where fractured plaster exposed rotting laths. Oh Lord, what had she got herself into? An acrid stench of sheep dung rose from the floor as she made her way gingerly to the hall, her eye caught by a line of rusting wires straggling along the plaster coving to connect with long-vanished bells. A wide staircase had once curved elegantly to a half-landing, lit by a glass rooflight, but this was now open to the elements and, through the jagged hole, she could see broken roof beams, angled like the misaligned spars of a wrecked ship. Clouds drifted past. *Dear God!* Splintered stair treads and drunken banisters led to the second floor, but there was no way she was going to trust them.

She had been warned, she reminded herself, as she peered into dark rooms opening off the hall, rooms where the window boarding remained intact. The lawyer acting as her grandmother's executor had told her the place had been empty for many years and would need work. But she hadn't expected it to be just a shell, pillaged and empty.

Nightmare.

Returning to the first room, dry-mouthed, she had to fight a rising panic. Like it or not, all this was now *her* responsibility. She'd better go and find Ruairidh Forbes, and then do some hard thinking. She had a knee on the windowsill preparing to climb out when she heard an engine again and leant out to see a Land Rover pulling up the foreshore towards the house. It looked like the one she'd watched racing the tide the night before—a farmer, perhaps, come to check on grazing livestock.

She pulled back to avoid being seen. Perhaps there was another way out? Back in the hall, she saw a passageway to the rear and started towards it, but then she saw a slit of daylight through one of the doors off to the right and turned to investigate.

She found it was coming not from the room itself but from some sort of small annex built on, so she went through and then stopped at the doorway of a little room. It too was boarded up, and the light was coming from a hole in the sloping roof through which it lit a wheelbarrow, a spade, and recently disturbed ground covered by planks and boarding. What on earth was going on?

And then the hammering started.

She turned her head at the sound. It must be coming from outdoors, close by. But what—? Then she saw that the light from the hall behind her had disappeared and remembered the unboarded window. She rushed back across the hall, shouting out, tripping in her haste, and began banging with her fists on newly fixed plywood which now covered her escape.

The hammering stopped abruptly, she heard a curse, and then the sound of nails being wrenched out. The boarding shifted, and she found herself face-to-face with a man with dark hair and angry eyes.

'Can't you read, for Christ's sake?' He rested the boarding against the wall, kicked the fish crate back into position under the window, and jerked his head. '*Out.*' And he stood back, offering no assistance, watching her clamber, wrong-footed, back across the ledge.

'Wait. Let me explain. I'm not trespassing, I—' Her jeans caught on a protruding nail and tore. Damn. 'Look, it's really alright—'

The man was not listening, and as soon as her feet touched the ground he tossed the fish crate back into the thistles and lifted the boarding again. 'There's nothing left to steal in there anyway.'

'*Steal?* No! You misunderstand. This is my—' Why was that so difficult to say? *This is my house.* She winced as staccato hammering drowned out her words, but then the man seemed to catch their meaning, and he stopped and looked over his shoulder at her. He lowered his arm, his eyes narrowing, and she found herself being scrutinised with a disconcerting intensity. His lean face bore the signs of an outdoor life, and beneath the old woollen jersey she sensed physical strength. 'Are you Ruairidh Forbes?' she asked, struggling to regain some measure of control. What a start.

'No.' The man continued his inspection. Then: 'So why go through the window? Haven't you got keys?'

'Not yet. He has them. Mr. Forbes, that is—' She dug her nails into her palm. The man clearly thought her a fool, damn him. 'I'm about to go and call on him.'

But he was now looking past her, over her shoulder, back

towards the strand, and she saw his expression lighten. 'No need,' he said. 'He's come to call on you.'

She turned to see that another vehicle, an ancient Saab, was coming up the track towards them. The driver halted below the house, perhaps not wanting to risk the low-slung vehicle on the rutted track. He slammed the car door and came towards them, followed by a black-and-white collie. 'Right on cue,' said the first man, leaning back against the Land Rover, his eyes alive with amusement. 'Morning, Ruairidh. Let me introduce Muirlan House's new mistress. I've just evicted her.'

His tone made her flush, but the newcomer looked at her with sharp interest and came forward. 'Harriet Deveraux? I'd no idea,' he said, and held out his hand.

'Hetty,' she said, taking it.

He looked about forty, several years older than the first man, a few stone heavier and, on first showing, a damn sight nicer. 'Had you written again?'

She shook her head. 'A spur-of-the-moment decision.' Triggered, as it had been, by an intense desire to leave London. And Giles— 'I was going to wait until June when I had more time.'

He held on to her hand a moment, then relinquished it. 'I'd have met the ferry had I known. Have you somewhere to stay?'

'Yes. Just over there.' She gestured across the sand towards the cottage.

'Diighall's place? Well, well…'

He lowered his bushy eyebrows to cover a glance towards the other man who, she knew, was continuing to stare at her. But he now stepped forward and put out his hand. 'James Cameron.' She took it and waited for an apology. 'You took a risk, you know, going in there.' He turned to put his tools back in the Land Rover and described their encounter to the newcomer with ill-concealed amusement, adding, 'The place is a death trap.'

No apology, then.

Ruairidh Forbes shook his head with kindly concern. 'Dear oh dear! What a welcome.'

'If something had fallen on you, it'd be your—' He now glanced at the other man and stopped midsentence. 'You'll have to tell her, Ruairidh.' He shut the back of the Land Rover and leant against it again, arms folded. 'Sooner or later.'

The other man looked unhappy. 'Aye. I know.' And as he told her, she understood why.

'*Human* remains?' she said, when he had finished. Whatever else she had expected, it had not included this. 'Who? Do you know?'

'No idea. Just bones. You see, James only found them yesterday, and we couldn't get back across until now, so I've not seen them. I'll have a quick look, then contact my colleagues on the mainland.' She nodded dumbly, thinking that when she'd learned that her key holder was a part-time police officer she hadn't expected to need his professional services.

'A tramp, perhaps?' she ventured, a derelict who'd taken shelter, or drunk himself to death. Surely no one could actually get *trapped* inside, could they? Unless— Oh God. 'Was it... Did something fall on—?' Her mind raced towards negligence claims and lawsuits.

She'd had ownership for less than a couple of months, but what would her position be?

'The corpse was stashed under the floorboards, so no.' James Cameron was still slouched against the Land Rover, watching her, and the significance of his words took a moment to hit her.

'*Under* the floorboards?'

He nodded.

The policeman returned her another apologetic look. 'A bad business,' he said, and gestured to the Saab. 'Why don't you sit in the car, miss, while we take a look?'

She stood, staring back at him, then shook her head quickly. 'No. I'll come. I'd better see—'

James Cameron straightened and produced hard hats from the back of the Land Rover, shutting Ruairidh's dog inside the vehicle, and went to unlock the heavy padlock on the front door. He stood aside as she made a more conventional entrance, then followed her in. Dazed still, she paused just inside, and in that instant she had a fleeting image of past splendour, seen through sunlit shafts of suspended dust... But the men were waiting for her.

James went on ahead, and Ruairidh ushered her through to the little annex where she had seen the wheelbarrow and tools. James was crouched beside them, his dark hair falling forward as he pulled aside the plastic sheet which was covering the disturbed ground.

They went and stood beside him, and looked down at pale bones lit from above, at the damaged skull lying on its side in a parody of sleep, the empty eye socket forlorn and sorrowful. Hetty felt a tightening in her chest. A heavy pall seemed to hang in the air, and it all felt unreal, and wrong. Dreadfully wrong.

'Poor devil,' the policeman said, crouching down. 'A bad spot that, just above the temple.'

Only the upper part of the skeleton was visible, and James Cameron was scraping gently with a penknife at the soil and mortar which framed the skull. 'See what I mean? It looks as if the bedding material was packed around and on top of the body, and then the floorboards were laid on top.'

The scene was almost unimaginable.

'To have been buried there, and no one knowing.' Her words fell into a pool of silence.

'Someone knew,' said Ruairidh after a moment, then he straightened, dusting his hands together. 'Let's cover them up again, Jamie.'

She stepped aside to give them space, but almost immediately she heard the younger man exclaim, and she turned back to see him pointing with the tip of his knife blade at something glinting amongst the sand and rubble. Ruairidh crouched again. 'Can you free it?' he asked, and they watched as James scratched the sandy soil away to reveal an oval locket strung on a gold chain. 'Is it a woman, then?' The policeman's voice was grim. Clouds covered the sun, dimming the light, and Hetty looked up through the broken roof. A woman?

'An expensive piece.' James turned the locket over and rubbed his thumb across a scrolling pattern of initials. 'What is it? BJS, SJB? Can't tell when they're all on top of each other. Do I open it?' He looked across at the other man, who hesitated a moment and then nodded. He slid the blade between the two halves of the locket.

Inside lay a curl of hair, and underneath it, a feather. Nothing else. No further inscription, no picture, just a lock of hair tied with thin twine and the feather, reduced to little more than a few spines and dust.

Chapter 3

≈ 1910, Beatrice ≈

Beatrice stood on a little headland and saw the house at last, lit by strong sunlight. Fine-weather clouds cast fleeting shadows over the wet sand as they sped across the sky, drawing her on towards the island. But a moment later a darker one skidded over the sun, plunging the house into shade, and she looked around her thinking of Theo's paintings, which had, after all, only hinted at the extraordinary quality of the light. Intense and ever-changing.

A sharp breeze reminded her that the year was still young and untried, and it carried a sour tang from the seaweed piled up on the high-tide mark. A bird circled her, emitting an urgent, piping cry as she stood there, the wind tugging at her skirt, lifting the brim of her hat. She spent a moment tying the ribbons more tightly, and when she looked up the cloud had passed and the house was once again flooded with light. A faint heat haze shimmered off the sand, blurring the shoreline ahead.

The scene held her transfixed until she heard her name called, and she turned to see her husband beckoning. She had left him overseeing the transfer of their trunks to a waiting farm cart, cautioning care with his painting materials, and had picked her way down to the shoreline. He watched her as she returned to him, searching her face as he assisted her onto the trap, before springing up beside her, taking the reins, and guiding the horse down onto the sand. 'Edinburgh's in another world,' she said, and he smiled at her.

Just two days ago she had sat at the window of their private compartment, engrossed, watched indulgently by Theo as the train steamed out of Waverley Station, leaving Edinburgh behind them. This journey might be nothing to someone as well-travelled as he, but Beatrice had rarely left the city, and the sky-hued flush of bluebells on woodland floors and the gorse aflame on the fells had filled her with delight.

But nothing in her experience had prepared her for the rugged grandeur of the Highlands, for the great procession of mountains sweeping down to tongues of glittering water which spread wider as the train headed west to become the ocean itself. Nor had the small ferry across the narrow strait to Skye prepared her for the sea crossing to the islands. 'It'll be rough,' Theo had warned, 'and I expect you'll be sick.' But he had been wrong, and she had remained on the oil-stained deck throughout, warm in her travelling coat, untroubled by the noise and smoke from the mail boat's engines, captivated by the blue-grey sea and the islands spread about her.

'Theo, I had no idea—' she had breathed, catching at her escaping hair.

He had stood beside her, a tall, well-made man, his hands grasping the rails, the wind blowing his hair across his brow, eyes narrowing to follow a line of gannets heading out to sea, shedding his city veneer before her eyes. But what was he thinking, she had wondered, this two-month husband of hers. One could never be quite certain, his face hid his emotions too well. A moment later he had turned back to her, his eyes warming a private smile as he bent to kiss her.

As the trap crossed the sand on this final stretch of the journey, she resumed her study of him. He was a handsome man, without a doubt, but so far she had known him only as a creature of the Edinburgh drawing rooms and galleries where they had met, and where he was an established figure, confident of the position which his money, intellect, and talent had earned him. But here, out of context, she found he was a stranger again.

He had been animated as he prepared for their departure, and purposeful, ensuring she packed suitable clothing and footwear, breaking off to explain to her the workings of the camera he had bought. 'But you will paint too?' she had asked, and he had answered with a curious fervour that he certainly hoped he would. And there had been an energy, an eagerness in him on the journey as he had overseen the porters dealing with their trunks at the railway stations, and he had been impatient at the late departure of the mail boat. But as they approached the long line of islands, he had fallen silent, and she had sensed him detaching himself from her.

'It has an almost Aegean quality on days like this,' he said suddenly, his expression lightening. 'But wait until the westerlies strike up. Then you'll change your tune.' She dismissed the westerlies with an airy wave and slipped her hand under his arm, drawing close, and he smiled down at her again. And now, with their destination in sight, she sensed excitement growing in him, and she stretched her eyes across the strand to Muirlan Island, on the edge of the world.

This was how he had described it to her. 'And beyond there be dragons!' he had said, his eyes glinting in the way she had grown to love. It was his refuge, he had said, a place of wild beauty, a special place, with endless stretches of bone-white sand, vast skies, and the sea—an ever-changing palette.

Then he had returned to practicalities. Although the house was large by local standards, they would not be living in grand style. 'Perhaps you'll find it primitive.' He did not retain a large staff; she must make do with local girls recruited for the summer from amongst the tenants, who would be overseen by Mrs. Henderson, the housekeeper. 'There's no Mr. Henderson, by the way. Never has been, so don't ask.' She looked blank. 'There's a daughter, you see.' The estate and the tenants, he continued, were managed by the factor, John Forbes, who farmed the estate on Theo's behalf. 'A very competent fellow. His father came as factor from Paisley with my father, but John's an islander to his marrow. We were boys together.' The factor was assisted by a grown son, and a daughter who kept house for them, his wife having died many years ago. Another son was in Canada.

'They've been more or less running the place for years.' And he had frowned suddenly—his Edinburgh face. 'They'll have to adjust, and there hasn't been a mistress in the place since my stepmother fled the island.'

'*Fled* the island?'

'She did find it primitive.'

He had given her a thin smile, and doubt had flickered across his face, but she had tugged at his sleeve. 'I'm entirely out of sympathy with Edinburgh, Theo. I want something quite, quite different.' Did he fear a repetition, she wondered, thinking that she too might turn and flee? She had met his stepmother and knew that Theo held her in contempt, but if it was his father's remarriage that had driven him away as a young man, what had prevented him from spending time there since his stepmother had left? She realised that he had a deep bond with this place, and it was the inspiration for so many of his early paintings, yet in recent years he'd told her that his visits had been infrequent and fleeting. And now, as they passed the midway point across the strand, she saw his face had taken on a strained look and his eyes were fixed on the house with the keen look of a hawk as it reckons its chances of success.

Puzzled slightly, she turned her own attention back to the house. It stood on a low ridge, its walls rising high above the landscape, out of all proportion with its surroundings. She could see a small roof turret at the front, crow-step gables, and long windows glinting in the sun. What on earth had inspired Theo's father—a textile manufacturer, not a belted knight—to build such a house? Here, in this remote place... And whatever must the islanders make of it? She thought of the low rough-hewn dwellings they had passed, which she had assumed were barns or byres. When she had asked Theo where the people actually *lived*, his explanation had astonished her, and she had studied the next ones more closely, trying to imagine what life must be like for the gap-toothed women who gossiped under low eaves, swathed in shawls, or bent over tin tubs, some straightening to follow the trap with shaded eyes. Dirty children ran out into the track, leaving little ones watching from behind peat stacks; a few returned her wave. And she had thought of the trolley buses and motor cars on Edinburgh's streets as a small donkey, struggling under peat-laden baskets, was jerked aside to let them pass. Expressionless stares had followed them.

And now, as the trap left the strand, Muirlan House came sharply into focus. It appeared more forbidding as they drew close, but she declared stoutly that it combined all the charm of a Walter Scott novel with the romance of a desert island. 'Will you feel the same in six months' time, I wonder?' Theo responded, and she was thrown against him as the trap pulled up the rocky foreshore.

Ahead of them the track forked, one branch leading off to the factor's house and farm buildings a little below the ridge, the other becoming a more conventional drive lined with bushes alive with the twitter of small birds. They passed between two stone pillars where a number of men in rough clothes stood beside the open gate. The tenants, she thought, scanning their bearded faces, and they looked back at her, pulling off their caps as Theo raised a hand in greeting. Then the men turned away to follow the laden farm cart round to the back of the house.

'John's rallied the forces to welcome you,' said Theo, nodding towards the front entrance, where several women were assembled, their skirts and white aprons blowing in the breeze. The trap came to a halt beside them in the shadow of the entrance porch, and an imposing figure in dark tweeds detached himself and stepped forward, followed by a younger man, who took the reins from Theo. 'Welcome home, Mr. Blake,' he said, and nodded respectfully at Beatrice. 'Welcome, madam.'

'Good to see you, John.' Theo stepped down from the trap to shake his hand. 'And *what* a welcome.' He acknowledged the waiting women as he walked round to Beatrice's side to assist her descent. 'Beatrice, my dear, this is Mr. Forbes. John, my wife.'

The factor's smile lit brown eyes above a full beard with an unexpected warmth, and he held out his hand. 'You're very welcome here, Mrs. Blake.' His voice was a low rumble and his handclasp firm. The youth, a slimmer version of the factor, was introduced as his son Donald, who murmured an inarticulate greeting as he clung doggedly to the reins. Then Theo went forward to greet a woman who had stepped forward, and Beatrice followed him, glancing anxiously up at the house. Was she to be mistress of such a place? Theo Blake, her mother had told her, would have expectations of her— But he seemed unaware of her apprehension, introducing her to Mrs. Henderson, the housekeeper, who seemed a pleasant woman, and nodded again to the other women who stood in line behind her. As he turned back to speak to the factor, Beatrice looked about her, taking in the terrace and a sunken rectangle where there had been some attempt at a garden. In one sheltered corner, a rustic seat, framed by trelliswork, was under construction. A garden, she thought, seemed a good idea.

She turned back as the housekeeper began herding the staff round to the rear of the house, and saw that another figure was approaching the house on the rough track which led to the farm buildings. It was a young man, walking quickly, a lean young man in dark trousers and a white, wide-sleeved shirt. He was hastily pulling on a jacket as he strode towards them, a brown pointer bitch at his heels, and he pushed open the side gate, entering the curtilage of Muirlan House, and let it clang behind him.

The factor turned at the sound and frowned, censuring the latecomer. Theo also turned, and he broke off abruptly in midsentence to stare at the young man. Then he swung back to the factor in startled enquiry.

'Aye. Cameron's come back, sir. About a week ago.'

The young man gave a curt order and the dog dropped to the gravel, panting slightly, and Beatrice saw that he was quite openly, almost brazenly, inspecting her as he approached.

And Theo stood, very still, and watched him come.

The newcomer switched his attention to Theo, gave a slight bow, and held out his hand. 'Welcome home, sir.'

Theo looked down at the hand, then took it. 'Welcome home yourself, Cameron.' He spoke slowly, almost carefully. 'I hadn't heard—' His eyes seemed to explore the young man's face before he turned to Beatrice. 'This is Cameron, my dear. Mr. Forbes's elder son. Returned from Canada, it would appear.' The young man gave another small bow. 'And this, Cameron, is my wife.'

Chapter 4

Ruairidh Forbes offered Hetty a lift back to her cottage, hastily brushing sand from the seat of the Saab and tossing an oilskin into the back, while he apologised again that her first encounter with the island had been so unpromising. 'A very poor welcome for you,' he repeated, glancing across at her from the driving seat.

'It's a shock.'

A shock. The word came nowhere close. She found she was gripping the door handle and so released it, flexing her fingers, and made an effort to smile. 'And for you too, I imagine.'

'Aye. Incredible.'

From the car she watched James Cameron pushing the wheelbarrow back down the slope towards the other house and outbuildings. Were those shutters at the window? 'Does someone still live there?' she asked.

Ruairidh followed her gaze. 'Not now. The farmhouse belongs to my grandfather, together with the outbuildings. He was born in the house and he'd live there still if my grandmother hadn't put her foot down.' He laughed suddenly, and she decided that he was a nice man. As they drove across the strand, he told her more: the farmhouse had been the laird's house long before Muirlan House was built, and his family had served as estate factors for three generations until the big house was closed up. 'I farm the land myself now, and use the outbuildings,' he said, 'which is probably why I hold the keys for Muirlan House. Old habits die hard.'

By then they had reached the opposite shore and rejoined the road which skirted the bay, and he pulled up on the rough ground outside her cottage. 'You've had a poor start, Miss

Deveraux,' he said, 'but will you come and eat with us tonight? You'd be very welcome.'

'I'd love to.' She smiled back at him. 'If you'll call me Hetty.'

'Aye, Hetty, then I will.' He drove off with a wave, promising to come and collect her later that evening.

She watched him go, then sighed and put her shoulder to the cottage door. After a couple of good shoves, it opened, and she was greeted by the musty smell of damp and soot which seemed to characterise the place. It had advertised itself as having fine views across the strand, which was why she had chosen it, but it was decidedly bleak. The kitchen floor was sticky, the lino in the bathroom glacial, and nothing was quite clean. She forced the door shut again and then stood a moment, staring across the room at last year's faded calendar. *Highland Games. Antigonish, Nova Scotia.* Swirling kilts and skirling pipes. A fantasy Scotland.

She put the kettle on and half an hour later sat with her hands clasped around a mug of tea, her legs tucked beneath her, staring into the empty hearth and taking stock. *A very poor welcome*, Ruairidh Forbes had said, and the image of the cracked skull rose before her, the empty eye socket reproachful and forlorn. And so, in this place where she had sought refuge, she now confronted another violent death— And who, if anyone, had mourned that loss?

Suddenly it hit her again, that storm surge of grief, the yawning gap, a sense of being adrift that had stalked her ever since her parents' death. An accident, yes, but sudden and violent, and even now, three years later, the thought of it could still overpower her.

Loss, was what people called it.

Such a little word.

But with enough potency to blow a hole right through her as it had done that day when she had answered an early morning phone call. A failed take-off, and then a crash, just beyond the runway. It had been weeks before the raw shock had begun to fade into grief, and even as grief numbed into acceptance, the void remained. Then her grandmother's death two months ago had finished the job which dementia had begun years earlier, and she had found herself quite alone.

Sometimes she felt that she'd been sleepwalking ever since.

She went over to the window and looked out across the strand. The sky was overcast and the scene before her colourless. Coming here, without Giles, was the first real initiative she had taken in three years. The planned restoration work would give her a focus, she had told herself; it would mark a new beginning. But now this! She watched two sheep pass in front of the window, then stop to crop the grass on the little headland.

The bones didn't actually *change* anything, of course, and were a matter for the police. Ruairidh Forbes seemed to think that the crime was an old one, but even so… And coming so soon after seeing the appalling state of the house, it felt as if her new start was over before it had begun.

She turned away from the window. Perhaps a fire would lift her spirits, if she could get the wretched thing to light. Last night the unfamiliar peat had defeated her. But it was worth another go, so she knelt at the hearth and began assembling paper and kindling, thinking that no one had explained to her how it was that James Cameron had been digging into the foundations in the first place. She'd have to ask. And she imagined the guffaws there'd be at the bar if he chose to describe the ludicrous picture of her climbing through the window, tearing her jeans as she was ordered out of her own property. It had evidently amused him at the time— Perhaps she'd ask Ruairidh Forbes instead. She'd warmed to him, a kindly man in this strange new world.

She watched the flicker of a flame come to life in the hearth, and remembered that surge of optimism she had felt the day before, when she had felt the *rightness* of coming here. For a while, as the hills of Skye faded over the churning wake of the ferry, she had been left in a sort of limbo where all around her the margins of sky, sea, and land had merged into a blue-grey wash, masked by clouds. But as they drew closer, the sun had backlit the clouds with a mother-of-pearl sheen and slowly burned through the veil, revealing the low contours of islands in a glorious welcome.

And arriving that way, at the end of a long journey, had seemed the *right* way to come, giving her a true sense of the remoteness of the place. Of its separateness.

Giles had tried to persuade her to come directly after her grandmother's funeral. 'Just to look. Get a measure of the place?' There was an airfield on a neighbouring island, he told her; they could fly up. 'And there's bound to be some old banger to hire once we get there.'

But that would have made the transition too sudden, and difficult as it was to make him understand, she had needed to come alone.

Giles had been enthusiastic about her plans for the house from the start, too enthusiastic. This was to be *her* scheme, *her* new beginning. And if he'd come with her he'd have taken control, taken the initiative away, as was his wont. She'd tried to explain to him how she felt, how she wanted to take things slowly, to consider, but he thought she should push things along, get started, and he'd offered to find investors, maybe put money into it himself. Typical Giles behaviour.

She stared into the fireplace, where the flame was faltering, and tried to see Giles up here, in this remote and windswept place. Giles, in every essential, was an urban animal— And she thought again of the incident which had provoked her sudden flight. They had gone to a party held by an associate of Giles's at a chic apartment overlooking the Thames, and the proud new owner had led her, a bottle tucked under one arm, the other uninvited around her waist, to look through a vast sheet of glass at the sun setting upriver towards London. 'Turner-esque, don't you think? Or should I say Blake-esque. Giles tells me Theo Blake was your great-grandfather.'

'No. My great-grandmother, Emily, was his sister. Half-sister, in fact.'

'Oh, I'd stick to the direct line if I were you. Great cachet, my dear. Flaunt it!' His protruding eyes shone at her. 'Theo Blake, the mysterious recluse. Such extraordinary early talent and then the merely commonplace. Was he crossed in love, or did he drink?' His tone had nettled her and she had felt suddenly protective of the artist. Blake was a vague character in her family's annals, but a painting of his, a wonderful and cherished seascape, had always hung in the bedrooms of her childhood.

Her host's expensive aftershave had wafted over her as he inspected her glass, and she had pulled away. 'As I said, the relationship's fairly distant.'

'But you've got his house, I understand,' he said, leaning close again to refill it. 'Lucky girl!' How like Giles to have told everyone. She wished he hadn't. 'And the classy hotel idea is marvellous. We must get you onto the gallery circuit, making the right contacts. I'll speak to Giles about it. With your looks and pedigree, darling, the punters will flock to you.' Pedigree? Good God! 'And I'll be your very first guest.' His palm slipped from her waist to her hip, and she had looked around for Giles. The big brush-off would no doubt offend the man, but did she *have* to put up with him? Giles was watching from across the room, clearly entertained, and showed no sign of rescuing her. He just blew her a kiss and turned back to give his attention to a dark-haired girl beside him. Hetty felt a hand slip to her thigh, and as she turned sharply back, her host planted an amorous kiss on her lips, chortling as she pulled away, stiff-necked with affront. 'Be nice, now,' he had said, and returned to the party.

Giles had come over then and flicked her cheek. 'Lighten up, darling. It's just his way.'

'Really.'

'And he's a useful man to have on board. A big noise in art circles, you know, got all the right contacts.' She had turned aside, biting back a tart response, and watched as the party gathered pace and tempo: men in sharp suits moving in on women sleek in tight-fitting couture, working hard at image and impact, at being part of the tribe. But this was not where she wanted to be, and she had said so.

Giles, exasperated, had refused to take her home and had reentered the throng. She had stood there a moment, watching him, then slipped from the room and found her coat, leaving the buzz fading behind her. As she descended in the external lift, she had looked along the Thames to the lurid sunset and thought again of Theo Blake's painting, of white sands and the low sun dazzling across the water, and the idea of just leaving and coming up here, without Giles, had presented itself. Independence was one of the pluses of working freelance, and the only plus of having little work coming in. Copy editing, she was learning, would never make her rich.

And the idea of flight had grown as the taxi sped through the London streets to her flat. She could simply cut and run.

The flame in the hearth flickered, and then guttered, leaving a thin trail of smoke. But the grand gesture seemed to have stalled, foundering on bleached bones beneath the floor of a wrecked house. Would there be no fresh start? Would she have to return to London and find herself a real job, one that paid? The money her parents had left her, significant though it was, wouldn't last forever.

Quitting her job on the magazine after the accident had been necessary at the time but, in retrospect, reckless, and getting back into that sort of work was not proving to be easy.

She put aside her empty mug, restless suddenly and needing to be outdoors. Ruairidh Forbes had pointed out a co-op a mile or so down the road where she could get basic supplies, and a walk would clear her mind. And up here, under these big skies, she could think— By now Giles would have heard the brief message she'd left on his answerphone before catching the northbound train, and she wondered fleetingly what he would have made of it. She hadn't told him where she was going, simply that she would be away, out of town, for a while. He might choose to think, or at least to report, that it was work related. She yanked the door open. And here, where there was no Internet or mobile phone signal, he could neither find her nor contact her, and she had gained the space she needed.

Chapter 5

≈ 2010, Hetty ≈

Later she fell asleep in one of the armchairs and was woken by a sharp knock on the back door. She sat up, momentarily confused, to see that the light was fading across the bay. The knock came again, and she rose, glimpsing her unruly hair in the mirror as she went through to the kitchen, calling, 'It's open. Push at your side. It jams,' and she heard the thud of a shoulder against the door. It opened abruptly to reveal not the friendly policeman, as expected, but James Cameron, the collar of his donkey jacket turned up against the wind.

'Hallo again,' he said, examining the doorframe and running his fingers along the edge to find the sticking point. 'Ruairidh's been called to duty. Sends his apologies.' His hair blew across his eyes. 'Murder and fire-raising in the same day, eh? It's not always this exciting.' And he stepped uninvited across the threshold, followed by the cool evening air.

He seemed to fill the little kitchen, and he looked around with undisguised curiosity, taking in the chipped Formica table and rusty rubbish bin. 'Diighall doesn't go for the luxury end of the market, does he,' he remarked, raising an eyebrow. 'What does he charge these days?'

There was something disconcerting in his manner, and she ignored the question. 'Fire-raising?' she asked instead.

'Arson.' He continued his survey of the room, kicking experimentally at a split in the curling lino floor, grimacing at the calendar. 'A young ne'er-do-well celebrated his release by torching his family's house. Seems his woman had found solace while he was inside.'

Arson? Such behaviour seemed out of place here. 'And Mr.

Forbes is taking him in?'

He shook his head. 'Someone else'll do that. He's just dispersing the spectators and then he'll be along, but he asked me to come and pick you up.' She murmured her thanks while he looked through the open door into the shabby little sitting room. 'And I'll give you these before I forget.' He dug his hand into a pocket and put a set of keys on the table between them.

'But won't he need them?' she said. 'To let the police get in, to take away—?' She faltered, staring at the keys. Going into the house alone now seemed impossible.

'He's still got his. These are mine.' She looked up in surprise. 'I've had them ever since thieves got in some years back and stole the fireplaces. Rather after the event we put better locks on and replaced the boarding. It still gets ripped off, of course, and then all sorts get in.' Amusement flashed in his eyes again, and she turned to get her jacket, not sure what to make of this man. 'Some nosey soul must have seen I was working up there. Local lads, I expect, short of entertainment.'

'Working up there?' The words came out more sharply than she intended. 'Doing what?'

He regarded her a moment before answering. 'Checking the foundations. As instructed.' The amusement had gone and there was an edge to his tone.

'Instructed by who?'

'Dalbeattie and Dawson, of course.' He leant back against the kitchen unit and folded his arms, giving her a straight look. 'Emma Dawson, to be precise.'

She stared back at him. There was no of course about it. 'You'll have to explain,' she said, though she began to think she could guess. Dalbeattie and Dawson were old associates of Giles's who had set up business on Skye, and who, on his advice, she'd engaged as agents. She'd spoken to Emma Dawson a few times on the phone, and that purring voice had been pushy, employing charm as a wedge, aware of her inexperience and exploiting it, and Emma Dawson, it appeared, had jumped the gun. During their last conversation she had offered to look for someone who might begin to gather costs, and that was enough, apparently, for her to have gone ahead and instructed James Cameron to make a start.

'You didn't know?' He looked incredulous, as well he might. 'So you won't know what I told her?'

'No.'

'I told her there's a bloody great crack tearing the west wall apart, and a few more storms will finish the job. And when it goes, it'll bring the main gable with it.' He paused and gave her a sharp look. 'I told her the job shouldn't be contemplated, but she wouldn't have it and told me to find out why the wall was cracked. So I did, and I got rather more than I bargained for.' He leant back, regarding her steadily, and when she failed to comment, he added, 'You've got big plans, Miss Deveraux. A grand hotel, fine cuisine, shooting parties, golf…'

Was that disapproval in his tone?

'They're options I'm considering,' she replied, maintaining eye contact as long as seemed civil, and then reached over to pick up the keys as an excuse to look away.

He was silent for a moment, frowning at the place where the keys had been, then looked up again, eyebrows raised. 'And now you've seen the state of the place?' he asked, then added, 'Forgive me, but have you any idea what you're contemplating?' She sensed a genuine effort to strip the words of offence, but his question hit the mark too keenly for comfort. She had no reply. 'I've known that house all my life and watched its decline. It's past saving.' She turned aside and reached for her handbag. Perhaps Giles *should* have come.

'It's very early days, Mr. Cameron,' she said, banishing the craven thought, and gave him a tight smile. 'And I'm only just starting to gather the facts.'

~

Inside Ruairidh's house, James introduced her to Agnes, Ruairidh's wife, who came forward, wiping her hands on a striped apron before tucking wild red hair behind her ears, and shook Hetty's hand. 'Call me Ùna,' she said with a smile. 'Everyone else does.' Beside her, the black-and-white collie thumped its tail in greeting. Pan lids rattled on top of a Rayburn, steam rising to lose itself amongst countless socks perched like starlings on a drying rail above. A table stood in the middle of the room, and a candle had been lit, intended perhaps to draw the eye away from piles of ironing and the evidence of hasty food preparation. A boy, introduced as their son, was laying four places, and he regarded Hetty for a polite moment before transferring his attention to James Cameron, swamping him with a torrent of Gaelic. The man listened gravely and nodded, and the boy then grabbed a torch, pulling him back out into the darkness, followed by the dog.

'Alasdair and his dad are repairing an old boat, and James has to admire progress,' his mother explained as she led Hetty through to the sitting room and offered her a drink. 'Are you alright at Diighall's?' She moved a pile of papers and gestured to a chair beside the fire. 'I don't expect he spends much on comforts.'

'Oh, I'm fine,' she replied, and after pouring two drinks, her hostess excused herself to check her pans.

Hetty sat and surveyed the chaotic room. The papers looked like pupils' exercise books and a marking sheet. Primary school. An eclectic collection of paperbacks filled various bookshelves while paintings and photographs occupied the spaces in between. A bleached vertebra from a sea mammal leant against the mantelpiece with letters and bills stuffed behind it, while on a side table the reel from a fishing rod was under repair. Rectangles of peat stood drying in the hearth.

Islington belonged to another world.

Then she saw, hanging in an alcove, a very familiar painting, and rose to stand in front of it. *The Rock Pool, 1889.* It was Blake's best-known work, his early romantic masterpiece, and even reproduced as this modest print before her, it was exceptional.

She had seen the original in London three years ago as part of a touring exhibition, and she had been standing in front of it, lost in admiration, when she had felt a tap on her shoulder and turned to see Giles Holdsworth smiling down at her. They had met only a few times then and always in his firm's offices, where the details of her parents' estate were being unravelled.

'I was going to tell you about this exhibition, but you clearly knew,' he said. And later, over a cup of tea in the café, he'd explained that he was at the gallery on business. 'But I skived off after the meeting to have a quick look once I heard *The Rock Pool* was here.'

Afterwards they had gone back to look at it again, and he had bent to read the label. 'Painted in 1889, and it says he was barely twenty. How extraordinary.'

Extraordinary indeed, and yet so simple.

The painting depicted a young girl in simple clothing, standing beside a rock pool, bracing herself with one hand against the rock face and leaning over the water, lifting her foot from the ripples. A single drop of water had fallen from her toe and bounced off the pool's surface. With her other hand she was clasping her clothes to her, raising her skirts away from the water, her dark hair falling forward across her face. Blake had caught her just at the moment she was turning towards him, and a tiny spot of brightness showed the gleam in her eye as she raised her face to him. It was a beautiful, sensitive piece invoking a stillness, a promise, a moment in time that would frame a lifetime.

~

The door opened and Ruairidh came across to clasp her hand with both of his, full of apologies. The fire-raiser had been despatched to the mainland, he reported, and the stunned family taken in by relatives. 'You can't blame the lass for leaving him,' he said, 'but it's a shame. He was a decent enough lad until his mother died.' Then the door opened again and James Cameron entered, poured himself a drink, and sat down beside the window, glancing briefly at a discarded newspaper.

The fourth place at the kitchen table, it transpired, was laid for him, not the boy, who had vanished with the dog, and she found herself sitting opposite him.

They were cousins, Ruairidh told her, as he ladled potatoes onto her plate. 'But then everyone's related on the island, one way or another, going back generations. And everyone knows everyone's business.' He paused, the spoon half-raised, dripping butter. 'Which is why these bones come as a shock, you see, because *someone* must have known.'

'And old gossip gets handed down,' his wife added.

Hetty looked around the table, observing the bonds of kinship but sensing something wider and deeper—an understanding of how their community functioned and had always functioned. It gave her a dart of pleasure, for this was what she sought—a community. And a community was not the same as a *crowd*, like Giles's networking friends; it was a more complex fabric woven from mutual need and common interest, and a shared past. It was something more tribal.

Hetty had never had that sense of belonging. Her father's job with the foreign office had meant that home was not a *place* but a transient thing, and her childhood had been spent flying backwards and forwards from boarding school. A new posting, a rapid withdrawal following a coup, or the need to replace an ailing colleague—it all boiled down to a different view from her bedroom window, a different language in the streets, and unfamiliar food. It was only later in life that she recognised how unsettling this had been.

'You've no idea who—?' she asked, coming back to the moment.

'None at all. There's no one *missing*, if you see what I mean.'

'A visitor, perhaps? Though I read that Theo Blake was something of a recluse.' They ate in silence for a moment, and she wondered if perhaps the tribe was closing ranks.

'He was, towards the end,' said Ruairidh, lifting his glass to drink. 'He spent his last twenty years alone in the house, letting it fall apart around him.' James Cameron glanced briefly at her. 'But there used to be smart house parties, folk who came up to shoot and fish. Before his wife left him, that is.'

'If she did.' James Cameron had said little so far.

Ùna Forbes gave an exclamation. 'You think it's his *wife*, then, Jamie?' She reached for the bottle and smiled at Hetty as she filled her glass. 'And that he stuffed her under the floorboards! *Very* Gothic.'

James shrugged.

But Ruairidh was chewing thoughtfully. 'No. It was always said that the Blakes left the island together, although *she* never returned.' He loaded another fork. 'I've contacted Inverness, by the way, and they'll send someone over.'

She thanked him but wanted to continue the earlier discussion. 'If Theo Blake spent his last years alone, then surely someone *could* have disappeared, and no one knows?'

Ruairidh leant back in his chair, cradling his glass on his generous stomach. 'True enough, but who? He shunned visitors towards the end.'

Since inheriting the house, Hetty had been trying to learn more about Theodore Blake, scouring libraries and the Internet for information, but had had mixed results. While his artistic achievements were well documented, there was frustratingly little written about his personal life, and his later reclusive years were unrecorded, except for the fact that he had drowned, as an old man, while crossing Muirlan Strand.

His father, she had read, had opposed his ambition to be a painter, but the young Theo had been determined to go to Glasgow, where he was attracted by the Glasgow School and their commitment to exploring realism. It was his early paintings, his Hebridean collection, which had made his name while he was still very young, but later, like so many of his contemporaries, he had gone abroad, where he had produced less innovative work, and his fame had dwindled. In his middle years he had limited himself to illustrations of native birdlife, completing a catalogue begun by his father, which had been well received but was long since out of print.

'I've a copy here,' said Ruairidh, when she mentioned it, and he rose to fetch it. 'He loved his birds, did Blake. Started one of the country's first reserves.'

'And when did he paint those others?' asked Ùna. 'You know, the weird ones.'

The weird ones—Hetty did know which she meant. There had been one such in the London exhibition, a chilling, wild scene of an anguished face looking from the shore to a goggle-eyed head rising from a cauldron of surf. The work of a deranged mind, some critics said. 'I read they were done in his last years but that there aren't many of them.'

'There were paintings burned when the house was closed up.'

James spoke softly, tilting his glass as if to study the candle's reflection on the wine. 'Your great-grandmother didn't like them, I'm told.' He glanced up briefly and then continued mopping up the last of the casserole with a chunk of bread, leaving Ruairidh to explain about the bonfires and what the old folks had said.

Ùna began clearing away the plates. 'She was being protective, I expect, like a good sister. He was quite barmy at the end, you know.'

'Makes you wonder, though.' Ruairidh refilled their glasses.

'Barmy?' This was news. Or was this a judgement foisted unkindly on a reclusive man? 'But he can't have been entirely alone up there, surely?'

'Aye, that's true,' said Ùna. 'I don't suppose he washed his own socks and peeled his own tatties.' She flashed an arch look at her husband as she cleared space for an apple pie. 'And folk would have mentioned bodies being stuffed under floorboards, you can be sure of that.'

'Donald Forbes was living at the farmhouse with his family then,' her husband said, 'and they kept an eye on him, I understand.'

'So have a word with Aonghas, he loves a good old gossip,' said James.

'My granddad,' explained Ruairidh. 'Turned ninety but sharp as a pin. Donald was his father, you see, and he remembers Blake's sister coming up for the auction when the house was closed up.'

At the end of the evening, James took her home.

And as she stepped out of Ruairidh's house, she felt the darkness engulf her—but it was a soft velvet darkness, not the flat dullness of a London night punctured by street lighting and the tracer light of car headlamps. It was still and quiet, and she breathed in the complex smell of the outdoors, looking up to see a million stars arching above them in the clear northern skies.

'Not a sight you'll ever get in London.' He stood holding the Land Rover door open, watching her. 'It was the thing I missed most working down there. The big skies.'

'Were you there long?' she asked, as he went to the other side and slid in beside her.

'Two years. It was enough.' The engine roared into life and they jolted off the verge and back onto the tarmac road.

Over dinner in Ruairidh's cottage, she had felt a warmth stealing over her as they described what was known of the house in its heyday, of her family and theirs, realising with delight that she had a stake in this shared past. But James's words reminded her that she was an incomer, recalling her to the sudden silence which fell when she referred to her plans for the house. Ruairidh had deftly moved the subject on, but not before she had seen the quick exchange of looks around the table.

'You didn't see much of the house, I suppose, before I chucked you out.' James kept his face forward but she sensed the glimmer of a smile. 'I'll take you back over in the morning, if you like. Show you the problems.'

'Shouldn't we keep away until after the police have been?'

'Can't see it matters.' He slowed as a sheep stepped into the road and stopped, its eyes eerily lit by the headlamps. 'If we asked Ruairidh, he'd have to say no'—he looked across at her and surprised her with a sudden grin—'so we won't ask.'

Chapter 6

He was on her doorstep early.

'We've only got a couple of hours because of the tide,' he explained as the Land Rover rocked over the rough track and then sped across the pristine sand. He steered carelessly with one hand, glancing occasionally at her but saying nothing more, and she turned her head to look out of the window, matching his silence with her own.

White sand, shallow water, and clear blue skies created a spectrum of shades, dark turquoise and aqua blue blending with chalky pastels. To the west she could see open ocean, while to the east the curve of the shoreline masked the other entrance to the bay, set against a backdrop of misty hills rising from neighbouring islands, and she twisted in her seat to encompass the scale of her surroundings, awed by its beauty. 'Have you been up here before?' he asked, breaking the silence, and she shook her head. 'It's got a special magic on days like this,' he said.

And he was right.

As they swept around the last rocky seaweed-clad mound, the house was directly in front of them. It was a tribute to unapologetic mid Victorian self-confidence, built to impress by its scale with a vigorous appreciation of the romantic, redolent of Abbotsford, or Waverley, with stepped gables and a little roof turret above the front porch. Built, she had read, to celebrate a very Victorian type of success in the textile mills of Paisley where Theodore Blake's father had woven thread into cloth of gold. But the gaunt shell looked so bleak now, like an abandoned film set without purpose or meaning.

'Rather dominates the landscape, doesn't it?' he said, and she felt his eyes on her again as the Land Rover left the sand and bumped up the sloping track to the house. 'Closing up the place had a bigger impact around here than the end of the war.' He swung in between the entrance pillars, the wheels skidding on mud. 'The bonfires burned into the night with stuff left after the auction. It was said they could be seen for miles. Armageddon, Hebridean style.' She nodded, then pushed the image aside and indulged in a moment's fantasy, seeing the house restored, alive again, the windows free of boarding, open to the peerless view. 'There've been rumours of all sorts of buyers over the years,' he continued, 'rock stars, hippies, religious groups... But nothing ever happened, and then the November gales started to take the roof off.'

The fantasy vanished and she looked away. 'And now you say it's too late.'

He pulled on the hand brake, reaching back for hard hats and a large torch. 'Fraid so.'

When he had come to pick her up that morning, he had pocketed the keys which lay where she had left them the day before, and he used them now to unlock the padlock on the front door, slipping them automatically into his pocket as he cautioned her to tread warily. Would he remember to give them back? she wondered.

They crossed the hall in front of the main staircase once again, and he pointed out where part of the landing was collapsing, leaving the front bedrooms marooned and unreachable, their fireplaces hanging above vanished floors. Splintered wood panelling and a few shreds of wallpaper, leached of colour, still clung to upper walls. But at least today she was prepared, resolute against disappointment.

'This was the drawing room.' He stood in the doorway of a well-proportioned room at the front of the house and played the torch beam around the void. 'There're some old photographs at the museum which show what it was like. You should take a look.' The light rested on a gaping hole in one wall. 'There was a splendid granite fireplace there once, a beauty, but it went with the others. And a grand piano stood over there in the corner, a chaise longue against that wall next to an old gramophone with a great morning-glory horn. And that's all that's left of a window seat.' The light lingered on a rusty rod of iron hanging loose beneath the window. 'Not a bad sort of life, was it, curled up beside the window with a Scotch, the gramophone crackling away, and one of the best views in the country.' She glanced sideways at him. The enthusiasm seemed out of character, and his tone had lost its laconic edginess. He sounded almost proprietorial.

He guided her into the next room. 'Dining room,' he said. 'There's a photo showing a great long table in here laid for some classy meal—white linen, some great silver exuberance in the middle, crystal, fine china, the whole bit.'

'Quite an achievement out here.'

'Which you intend to match,' he remarked. The edge was back, but she decided to let it pass. What exactly was his problem? When she made no reply, he shrugged and led her into the next room, the one she had broken into. 'Blake's study,' he said, stooping to pick up the splintered remains of the old window boarding. 'Probably where he did his bird catalogue.' And she thought of the exquisite illustrations in Ruairidh's book, imagining the painter bent to his task, lifting his head to watch the birds circling out over the strand. 'I suppose it filled the man's time. He'd nothing else to do, of course, not being troubled by making a living.'

He propped the broken boarding against the wall and tested the strength of his handiwork from the day before.

'I wonder why he didn't go back to his landscape paintings,' Hetty said.

He shrugged. 'Maybe he became as obsessed by birds as his father. That was why old man Blake bought the estate in the first place, you know. He'd made his fortune, so he built this pile to indulge his interests in comfort. First wife died, and he did a bit of social climbing and pulled wife number two from the impoverished gentry, then he built this place and indulged his fancies.' He turned back to the doorway, lighting her route with the torch beam. 'A man of his time, was Duncan Blake, same as his son.'

They went next to stand at the door of what he told her had been the morning room. 'Although Aonghas said in his day it was used to store lumber—and turnips.' He shrugged at her puzzled expression. 'And the bit added on to it, where the bones are, had been intended as a conservatory but was never really finished. Whoever built it were complete cowboys, unskilled tenants probably, and what they did compromised the original wall. Come outside and I'll show you.' And he took her round to the side and pointed out a great crack, which spread up the wall above the sloping roof of the conservatory, fissuring and branching under windows and eaves. 'It's my guess the foundations shifted after they levelled the ground.' He gave her a long look. 'They broke its back, you see, and if that wall goes now, it'll bring the rest with it.'

She nodded slowly. 'So what do you suggest?'

'Unless you're prepared to spend a fortune, there's only one option.' He hesitated, watching her face. 'Pull the whole thing down.' She looked up sharply, in disbelief, every part of her protesting. 'Salvage what you can, build yourself a cottage on the site, and consign Muirlan House to history where it belongs.' And he walked on, round the back of the house, giving her space to absorb the blow.

She stood where he had left her, staring at the damaged wall, and saw her plans splintering into similar fractured pieces. And the house seemed to stare back at her, indifferent to its fate, past caring.

Eventually she followed him and stood, only half-listening, as he pointed out the various outbuildings—the scullery, the wash-house, and the stores—unwilling to be convinced by his verdict, and resisting. Then she waited as he secured the padlock on the front door, dully watching him pocket the keys, searching for the words to challenge him.

'I've seen places in a worse state on those restoration pro-grammes,' she said, but even to her ears this sounded weak.

'Have you?' was all he said.

~

So she said nothing more as he drove her back across the sand but thought again of that first evening when she'd seen the house, lit by the evening sun, and been enthralled by the sight. She had only this man's opinion, after all, and she sensed there was something else driving that opinion. Some agenda of his own— She knew what Giles would say if she told him. *Get someone else, for Christ's sake! Get Emma onto it—or leave it to me. I'll find someone.*

But she wasn't going to tell Giles.

She straightened her shoulders as they drew up outside her cottage. Not yet, anyway. She wasn't prepared to give up that easily.

First off, she needed to get the keys back and turned to ask him for them, but he forestalled her. 'Let's look at the report, shall we, while it's all fresh in your mind.' And he reached into the back of the Land Rover and pulled out a briefcase.

'What report?'

He looked at her. 'The one I sent to Emma Dawson.'

'When?'

'A week or so ago.' He raised an eyebrow at her expression, then got out and came round to open her door. 'You haven't seen it? I thought that was why you'd come.'

Damn Emma Dawson! She unlocked the cottage door, which stuck again, and watched, wrong-footed once more, as James shouldered it open and then stood aside to let her pass.

They were met by a chill dampness which suggested that the cottage's night storage heaters had defeated her as comprehensively as the peat. She apologised for the temperature and gestured him into the sitting room while she made tea. Why hadn't Emma told her she'd received a report? Or had she told Giles instead? She frowned as she selected the best of the cheap mugs, remembering other occasions when this had happened.

Reversing through the door with the laden tray five minutes later, she found James crouched by the fire, effortlessly coaxing the peat into life. He straightened as she entered and brought his briefcase over to the table, pulled out a chair for her, and sat down opposite, tossing his jacket aside. He accepted a mug of tea with a nod, rolled up his sleeves, and his whole demeanour seemed to change. He became serious and professional, waiting until she was settled and then going through the report page by page, explaining his points clearly and carefully, looking at her to check each time that she had understood, drawing neat, concise diagrams with a sharpened pencil if he thought she hadn't, demanding her full attention. By the end of an hour, she had to admit that his survey had been thorough—and it was damning.

He sat back at last, tapping his teeth with the pencil end, and looked at her. 'So, there you have it,' he said after a moment, and gestured hopefully towards the teapot. 'The problems go back a long way, and Blake let things slide badly in his later years.' He spooned sugar into the replenished mug, stirring it slowly. 'And since then all the original features have either been nicked or relocated throughout the islands, though I imagine the fireplaces were fenced through Glasgow.' He studied her face for a moment. 'I'm not saying restoration *can't* be done, like the projects you've seen on the box, but what you're planning will cost you the thick end of a million. Minimum.' He sipped his tea, watching her absorb this, then asked more gently if she had considered the costs of running such a place. 'No one lives out there now for a reason, you know, and providing even the basic services will be a huge expense. It never had electricity, and drinking water had to be piped across the strand from a pump house on the main island. They say it took eighty cartloads of peat to heat the place in the cold months, so translate that into oil at today's prices if you will.'

He sat back again, still watching her over the rim of his mug, and there was silence between them. Then the peat shifted in the fireplace and warmth began to spread through the room. 'You must think me very naïve,' she said at last.

'You hadn't seen the place, had you?' He set down his mug. 'And you got swept up with a dream. Nothing wrong with that, of course, we all need dreams, but even dreams need foundations.' He began gathering his papers together, giving her a twisted smile. 'I'd an idea to try and save the house myself a few years ago.'

'*You* did?'

'Presumptuous, wasn't it?' His eyes glinted briefly as he took in her expression. 'We didn't know there was any of the family left and thought we'd get it for a song.' So was this the problem? Had she somehow thwarted him? 'But after the fireplaces went, Ruairidh managed to track down your grandmother's solicitors. And then, well, other matters intervened.' She waited for him to say more, but he didn't. 'Even then a cursory inspection showed it would be impossible—or at least with the budget I could muster, and now the roof's going, it's quickening the end.' He paused. 'So if you don't pull it down, nature'll soon do the job for you.'

Later that day she strolled along the shore and looked across at the island, remembering his last words as he turned at the door. 'Ruairidh and I spent our childhood playing around the two houses and it got into the blood, so to speak.' He paused. 'And there's a sadness now, seeing it fall apart, like watching a great beast roll over and die.' Rolling over and revealing its secrets—and for a moment his eyes had held hers. 'It's hard, I know, but when you think about it, it always was an aberration. A place like that, up here? Crazy. Just let it go.'

She looked now along the shoreline, to where an unmarked police vehicle was parked at the end of the track, awaiting the return of the inflatable which had crossed the tide-filled bay, taking a police inspector out there an hour ago. But letting go was no longer possible; she couldn't just take some photographs and walk away, it was now in her blood too. She'd been drawn by a thin familial thread to this place, and that thread had led her to the bones, and she was now responsible, compelled somehow to trace the thread back, and maybe understand.

And there was now too a lost soul to lay to rest.

She looked to the west and saw that the sun was sinking behind a distant cloud bank, and the water was a gunmetal grey, flecked with white. She shivered, remembering what Ruairidh had said last night about Blake's death, about how his body had been found when the tide had ebbed, caught amongst rocks in the middle of the strand. Had he misjudged the tides? she'd asked, but he had shrugged. No one had been there, no one had seen.

Then a low buzzing sound caught her ear, and she looked back to see that the inflatable was leaving the island, heading towards her, leaving a shallow wake. As it drew close, she saw Ruairidh raise the outboard clear of the shallow water as James leapt out onto the sand, and she went down the foreshore to meet them.

'I'll let you know if there's anything relevant in the missing person file.' The inspector and the two island men had found places to sit in her tiny sitting room, concluded the necessary formalities, and had been given tea. 'But don't hold your breath.' He switched his attention to James. 'Tell me what you said earlier about the time frame.'

James was sitting on the arm of the chair occupied by his cousin, his long legs stretched out in front of him, swallowing his tea. 'You saw how the skull was up against that big rock in the foundations? Well, that rock was frost-fractured and split, so I think they'd removed the rest of it to level the land before they built the conservatory. A daft thing to do, given the sandy soils, but it left that hollow—'

'So during those building works, you think?' The inspector stopped writing to look up at him.

'Makes sense.'

'Any chance of finding out who did the work?'

'I doubt it. There's no estate archive to speak of.'

'But you reckon it was carried out when?' He began writing again.

'Early photos show there was open ground there before the conservatory was built, and they're pre-war. First war, that is.'

'Earlier,' Ruairidh interjected. 'The Blakes left the island in 1911 and stayed away for years. There'd be no building work after they'd gone.'

'When did they come back?'

'Donkey's years later. And by then Blake was on his own.'

The inspector looked up. 'The wife?'

'She'd left him.'

'Children?'

'None.'

Hetty scanned their faces, remembering what Ùna Forbes had said. 'Do you think it could be her? His wife, I mean?'

'Ach, it could be anyone,' said the inspector, giving her a brief smile as he put away his notebook. 'The locket suggests a woman, but the lab will be able to tell us in due course. They'll collect DNA too and see where that leaves us. If you'd be willing to give a sample, it might show if there's any Blake connection.' That frail thread, gossamer thin… 'Though it won't help if it is Blake's wife.'

'Take mine too,' said Ruairidh. 'My family's been on the estate for generations, and his lot are connected too.' He pointed to James with his spoon.

'Take mine by all means, but you could have the whole island's DNA and be no wiser,' said James. 'We've been marrying our cousins for centuries. No new blood since the Vikings came, the traffic's been all the other way.'

Chapter 7

∼ 1910, Beatrice ∼

It took a moment or two before Beatrice's eyes adjusted after the strong sunlight outside. Her city heels clicked across the tiled hall ahead of Theo, and she halted at the foot of the stairs, swinging her hat, taking in her surroundings while he gave instructions regarding the trunks. A red deer, glassy-eyed and arrogant, snubbed her from the half-landing while a fox crouched warily on top of a bookcase. Other eyes were watching too, a host of baleful creatures, staring blankly. Had they also assembled to inspect her?

She looked around her. The hall seemed faded and dusty, lulled to sleep by the tick of the longcase clock and the heavy scent of burning peat. Fine cobwebs criss-crossed the red deer's antlers, overlooked by a hasty housemaid, and a mustiness rose from the horsehair settle. She looked up at the glorious light which flooded from the raised glass rooflight, catching floating dust motes in its path. 'Where shall we start?' Theo called across to her, and she smiled over her shoulder at him, privately conjuring up a vision of the hall in a pale sunlit yellow with bowls full of flowers from the garden she intended to nurture.

Her resolve grew as they toured the house. Little had been done since Theo's father had established his household there half a century ago, and he, she surmised, had valued things for durability, not style. There was so much she could do, but for now, she politely acknowledged and admired, conscious of Theo's anxiety and his desire that she would be pleased. 'I suppose it's all a bit old-fashioned,' he admitted, looking about him in consternation, and she smiled, saying nothing.

From the dining room there was a wide, sweeping view where

the blue hills of the next island rose beyond the bay, and she went across to look out of the window. 'Oh, exquisite!' Below her she heard male laughter and, glancing down, she saw the factor's sons on the path below. The younger one dropped his head when they saw her, but the older one raised a hand in a friendly salute. Something told her that their laughter was connected with herself, and she turned aside, the salute unacknowledged. Then her eye was caught by a display case above the fireplace, where an unusual bird, the size of a goose, sat on an untidy nest. 'What extraordinary colouring.' She went closer. A bright red eye stared out of a black head above a necklace of black-and-white feathered patches, a pattern which continued onto its body, giving the effect of dappled light reflecting off still water.

'Aha. *Gavia immer*, my prize.' Theo came and stood beside her, his hands in his pockets. 'I got him just off the headland to the east, many years ago. But the display is contrived, I confess; they don't breed here.' He guided her back across the hall to another room. His study.

'Good heavens!' She stood, aghast, at the threshold. It was a large room, overlooking the strand, and should have been beautiful, but was choked with desks, bookcases, and cabinets, and on every surface stood stiff, lifeless birds, arranged in varying poses, their eyes dull and unfocussed, and their very stillness was numbing. In other wall-mounted cases, the scientific intent was more obvious, and the displays more brutal. Wings, which carried light bodies on soft breezes, had been severed, splayed and pinned to show the mechanics of flight; tail fans, designed for balance and courtship, had been treated likewise. Their dusty staleness gave an odd atmosphere to the room, and again she felt under a silent scrutiny.

She glanced at Theo as he examined a parcel on his desk and thought how strange it was to destroy wild creatures only to fix them again indoors in a semblance of life— Then she saw an easel beside the window and went over to it, feeling more comfortable with the painter than the collector. She picked up a half-finished sketch which, at first glance, seemed to show a young girl, but on closer inspection she saw that it was a boy, a naked youth, graceful and slim, water glistening on his back as he emerged from a rock pool. 'A masterpiece in progress, Theo?'

He looked up and frowned slightly. 'Hardly,' he said, coming over to join her. 'A mere scribble. I shan't finish it.' And he took it up, glanced at it, then tucked it into a pile of old canvasses, burying it from sight.

~

The following days passed in a pleasant idleness as Beatrice explored her husband's refuge and found everything delightful. The house, of course, was impossibly old-fashioned and could be made so much brighter with a light tone of paint and the banishment of heavy oak furniture to attics or outbuildings. But for now she kept such thoughts to herself— After years of frugality at home, spending Theo's money was something she was cautious about, despite the carte blanche he had given her to order whatever she wanted, and change whatever needed changing. 'Except in my study, of course,' he had added hastily, and she had laughed at his expression.

About a week after their arrival, she had awoken as the early morning light shafted through her window, and yawned self-indulgently before opening her eyes, resting her arms in an arc above her head. She lay a moment listening to the gulls, then slid a hand across the bed, but Theo was gone, long gone, the sheets grown cold. She rolled over, sweeping her hair aside, to look where his head had dented the pillow beside her, wondering again where he went these early mornings. She had seen him once returning across the strand and had chastised him for not waking her to join him. 'I often rise early up here,' he had said, and given her his wistful smile as he bent to kiss her. 'But that's no reason to rob *you* of sleep.'

She threw back the covers and went across the room to the little turret which gave her views in three directions, resting her hand on the wall. Theo was a perplexing man. Here, where they were thrown back on each other's company, and without the structure of city life, she realised how little she knew him. He had seemed elated upon arrival, delighted to be here, and she had watched him walk down to the foreshore and then linger, talking to the factor's son.

But she had become aware of his moods here. His silences.

Yesterday they had strolled along the shoreline, hand-in-hand at first, then walking side-by-side, stepping between clumps of pink sea thrift and hummocks of coarse grass. 'Earnshaw wants us to go across and have dinner with them, but I put him off. Do you mind?'

'Not if you don't care to go.'

'I don't, not at the moment— It's a bit of a trek, and we'd have to stay one night at least, although they'd expect us for longer, and it'll all get immured in politics.'

'Politics! Up here?'

He had groaned, giving her a hand over the slippery rocks. 'You've no idea. Century-old disputes over land, and I didn't come up here to get dragged back into the debate.'

'No indeed! You came to paint. Did you tell him so?'

'I imagine he'd think I'd other reasons for declining.' He had given her a dry smile and led her towards the tumbled stones of an old ruin. 'Come and have a look at St. Ultan's chapel, my dear, before it erodes away completely.' He pointed out the old gravestones clustered about the ruins, one inscribed with a sword, another with a simple ship. 'My father started cataloguing them all once, scraping the lichens away to see the inscriptions. He had this uncontrollable urge to list things—birds, tombstones, or profits and losses.' There was always an edge to Theo's voice when he spoke of his father, who had remained indifferent to his talent. This much she had learned in Edinburgh from Theo's sister, Emily, and had observed the coldness between Theo and his stepmother for herself. 'The lichen's beginning to grow back, thank God. Just look at that colour, quite luminous.'

She agreed that it was lovely, and had watched him as he examined the overlapping pads of moss and lichen on the fallen cross. 'Who was St. Ultan?' she asked.

'An Irishman. He gave succour to infants, I'm told, especially orphans.' He had come and sat beside her, leaning his back against the wall of the ruin, and she felt the warmth of his shoulder next to hers. 'My mother wanted to bury her stillborn daughter here, but my father wouldn't have it, said the babe wasn't an orphan. He had a plot made on the ridge behind the house, and then two more joined the first, poor wights. Mother hated them being there, exposed to every gale, all alone.'

Theo rarely spoke of his mother, except to say that she used to draw pictures with him when he was a child. And he, so young when she died, must have felt her loss keenly. 'But she's with them there now,' she said carefully.

'She'd rather be here, nevertheless.' He got abruptly to his feet. 'Come on, I felt spots of rain,' he said, and he had set off, leaving her to follow.

So far he had shown no inclination to paint, but had been boyishly enthusiastic about his new camera, prowling around the house experimenting, startling housemaids whom he commanded to remain motionless, and self-conscious, in his compositions. He had surprised her too as she sat at her dressing table one morning. 'Raise your arms to your hair again. As you were. No. Wait! Yes, there.' And he told her he had captured a thousand images of her, reflected in the angled side mirror. 'But what will I do with a thousand Beatrices?' he asked, putting aside his camera. 'Just one has all a man could ask for.' And he had swept her laughing from the stool and carried her back to the rumpled bed. The poor girl who had come to collect her breakfast tray half an hour later had been mortified.

Lifting her head now, she saw him from the window, out on the drained sand, walking towards the house, a dark figure backlit by the low sun, and reached for her clothes. She would join him, if only for the last stretch up to the house. Grabbing a shawl, she looked again at the approaching figure and then stopped, the shawl loose in her hand. For it was not Theo, after all, but the factor's elder son who was striding across the beach towards the house; the long shadows had deceived her. And as she watched she saw him raise a hand to his mouth and heard a piercing whistle, which brought Bess, the brown pointer, tearing from the shore, circling him in delight. He bent and twisted, hurling a stick far out onto the strand. The dog pelted after it, sending up sprays of diamonds from the shallow water, and she found herself wondering if Theo had ever played so lightheartedly across the sands.

Halfway down the stairs, she met Mrs. Henderson with her breakfast tray. 'I was just bringing this up, madam, with a message from Mr. Blake. He's ridden over to the manse but says he'll be back for dinner.' Beatrice smiled brightly and thanked her, agreeing that she would take breakfast in the morning room, and entered just in time to see through the window as Cameron Forbes disappeared around the back of the factor's house, followed by his dog.

She poured her tea and bit into the toast, looking round, resolving again that a pair of dusty lapwings over the fireplace would be better suited elsewhere. But she must be patient, not try and change things too quickly, and in the meantime she must find some occupation, for Mrs. Henderson's competency left her with little to do. 'We're damned lucky to have her,' Theo had said, explaining that she had been trained in one of the big houses on the mainland and had returned to the islands 'in trouble.' Running Muirlan House for them was child's play.

She pulled out a half-finished letter to Emily Blake and picked up her pen. *Your brother has not yet dipped brush in paint,* she wrote, *but spends his days either out on the estate or closeted in his study with the factor's son. Still settling in, he tells me. Do you think you will come this summer? You mustn't think you intrude…*

When Theo had first suggested they spend the summer on the island, she had felt a stab of disappointment, hoping he might have suggested Europe. 'Venice stinks in summer,' he had said, 'and Rome's full of foreigners.' And something in his face had told her that coming here was important to him. *The island is as lovely as you described and I confess that I don't miss Edinburgh one bit.* She paused again, thinking back to the endless, deadening round of social occasion and intrigue, driven as she had been by the cheerless imperative to find a husband as her father careered towards financial disaster. He had led a reckless life, with a circle of ramshackle friends, and his love of the racecourse had never been equalled by his successes there, but her mother's frank revelations regarding his debts had come as a shock. 'Don't fall for a charming smile, my dear. We must find you a man of substance, and *quickly.*' Her mother had made an unequal match, marrying against her family's wishes, and Beatrice had watched, mortified, as she used all her remaining connections to thrust her daughter forward before her husband burned through her remaining inheritance.

Beatrice had tried to play by the rules, hating the whole business, and had a number of admirers, but when her first close association was found to have considerable debts of his own, and a rather unsavoury past, she had been whisked away, narrowly avoiding a personal disaster.

And it was then that she had met Theo Blake.

She knew his name, of course, as well as his reputation, and had been pleased to be invited to a private viewing of his recent work, completed during a long stay in Europe. He had been pointed out to her upon arrival, a strikingly handsome man, bronzed and healthy-looking among the pale city dwellers, moving amongst them with an assured nonchalance. But as she wandered through the exhibition, examining his paintings, she was conscious of disappointment. They were mostly rural scenes, goat herds amongst sage scrub on parched hillsides, ochre buildings decaying in golden sunlight, a dog asleep in the shadows. Beautifully executed but unremarkable.

And then she had been drawn to a painting which hung in a corner, away from the others, a painting she now recognised as the view from the foreshore in front of the house. It showed two ill-defined figures walking across the strand, through contrasting patches of light, shadow, and mist, walking in parallel, slightly apart from each other, and somehow clearly a man and a woman. But were they coming together or drifting apart? The painting left it unresolved, and she had been arrested by a sense of deep poignancy. She stood looking at it for a long time, then spoke to the companion she imagined stood behind her. 'Why, this is quite ethereal. A mirage—'

'A mirage, you say?' A deep voice spoke across her shoulder. 'Something you're compelled to reach for'—she had turned to find the painter himself looking at it over her head, his eyes sharp and intense—'knowing you can never grasp it.'

Introductions were swiftly made, and he had explored her face with an unsettling directness, then others had stolen his attention and she watched him accepting congratulations with urbane dismissal, his manners easy and smooth. And she had detected a hint of disdain, as if he held neither their flattery nor the paintings in any great esteem. His single state, his established reputation and, more particularly, his controlling interest in his deceased father's textile mills had made him the subject of considerable interest in Edinburgh society, and she watched predatory mamas calculating their chances.

And then he was beside her again. 'I sense indifference, Miss Somersgill.'

She looked up guiltily to find that he was smiling. 'Not indifference, no. Only… only these are so very different from the other one.'

'That's because these, you see, are exercises in technique designed to'—he opened the exhibition catalogue—' "demonstrate complete mastery of brushwork and perspective, an eye for the charm of the commonplace, a superior understanding of tonal quality.'" He lowered the catalogue and smiled over the top of it. 'And to remind people that I'm still alive.'

'And the other?' She smiled back at him. 'To remind *yourself* that that's the case?' She had spoken without thinking and was startled by his changed expression. 'There's a greater... a greater sensitivity, a depth of feeling—' she added, faltering and confused. 'I like it better.'

'So do I.' Again that searching, unsettling intensity. 'Let me help you to the refreshments. You've spoken the first sensible word I've heard tonight.'

And so it had begun.

Chapter 8

≈ 1889, Theo ≈

He stood motionless on the top of the dunes and stared out to the horizon, and the world was still and quiet around him. Below him the sea was a dark wash of ultramarine tipped with white stretching clear to the horizon but an icy jade where the waves rose to meet the shore. He watched, transfixed by the sight, by the relentless energy, seeing veils of spray flung back as each wave raced ashore. Torrann Bay—at last! Here was the very essence of the island, its elemental spirit. Mystical at dawn, blazing white hot at midday or drenched by showers, and an awesome symphony of light as the sun drowned in the western sea.

Twenty years ago he had set up his easel just behind where he now stood and had painted the scene. It felt like yesterday, and the sound and the smell of the place had haunted him throughout his self-imposed exile.

After a while he turned away and sat on a stone, his customary seat, and leant against the wall of a ruined croft house, closing his eyes and losing himself to the sound of the waves and the wind rattling through the dune grasses.

The sun had not yet tipped the peak of Bheinn Mhor on the main island when he'd reached the dunes this morning, and he'd been panting by the time he'd climbed to the top. City living had taken its toll. Or was it age? Forty, by God! He'd looked back across the machair towards the house, where he had left Beatrice sleeping. Content, it seemed, to be here. Or was it simply the novelty? Or to please him? Beatrice, bless her, was eager to please. He smiled slightly, his eyes still closed, savouring the thought of her, and this perfect moment, before the land was flooded with light. A calm, expectant moment, a moment of quiet solitude.

To reflect.

And slowly, as he sat there, he felt the sanctity of the place wrap around him, and knew that he had truly returned.

He had not dared to come here until now.

His eyes remained shut.

But even with them closed, he could clearly see Màili standing where he had just stood, and where he had once sketched her, skirt flattened against her bare legs, outlining the curves of her form. A few deft strokes, a little light shading, and he had captured her—or so he had thought.

But she had slipped away, as surely as a selkie maid.

Once, as they had lain lazily in a sandy hollow just below here, where dunes became beach, she had told him the island legend of the selkies, the seal people who came ashore at midsummer, shedding their skins to dance on the beach. Unwary fishermen would fall under their enchantment, she had told him, her eyes wide and believing, and then steal their skins, binding the creatures to them, compelling them to stay ashore as wistful wives, forever seeking their lost pelts, their only chance of returning to their ocean home. She had been stretched out on her stomach plaiting the coarse dune grasses as she told the story, and he beside her, watching her nimble fingers twisting the blades. 'And are you weaving binding spells in the marram grass?' he asked, capturing her hands and ruining her handiwork as he pulled her to him. 'Strong magic, Màili.'

But no spell had been needed; by then he was already bound to her, hand and foot and heart.

And it was here, on another occasion, that they had stood together and looked up to the sky and watched two sea eagles twisting and turning in a strange, violent dance. 'Are they fighting?' Màili had asked as the birds came together, locked talons grappling, tumbling, and rolling over each other, doing cartwheels through the air, their wing pinions fluttering and feathered legs swinging out below.

'Courting, not fighting,' he had replied.

They had watched as the birds plummeted, apparently out of control, until the last moment, when they had recovered and climbed again, only to repeat the performance.

Then she had given him her slant-eyed smile. 'And I thought courtship was a gentle business.'

But he had not heeded her words. And later that day he had sketched her lying on the sand below the dunes, her arm out-stretched and her hair entwined with the tangle, becoming part of it. She had laughed at his sudden intensity, but the composition had excited him: dark curls merging with trails of seaweed, bare legs the colour of shell sand, and he had begged her to let him paint her, in that same pose, unclothed: 'A true selkie. Please, Màili.' But she had shot to her feet, dark eyes enormous and cheeks crimson, ready to flee.

Theo opened his eyes and stared, unfocussed, over the surface of the sea. Only once did he allow his gaze to stray to the headland, where hidden amongst the rocks and grassy tussocks was the rock pool, with its cushions of pink thrift rooted in the cracks and crevices. It was after *that* day that things had changed. After that day she had gone seeking her pelt, and then slipped away.

He took a deep breath and, after a moment, pulled his field glasses from their worn leather case and began raking the shoreline for birds, dragging his mind back from the past, and began mentally ticking off the species as he saw them. At least some things in this charmed place remained constant— He followed the flight of a pair of shelduck which had risen near the rocks, and then paused to fix upon two dark shapes beyond. He sat forward and watched them intently for a while until he was certain, then he lowered the glasses, smiling with a deep satisfaction. Divers. Immature males, overwintering, no doubt. They would leave soon. Or did they, like him, intend to stay, look for sweet-tempered mates, and settle? It was too much to hope for.

He looked about him once more. Surely he could come back here now and paint again, really paint, not just go through the motions in some Parisian atelier or picturesque French village. This was where he belonged, where he had first found that compelling absorption, that sense of purpose, the intense, slow burn of passion.

And he would bring Beatrice here.

Soon. Very soon—

He smiled again at the thought of Beatrice. Lovely Beatrice, with her calm manner and her poise. She seemed delighted by all he had shown her, and she seemed to *understand*, as he thought she might when he had first seen her at the gallery staring with such intensity at his painting. 'A mirage,' she had said, seeing it for what it was. He'd been chasing mirages across the world for far too long! That painting had been a wrenching farewell to his old love, conceived in grief, but Beatrice, of course, could not have known that.

He released another deep breath. It had taken a long time to work up the courage to come back to the island for anything more than was necessary to keep the estate in order. Pitiful! Such wretched cowardice. But now Beatrice offered him a new beginning. New hope. They would spend every spring and summer here and leave with the corncrakes in the autumn.

He lifted his face to the sun, closed his eyes, and let the light flood around him, seeking strength from its energy. There must be no more fruitless grieving. He would be resolute and put it all behind him, for Beatrice was here with him, his shield and his talisman, untouched by the past.

A past that could be put aside at last.

But for Cameron.

The thought brought him back to earth and he opened his eyes, a frown creasing his forehead. How the *devil* was he to cope with Cameron being here? When he had appeared so suddenly that first day, without warning, Theo had felt the impact like a blow, and could only stand, winded and off balance, and watch him approach. That familiar, confident stride—and when he had raised his eyes and smiled, extending his hand, it had been Màili who had looked out at him.

He got to his feet and went to stand again at the edge of the dune, his hands thrust deep into his pockets, and stared down at the beach below him. Those eyes had always been a conduit back to Màili, a thin and precious thread. And once, years ago, he had stood here with Cameron, a boy who barely reached his shoulder and who had pulled urgently at his sleeve. 'Look, sir! Sea eagles.' And together they had watched them, perhaps the same pair, for they were long-lived creatures. And as the lad lifted excited eyes to Theo, he had looked down at him and been swamped by a powerful emotion, the strength of which had never left him.

Having him close had been like having Màili, again.

He turned away from the sea and bent to pick up his field glasses, shaking his head to rid himself of impossible longings. And it was time to be heading back; the sun was up.

The lad had altered, he thought, as he walked along the ridge of the dunes. Or was he just two years older? He looked well, though, very well, and Theo wanted desperately to talk to him, hear of his travels, his impressions, get to *know* him again, but he sensed in Cameron a new reserve and a greater assurance. Almost challenging— though that was nothing new! And he smiled, remembering Cameron as a boy with his precocious self-confidence. But what had drawn him back here? Canada must surely have offered opportunities for a young man like him. John Forbes had been ill last winter. Was it that which had brought him back? Or was it the pull of the island itself? God knows it gave a powerful tug!

There was an irony, though, that their returns had coincided so closely, as if the same force had simultaneously reeled them both back in.

But would he stay?

If he did, they could work together again. Donald was old

enough to help his father now, freeing Cameron to assist Theo. He was intelligent and had good prospects here, he must be made to understand this, and Theo could advance his interests in many ways. He plunged down the landward side of the dunes, his feet sinking deep in the sand, watching as the sun reached the top of Bheinn Mhor and the sweet tang of the damp grass rose to assail him. He would speak to him, and to John, and if he could persuade Cameron to stay, he would have all he could hope for. And in this mature contentment he would rediscover the island. Reclaim it for himself, on his own terms. Timeless and unchanging.

And he would *paint* again.

Chapter 9

'Yes, I think that is all, Mrs. Henderson. Thank you.'

The housekeeper gave a smile and a nod, and then withdrew, closing the door of the morning room behind her, and Beatrice smiled. It was something of a charade, this morning ritual when Mrs. Henderson came to her for instructions, knowing better than she did what needed doing. She always brought a list of suggested meals for the day, and occasionally would offer Beatrice a choice while managing to convey a sense of what she felt would be more appropriate, and Beatrice appreciated her tact. In Mrs. Henderson she recognised an ally. Gradually, and tentatively at first on both parts, they had begun to discuss how they might tackle the house, bring it more up to date and make it more comfortable. They had got as far as making lists for each room of which furniture required a thorough clean, which perhaps could be refashioned or reupholstered, and which ought to be removed altogether, and discovered that they were largely in agreement.

'I was just a housemaid when the first Mrs. Blake was here, and everything was still quite new then, and these heavy furnishings were more in fashion. Most had been sent up from Paisley,' she told Beatrice. 'But I was working on the mainland when the dear lady died, poor thing, and the second Mrs. Blake was never really happy here.'

'Theo—Mr. Blake said she found it... remote.'

'Aye, she did, so she never cared enough for the place to keep it up. And by then old Mr. Blake was quite set in his ways and didn't like changes.' Beatrice hoped his son was not going to prove to be the same. 'And Mr. Theo, of course, hasn't spent much time here in recent years.'

Beatrice wanted to ask why that was, but this was a subject to be approached obliquely. 'And yet he clearly loves the place! His paintings show that.'

'Oh yes! I remember him as a lad, always with his sketchbook. His mama would take him out and they would sketch and paint together, it was lovely to see! But when I came back, everything had changed. She had died, Mr. Blake remarried, the old factor was sick and John Forbes was trying to do his job, a man's job, it was, though he was hardly more than a lad then. He and Mr. Theo had been firm friends from childhood, you know, and old Mr. Blake saw to it that they had lessons together. They were always off somewhere, with Màili Cameron, the schoolmaster's little girl, chasing after.' She smiled a moment at the memory. 'Happy days, those. But in the time I was away, everything had changed, and Mr. Theo was so quiet, still grieving for his mother.'

There was much more that Beatrice wanted to know, but Mrs. Henderson had stopped at that point and asked what Beatrice wanted done with the linen. 'Some of it is so thin, madam, you'll have your feet through. If you and Mr. Blake have guests to stay, I'll be hard-pressed to make the beds.' They had agreed to order more linen and find time to sort through the old stuff, and then Mrs. Henderson had left her.

Beatrice went over to the window and saw the factor setting off down the track, and tried to imagine Theo and him as carefree boys together, escaping lessons. An old friendship must bring with it trust, and so Theo had felt able to leave the estate to his care over the years. And yet, while she had observed that John Forbes was unfailingly respectful, he was never familiar, and his exchanges with Theo seemed limited to estate matters.

She went over to her bureau and sat, pulling out the letter to Emily which was still unfinished, and found herself hoping very much that she would come up and stay— Then she glanced again at the window and saw that the clouds had lifted and the weather looked set fine, too fine indeed to be indoors. Emily's letter would have to wait, she decided, and shut the lid of her bureau and went to find her hat.

Piece by piece, little by little, she was beginning to put together a picture of her husband's past, she thought as she pulled the front door closed behind her and went down towards the shore. From Theo himself she had learned only the basic facts of his existence; the rest was hidden behind an impenetrable reserve. Mrs. Henderson would perhaps tell her more as they got to know each other better, and Emily too might fill in the gaps, although Theo must have been a man already grown and gone before she really knew him.

And Beatrice felt she barely knew him herself.

He had seemed quite formidable at first, she thought, as she walked down to the foreshore, rather aloof and often ironic, and she had felt shy with him. But she had also been drawn, intrigued by an enigmatic quality, sensing a depth and a restrained passion. She remembered the buzz of astonishment when their engagement was announced a few weeks after they had met at the exhibition. Envious friends had congratulated her on his wealth and sighed over his handsome face, while spiteful ones had commiserated with her for marrying someone almost twenty years her senior. 'But you can always take a lover in a year or two,' one bold young matron had told her, and Beatrice had pulled away, resenting such cynicism. Besides, Theo did not seem old to her. Only his eyes, perhaps, remote sometimes, staring off into some distant, private world.

When the exhibition of his work had finished, she had asked him if she could keep the painting over which they had met, not sell it—and an unexplained shadow had darkened his face. But later he agreed and had written a dedication to her on the back, and it hung now in the drawing room in Muirlan House. She often stood in front of it seeing how, through observation and consummate skill, he had captured the island's unique quality. His works spoke of space, of light and of limitless horizons, a restless landscape—and they resonated with her present mood. She stopped a moment, elated as the wind flattened her skirts against her legs and loosened the ribbons of her hat, and she felt like a newborn creature, discovering stiff, untried limbs. And here, amidst the backdrop and the inspiration of so many of his paintings, she could appreciate more fully the complexity of his work.

She walked on, feeling liberated by her swinging skirts and sturdy shoes, and heedless that the skies immediately above her were filling with a rasping, clicking sound. By the time she looked up, it was to see a cloud of delicate, black-capped white birds with long forked tails hovering directly overhead, screaming at her. There could be no mistaking their hostility, and she hesitated, unnerved, then took a hasty step and missed her footing, dropping her head just in time to avoid a sudden dive. Another swooped, beady eyes enraged, as the wind snatched off her hat, cartwheeling it away, and she went in pursuit. The birds followed, scolding furiously, until a sharp stab on the top of her head brought her up short, and she looked up to see a white fury hovering overhead, its red beak shrieking a warning.

Panicked now, she bent and had started to run in pursuit of her hat when she heard a shout and looked up to see three figures at the edge of the field, waving and calling, their words carried away by the wind. The factor and his sons. Then another beak struck, sharper this time, and now two of the figures were running towards her; one veered off after her hat while the other continued into the melee of feathers and rage, stripping off his jacket. Another bird dived.

'Keep your head down, or they'll have your eye out!' Cameron Forbes warned as he threw his jacket over her head. 'Grab the sleeve.' He held on to the other and put his arm around her waist, propelling her firmly up the beach until the furious birds dropped back, one by one, and he released her, his eyes alight with amusement.

'Are you alright, Mrs. Blake?' The factor was striding towards them. 'You were struck, I think?'

She found a sticky patch on her head and looked at her red fingertip in astonishment. 'What on earth are they?'

'Arctic terns.' It was his son who answered. 'And they can skewer fish with those beaks.'

'But why did they attack me?'

'They will, you see, if they've eggs and young chicks.' The factor's tone was apologetic. 'And you'd strayed into the heart of their territory, not knowing—'

'If we hadn't seen you, there'd be nothing left to find but strips of flesh and a handful of rags.' Cameron Forbes stood with his jacket tossed over a shoulder, a finger hooked into the collar, the other hand reaching down to fondle his dog's ears, a smile still playing across his features.

John Forbes frowned at his son. 'May I take a look at your head, madam?' he said, and she dropped her chin. 'You must have some ointment on that cut,' he said. 'Cameron, take Mrs. Blake back to the house and tell Mrs. Henderson to attend to it.'

'Of course.' The young man pushed an arm back into his jacket sleeve and whistled to his dog. Donald returned too, and held out her hat.

She took it from him and crammed it back onto her head, thanking him briefly, feeling foolish, like a child being taken home after a silly mishap, nettled by his brother's obvious amusement.

'In a few weeks they'll have flown and the beach will be empty again,' he said in a conciliatory tone as they rejoined the track.

'And has the island other forms of vicious wildlife I should know about?'

He seemed to consider. 'Eagles or buzzards will attack a lamb or a newborn calf, but I don't imagine they'll try to carry *you* off, madam.' She looked up sharply at this familiarity, still conscious of the way he had propelled her up the beach, and met a cheerful, uncomplicated smile. 'Nor would the terns have done you any real harm.'

She found herself responding to him. '*Not* reduced me to

rags and strips of flesh?'

'Not for a first offence,' he said gravely, and she dropped her head to hide a smile, wary of encouraging him. After a moment he added, 'Edinburgh must seem a long way off, madam.'

'Another world.' And they talked of Edinburgh, which he had visited once, and this led on to his wider travels, and Beatrice was struck, as she had been on earlier occasions, by this young man's easy manners and style of address. Theo, to her surprise, seemed to give him that license. When Cameron's attention was taken by the dog, she glanced across at him. There was something about him, something which set him quite apart from servants she had known at home or in Theo's Edinburgh house. It was more than just the way he carried himself, shoulders straight and assured; it was something in his expression. His directness. Theo seemed to use him as some sort of secretary, so perhaps he did not consider himself a mere servant.

'What was it you were doing today,' she asked, intrigued by him, 'with your father and brother?'

'Deciding where to build sand fences to halt the erosion. Futile, really, as the storms will have their way in the end.'

So he was a farmhand too! 'But it makes a change from Mr. Blake's catalogues and ledgers.'

'And provides a chance to be heroic.' This time she allowed herself to return his smile.

Later she questioned Theo about Cameron's role, but he was dismissive. 'I'm employing him to assist me, when he can be spared. He has a neat hand and knows my ways. He's worked with me before, and I trained him, so to speak.' And with that she had to be content.

But she found that she often came across them together, heads bent over dried specimen in the study, discussing books and articles, like tutor and scholar, absorbed by common interests. Or she would watch them heading out together onto the estate with sporting guns, sometimes with John Forbes, or Donald, but often just the two of them. And yet she sensed a current of tension between them, and once she had met a wrathful Cameron in the hall following a curt dismissal. Earlier there had been raised voices in the study, and from the little she had overheard, it was not natural history that had been under discussion.

Chapter 10

~ 2010, Hetty ~

Hetty stood drumming her fingers on the windowsill and looked across to Muirlan Island, where clouds hung low, threatening rain. She stooped to pick up a mug left under a chair and took it through to the kitchen. She wanted to go back across and have another look around, on her own, but was thwarted now by tide and police prohibition. No one was to go near the bones again, the inspector had warned, and nothing was to be said until the forensic team had removed them. Any interest caused by unusual activity up at the old house could be explained away, if necessary, by Hetty's arrival.

But no one was going over the strand this morning, anyway, and Ruairidh's tide tables suggested it would be hours before it was safe to cross. She needed a walk, though, and decided she would explore along the shore following the edge of the bay to where she'd seen the tide pouring in between the two spear points of land, and take some photographs.

She thought again about James Cameron's report as she pulled on her jacket and reached for her camera. In fact, she thought of little else— His estimation of costs was quite unreachable, but then Giles had once spoken of partnerships, ways and means of raising finance to make the project viable, but she had resisted the idea. Once the restoration was done, she had hoped the hotel would cover its own running costs, but James's view suggested otherwise. She would, after all, have to ask Giles to explain her options in more detail. Finance was his forte.

But how far did she want to involve Giles? The question couldn't be dodged forever.

Almost without her noticing, over this last year Giles had

drawn her into his world and become part of her landscape. Or, rather, she had become part of his. She was fond of Giles, and grateful to him. He had been there when her need had been the greatest, first in a professional capacity but later, after that encounter in the art gallery, he had stepped in and supported her at a time when she was overwhelmed by the relentless bureaucracy of death, steering her through probate, the house sale, even helping her find a suitable home for her grandmother as her dementia deepened. And they had been seeing each other, off and on, ever since. They met two or three times a week these days, for a film or a drink, had holidayed together twice, and now almost invariably spent the weekends together, at either his flat or hers, although she had resisted his entreaties that she move in with him. She was not ready for that. Her friends told her she was lucky. Nice man, well set up, clearly devoted, and he had started to talk about the future.

She paused, balancing on a slippery rock. Friends might see them as an established couple, and perhaps they were... but it was hard to explain to them how she felt as if Giles could drain the oxygen from a room, and it was this characteristic which made her hesitate. He meant well, of course, but even in the darkest days she had needed her own space, and she needed it still. He was only trying to help, he told her, but— It seemed her thoughts always stalled with that blunt little word, like a railway buffer at the end of a track.

Was that what they were approaching? The end of the track?

A shaft of sunlight split the clouds, turning a pool of water on the strand to hammered silver, and she pulled out her camera, pushing Giles into a siding for the moment, as she tried to capture the image before it faded. From here the house looked almost intact. Ahead of her there was a small headland from where she might get an even better shot, across the water, so she walked on, towards an old croft house which stood at the end of the headland, stoically facing the bay.

It was one of the traditional stone dwellings, with two

rooflights and two lower windows, the front door hidden on the landward side, and a miscellany of floats and lobster pots scattered amongst bog cotton and coarse grasses. A neat peat stack stood, somewhat incongruously, beside a propane tank, and a traditional-looking wooden boat was pulled up above the high-tide mark between two large boulders. Did the occupants still survive by fishing, she wondered, or did they have land elsewhere? Sheep, perhaps, or cattle. Island life was a mystery to her.

But she could learn.

It wasn't clear to her where the beach began and the croft land ended, and ideally she would climb onto the larger boulder for her shot. There was no sign of life, however, and perhaps the owners wouldn't mind. So she tucked her camera inside her jacket and scrambled up, experimenting with the zoom until, right on cue, a shaft of light raced across the low-lying land and lit the walls of Muirlan House. Brilliant!

'Should be good.' She jumped at a voice behind her and turned to see James Cameron leaning out of one of the upstairs windows, his arms folded on the sill. 'Never the same light twice.'

'Oh. This is your—?' But he had vanished. She climbed down from the boulder, putting her camera away, and wished it had not been his house. Wrong-footed yet again. He reappeared a moment later from round the side of the house, and she apologised. 'I'm probably trespassing.'

'Yep,' he agreed, 'so you'd better come in and account for yourself'—he gestured open-handed round the side of the house, and there was the Land Rover parked in the shadow of the far wall. How had she not seen it?—'and have a cup of tea.'

She could hardly refuse. Was he the boat owner too? And the lobster pots? She followed him round the side of the house, wondering where on earth Emma had found him. Was he even qualified to have a view on restoring Muirlan House?

She stopped at the door of the cottage and looked inside, and felt at once that her question had been answered. The interior was stunning—the ground floor had been knocked through and opened up, and a new wooden staircase now separated a cooking and eating area from what had been the small parlour. Original features, including the kitchen range and parlour fireplace, had been carefully restored, and the narrow wooden panelling on the walls was freshly painted and expertly lit. A clever blend of the old and new, practical and minimalist, yet striking, and what he had done had taken skill, and taste.

He offered her tea. 'Or coffee?'

'Tea, please,' she said, just as the phone rang.

'Half a mo, but I need to get this.' He gestured her into the living area and, juggling a diary and a pen, the phone clamped under his chin, he began to discuss ferries and delivery dates.

She continued her assessment of the cottage, now intrigued by the man. The walls were covered with photographs, arranged at all heights, large frames and small, a mixture of nineteenth-century sepia prints and more recent modern landscapes, many monochrome and of very high quality. And she recognised views of the island, of the strand, and of Muirlan House itself, taken from where she had stood a moment earlier. 'Your work?' she asked, when his call was finished, and he came across carrying two mugs, placing hers on the hearth where a peat fire smouldered in a bed of ash. 'They're very good.'

'You can't go wrong up here. With this light.' She continued to move round the room, studying the pictures. Landscapes and seascapes, sunsets and storm clouds, all cleverly captured and sympathetically framed.

And then she came to two small pencil sketches tucked into an alcove. One depicted a young girl lying on her back in the sand, dark hair spread fan-like, mingling with the seaweed, one arm stretched voluptuously above her head, apparently asleep—but she wasn't. A little smile played around her parted lips, and beneath half-closed lids one imagined her eyes were dancing. The pencil had stroked the swell of her breasts beneath a light blouse, and her skirts were rumpled, offering a shadowed glimpse of a dimpled knee. In the other, the same girl was standing on the edge of the dunes with her clothes framing her form as she leant into the force of the wind.

'These are *brilliant…*'

He came and stood behind her. 'Aye. But the talent's in your genes, not mine.' She looked round at him, then took his meaning and turned back, peering closer, searching in vain for a signature. 'Others in the sketchbook were signed,' he added.

'Others?'

He went over to a small desk in the corner and came back with a worn sketchbook, which he handed to her. Reverently she turned the pages, seeing half-finished sketches, studies, exercises in tone and shading and, on one page, several attempts to produce a flourishing signature: *Theodore Blake*, and on another, a date: *1889*.

'They came out of this?' She looked up at James in astonishment, and he nodded. 'But… but should you have taken them out? This must be worth a fortune.' He shrugged, his eyes unreadable. 'Where did it come from?'

'It'd been kicking around the old farmhouse for years, and no one had given it a thought. Aonghas gave it to me to scribble on when I was a kid.' He grinned at her expression, then turned to the back of the book and showed her childish drawings of aeroplanes and rocket ships. 'That's my contribution—I suppose the book came from the big house when they cleared it out. I found it again when we moved Aonghas out of the farmhouse and realised then what it was. I liked those two particularly.' She turned back to study the drawings, and even as the thought struck her, he spoke again. 'It's the same girl as in *The Rock Pool*.'

'Who is she?'

'Not sure.' He shrugged and gestured to her mug on the hearth.

'Could it be his wife?' She reached for it and noticed that the file on the floor lay open at the illustration of the cracked wall of Muirlan House.

'No. He married late. He was only nineteen in 1889, and the clothing suggests an island girl. Painters often used local people in their compositions.'

'But there's more, surely. There's a familiarity…' she said, looking more closely.

'—with the form beneath the clothing?' His eyes gleamed a moment. 'I know what you mean.' Then he nodded towards the kitchen area, changing the subject. 'That phone call was from a supplier on Skye. Apparently the ferry's had to turn back with engine trouble, so if the police team were on board, they'll not be here until tomorrow.'

But she was still looking at the girl stretched out on the sand. 'I wonder if they'll be able to find out who it was.'

He shrugged again. 'Who knows.'

The peat settled in the fireplace as he sat down opposite her, placing his mug on the hearth. Neither spoke for a moment, then she gestured to the open report on the floor. 'Were you having a rethink?'

''Fraid not. The facts remain.'

Was it just the facts? She sipped at her tea, looking at him over the rim. Or something else. Something hidden.

She hesitated, then decided to probe a little. 'You don't approve of my plans, do you?'

He looked taken aback and picked up his mug again, taking a moment to reply. 'Doing anything with the old place would cost you a fortune.'

'Yes. You said.'

He smiled, swirling the tea around in his mug and staring into it. 'Nothing's going to change that, you know. No amount of dreaming or planning. It's a wreck.'

She picked up the report from the floor and flipped through the pages, piqued by his manner. 'Perhaps I should get a second opinion.'

'By all means.'

She turned his illustration of the cracked wall on its side, pretending to study it again. 'There's something you don't like about the project, though, I can tell. And I bet you have an idea who the bones are,' she added, flicking a glance at him.

'If I knew—'

'I didn't say *know*, I said *have an idea*. Or can guess? Or maybe Ruairidh can.'

He sat back, nursing his mug against his chest, considering her. 'Like we said, there's no island lore about someone disappearing, unaccounted for.'

She glanced again at the sketches, then added, 'But identifying the bones is only one question, isn't it?'

'Meaning?'

'Someone else did the killing, and the burying. Maybe you have an idea about that?'

He seemed amused by the interrogation. 'Tricky one, that, not knowing who the victim is. Next question?'

She hesitated. 'Alright. Tell me what island lore says about Theo Blake. I'd like to know.'

'Would you?' He got to his feet and brought the teapot over, refilling both mugs, then he reached up to one of the photographs hanging on the wall and passed it to her. 'Recognise this?'

She took it, a faded sepia image of a collection of low houses, clustered together like the encampment of a primitive race, with smoke rising from thatched roofs. At one side, only half in shot, was the wall of a larger stone building. She shook her head.

'Then try this.' He handed her another photograph. No mystery there. It was Muirlan House, newly completed, raw and pristine, the encircling wall intact, the gravel on the drive raked smooth. And to one side was the wall of the same stone building. The factor's house. 'Got it?'

She nodded slowly.

'That's what island lore remembers. Theo Blake's father, who flattened their forebears' houses to build Muirlan House, giving them the choice of poor land elsewhere, or emigration. And they remember his son, who came to paint or fish or shoot, and entertain wealthy guests. A man who demanded rents and had the power of God over them.' He nodded towards the sketches of the girl. 'And maybe even seduced their daughters. Who knows.'

She handed the photographs back and he rehung them on the wall. Was that it? 'And so you don't want to see his house restored. Is this some sort of delayed revenge served, in this case, very cold indeed?'

He gave her a straight look back and answered quietly, 'You asked for island lore, not my views.'

'But you—' The phone rang again and he went to get it. Saved by the bell, she thought, as she looked again at the two photographs. There was something appalling about them, seen together like that, a depiction of unbridled power and wealth descending like a giant boot to obliterate the simple dwellings. But for goodness' sake, it wasn't even Theo Blake's doing; it was his father's, and well over a century ago. Surely—

'Aye.' James came back into the living area, the phone clamped to his ear. 'I know exactly where she is,' he said, looking across at her. 'I found her outside here, trespassing.' He raised a mocking eyebrow. 'Hang on.' He lowered the receiver. 'Ruairidh wants to know how long you're staying.'

'Until the weekend, at least,' she told him, and he relayed the message.

'Aye. Right.' He hung up. 'The forensic team *was* on the ferry, and by the time they got back to Skye something else had cropped up. It'll be a day or two before they get back here.'

Later that afternoon, as soon as the tide allowed her, she walked back across the strand to the island, wrestling with this new angle on the past, unsettled by the thought of the cluster of low dwellings in the photograph, the homely drift of peat smoke. A vanished community.

She had glimpsed other ruins on the island the day before, and when she reached the other side she set off along the shoreline away from Muirlan House to find them. But there was little enough to see when she got there: tumbled walls and empty doorways, cobbled thresholds and fallen lintels, and a light snowfall of daisies tracing the outline of old lazy beds amongst the clover. *The choice of poor land elsewhere*, James had said, *or emigration*. Had these places been abandoned at the same time, or later, as the population on the island declined?

Down by the shore she saw low mounds marking ancient graves, a cross covered with moss and yellow lichen fallen in the corner of another ruin, which was eroding onto the beach. Some graves were more recent and a few had headstones. She studied them, seeing the same family names repeated over and over, generation succeeding generation, marking the passing of time. Amongst childbed deaths, losses at sea, and fallen soldiers, there were others whose lives had spanned eight or nine decades and seen the world change around them. Some had been scraped clear of mosses, and she traced an almost unbroken sequence of MacPhails, the earliest stone bearing a date of 1698 carved in irregular letters. Those graves had been kept trim, still venerated—the bond was strong.

But Theo Blake's grave was not to be found here, amongst the islanders. Ruairidh had told her that he lay with his parents in the family plot behind Muirlan House, as removed in death as he had been in life from the people his work had immortalised.

She sat a moment, resting against the wall of the old chapel, feeling the warmth of it, and listened to the jangling of the skylarks high above. She closed her eyes. It all came back to that question of belonging. Perhaps her own sense of connection with this place was no more real than Blake's had been, just wish fulfilment, spawned by a need to belong. For it was that, she realised, which had brought her here. She had come here with a view to making a new start but also with the half-formed belief that she could honour Blake's memory by preserving his erstwhile home. Giles had encouraged the idea. 'It's part of our heritage, darling, as well as your own past, and these places are important, like Dove Cottage or Brantwood.'

But Theo Blake had been no Wordsworth or Ruskin, and here, according to James Cameron, he was remembered rather differently, as an idle despot who demanded rents from the islanders, and had the power of God over them.

Chapter 11

≈ 1910, Beatrice ≈

Beatrice came across the mourners without warning. They were clustered around a new grave beside the chapel ruins, and the soft sound of committal prayers drifted towards her. Men stood, hands clutching doffed caps, the wind whipping at their dark clothing, lifting the hair on their bowed heads. She halted abruptly, recognising the factor and his sons among them, and one or two of the tenants. The rest were strangers.

She had begun backing away, not wishing to intrude upon private grief, when one of the men at the graveside raised his head. He scowled across at her, an expression of such dark malevolence that it seemed to leap across the open ground to strike her, and she recoiled. One or two others lifted their heads, and she felt a wave of more muted hostility. A flock of choughs rose like dark spirits to fly between them, and Cameron Forbes looked up, his face solemn as befitted the occasion. He nodded slightly to her before dropping his chin again, but even he managed to convey the message that she should not be there. She withdrew quickly, pulling at her skirt which snagged on a clump of thistles.

Later she stood at the drawing room window and watched a group of men leaving the factor's house, casting long shadows as they set out across the wet sand. Theo appeared at the door, and she called him over. 'I saw them at a burial down by the ruined chapel. Such a lot of people.'

He came and stood beside her, watched them for a moment, and then turned away. 'Anndra MacPhail was buried today'— his face was expressionless—'and John must have provided the mourners with a cup of tea.'

She waited for more. 'Was he a tenant?' she prompted, her eyes following the retreating figures.

'Years ago. In my father's time.'

'But he wanted to be buried here?'

'So they told me,' replied Theo, sitting down and opening his book. His face had that shuttered look which she had begun to recognise, signalling that the subject was closed.

But the incident stayed with her, and next time she encountered Cameron Forbes alone in the study she decided to ask him instead. 'Mr. MacPhail must have been a well-regarded man,' she ventured.

Cameron was sorting through old leather-bound ledgers, and he hesitated, his face impassive, hard to read. 'He was very well-known on the island, madam.'

'Mr. Blake said he used to live here?' Her finger idly traced the delicate curl of a lapwing's crest.

'Aye. He did,' he replied, then lifted his head and smiled at her. 'You're becoming quite a walker, madam. I see you all over the island.'

She had been deflected again. 'I enjoy the exercise,' she said coolly, and withdrew. There were things, it seemed, that would not be explained to her.

It was later the same day, as she crossed the hall, that she again overheard Theo's raised voice coming from the study.

'This is not your concern, Cameron. Nor is it an estate matter.'

'But if you saw how they were living, sir. Crammed into two damp rooms.'

She paused, making a play of arranging ornaments on the mantelpiece above the hall fire, and listened.

'I'm sorry for that, but if I provide land for them, I'll have others demanding—'

'Surely they have some claim,' Cameron cut across him. 'MacPhails have worked this land for generations.'

'No!' Theo spoke sharply. 'Duncan MacPhail has no claim on me *whatsoever*. His father was only a child when the family left.

Almost fifty years ago. Before you were born. Before *I* was born, for God's sake.' She drew closer to the study door. 'What would you have me do? Tear down the house and let them retrace the old run rigs?— For God's sake, Cameron, accept that things move on.' He paused. 'I knew that burial would stir up ill feeling. The MacPhails leave a legacy of ill will.' This was followed by a silence, and when Cameron spoke again it was in a low, conciliatory tone, and she had to strain to hear his words.

'Duncan doesn't care whereabouts the land is, sir, and he's prepared—'

'*Enough*, Cameron.'

'And Aonghas MacPhail gives you no trouble.'

'Aonghas's croft came to him through his wife; he'd no more claim on me than his brother. If Duncan wishes to stay, and if Aonghas will house him, he can take what seasonal work there is, though I doubt it'll be enough to support a family.'

There was a short silence. 'I told him in Glasgow that I'd speak for him. He came up for the funeral hoping that—'

'Cameron.'

'Sir?'

'I said *no*. If you raised his expectations, you should not have done so. And that's an end to it.'

'I wouldn't be so sure.' Cameron's voice had taken on a different tone. 'As far as the Land League's concerned, there won't be an end until—'

She heard the scrape of a chair on the wooden floor. 'Damn it, Cameron! Do you imagine you help Duncan MacPhail's case with veiled threats? The League is *not* concerned, and I mean it to stay that way, so be off with you.' Beatrice withdrew hastily to the morning room as Cameron left the study.

I'm planning a garden... The letter to Emily was still unfinished... *though Theo says I'm mad and that the first gales will destroy it. Are the storms really so fierce? I can't imagine...* She was finding much was unfamiliar in this new world, different rules applied. *Theo says this settled spell won't hold much longer, so perhaps I'll see for myself...* Even the physical boundaries were ill-defined, the separation between sea, sky, and land hidden beneath clouds, and the long hours of daylight merged into darkness, a soft lingering twilight alive with birdsong. And the sea set its own rules, marooning and releasing the island twice a day, following its own irregular rhythm. *I try and imagine the childhood you described, and I want my children to grow here too, where they can run wild...*

Until she came here, the sea had been something to be admired from Portobello pier or promenade, unchallenging and tamed, but here the sea was master, governing the daily round, dictating when cattle could be taken across the strand, when cockles could be gathered or fishing lines set out in the sea pools, determining whether they reached church on Sunday in the trap or by boat. *I love walking along the shore watching the sea creep over the sand, listening to the sound of it hissing, deepening as the tide rises, especially on rough days when the waves boom into the rocks, sending spray high into the air...*

She had taken to sitting and watching the pulsing of the waves as they filled the rock pools below the ruined chapel, reawakening the crimson anemones and stirring the bright green fronds. And as the tide pulled back, she would watch the anemones retreat inside their glistening sheaths, the barnacles closing their hatches as the strand once more became an ebb flat of worm casts and ripples in the sand.

She had been sitting there one day, staring into the miniature tide-pool world, reaching in to catch a darting fish, when she had heard a laugh behind her. 'I must find you a net, madam.' She had spun round to see Cameron Forbes standing at the edge of the field watching her, and had flushed, wondering how long he had been there. But he had come down and sat opposite her, his reflection darkening the surface of the pool, accepting her pastime as quite natural. 'I used to spend hours down here with my mother and Donald, lying on the rocks looking down into the pools, with their own order and sense.' And he had shown her how the anemones would close around a probing finger and how hard the limpets gripped the surface of their stony territory, while a periwinkle slowly grazed its way across the rock pool floor.

'…I think I told you that the factor's elder son has returned from Canada. Theo was surprised to see him but seems glad of his help in the study, though I wonder that the young man doesn't prefer to be outdoors.'

She tapped the pen against her lips, remembering what Emily had told her, how she and her younger brother, Kit, had spent their childhood days with the Forbes children, Theo already a grown man.

A noise in the hall disturbed her, a child's voice, and she went to investigate, pausing at the open door of the study. Theo looked up and beckoned her in. 'See what Tam has brought me,' he said, gesturing to a basket held by a boy she had seen around the estate. Cameron stood beside him, yesterday's quarrel apparently put aside. 'Red-throat's eggs, a whole clutch of them, from the small loch just across the bay. They've never nested there before.'

Three speckled eggs lay in the fleece-lined basket. 'Won't it discourage them if you take the eggs?'

She spoke without thinking, and Theo frowned slightly, handing the boy a coin. 'Remember what I said, there's a guinea in it for you.' He waved a hand in dismissal as the boy pocketed the coin and left.

'A guinea, Theo!' Beatrice looked at her husband with astonishment. 'You'll have small boys robbing every nest on the island for that. A *guinea* for three eggs…'

He looked down his nose at her. 'That was thruppence, but I've promised him a guinea if he can find me a nesting Great Northern diver, like the one in the dining room. I need a good specimen of a sea eagle too; the moths have got at the one my father took.' He turned back to examine the eggs. 'But I think your guineas are safe, my dear, divers haven't nested here for over a century.'

'And that's only hearsay, sir,' said Cameron. 'There's no proof.'

Theo swung round to him, his face brightening. 'Yes, but they're here again! I saw two of them off Torrann Bay the other morning. Immature, probably both males. But if one of them finds a mate, they might breed.' He disappeared behind one of the bookcases to replace his book.

'And if they do, will you take *their* eggs too?' she asked indignantly, directing her remark to Cameron, who looked taken aback, then glanced towards Theo.

'*I* wouldn't.'

'Cameron disapproves too, my dear.' Theo spoke from behind the bookcases. 'He says if we find a nest we should just record it, see if they're successful and return.'

'Isn't that a good idea?'

'Up to a point,' Theo replied, stepping back towards the desk. 'Photographs are all very well, but there's a limit to their usefulness.' He gave Cameron a stern look. 'We've no proof they've ever nested here because no one gathered proof. Eh, Cameron?' Cameron looked down at the basket of eggs, saying nothing, and Theo, his point made, seemed to relent. 'Go and see for yourself—they were off the headland towards the Bràigh. And take Mrs. Blake, she's not seen Torrann Bay yet.' He turned to Beatrice. 'It's about a mile or so, my dear, but you like a walk.'

'Can you not come too, Theo?'

'Another time. I'm still catching up.' He gave her a tight smile and turned back to Cameron. 'Join us for lunch, and then go this afternoon. This weather won't hold forever.'

Lunch was a simple affair of soup and rolls with cold meat left from last night's dinner, and Cameron pulled out a chair for Beatrice before taking his place opposite. 'I was working for a mining company north of Lake Superior,' he said in answer to her question, as she ladled soup into a dish. 'They'd struck gold and we were set to make our fortunes.' He pulled a wry face, taking it from her. 'Maybe next time.'

'Fool's gold,' Theo remarked from the head of the table. 'I tell you, you'd be better staying here.' Cameron dropped his eyes to his soup, giving an evasive response, and Beatrice looked across at her husband, intrigued again. He had told her of his previous attempts to secure Cameron as an assistant, how he had lent John Forbes money to help pay for his education, and of his subsequent disappointment when Cameron had left for Canada. 'He turned me down. Very grateful and all that. Tiresome, after all I'd done for him.' And now Theo seemed to be renewing his efforts to persuade Cameron to stay but appeared to be meeting resistance.

'Did you see much wildlife there?' she asked, to fill the silence.

'A great deal, madam.' Cameron looked up again. 'It's still mostly wilderness where I was, teeming with birds and animals, and it made me think what we have already lost, or are losing, here. Ospreys, sea eagles…' He glanced towards Theo. 'Which makes places like this so vital, they offer sanctuary.'

'Exactly. So you don't have to go traipsing halfway round the world to study them.' Theo reached across for the butter. 'I learned that for myself.' And they were soon engrossed in amicable discussions about the naming of variant subspecies on the two sides of the Atlantic, and Beatrice watched them as she lifted her spoon to her lips, all trace of animosity between them gone, leaving only the familiarity of a long association.

Lunch finished, Theo threw down his napkin and pushed back his chair. 'Enough,' he said. 'I've work to do. You must excuse me, my dear. Enjoy your walk.' From the door he called back over his shoulder, 'And find me my divers, Cameron.'

~

There was a sharp, almost astringent, quality to the air as they set off across open land, leaving the track behind them, and Beatrice drew deep breaths, revelling in the warm, heady smell which rose from the clover. Bess ran ahead of them across the pasture, a pale green wash spattered with the vibrant colours of wild flowers. Lambs ran from them, calling to their mothers, while lapwings and gulls competed for the skies, their cries blown by a breeze which sent ripples over the rough silk of the machair. She looked across at Cameron as he strode beside her with an athletic grace borne from long practice walking across this windswept terrain, and she tried to match her steps to his.

As they came alongside a long narrow inlet from the sea, he stopped suddenly and clipped an order to Bess, who dropped to her haunches in obedience. 'Look! Amongst the rocks, in the weeds. Otter. Come in on the tide.' He stood close beside her, pointing, and she saw the curve of a sleek back rise amongst the seaweed on the opposite bank, then the creature rolled over, lifting a whiskery face, and began to tear at something held between its front paws. They watched until it drifted too far away to be seen, then moved on, climbing up the leeward side of the dunes, stopping just below the crest, and Cameron parted the coarse grasses.

Before them lay a great white sweep of beach, bordered at both ends by low, rocky headlands. Waves which had broken further out at sea came in layer upon creamy layer, their rhythmic sound muted by the heavy burden of weed which had built up against the rocks. A lighthouse stood etched against the clear horizon, and in the distance lay the grey shapes of small islands and skerries trailing away like the fraying hems of a loosely woven shawl. She recognised the view from his painting and stood mesmerized by the dazzling light on pools along the sand. Cameron stopped beside her. 'It has a pull,' he said softly, 'even over three thousand miles.'

The dog settled herself in one of the hollows and began grooming, while Beatrice and Cameron sat resting against the wall of an old ruin, and Cameron scanned the shoreline through field glasses. 'He's right,' he said after a while. 'Look. There!' He pointed beyond the breaking waves. 'No. Gone. Wait and it'll be up again. Keep watching just beyond the weed, you'll see a neck and a body low in the water.' She waited and watched. 'There, now!' He handed her the glasses, and she followed the line of his pointing finger and saw a large bird with a short thick neck thrown back, its head held alert, questing.

'But it's plain and grey,' she said. 'Not like the smart fellow in the dining room at all.'

'Immature. They don their fine colours to go looking for a mate, and when they find one they mate for life.' The bird dived. 'They've a wild, haunting cry which echoes through the woods like a weird spirit. I stayed awake all night once north of Lake Superior, listening to a pair calling to each other. Some Indians say they're omens of death, and you can well believe it when you lie there in the dark with your hair standing on end.'

'But they don't nest here?'

'Occasionally, perhaps… We don't really know.'

Because Theo shot the one who might have tried, she thought as she passed the glasses back to Cameron. She studied his profile as he followed the bird's progress up the beach, thinking of the conversation in the study that morning and the quarrel the preceding day, and decided to quiz him a little. 'If you disapprove, as my husband said, I wonder if you *would* tell him if you saw one all decked out in his fine feathers.' She kept her tone light, but he made no reply. 'Would you?' she persisted.

He continued watching the bird through the glasses, saying nothing, but the crooked line beside his mouth suggested he was smiling. After a moment he murmured, 'Mr. Blake has a collector's instinct, madam, and a collector's—' He broke off, as if choosing his word.

'Ruthlessness?' she suggested, and waited for his reaction. He smiled briefly, scanning the ocean in the other direction, making no response. 'You didn't answer my question.'

'Didn't I?' He lowered the glasses. 'Mr. Blake takes the view that what happens on his estate is his own business, madam, and that includes the birds.' His voice had taken a different tone. A fulmar swooped low beside them, and he watched it lift on the breeze. Further probing began to seem unwise, so she turned back to the white sands of the bay and changed the subject.

'Tell me what else is out there now. My husband has been trying to teach me, but I fear I'm something of a disappointment to him.'

'Surely not,' he murmured, scanning the beach. 'Tell me what you see, and then we can decide what it is.'

She looked out over the glinting darts of light. 'I can recognise the gannets. Theo... Mr. Blake took me once to Bass Rock. But the gulls are impossible.'

'No more difficult than periwinkles and limpets,' he said, with his usual smile. 'You just need to learn what to look for.' And so they sat there, sharing the field glasses, while he pointed out the differences which distinguished the species, and she nodded, watching his face, amused by his determination to instruct her. 'And there are your tormentors, fishing this time,' he said, pointing to the flashes of white where the terns were diving just beyond the rocks.

They left the dunes and dropped down onto the beach, sending up a cloud of shore waders which rose only to settle again a few yards further on. And he guided her past a shallow scoop in the sand where three eggs lay camouflaged among the small stones, drawing her away as the parent bird appeared from nowhere, piping stridently, feinting an attack. 'Not again!' she protested, and he laughed. Then he saw that the diver too had made its way back along the beach, and they sat again, while the sun sank low over the sea.

Eventually he rose and looked over his shoulder to where they had left Bess in the dunes. 'Perhaps we should turn back,' he said.

She stood and took a last look at the wide bay, regretting again that Theo had not brought her here himself, for he had often spoken of Torrann Bay. 'You know, Cameron,' she said slowly, 'I think if you do see a diver looking for a mate perhaps you need *not* tell my husband. If they are lucky enough to find each other out here on the edge of the world, they deserve to be left alone, don't you think?' He raised his eyebrows in mock astonishment, saying nothing. 'Though you could tell me, of course,' she added lightly, dusting the sand off her skirt and looking around for her hat.

He retrieved it from behind a clump of dune grass. 'And you'd say nothing?' he asked, handing it to her.

She was conscious suddenly of disloyalty, off guard after a delightful afternoon; Theo would not thank her for inciting Cameron to further rebellion. But he did not press her for an answer, turning to whistle for Bess instead, and as the dog came bounding joyously towards them, they dropped down from the dunes to rejoin the clear track back to the house.

Chapter 12

∼ 2010, Hetty ∼

'I hadn't realised who you were.' Hetty had been on the point of going back across the strand when her landlord appeared on the doorstep and introduced himself, following up with what felt like an accusation. 'Have you everything you want?' he asked, stepping into the kitchen. 'If you don't like the peat, there's coal to buy at the co-op.' The peat was fine, she told him, now she'd got the hang of it. 'And there's extra bedding in the bedroom cupboard.' A thin blanket reeking of mothballs. She'd already rejected it, preferring a hot-water bottle. 'I'll be back to read the meter for the electric before you go.'

'I'm here until Sunday.' At least. But if she stayed away much longer, her few remaining clients would be wondering if she had emigrated.

'Aye, well. I'll come Saturday teatime, and we'll settle up.' He looked around at her meagre supplies and seemed reluctant to leave. 'I've croft land on the island, you know?' he said abruptly, like another assault. 'My grandfather's.'

'Have you?'

She waited for him to continue, but he kicked at the split lino instead and looked up at the water-stained ceiling, a pugnacious bottom lip thrust forward. 'I'd been thinking of doing this place up.' His red-rimmed eyes gave her a baleful look. 'But a big hotel'll take the business from me.' Really? She held the look and he dropped his gaze. 'And I've a closed-season licence for the geese.'

He nodded curtly, leaving her mystified by that one, and she stared at the closed door in consternation. Back in London, Giles had convinced her that her proposals would be greeted with enthusiasm by the locals, bringing jobs and prosperity to the area. 'You'll need professional hotel managers, of course, but there'll be jobs for chambermaids, kitchen staff, and the like, as well as groundsmen and ghillies, if they still call them that.'

But neither James Cameron nor her landlord came anywhere close to enthusiastic.

After he had gone, she set off, intending to go across to the island and visit the painter's grave, but as she approached the place where the track led down onto the strand, she found it occupied by a huddle of noisy children, jostling each other and running around in circles. Then she spotted Ùna Forbes amongst them, who raised a hand in greeting.

'Hello there!' A friendly face, thank goodness. 'Are you going across? We'll go with you.' The children gathered around, staring like curious calves, and Ùna smiled. 'Art and Nature, once a week, weather permitting, to suit the tides. Better than a stuffy classroom, don't you think?' She introduced her teaching assistant, a girl in her late teens, and then turned back to her flock. Whatever she said to them triggered a cheer, and they shot off as if she had drawn a cork, fanning out and zigzagging their way across the strand, her assistant following gamely. 'We use one of the old outbuildings as our studio, where we can make as much mess as we like, splash paints and clay around to our hearts' content, and then just rake over the floor.' She paused, adding cheerfully, 'I suppose we ought to ask your permission now, I hadn't thought of that. Do you mind?'

'Not at all.' At least, not yet.

'Good. The children love it. We collect stuff as we walk across and then make collages to sell at the school fete. You know, match-boxes with gluey shells all over them, that sort of thing.' Ùna caught at her hair and stuffed it into her hood as she scanned the open beach ahead of her, counting heads. 'And what about you? How are things coming along, after such a poor start?'

She gave a brief laugh. They hadn't improved. 'James Cameron says I should pull the house down and build a cottage, and my landlord's complaining that a hotel'll ruin his business.'

Úna gave a whoop of mirth. '*What* business? Propping up the bar? Diighall will be just fine.'

'But James was serious about the house. He says it's past saving.' She watched her companion's face carefully.

'Aye, he said as much to us.' Úna looked back at her. 'So what will you do?'

She hesitated. 'Get a second opinion, I think,' she said, realising that this might offend.

They walked on. Úna called out to one child who was spinning in circles holding a long band of wet green seaweed and causing squeals of delighted anguish from his companions. '*Fionnlagh, sguir dheth!*' Hetty smiled and reached for her camera, then realised she had left it on the table, distracted by her landlord's sudden arrival.

Order restored, Úna glanced at her from under her hood. 'James knows his stuff, though.'

'I'm sure he does, but I sense that he's against the whole idea.' Her companion walked on, head down. Would no one explain? 'He seems to think it would inflame ancient grievances.'

At that Úna looked up. 'Grievances? From before, way back?' She shook her head vigorously. 'No, no, it's not that. It's more a worry about what a hotel would do to the island now, today.' She gave Hetty a lopsided smile. 'I suppose no one likes change.'

'Is that all it is?'

The island woman hesitated. 'When you've grown up in a place like this, it's a rather big *all*.' They walked on, the gulls wheeling and turning above the children, who were scattered like plump shore waders across the strand. 'You see, we're not used to constraints here and do our best to avoid the rules everyone else has to obey. A hotel on the island would change that.' She gestured to the children. 'I taught in Glasgow for a while. Can you imagine letting children run wild like this anywhere else but here?'

Free spirits? They were an enchanting sight, but—'And when

they grow up? Won't they need jobs if they want to stay here?'

'A lot will leave, of course, they always have done, but some will come back. And the place never leaves you.'

Hetty walked on, digesting this new slant on matters. Surely there was some compromise to be reached, rather than just tearing the house down. Something more constructive, more positive.

Úna changed the subject. 'Ruairidh told you about the forensic team getting turned back?'

'Yes, he did,' she replied, then added, 'Did he have any more thoughts about who it might be?'

Úna called out to another child, whose gleeful stamping in a shallow channel was soaking his companions, and shook her head. 'No. And I guess we won't know for a bit.' Again it seemed impossible to press the matter. 'You're sure you don't mind us using the old croft house?' she asked, shaking her hair free of the hood as they reached the island. 'We'll move our stuff out if you like?'

'It's fine, really.' She felt awkward, mindful of her new status as landowner, potential developer, incomer, outsider. Finding a place here was not going to be easy after all.

'Fantastic,' said Úna. 'Drop by and see for yourself, if you've time?' They caught up with the children, who were waiting obediently at the bottom of the track which led up to the house, and Hetty promised that she would.

She went off on her own and found the little burial ground without difficulty on a ridge behind the house, bounded by a low wall. Rusty iron hinges showed where a gate had once stood, but now the sheep had wandered in, cropping the grass. They bolted as she approached, like guilty spirits departing.

The painter's grave was marked by a simple headstone giving only his name and dates, and she stood a moment, looking down at it, seeking a connection to him. But this was a bleak place, and there was nothing of him here.

His headstone was in stark contrast with the ostentatious Victorian memorial, complete with weeping angels, which marked his parents' grave and that of their three infant daughters. She discovered too that the burial ground was shared with the Forbes family, underlining the close, if unequal, relationship between the two families. A ring-headed cross marked the grave of John Forbes, the one-time factor, and beside him was his wife, who had died several decades earlier. Just twenty-four years old, poor thing, buried with an infant who had survived her by a day. And then she saw that there was another inscription on the base of the cross shaft, and she bent to pull aside a wiry strand of heather. *In memory of John Donald Cameron, Argyll and Sutherland Highlanders, 1944.* Some forebear of James Cameron's, no doubt; Ruairidh had said that they were connected.

She sat down on the low wall, biting into the apple she had brought, and contemplated the grassy mounds. At least one of those slumbering here knew the answer to the riddle of the bones and had taken the secret to the grave. Had others known too? A conspiracy of phantoms? And she wondered if they were unsettled now by the discovery. If she hadn't come here, perhaps no one would have ever known. Muirlan House would have become just another ruin, burying its past under collapsing ceilings and a fallen roof.

She looked again at Blake's grave. Had *he* known?

He must have done.

But Blake was himself a tragic figure. From a meteoric rise which seemed set to place him amongst the greats of British art, he had fallen hard. A self-imposed exile, then a brief, childless marriage, followed by a long, slow decline which had ended in the clear waters of the strand. And somewhere in that broken life, another life had ended. But when? And why? She scanned the graves again, then threw the apple core into a patch of nettles and left the burial ground.

It was hard to reconcile any of this with the man behind the paintings. The seascape, which had been part of her childhood and which now hung in her flat, was shot through with brilliance, overflowing with talent and energy—and optimism. When she had described it over supper that first evening, the cousins had agreed it had almost certainly been painted at Torrann Bay. 'A great sweep of a beach to the west, a mile or so long. The sun sets along it,' Ruairidh had told her.

She decided to ask Ùna how to get there, and went down the ridge towards the house to find her.

The chatter of children drew her towards an outbuilding which looked as if it had been one of the old croft houses, now sporting a new tin roof with large rooflights. She stooped to enter the low doorway, and the buzz inside subsided and then resumed as Ùna came forward to greet her.

'You found him, then? The poor wee man. For all his money, he can't have been happy. It's no wonder he went barmy. Can you imagine it, living there alone with that under the floorboards for company?'

'I was thinking he must have known.'

'Aye. He must have.' Ùna dismissed Theo Blake and pulled Hetty over to admire the work of her young charges. 'Not quite up to his standards yet, but they're very keen.'

It was the usual array of childish daubs and collages: sea shells, crab claws, and dried seaweed, with a few more dainty arrangements of pressed wild flowers. 'This place is perfect for the children. Some of the dads repaired the old benches and fixed the roof, and the new rooflights are great. And we had a safety inspection so don't you worry—' She broke off to defuse a sudden quarrel between two of the small artists and to mop up the resultant spillage. Hetty joined in, drying the children's hands on paper towels, and then asked for directions to Torrann Bay.

'Less than a mile, straight across. It's a gorgeous spot, but don't tarry too long there or you'll find yourself staying the night. Be sure to cross back over by four.'

A sweet smell rose from the turf as she followed Ùna's directions. It must be the clover, she thought, and those yellow flowers, whatever they were. And there were signs of a crop coming through. Was it Ruairidh's? He said he farmed the land.

She headed for the dunes to the west and climbed to the top, emerging through the grasses into a scene that was instantly recognisable— her painting, laid out in front of her. The sun was already beginning its slow descent towards a distant horizon, reflected in the pools and rivulets left by the tide, and even the rocks in the foreground were where she expected them to be. Blake must have set up his easel right there, in that sheltered spot in the angle of a ruined wall, and she went and sat where he might have sat, in a place of stillness and calm, and listened to the waves coming ashore.

What a strange sensation it was, feeling the painting coming alive around her. It seemed to envelop her, drawing her in and binding her close with a sense of connection, strong and powerful. And it was here, not at the grim little graveyard, with the flung cries of the seabirds above her, that she felt the spirit of the young painter, restless and driven, glorying in his talent, before his world fell apart.

Chapter 13

～ 1910, Theo ～

Theo held the book open in front of him, feigning concentration. He improved the charade now and then by turning the pages, determined to avoid conversation. He wished now that he had ordered a fire; the room was cold. And too still, too quiet. When he was sure that Beatrice was not looking, he studied her, searching for clues. How much damage had he done?

She was sitting on the window seat, her chin cupped in her hand, looking out across the bay, a picture of tranquil thoughtfulness. But he wasn't fooled. There was little tranquillity behind that cool façade. He had seen the expression of hurt bewilderment on her face when he had snapped at her, and he cursed himself again for his lapse. He flipped over another page as she moved, drawing her shawl close, and frowned at his book with counterfeit attention, but she didn't turn to him. Thank God— He didn't want her to speak of it, to ask him to explain, for what could he possibly say without causing further damage? They must just forget the incident, bury it, and keep the surface smooth.

But there were already cat's-paws on that surface, and he knew that there would be further squalls. He had seen the way she had begun to look at him, puzzled and dismayed, as if striving to understand. He gripped the covers of the book, stifling a groan. He had not meant to speak to her as he had, but the sight of her standing there beside the pool, a parody and a cheat, had sent shock waves jagging through him, and for a moment he had lost control.

It was to have been a delightful afternoon, and he had set off determined to make it so, determined to put aside his frustration with Cameron and give Beatrice the attention she deserved. It had begun well too. They had picnicked on the sand, watching the seals playing off-shore, and after a while she had wandered off, leaving him sketching the gaunt bare ribs from a long-wrecked boat, half-buried in the sand. He had forgotten her as he became absorbed in his work but, as so frequently happened these days, he had become distracted, the painful scene in the study replaying itself in his mind. 'I'd understood there was no further obligation, sir,' Cameron had said. *Obligation!* Good God. It had come to that.

He had persevered with the sketch, but after an hour he had given up and sat brooding, gazing out to sea, wrestling with the hurt, and eventually he had gone to look for Beatrice.

At first he could not find her, but as he came from behind a large rock he saw her—and had gaped in disbelief. She was poised on the edge of a rock pool, one hand resting on a boulder, her skirts gathered in the other, leaning forward, dipping her toe into the pool, causing a flurry of ripples to break the surface. The blood had pounded in his ears, and it was not Beatrice he saw:

'For pity's sake, Màili. Stay still!'

'I can't. I'm just balanced on the edge.'

He sketched rapidly while she held her pose. 'Just a moment more, then I'll have it.'

But she stepped away from the pool and laughed at him over her shoulder. 'Will this one make you famous, Theo?'

'What on earth are you doing, Beatrice?' His shout had unbalanced her and she had straightened abruptly, letting her skirts dip into the water while he stood staring, his bag across his back, his heart still jumping.

Moving away from the pool, she dropped beside him, her chin resting on his shoulder, and the musky salt smell of her hair drove the sketch from his mind. 'I was stiff! Surely you can make the rest up, you've drawn me often enough.'

Beatrice looked across at him. 'Why, nothing. Theo—?'

'Well, come away.' It had been all he could do to regain

control. 'You've got your hems all wet.' His fault for calling out, of course, but she had stepped away from the pool, giving him a puzzled look. 'The light's changing. We should head back.' He gestured abruptly to her discarded shoes and stockings: 'I'll wait at the top of the dunes while you put those on,' and he had felt her eyes following him as he climbed up the dunes, his feet sliding backwards in the soft sand, struggling for control. But Màili's voice pursued him, carried on the wind:

'If it makes you famous, will I get talked about in Edinburgh?' she asked, and began plucking at the pink heads of sea thrift that grew from a cleft in the rock. He leant back against the rocks, pulling down the brim of his straw hat low across his eyes, and watched her, his pulse thudding.

He could remember every moment of that day.

'I'd rather they talked about the painting.' Retrieving his pencil he altered a few lines in the fall of her skirt, and in the round fullness of her breasts. And she laughed at him and flung a pink flower head into the pool, then watched the wind catch and spin it, breaking the calm of the surface.

By this time Beatrice reached him. 'Did you make good progress, Theo?' she asked quietly.

'A little.'

'Will we come back another day, in better light?'

'No. At least… I don't know.'

She had run her fingers through her hair and pinned her hat into place, glancing at him from under the brim, curious. 'I thought it quite a striking scene.'

'Barren, lifeless.' And too sharp a metaphor of his life! He had tightened the strap on his bag, hitching it higher on his shoulder, and she had followed him down the inland side of the dunes.

'Could you improve it at all? By adding people or birds, maybe?'

He had snorted angrily, still shaken, and too ready to be insulted. 'For God's sake, Beatrice! Why not a couple of palm trees and a half-buried sea chest? Would you like that better?'

A stricken look had crossed her face, and she had dropped her head again, shaking the sand from the damp edge of her skirt, but when she looked up, her face was expressionless and he had felt a pang of remorse. 'It's not a good composition. I'll try somewhere else.'

She had nodded coolly, and they began to walk back in a strained silence. If she had said nothing more, he would have managed somehow to smooth the matter over, but she had looked across at him and spoken again. 'I imagine choosing the right place must be difficult. And then framing the picture as you want it.' He had grunted in response. 'I was thinking as I stood by the rock pool how difficult it must have been for your girl in the painting.'

His girl.

'Meaning what?'

'To stay still for you, to hold her position as you wanted her.' To hold her position... He had strode ahead then, forcing her to quicken her pace.

Dear God! He lowered his head to the book to hide his pain. What mischievous sprite had put those words into her mouth? Màili had not held her position, nor kept her promises. When he had explored the hidden beaches and coves with Màili, his sketchbook had been a lure, a fig leaf to hide his desire, while with Beatrice it had become a shield he held up to keep her at a distance. The contrast was too great, too painful; he must never take her with him again.

God knows he had meant to make it work, he thought despairingly, as he got up to refill his empty glass, but the past still had its claws into him. Just rounding the corner and seeing her standing there... And her averted face now signalled the distance he had put between them.

He could never explain. For Beatrice, *The Rock Pool* was a painting, nothing more. But for Theo, it had changed everything.

For that day Màili had become for him the beating heart of the island, inseparable from his art. When he had first returned from

Glasgow he had come across her scattering food for the hens outside the schoolhouse, backlit by the sun, and the smile she had given him that morning had lit in him the joy he felt seeing diamonds of light trembling on the cusp of a wave, or sunlight on a gull's wing, or moonlight low over the strand. But from that day, beside the rock pool, she had become his whole world.

'I love you, Màili.'

She glanced at him, saying nothing, and pushed aside her hair in a characteristic gesture. His artist's eye caught the glints of gold amongst the brown, and he caught at her arm, pulling her towards him, and she resisted for only a moment. 'Do you love me?' he had asked, desperate to hear her say so, and she had nodded, her breath on his cheek, as his lips sought hers.

And as he held her, easing her back into the soft grassy hollow, a fickle breeze sprang up, sending ripples across the rock pool. 'Màili—' He had looked into her eyes, seeking confirmation there, and believed that he saw it. And as his lips parted hers, a flurry sent the discarded flower heads skimming over the water until one came to rest in the shadows, hard up against the rock.

He drained his glass and shut his eyes in a futile effort to block the memory— Then, through half-closed lids, he stole another look at Beatrice. In Edinburgh, her calm beauty had attracted him, but it hadn't proved enough to drive Màili's more vibrant shade away. She was everywhere, a fleeting will-o'-the-wisp, a light across the peat bogs, drawing him on—and he knew himself still possessed.

He ducked back to his book as Beatrice stirred beside the window and then rose. Her shoulders seemed to straighten, and he remembered her icy coolness as they walked back to the house; for a moment he had glimpsed steel beneath the gentle skin.

'I'll retire now, Theo,' she said quietly. 'The fresh air has made me tired.'

'Good night, my dear.'

'Good night.'

And as she withdrew, she left something of that coolness behind her. Theo tossed his book aside and sank into his chair. Dear God. What a confounded mess! He had believed he could love Beatrice, but he was making the poor girl unhappy— Coming here had been a mistake, after all. They should leave, not stay the summer. Perhaps go to Italy, or Turkey, somewhere foreign, to a place that was not haunted by Màili and where Cameron was out of sight.

Each day the knot of frustration with him tightened, and Theo sensed him pulling away, censorious and defiant. And although part of him wanted to acquiesce to Cameron's demands, and gain his approval, he would not be browbeaten. So now they argued at almost every encounter, and yet... and yet, still, amongst it all he wanted Cameron to stay.

But he and Beatrice should leave, before there was further damage.

Then he remembered the visitors who were arriving next week and cursed aloud. *Damn* them. He couldn't leave! Not yet, anyway, so somehow they must stagger through. And he sat there, shoulders hunched, staring ahead, lost in anguish, while the evening shadows lengthened.

Chapter 14

~ 1910, Beatrice ~

Beatrice put a hand to her escaping hair as she reached the top of the dunes, and there she stopped, breathless, and looked down at the shoreline in surprise.

She had left the house early, craving the windswept solitude of Torrann Bay, where she might be alone to think and try to understand. Theo had slept in his dressing room yet again, and she had not seen him this morning. He had left the house early and gone to wherever it was that he went.

But solitude was to be denied her, it seemed, and she bit her lip in consternation. Below her, the sands of Torrann Bay were occupied by a large group of men and women, with horses and carts at the water's edge, all engaged in some strange activity. They seemed to be gathering seaweed, using long-toothed forks and rakes to heave it onto the beach, and others were lifting it onto the waiting carts. A third cart was being unloaded higher up the beach, and its contents were being spread on the rocks.

Distracted, she went closer to watch, and as she stood there, a rider approached along the beach, dismounted, and began an animated discussion with the labourers. A group soon gathered round him, and she could hear them arguing. Then one of them spotted her and they fell back, revealing the rider to be Cameron Forbes. They all stared at her a moment, then dispersed. One of them went across to the group unloading the cart, while Cameron remounted and trotted over to her.

'You're a long way from home, Mrs. Blake,' he said, sliding off his pony beside her. 'Have you come to help?'

She had grown used to Cameron's easy manners, and smiled. 'Whatever's going on?'

'They're harvesting seaware.' She looked blank. 'Kelp.' She was no wiser. 'But they're spreading it too close to the beach; a big storm, and we'll have the work to do again. I was telling them to take it further back.' He looked over at the group on the rocks and grinned. 'They were grumbling until they caught sight of you.'

'Why should *I* make a difference?'

'Word might get back.' He gave her a wry smile, then shouted something across to them. One giant of a man returned a laconic, sarcastic reply, to which Cameron gave a brief response and raised a fist, provoking a spurt of general laughter. He turned back to her, still grinning. 'A calm day like this is ideal; it's far harder if there's a swell on the sea.' But it still looked arduous, the seaweed slippery and heavy.

'But what's it for?'

He crouched down and took a handful of almost solid material from a burned ashy spread at her feet. 'Easy money,' he said, holding it up to her. 'Hebridean gold.' He squeezed it between his fingers like putty. 'Or it was, once. For the landlords, that is. The tenants never saw the profits.' He wiped his hand on the turf and straightened. 'It's not worth much now, just a few extra shillings, and if the price is very bad we spread it on the fields ourselves. A lot of hard work'—she watched the women stop to straighten up and stretch their backs—'for a very small return. But if there's a good spell of sunshine and a warm breeze, it'll soon be dry enough to burn.' His eyes glinted briefly. 'And then you'll see this ridge transformed into the gateway to hell, with Lucifer's henchmen feeding the fire, blackened faces, and a thick grey smoke, pitchforks and all.'

'How terrifying.' She smiled. 'I must come and watch.'

'Aye, nowhere's safe for idling anymore, with such an energetic mistress.' His teasing smile was a balm to her spirits.

They strolled back towards the track where he had left the pony. 'You've a party of guests arriving soon, I understand,' he said, as he reached for the halter, and she nodded. So far their only visitors had been local landowners, or their factors, but a party of three couples from Edinburgh was expected soon, their first mixed house party. Theo's long-time patron, Charles Farquarson, was one of them and had persuaded Theo that an invitation to the others would flatter their conceit and open their purses for a new gallery he was planning. Beatrice was daunted by the prospect, but Theo had airily dismissed her concerns, and later, as they sorted through bed linen and blankets too long in store, Mrs. Henderson had been reassuring.

'You'll be glad of the ladies' company, I expect,' said Cameron, running his hand along the pony's back, watching her face.

Beatrice considered for a moment before answering. 'I suppose I will be, but I've got out of the habit. The social dos and don'ts.' He said nothing but continued to watch her. 'All the little rules and rituals.' She hesitated, then confided, 'I've got used to wandering around in simple clothes all day, you see, pleasing myself. It's like a release from bondage.'

Cameron raised an eyebrow and looked across at the kelp workers. 'A benign form of slavery, nonetheless, madam,' he said.

She followed his glance and bit her lip. What a stupid thing to say. 'I meant only the social stranglehold.' But when she looked back at him, chastened, she saw that his eyes were fixed on something over her shoulder, his expression wary, and she turned to see Theo approaching along the field track in the horse and trap.

'You're all the way out here, my dear,' he said as he drew up, his eyes searching Beatrice's face, and she felt a jolt of pleasure. He had come looking for her! 'Someone said they'd seen you heading this way. Very ambitious!' Then he turned a stony face to Cameron, who had stepped forward to take the reins. 'I'd expected you to be working with me this morning, young man. I *didn't* expect a message saying you were engaged elsewhere and that I'd have to come looking for you.' So was it Cameron he had sought, not her? She swallowed a pang, then saw that his attention was fixed on the kelp gatherers. 'Is it really worth the effort these days,' he muttered, 'for a few shillings?'

'They need the shillings, Mr. Blake.'

Cameron spoke quietly, but Beatrice saw Theo's eyes snap. 'And aren't they spreading it too close to the beach? Surely they realise—'

'I've spoken to them. They're going to bring it higher up.'

Theo grunted and took up a pair of field glasses, first scanning the workers on the beach, then swinging round to the fields and pausing to study them more closely. Beatrice sensed Cameron grow still and watchful, and when Theo lowered the glasses he fixed Cameron with a hard look. 'Who are they?'

Cameron held the look. 'They came across this morning, sir, looking for work.'

'Does your father know they're here?'

'I'll explain to him this evening.'

Theo's frown deepened. 'You'll oblige me by explaining *now*. Where are they staying?'

'With relatives, for the most part,' Cameron replied coolly. 'The tangle is well in and there's a good on-shore wind, so extra hands are a blessing.'

Beatrice saw the muscles in Theo's jaw tighten as he lifted the glasses again. 'I see Duncan MacPhail is amongst them.'

'You said we could offer him work, sir.'

Theo lowered the glasses and gave him a dark look. 'I did, but if you've offered work to these other people without your father's agreement, you've exceeded your authority. As you *damn* well know.' Cameron looked aside, but not before Beatrice saw a correspondingly angry brightness in his eyes. 'Given recent events—'

'They're not here to make trouble.'

Theo continued to scowl at him, then gestured to Beatrice. 'Step up, if you will, my dear, and I'll take you back to the house.' He pointed the handle of the crop at Cameron. 'And I hold you responsible, Cameron. See that they leave as soon as they've been paid.' He gathered up the reins. 'And, in future, you'll not offer work on the estate without my agreement. Or your father's.

Do I make myself clear?' Cameron gave a curt nod, and as he offered Beatrice a hand up, his face was shuttered and blank. 'Ask your father to come and see me this evening.' Then Theo flicked the reins and they pulled away.

She watched Cameron mount his pony and ride back down the beach, then glanced at Theo's stern profile. Why so angry? And why had Cameron responded as he did, with defiance hovering just below the surface? No Edinburgh servant would have dared speak as Cameron did, nor would Theo have tolerated it.

His face discouraged conversation, but she was anxious to understand. 'What recent events, Theo?'

He gave an exasperated sigh. 'You must remember the fuss over land raids a year or two back? The same sort of thing rumbles on. Endlessly.'

She did remember. She remembered the outrage on both sides of the argument, and a newspaper photograph of men from a nearby island, stoically defiant in ill-fitting suits borrowed for a trial which had led to their imprisonment. Punishment for illegally occupying estate land. 'The land problem is *being* addressed,' he continued, 'but not fast enough for some hotheads who take matters into their own hands.' He briefly acknowledged a woman, dwarfed by a creel of fishing net on her back, who had stepped aside to let them pass. 'Agitators, stirring up bad feelings. Occupying farmland, driving in stakes to mark out crofts. The MacPhails—' He scowled and broke off. 'I would far rather Cameron had sent the boatload back to wherever it came from.'

'But if we have work for them and they need the money?' The tenant houses she passed on the island seemed pitifully poor. Did some people actually have *less*?

Theo was not listening. 'Cameron can be very impetuous.' He flicked the reins angrily, and the trap jolted her forward along the uneven track back to the house.

His temper did not improve as the evening progressed. The

factor had come just before dinner, and she heard Theo's raised voice in the study, interspersed with the islander's calmer tone. He hardly spoke during dinner but sat there, unreachable, irascible if she questioned him, and then retreated into the study immediately afterwards with only the briefest apology, leaving her no choice but to fret in the drawing room alone, or to retire early.

She had chosen the latter, closing the bedroom door and leaning against it for a moment before sitting at her dressing table, slowly easing her feet from her shoes, searching for an explanation. Her head ached abominably. She began to undress, steadying herself before stretching out on the bed to stare up at the ceiling. First his strange behaviour yesterday, and then again today. Somehow it was all of a piece—something was wrong, some discord ran through the house, intangible but real. And even before that bewildering incident at the rock pool, she had felt a change in him. The energy, the delight he had displayed upon arrival, had evaporated, to be replaced by a detached silence and a shadowed brow. She could almost feel him withdrawing, leaving her stranded like the clouding jellyfish she came across high above the tide line, not knowing how to save the situation. She lay there, nursing a bruised emptiness, listening to the night sounds through the open window, a foreigner marooned amongst strangers.

Her heart had leapt when she had seen the trap approaching the kelp workers. He had come to find her, she had thought, to explain. But no, he had been looking for Cameron, inexplicably angry with him again. And yet it seemed that the hours he spent in the study with the factor's son gave him the most satisfaction; he apparently preferred Cameron's company to hers—

Her thoughts faltered, then jarred, and a hot sensation rose up her neck, suffusing her face. No, no. Surely not. She became fixated by the crack in the ceiling, stunned by the thought. *Was that it?* She sat up, her arms clasped across her chest, hunched forward, her pulse thudding. *Surely not!*— But other incidents began tumbling into her mind. Theo's oddness the day they had arrived, when he had expected Cameron to be abroad. He'd been thrown off balance, his reaction to the young man's appearance so marked. And he had provided the money for Cameron's education, a loan that he had told her John Forbes had repaid with almost offensive swiftness. And then Cameron had rejected Theo's offer of work and left for Canada. The half-finished sketch of the naked boy she had seen that first day suddenly took on a shockingly different meaning, and her head began to pound. She recalled Theo's outrage when a fellow painter had been ostracised, forced to leave Edinburgh, taking with him the olive-skinned boy he had brought from the south of France. *Monstrous bigotry,* Theo had called it.

She rose and went to the little turret, dragging a shawl around her, shivering uncontrollably. She knew little of what might draw two men together, but she knew enough— And she recalled the time when a friend of her father's had suddenly vanished from their circle, remembered the overheard gossip, and her astonishment when the extraordinary explanation reached her.

So was Cameron Forbes the reason for Theo's long bachelorhood? A bachelorhood which ended only after the young man had left the island, supposedly for good. And Theo had exiled himself to Europe— Had he married her upon his return not for herself at all, but as a cloak against suspicion?

She pressed her fingers to her temples, fighting a growing panic, as she explored the intimate reaches of their own relationship, looking for clues. At first Theo's lovemaking had been considerate and restrained, making allowances, she had thought, for her modesty, but he had become increasingly ardent, and she found herself responding with delight. But lately… Her face crumpled as she faced the fact that lately his attentions had been infrequent, defined by a courteousness which distanced her.

And she had seen his eyes following Cameron.

Out across the strand, the call of seabirds filled the growing darkness, and she recalled snatches of overheard conversation.

'There's work for you *here*. It won't always be catalogues and dead birds, I promise you...' She had heard the frustration in Theo's voice. 'At least *think* about it, Cameron. It was what I'd hoped for.'

'I'd understood there was no further obligation, sir?'

It had been clumsily said and Theo had reacted violently. 'Good God, no! You must forgive me.' But even then she had sensed something else behind the heavy irony. 'No further obligation, I assure you.' She had imagined it to be annoyance, but perhaps it had been pain.

She heard footsteps in the dressing room and saw the light move under the connecting door and heard the sounds of Theo undressing, then silence. She slipped back beneath the chilly sheets and waited. She could almost see him hesitating on the other side of the door, but then the springs of the daybed creaked, and the light beneath the door was extinguished.

Chapter 15

∼ 1910, Beatrice ∼

Whatever should she do? Next morning, Beatrice sat at her dressing table, slowly brushing her hair, staring at her drawn, sleep-starved reflection. Should she write to her mother, perhaps? But putting her fears on paper was unthinkable and, besides, it would be weeks before she might expect a response. Her parents had left for Italy immediately after the wedding and were moving rapidly from one apartment to another, their letters brief and erratic. And Emily Blake was her only other confidante.

She asked for a fire to be lit in the morning room and later huddled beside it, a book in her hands unread, her tea growing cold. Perhaps she was mistaken? She had so little experience of the world. The association between the two men went back a long way, to Cameron's childhood, so perhaps that alone accounted for their unusual familiarity? And perhaps Cameron's determination to resist further patronage, and thus frustrating "Theo's objectives, was enough on its own to explain Theo's dark humour? She took up her cup, staring into the fire, quite at a loss.

After a moment, she put her book aside and went to stand by the window, watching the droplets of rain course down the pane until, at last, it slackened to a drizzle and she felt the need to be outdoors.

Half an hour later, however, and quite unexpectedly, she found herself being ushered into the farmhouse kitchen by the factor's daughter. She had come across Ephie Forbes bottle-feeding two lambs in a small enclosure beside the stables as she walked past, heading for St. Ultan's chapel. She had been distracted from her thoughts by the lambs as they butted each other from the teat, their tails on springs, and had stopped. Ephie then shyly invited her to come inside and see an even tinier one, rescued from near death the night before.

The kitchen was filled with the comforting smell of Ephie's new-made scones, and Beatrice looked around her, enchanted by the purposeful simplicity to the room. Boots stood beside the door, oilskins hanging above them, and there was a clutter of fishing rods propped against the wall, surrounded by buckets and creels. Bent-grass chairs were pulled up before the range, and a bowl of primroses stood on the large scrubbed table. Ephie's defiant splash of femininity in her masculine world.

'It's over there, madam, by the range. Cameron brought it home in his pocket last night.' And Beatrice saw the orphan curled up on an old shawl, lit by a shaft of sunlight from the open door. She went across to it and crouched down, reaching out her hand, and felt a faintly pulsing heartbeat through the curls of wiry wool. Such a little scrap, clinging so resolutely to life.

'Any closer and it'll be in the oven.' She looked up sharply to see that Cameron had appeared and was leaning against the doorframe, wiping his hands on a rag, and she dropped her head, her cheeks aflame. 'Not much meat, maybe, but nice and tender.' His face was dirty and his clothes were covered with gore from calving.

Ephie shooed him away. 'Don't listen to him, madam. He stayed up half the night until it fed. He'll not eat it.'

'Will I not?' And they heard him laugh as he retreated.

Beatrice smiled slightly, glad that he had gone, not yet ready to face him, and turned back to the lamb. But Cameron soon returned, washed and changed, and he came towards her. 'Will you see if he'll take some milk, madam?'

She half rose in confusion and shook her head. 'I don't think—' she started to say, but he stood, blocking her route to the door, and smiled down at her in his friendly manner. He pulled out one of the chairs, giving her little choice but to sit, then lifted the lamb and placed it, shawl and all, on her lap. It weighed almost nothing and she drew the shawl protectively around it, and watched as Cameron took a pan of warm milk from the range and poured the contents into a bowl.

Then he crouched beside her chair, showing her how to drip the tepid liquid onto the lamb's nose and mouth from a soft rag. She became absorbed by the task, forgetting Cameron, watching as the orphan gradually woke to the smell and taste of the milk, its tiny tongue first licking, then tasting, and eventually settling down to suck. Beatrice looked up in delight to find that Cameron was watching her. 'Well done,' he said.

∼

That evening, Theo did not retreat to the study but sat beside the fire in the drawing room, a brandy beside him, leafing through a book. Once she had enjoyed the quiet intimacy of these evenings. She would write her journal or letters, while Theo sat opposite reading, the lamps filling the room with a soft glow. If the weather was fine, he might light a cigar and wander onto the terrace or down to the foreshore, and sometimes she would fetch a shawl and join him, tucking her arm in his, and he would smile at her. But lately, when the business of the day was finished and they were alone together, a glass wall seemed to descend between them, and the silence was no longer companionable.

'We talked of doing things to the house, Theo,' she began tentatively, exploring how things now stood between them. 'To brighten it up.'

He barely lifted his eyes from his book. 'There's really little point, my dear. I'm not sure we'll come here every year.'

'Will we not?' She stared at him; they had talked of coming every summer.

'Besides, I've got used to it this way.'

'But you had plans, Theo. To finish your catalogue. To paint—'

He smiled briefly. 'And you wanted to see Venice and Rome.'

He sat with his long legs crossed, wearing a comfortable old jacket, outwardly relaxed, but she sensed a tension in him.

After a moment she tried again. 'How does the catalogue progress, Theo?'

'Am I neglecting you?' This time he lowered the book and looked over the top at her.

His directness stalled her. 'I thought perhaps there was something I could help you with.'

'Thank you, my dear, I'll bear it in mind.'

It was a masterly deflection, but she would not leave the matter there. 'I'm sure I could do whatever it is Cameron Forbes does, checking lists and marking up illustrations.' He acknowledged her words with a nod, implying that he would consider it. 'And then he'd be free to go back to Canada.' At that he raised his eyes. 'He must be keen to be off, now his father is well again.' She clamped her teeth together awaiting his response.

Theo lowered his book, staring past her to the window. 'He's agreed to assist me for the summer,' he said after a moment. 'Then get a passage in the spring.'

'But surely he's more useful to John out on the estate now, while the weather holds. I could help—'

Theo switched his gaze to her. 'Do you dislike having Cameron in the house, my dear?'

'No, not at all. By no means.' Again his directness wrong-footed her.

'I hope not, because I'm trying to persuade him to stay on. Having helped educate the blighter, I'd like to reap the rewards.'

The throbbing in her temples started again. 'But if we're only here for a few weeks—'

'There's a role for him in Edinburgh too.'

Her heart lurched violently. 'Is there?'

'I believe so.' And with that he returned to his book, reading doggedly. But after a moment he rose, selected a cigar from the ebony box on the sideboard and trimmed it briefly, before making for the door. 'I'll take the air a moment, my dear, before retiring.' And she watched him walk onto the terrace, shoulders hunched as he lit the cigar, and then, one hand in his pocket, and his collar turned up against the wind, he strolled down the drive and disappeared through the gateposts, out onto the strand.

Chapter 16

Hetty emerged from the cottage next morning to see the red Saab pulling onto the grass verge. 'Were you away out?' Ruairidh Forbes asked, opening the car door.

'I'm going over to the island again. I forgot my camera last time.'

He looked across the strand and then at his watch. 'You'll be alright for a couple of hours or so. I just dropped by to let you know they came and took the bones away early this morning. But I won't keep you.'

'So they've gone.' She looked towards the house, glad that she had not known.

'There'll probably be something in the papers, but let me know if anyone bothers you.' She nodded gratefully. 'And I've had a word with Aonghas, my granddad.'

She had forgotten about the old man. 'Could he help?'

'Not a lot, I'm afraid. Blake's wife was called Beatrice, he's certain of that much. And as far as he knows she left the island with her husband, but it was years before he was born, of course, so it's all hearsay.' He ran his hand through his hair, scratching the back of his head. 'And he's certain that when Blake came back, years later, he came alone, and he never saw a woman up there. Blake was in a poor way, he said, by the time he died. Hardly ever came out of the house, leaving matters to Aonghas's grandfather and latterly to his dad, though he remembers the bird reserve being set up because he helped drive in the boundary markers.' He glanced across the strand again. 'Anyway, I mustn't hold you up, these westerlies bring the tide in fast, so keep an eye on the time.' He lowered himself into the car, giving a friendly wave as he drove off.

So the bones had gone, she thought, as she crossed the strand, conscious of spots of rain on the wind. Torn from their sandy grave to be transported to some impersonal laboratory hundreds of miles away, labelled and packaged, another job number. Perhaps it would have been better if they'd been left in peace, their story untold.

She didn't linger in the burial ground this time, and having taken her photographs she set off to explore in the other direction, away from the house to where the wind and tides had sculpted the shoreline into small coves and headlands linking wide expanses of sand. She saw more ruins as she walked, almost a small hamlet, and was reminded again of the sepia photograph on James's wall. Had Blake's father cleared these people off their land too, or had they left to find an easier life? Past wrongs had a lasting potency, if James's attitude was anything to go by, a bitterness which lingered. Did he, and her sullen landlord, cast her in the same mould? Despoiler. Oppressor. The idea was ludicrous.

She walked for perhaps a mile, then stopped when she rounded the next headland, puzzled by the sight of another old black house, tucked into the shelter of the cove. But this one was no ruin. It had been carefully restored, the roof recently thatched, weighted down by ropes and large stones, and glass shone from the deep-set windows. A pair of sturdy boots stood beside a peat stack near the door, and beyond the house she could see a patch of turned ground where a leafy crop was coming through. There were no cables, no propane tank, only a tin water butt, and two pairs of socks leaping energetically on a washing line. It needed only a few hens scratching at the threshold or a black-and-white collie chained near the door to be the subject of one of Blake's paintings.

She stood and stared, her brow puckered. She'd been told that the island was uninhabited, and as far as she could recall from the map Emma Dawson had sent her, this part of the island was estate land. Yet someone was clearly living here. Should she go and knock on the door? She shrank from the thought of another confrontation. Then the cry of a gull overhead recalled her to the present, and she glanced at her watch and saw that it was time to turn back. She'd ask Ruairidh and take the matter from there.

Distracted by this new concern, she must have mistaken her route, and found herself on a track which brought her not to the bottom of Muirlan House drive but down the slope to the farm buildings behind the factor's house. And there, in the middle of the farmyard, stood the battered Land Rover.

As she hesitated, considering whether to slip away unseen, the back door of the old farmhouse opened and the Land Rover's owner emerged, a toolbox in his hand. 'Hallo there,' he said, banging the door closed with his foot and locking it. 'Been up for another look?' He tossed the tools into the vehicle, wiping his hands as he came towards her.

'I came to see the burial ground, then had a walk.'

He glanced back up the ridge. 'Aye. They're all up there, saints and sinners.' He opened another door, took out a shovel and a small pickaxe, and carried them to the Land Rover. 'By the way, the boys in blue have been.' And he nodded towards the tools.

'I know. Ruairidh called by.' Had James been there when the bones were lifted? She hoped so; it made the business somehow less impersonal.

'Where did you walk to?' he asked.

She remembered the occupied house. 'Just along the shore for a mile or so'—she hesitated—'and in one of the little bays I saw a house.'

'A house,' he repeated.

'A restored croft house, with people living there.'

He bent to scrape mortar off the shovel blade. 'And did you see anyone?'

'No, but there was washing on the line.' He carried on scraping, saying nothing. 'I thought you said no one lived over here?'

He glanced up, giving her an odd look. 'Then you've yet to encounter your one remaining tenant, Miss Deveraux.'

'No one mentioned a tenant.'

'No? Well, you'll meet him soon enough.' And there was a glint in his eye as he turned away. 'Have you been to see the photographs in the museum yet?'

'No.' Was James Cameron playing games?

'And you're away soon?' he added, as the shovel joined the other tools in the back.

'Yes. But I'll find time to look,' she said, 'so I can see what the interiors were like. And get some inspiration.'

He looked round then. 'So you're going ahead?' The glint had sharpened, but she held his look.

'I haven't discussed your report with my agents yet,' she replied, and he leant against the Land Rover, his arms folded. 'And they might have other ideas.'

'Such as?'

'Getting a second opinion, perhaps.'

He nodded, still watching her.

'And you said I need capital. My— I have a friend who's an accountant. He understands finance.'

'Does he.' He straightened, evidently unimpressed, and went round to the driver's door. 'Hop in, I'll take you back over.'

'Thanks, but I'll walk.'

His head came up, and he looked across at her, eyes narrowing. Then he glanced over the bay and seemed about to insist, but he gave his maddening shrug instead. 'Suit yourself. But get a move on. The tide moves fast with a westerly behind it.'

∼

She regretted her refusal of his offer almost as soon as she left the shelter of the courtyard, for the wind across the strand was biting, studded with rain. Damn the man, with his silences and evasions, she thought as he passed her on the track a moment later with a toot on the horn. He confused her.

The tracks of his Land Rover had disappeared under shallow water by the time she was halfway across, and she realised that he was right—the tide did come in quickly! By the time she reached the last channel, it was deep and filling fast, so there was nothing for it but to roll up her jeans and get wet. She waded across, emerging wet above the knees and her feet numbed by the icy cold. As she sat on a rock, drying them as best she could on her socks, she heard a familiar engine roar and looked up to see the Land Rover move off from where it was parked fifty yards down the road. She watched it drive away, and annoyance reignited. So he'd sat there and watched her, the wretched man! And he now had another story to entertain the bar with, about the stupid English woman who was, quite literally, out of her depth.

She got back to the cottage to find that the storage heaters had cooperated this time, and the place was warm, so she heated some soup and drank it from a mug, looking out at driving rain which slanted past the window. There was no sign of it slackening, so this afternoon seemed as good a time as any to go and see the photographs that James had described.

Half an hour later she drove past bedraggled sheep which stood chewing beside the road or huddled in groups under the protection of low walls. She retraced her route from the day she had arrived, climbing to the high point and then dropping down on the eastern side of the island. A mile or so from the small town, she recognised the single-lane causeway she had crossed over a tongue of water, and slowed as she approached it—and then, with a jolt, slammed on the brakes.

There was a man standing in the middle of it madly waving his arms at her, and she skidded to a halt, straining to see through the wet windscreen. Behind her another car stopped, and the driver got out and joined the arm-waving man, both of them running erratically as if herding invisible sheep. What on earth?—Then she saw. A family of shelduck were scattered across the causeway, hemmed in by walls which cut them off from the sea, the two parent birds and seven or eight half-grown ducklings, panicked and running in all directions. It was an absurd scene, and she smiled, watching as the birds led the two men in a merry dance before they got the ducks all heading in the same direction, towards safety. Then, at the last moment, one duckling doubled back towards her, and there was nothing for it but to leap from the car and do her bit. She headed off the maverick and sent it back again as breathless, but laughing, the first man came towards her.

'Thanks! Neat job.' He was an elderly man with a craggy face and grey hair, and he was panting, the accent somewhere mid-Atlantic. 'That one was the wild child.' Then he threw back his head and gave a tremendous laugh. 'But where else on earth would a bunch of ducks bring all the traffic to a halt?' His laughter was infectious, and then she saw that two more cars had pulled up behind her. 'Better move on, I guess, but thanks again,' he said, and in her rear-view mirror she saw him continuing slowly on foot.

The museum, when she found it, was housed in an old manse, to which had been added an extension for the archives and a café. Two women sat behind a desk in the hall, deep in low conversation, but they broke off as she approached, nodding enthusiastically when she explained what she wanted. Yes, they had photographs of Muirlan House, in digital form, and they could be viewed anytime, although just now one screen was broken and the other one was in use. The woman gestured to the room on the right where an A4 sheet of paper was stuck over a screen. And at the other sat James Cameron, regarding her thoughtfully.

Hetty nodded briefly and turned to leave, but he rose and came towards her, cutting off her retreat. 'I wondered if you'd come.'

'It was raining, so—'

'That's what I thought.' He pulled over a second chair. 'Have a seat.' She wasn't pleased to be so predictable, but she could hardly refuse, so she sat down beside him and smiled her thanks to the woman who hovered a moment and then withdrew to whisper to her colleague. James flicked back to the title page, making no further comment, and began to scroll through the images.

She'd always loved old photographs, those little imprints of the past, and was soon drawn in. And she forgot James beside her as a century dissolved before her eyes and the stark ruin of Muirlan House became whole again, peopled and furnished in muted half-tones: a lost world. Rugs appeared on polished floors, a carpet covered the stairs, held in place by brass stair rods, and a great stag's head peered down from the landing. A housemaid stood stiffly in the morning room, a woman's hat lay cast aside on a hall table, a fishing rod slipped sideways on the porch, and a bowl of wild flowers drooped on a windowsill. The emotive trivia of life—how strange it was! And how impossible that the simple passage of time had blown it all away.

'Bit of a house of horror if you don't like stuffed birds.' James's words broke the spell.

He was right. There were birds everywhere, on shelves and bookcases, under glass domes and on plinths, reminiscent of old museum displays. 'Some of them are through there.' He gestured behind her to the museum. 'Bought at the auction and later donated. Probably the last Hebridean sea eagle amongst them, a bit bedraggled now, poor beast.' Then the photograph he had told her about appeared on the screen, the dining table draped with white linen, a fluted silver centrepiece, fine crystal and silver, and the windows thrown open to an unchanged view. That at least was constant, but everything else had gone, and she felt again a deep sense of regret.

She must have sighed aloud. 'It's no good, you know,' he murmured beside her. 'It can't be done, not without millions,' and he scrolled on, stopping at a photograph of a shooting party posed at the front entrance. Two of the men had struck jaunty poses with feet on the lower step and guns over their shoulders. 'That's Theo Blake there.' He pointed to a tall, rather imperious figure on the top step looking over the heads of his guests with a self-confident, patrician air. The image was small and the figure distant, but it was enough to see a well-made man, with a large, flat, pancake-like hat, in the style of the times, covering most of his features. 'And that big fella there is John Forbes, the old factor.' He was a broad-shouldered man who stood to one side, and she could see the resemblance to Ruairidh in his build, although his face was obscured by a full beard and moustache. An island patriarch, Ruairidh had said, and she thought of the ring-headed cross in the graveyard.

Then came the photograph of a young woman wearing a pale silk blouse with a wide lace-edged collar and loose sleeves. She was seated on the window seat in the drawing room looking out of the open window, her face in profile, her chin resting on her hand, a picture of gentle femininity. Around her neck were two long strands of beads, unevenly spaced, and her fair hair had been swept back, held in place by combs from which a few wisps had escaped. Pearl drops hung from her ears, and her lips were slightly parted. *Mrs. Theo Blake at Muirlan House c. 1910* read the caption.

'Beatrice!' said Hetty. 'She's lovely.' And then the terrible thought—the pale bones, the sandy grave, and a locket shining amongst the rubble. 'Do you think it *is* her?'

'We'll know soon enough,' he replied, and they studied the photograph a moment, then he moved on, scrolling through similar shots before stopping again at one of a group of three men and two women, all well-dressed and stylish, posed outside the front entrance. *The Blake family, Muirlan House 1910.* This was a better image of Theo Blake, and Hetty leant forward. The painter had a lean face, handsome, if somewhat austere, with slightly hooded, intense eyes, and he exuded self-confident authority. His wife stood beside him and, as in the other photograph, she had a delicate quality about her, somehow belied by her enigmatic smile.

James pointed to the other figures. 'Kit and Emily Blake, Blake's younger half-brother and sister.' He glanced at her. 'She's your—what is it—*great*-grandmother?' He zoomed in on her face and leant forward. 'Hmm. Same smile.'

'As whose?'

'Yours.' That was unexpected, but he gave her no time to respond. 'And judging by the proprietary stance of the man beside her, that's her first husband. Armstrong was her second, according to Aonghas.' A tall, distinguished-looking man stood beside Emily Blake, while a younger, slighter man languished against the wheel of the pony trap.

'What happened to him?'

'Don't know.'

Emily. Hetty studied her great-grandmother, and greeted her silently. After all, it was Emily who had brought her here, pulling gently on that thread woven through the generations, and validating her right to be here. The photograph showed a trim young lady of about her own age dressed in a fashionable travelling coat and a matching long, narrow skirt. She was leaning slightly against the tall man, smiling directly at the camera, and Hetty found herself smiling back, touched and encouraged, as if the smile had been meant especially for her. *Same smile*. 'How strange it is.'

James glanced at her, saying nothing, but after a moment he moved on through the next few frames, stopping at an image of three men taken on the track just in front of the stone gateposts. One had a sporting gun, and another, now identifiable as John Forbes, carried a number of wildfowl. *The factor and his sons*, the caption read, and James pointed to the bigger and broader of the young men. 'That's Donald Forbes, old Aonghas's father.' He looked as if he was in his late teens or early twenties, and stared stolidly at the camera in a slightly self-conscious way. 'And that's his older brother, Cameron.' This young man was as tall as his father and brother, but of a leaner build, and he stood, his feet slightly apart, with his head thrown back. An arresting figure. His hands were thrust deep into his pockets with his long jacket swept behind him, his gun resting on the crook of one arm, his stance somehow challenging. 'My own forebear.' As he zoomed in closer, the image became a little grainy, but she could see that Cameron Forbes had very dark hair and strong regular features, but it was his eyes which held attention. They stared steadily at the photographer with no hint of the self-consciousness of his brother.

'He's a fine-looking man,' said Hetty, and she glanced at James. Self-assurance seemed to have been passed down the generations. *Same eyes.* But she wouldn't flatter him by saying so.

He drew her attention to the next image, which showed the angle where the conservatory was to be built. 'This is the one I came to see. There's no sign of any building there, and if you look at this'—he pointed to a rake and wheelbarrow in a far corner of the garden—'and then go back to that'—the rake and wheelbarrow were in the same spot in the picture of the assembled family—'they must have been taken at the same time, and the date given is 1910.' He zoomed in on the ground surface. 'See how uneven it is? Rocks poking through? That's why they had to import sand to level it and get rid of the biggest of the boulders. It must have been a hell of a job digging them out and left them some pretty big holes to fill. And that one there'—he indicated a long rock, frost-cracked into several pieces—'is the very one. I'll swear to it.' Hetty sat back, and the photograph brought into focus the grim reality of what had been discovered.

James glanced at her. 'Had enough?' She nodded and he shut down the computer. 'Cup of tea?' She nodded again, and they left, thanking the two women at the desk. Conversation broke off as they passed and then resumed in low, excited tones as James ushered her through the door, smiling slightly. 'They've twigged who you are. The Blake heiress.' He looked her up and down, taking in her jeans and loose sweater. 'But they expected something rather flashier.' He grinned at her, then gestured to a free table by the window and went up to the counter. She took a seat and watched him as he leant against the wall, chatting easily with the girls behind the counter and making them laugh. James Cameron was clearly well-liked here, but he was sending her mixed messages.

A local newssheet lay on the table and she picked it up, idly skimming the headline. Something about a fishing competition. Then, *Reserve gathers forces to oppose hotel scheme.* No! She rapidly surveyed the other customers, but no one was watching her, so she read on furtively. *Attempts to get protected status for large parts of the west…*

'Well, hello again!' She gave a start as a figure paused at her table, and she turned over the newssheet. 'Been chasing any more ducklings?' It was the elderly North American from the causeway, and she relaxed.

'No, I—'

Then James was there with a laden tray, and the man looked up. 'James! Great. I need to see you.'

But James had stopped in surprise. 'You two know each other?'

The older man nodded his head. 'We met over an act of mercy.' Then he seemed to catch the expression in James's eye and glanced back at her, his eyes suddenly shrewd. But he smiled genially, nodding at the tray. 'Mona's shortcakes are a real treat. Enjoy,' he said and turned back to James. 'If you're home this evening, I'll call by.' He gave a polite nod to Hetty and left.

'So you got wet'—James slid the tray onto the table as she watched the older man leave—'this morning.'

Irritation returned. 'And you sat and watched me so you could say you'd told me so.'

He raised his eyebrows. 'Actually, I was making sure you got back alright. That didn't occur to you, I suppose?' In fact it hadn't. 'Those breeks have had a hammering, haven't they, what with one thing or another.' He laughed as she covered the roughly sewn tear in her jeans with her hand. 'Have you always been this stubborn?'

He was very direct. 'I like to make my own decisions.'

'Even if you're flying in the face of sound advice?' he asked, biting into a biscuit.

Stubborn? Was she? She reached for her tea, refusing to be drawn, and decided to match his directness. 'So what brought you here? Looking at the photos.'

'I hoped you'd come along, and I'm bound to have an interest, aren't I? Having unearthed the poor devil.' He dunked his biscuit in his tea. 'Besides, I wanted to check my Theory about that frost-fractured rock.' Pushing back his chair, he crossed his legs and chewed thoughtfully. 'And if, as they show, that conservatory was built after 1910, and the Blakes left together in 1911, we narrow the time frame down to a few months.' He began running his finger around the rim of his cup, staring at the table. 'And there were other things going on around that time—' He stopped, and then continued. 'Remember the photograph of Cameron Forbes? Well, the story is that Theo Blake threw him off the island in 1911, and he left for Canada.' He picked up the teapot and refilled both their cups. 'Never came back, as far as we know.'

'Do you know why?'

'No...'

His denial lacked conviction. 'Are you thinking it might be him? That he never went?'

'Oh, he went alright. He sent back letters.'

'So?'

'After two letters, a year apart, nothing more was heard. He disappeared.'

They sat in silence for a few minutes. 'Perhaps he came over with the Canadian forces and died in the trenches. An unknown soldier.'

'But why not keep in touch with his family? Tell them what he was doing?'

'A family quarrel?'

He shrugged. 'Maybe.' Then he leant forward again, his elbows on the table, his eyes on hers. 'Apart from those two letters there's nothing except'—he hesitated—'except he left a child, a boy. My grandfather.' His eyes held hers. 'John Forbes brought him to the island a few years later, from God knows where.' A noisy group of walkers entered the café and settled at the tables around them, shattering the moment. 'No one knows the whole story, but I'd like very much to know why he quarrelled with Blake.' He lifted his cup and looked at her over the rim. 'Finding a body under the floorboards cranks things up a notch or two, wouldn't you say?' Then he glanced at his watch, swallowing the last of his tea, and his expression changed. 'So you're pressing on with the hotel scheme, are you?'

She made a play of getting her purse out, scrabbling in her bag on the floor. 'It's very early days, and I think there's more behind your opinion than the state of the house.' She gestured to the newssheet. 'And apparently other—' She broke off as he reached across the table and gripped her wrist. Astonished, she protested, pulling away, but he held on, his eyes sharp and direct.

'Whatever you imagine I feel personally about this scheme, it doesn't affect my professional judgement. Restoring Muirlan House would cost you a fortune, far more than you can begin to imagine.'

'Let go,' she hissed. They were attracting attention.

'You'll get more than wet feet, I can promise you. It'll ruin you.' He released her as abruptly and stood up, waving aside the money she had got out. 'You discuss it with your agents, Miss Deveraux, but take care, and don't let them sink you. They might find you the capital you need, but big money brings big problems.' He dug his hand into his pocket and laid the keys to Muirlan House on top of the newssheet in front of her. 'Stay in control.' And with a curt nod, he walked away.

Chapter 17

'That's a fine bitch, that pointer of yours.' Robert Campbell, the hard-faced shipowner from Leith, had been watching Bess as she tracked an appealing scent. 'Will you sell her? I'll give you a fair price.' Beatrice heard Cameron quietly refuse, and the man gave him a truculent look. 'Blake said you wouldn't, but why do *you* need a first-rate gun dog? A collie would be more useful, surely. Like your father's.'

Theo's guests had been with them for three days now, and an expedition to a seal colony on an off-shore island had been planned for their entertainment. Cameron was striving to assemble the party, watched by an increasingly impatient Theo.

'Mrs. Blake, you may wish to think again.' Indifferent to Campbell's scowl, Cameron had crossed the drive and spoke to her in low tones. 'We are running late, and given the tides, we'll have to move fast. You may find it tiring—'

'You mean I won't be able to keep up?' She had hardly seen Cameron these last few days while she wrestled with her suspicions. Even Bess, she had learned recently, had been a gift from Theo.

'—And I'm not sure about the weather, there's rain on the wind.'

'Thank you, Cameron, but I need a day in the fresh air.' She had been watching the antics of one of the ladies, who was further delaying the party, and was desperate to escape. Cameron followed her gaze, met her eyes briefly, and nodded.

It had been clear from the outset that the guests would challenge her talents as chatelaine, and the whole household had found common cause in dealing with their demands. After displaying astonishment at the outlandish position of the house, the ladies had confided to her that they had had enough of trailing after husbands and longed only to stay at the house and rest. Pottering down to the foreshore was as much as they could manage before returning fatigued to demand tea or hot water for baths, taxing even Mrs. Henderson's equanimity. Theo had been away with the gentlemen each day, leaving Beatrice to bear the company of their wives, and she could take no more. To her relief, they had rejected the idea of joining today's party but expressed themselves content to be left to their own devices if Beatrice wished to go.

'Hey, Forbes!' Cameron turned, blank-faced, to Ernest Baird, who had appeared on the doorstep, a pear-shaped figure in sporting tweeds. 'What became of m'stick?'

'Think about it, lad.' Campbell tapped a finger on Cameron's chest as he passed. 'She's wasted up here.'

'You'll have to find it,' persisted Baird. 'I'll get nowhere without it. Quick now, man! Mustn't hold things up.' His tone was peremptory, and Beatrice saw the muscles in Theo's face tighten as Cameron disappeared back into the house.

Eventually they were ready, and Theo led them off at a cracking pace, Cameron striding out beside him, the others falling in behind. The earlier brightness had already faded, and the air had turned heavy and humid. Baird, red-faced and panting, threw Beatrice a grateful look as she slowed her pace to walk beside him, but after a couple of miles he sank down on a collapsed wall, mopping his brow, and clutched her arm. 'It's no good, m'dear, I need a rest. Ten minutes surely ain't going to make a difference.' She called out to Theo, and the others came back, glad of an excuse to stop. 'I need to catch m'wind, Blake.'

Ominous signs appeared again on Theo's face, but Beatrice saw Cameron draw him aside. He listened, scowling, glancing up at the sky and then over towards her; eventually he nodded and clasped a hand to Cameron's shoulder. Turning back to the guests, he announced that Cameron would return to the house, and that he and Donald would collect the party later by boat. 'That way we're not at the mercy of the tides and can slow the pace.'

'Thank God! We're not all as fit as you, Blake,' Baird cheered, and there were grunts of agreement. 'And, Forbes, get that little sister of yours to give you a couple of hip flasks to bring back with you.' He dropped his voice to a stage whisper. 'Or she can bring them herself if she likes, even if it means a bit of a *squeeze* in the boat.' He opened and closed his palm suggestively, nudging his neighbour.

Beatrice looked anxiously at Cameron, but Theo had moved between them. 'I think you'd better return with Cameron, my dear. The weather may play us false, and I think you'll struggle.' His tone gave little room for dissent, but she was content to go, finding the gentlemen as trying as their wives.

There was a dangerous brightness in Cameron's eye as they passed Baird, still mopping his brow, and began to retrace their steps. 'Will it take long to row back there, Cameron?' she ventured, glancing at his stony profile. 'It's quite a distance.'

'We frequently row further.'

They walked in a constrained silence for another quarter mile before she tried again. 'It's getting blacker by the minute.'

'Aye, the gentlemen will get a wetting.'

She turned aside to hide a smile at his tone, and they walked on, some few yards apart. The party had had the wind at their backs on the way out, but now the two of them confronted its growing force head-on, and it was not long before Beatrice felt the sting of rain on her face. Cameron halted and looked up at the sky. 'We'd better find shelter,' he said.

There was a small group of houses just ahead of them, and he led her towards one that was set back from the track. Black hens scattered as they crossed the cobbles, and Cameron called out a greeting. Almost immediately, a small, wrinkled woman emerged from the house to stare at Beatrice as she murmured anxiously, twisting her hands in a dirty apron. Cameron laid a reassuring hand on her shoulder and ushered Beatrice inside just as the first blast of slanting rain reached them.

The doorway was so low that she had to stoop to enter, and as she straightened she found herself entering an unfamiliar world, a world of earthy smells where acrid smoke hung like a low mist, and she stifled the urge to cough. The woman touched her arm, gesturing shyly to a low wooden chair beside the central hearth. '*An gabh sibh strùpag a' bhean-uasail?*' Beatrice looked at Cameron.

'Mrs. McLeod is offering you refreshment.' He sat down on a rough bench against the wall and added quietly, 'Milk, perhaps. Tea's expensive.'

'Milk would be lovely.' Cameron translated, and Beatrice was rewarded by a gap-toothed smile as the woman shuffled away.

Gradually her eyes adjusted to the gloom, and she saw that a shabby box bed with limp curtains occupied much of the space in the room, with a wooden chest at its foot. A dirty rag rug was pressed into the floor's uneven contours beside the bed, and a small dresser on rotting legs leant at an angle against the wall. There was not a shred of comfort: the fire, set about with cobbles, smouldered in a circle of white ash, and above it hung an iron pot, steam from its contents mingling with the peat smoke. But the smell of cooking was overlain by a musty dampness and a strong animal aroma, which caught at her nostrils. How could the poor woman live like this? The dwelling was little more than a barn, the only daylight coming from the doorway and a small window set into the thickness of the bare wall. Underneath the window was an old spinning wheel beside a broken creel of wool where a ginger cat lay suckling a ginger kitten. The black hens had retreated indoors and now pecked at the threshold. She looked beyond, but there was only darkness.

'That's where the cow spends the winter.' Cameron sat with his head thrown back against the bare stone wall, watching her from under half-closed lids. 'Mrs. McLeod is the poorest of your tenants, and the cow's her livelihood.' There was an edge to his voice, but before Beatrice could respond the old lady returned, panting quietly, carrying a cup of milk and a plate bearing a flat scone, which she offered to Beatrice. 'Take it or you'll give offence,' said Cameron quietly, as she hesitated.

She ate in silence, uncomfortable under the scrutiny of the old woman, smiling tightly at her, and was relieved when Cameron leant forward, his forearms on his knees, and addressed her. '*An cuala sibh bho Samaidh bho chionn ghoirid?*' The woman's eyes sparkled and she rose to retrieve a well-thumbed photograph from amongst the chipped crockery. '*Tha e a' coimhead math.*' He smiled, taking it before passing it on to Beatrice. 'This is her son. He went out to Cape Breton Island last year to find work in the coal mines. He sends money home.' Beatrice took it, unsure how to respond, and smiled at the woman. She beamed back and addressed a question to Beatrice. 'She asks if her granddaughter is giving satisfaction.' Cameron gave a dry look to her blank expression. 'Marie. She's working in your kitchens while you have guests.'

Beatrice barely recognised the girls who worked at the back of the house and was only vaguely aware that there were more of them since the guests arrived, but she answered quickly. 'Oh yes, she's a very good girl.' Another smile spread across the woman's wrinkled face when this was translated, but Beatrice's eyes fell before Cameron's sceptical look. She bit her lip and watched as he went over to the doorway, looking out at the sky.

'It's clearing,' he said, turning back. 'We should go before the next downpour.'

She rose, relieved to be going. The impoverished house and this new, hard-faced Cameron were both deeply unsettling. 'I've no money to offer her—' she murmured, holding out her hand to the woman.

'Good thing. It would offend,' he said, and clasped the old lady's hand with both of his, thanking her. '*Dia leibh agus taing dhuibh.*' They took their leave, and when Beatrice looked back the old woman still stood in the doorway, a pathetic figure in a shapeless black dress clasping a shawl around her thin frame, the ginger cat winding itself around her legs. The poorest of your tenants, Cameron had said, and she was living like an animal little more than a mile from her door.

They rejoined the main track, leaving the collection of houses behind them, and after a moment Beatrice broke the deepening silence. 'Do all the tenants live in such conditions?'

'Three or four families struggle. Others do better.'

There was still rain in the biting wind. 'How does she make a living?'

'She barely does.'

Beatrice began to resent this treatment. 'Explain to me, if you please. I should like to understand.'

He flicked a glance at her. 'What shall I tell you, madam? Mrs. McLeod's life story or how such people put food on the table?' She pulled her jacket around her more closely. Muirlan House had disappeared into the mist and the rough track was now her only guide. 'Makes little difference anyway, Euphemia McLeod's story or a hundred others.' He kicked aside a loose stone and fell into step beside her, but his closeness was not companionable. 'She's poor because her man and her two other sons are dead. They're dead because their fishing boat was lost in a storm. They had to fish because the croft was too small to support them, they'd have gone hungry otherwise.' Under this assault, Beatrice began to regret her persistence. Too late. 'The family had better land once,' he continued, 'but were evicted when the land was cleared to build Muirlan House. She'd just wed and had a bairn.' He stopped abruptly, then added, 'Five houses were demolished then, but hers still stands. It's where your husband skins his birds.'

Beatrice was mortified. They walked on in silence, but after a few paces, Cameron turned to her again. 'You asked me once about Anndra MacPhail, madam, after the burial. Well, he was evicted at the same time, and while the McLeods went quietly, Anndra MacPhail didn't. He was dragged from his house, fists flailing, curses flying, and it took four men to hold him down while they fired the roof. And his wife and children could only stand by and watch it burn.' Beatrice listened, appalled and exposed. 'And when he threatened to burn the roof off Muirlan House in return, he was thrown in prison and only released when he'd undertaken never to set foot on the island again.' Three hooded crows rose suddenly in front of them, and Cameron's eyes followed their flight before turning back to her. 'So what you saw that day was Anndra MacPhail reclaiming six foot of island land for his own, forever.'

Clouds rolled across the island, low and heavy, and they tramped on in silence.

Beatrice was deeply shocked but felt she couldn't leave matters there. 'Things are different now, though, and the remaining tenants are treated well.' Although if this was so, how could there still be such poverty? Cameron said nothing, and his silence was a further rebuke. 'I said my husband is a good landlord,' she repeated, demanding a response.

'He could do more, madam. If he chose to.'

They stopped walking, confronting each other, oblivious to the driving rain. 'How?'

Cameron met her glare evenly, as if calculating how far he could go. 'People need land, Mrs. Blake,' he replied, wiping the rain from his forehead. 'It's as simple as that. And those who were evicted are owed it. Their descendants want to return, they feel *bound* to the land. It's all they have.' Now the fragments of heated conversation in the study, the tension at the kelp gathering began to make sense. Was it *this* which lay at the heart of the discord between Cameron and Theo? And only this? 'A landless man like Duncan MacPhail wants to get his family out of the slums of Glasgow, to return here like his brother did, and have a croft of his own. Others too. But your husband won't have it.' He shook his head vigorously and began walking again, forcing her to follow. 'For him the island is just a backdrop for his paintings and a source of specimen for his catalogue. Nothing more. The rent's of no consequence.' He looked back across the fields to more roofless houses by the shore. 'But it could serve his needs *and* provide a livelihood for these families. Yet he chooses instead to entertain the likes of your present guests.' He did not trouble to conceal his contempt.

He had gone too far, much too far. She ought to rebuke him, adopt the haughty tone her mother used to address servants, and remind him of his position. And she should tell Theo— But the sour odour of Mrs. McLeod's poverty clung to her.

Then understanding came and she stopped abruptly. 'You took me there on purpose.'

Cameron stopped too, then shrugged and continued walking. 'We needed shelter, madam.'

'We did,' she conceded, not moving and forcing him to halt. 'But you chose the poorest house.'

'It was close by, madam.'

'There were others closer.' He said nothing. 'You took me there to make a point, to shame me.' She felt angry but confused, uncertain where to direct her anger. 'And you call me *madam* in that contemptuous tone to add a barb to that point.' He looked taken aback, arrested by her vehemence, then walked on, making no further reply, leaving her behind, and after a moment she followed him, humiliated and shaken. It felt as if Bess had suddenly turned on her, baring wolf's teeth.

By the time they reached the house, the rain was falling steadily and she was still considering her response. She dared not admonish him, yet surely matters could not be left as they were. But he preempted her. 'Excuse me, madam. I must find Donald and see about the boat,' he said and disappeared around the back of the house.

She crossed the hall and slowly mounted the curving stairs, thankful for Mrs. Henderson's news that the ladies had taken to their rooms. And as she trailed her hand up the banister, she had an image of the smoke trickling through a hole in the thatched roof, the sooty rain which fell from thinning patches, and she stopped to look out of the round window back towards the croft houses. It *was* shaming, there could be no question. But what of Cameron's recklessness? Had he assumed that she would not carry tales to Theo? Or did he consider himself immune to reprimand?

Chapter 18

≈ 1910, Beatrice ≈

'Beatrice, darling, is it the damp which puts the piano out of tune? I could have played for us otherwise.' Each scale produced a new discordant note, and Gertrude Campbell winced theatrically as she played.

There was more out of tune here than the piano, Beatrice thought, as she returned a bright smile. 'That would have been delightful. Theo has sent word to a piano tuner on Skye, and we expect him any day.'

'Good heavens! All that way…'

Ernest yawned and suggested cards, but no one responded. As their visit drew to a close, the guests were finding island entertainment thin, and Beatrice dug her nails into her palm, willing the woman to close the piano lid, wondering resentfully when Theo would reappear. He had withdrawn to the study, his temper decidedly frayed, abandoning the guests to her. She looked out of the window again and prayed the weather would clear.

After lunch it did, and Theo, with John Forbes and Cameron in attendance, took the gentlemen out with their guns, while the ladies withdrew to their rooms, leaving Beatrice to spend a restless afternoon in the morning room, trying to reply to a letter from Emily. *Do come! We're by no means swamped with guests. Theo will be busy with his book again when they're gone, and I long to see you.* Last night she had watched the guests at dinner and seen them as Cameron might have done, overdressed and idle, and the rich food had soured as her thoughts returned to the toothless old woman offering her simple hospitality on a cracked plate. Following dinner, she had summoned Mrs.

Henderson and asked her to send an appropriate gift by way of thanks. 'And can we not find work for Marie, even when the guests have gone?'

'There's always work, madam.'

'And if there are others who are in need, you must tell me,' she said, and the housekeeper had nodded in approval. She picked up her pen again. *I confess our current guests are tiresome, and seem no more content to be here than we are to entertain them. And there's so much I want to ask you…* But what could she possibly ask of her husband's sister? She sat looking out of the window, the pen idle in her hand, watching the gulls hanging in the air.

Later, the shooting party returned with their quarry, noisy and triumphant, and she went with the ladies out onto the drive to meet them. Cameron was just outside the front door when she stepped out, and he looked up quickly, but she ignored him and went to stand beside the others as they admired the hunters' bag.

'Oh, those colours! Such iridescence.' Gertrude's toe gestured to the blue-green neck of a fallen mallard laid out on the gravel. 'But they seem to fade so once they're on a hat.'

Beatrice felt her legs nudged aside as Bess asserted herself in between the ladies, sniffing at the dead birds. A low whistle brought her back to heel, and Beatrice realised that Cameron was standing just behind her.

'… try sulphur fumes to brighten them.'

'But the smell!'

'Mrs. Blake, I owe you an apology.' Cameron spoke quietly, and she half turned her head to hear him. 'I shouldn't have spoken as I did.'

'No.'

'… the silly girl *ruined* it. I said a *light* lather…'

'I wanted you to understand. It's important that you do.' Cameron pulled Bess back as she strained forward again.

'Understand?' She took a step back, away from the others.

'The realities behind all this.'

No one appeared to be paying them any attention. 'So you *did* intend to shame me?'

'Yes. It was unpardonable.' He gave her a twisted smile as he bent again to Bess and spoke more loudly. 'It's a cleg, I think, madam. That or a burr. She won't leave it alone.'

Diana Baird had moved to stand beside Beatrice and pointed to a delicate bird with striking plumage that lay beside the mallard. 'Now consider *that* for a dash of colour in a hatband, Beatrice. Rust and grey, just the thing for autumn. Who is this smart fellow, Cameron?'

'A phalarope, madam,' Cameron replied evenly, looking down at it. 'But that's the female, not the male. They were building a nest by the loch.' Beatrice remembered Theo's pleasure when Cameron had told him about the nest, and looked up quickly. Cameron responded with a slight shrug.

'Gaudy colours for a female, surely?' remarked Ernest Baird, who had strolled over to join them. 'For a female *bird*, that is, not a woman. *Lord*, no!' His wife gave him an admonishing rap on the arm, and Beatrice let her eyes follow a butterfly which landed on a patch of yellow vetch at the side of the drive.

'From what I hear from Mrs. Henderson, you've been very generous,' Cameron murmured, as the guests continued their raillery. 'So now I'm the one shamed for venting my foul temper.'

The visitors broke into general laughter as Baird continued to tease his wife: '… a pea*cock* not a pea*hen*, my dear.'

'You had been provoked, I think.'

Theo was standing a little way apart, talking to Charles Farquarson and the factor, but he now raised his head and caught Beatrice's eye, signalling a move indoors. Cameron caught the look and bent to gather up the afternoon's spoils, adding quietly, 'And for all that he could do more, Mr. Blake is a better landlord than many. I'm sorry for what I said.'

Then Theo called out and beckoned him over. 'We must think of something to entertain our visitors tomorrow, Cameron, if the weather's fine. Your father's joining us for dinner, so come too and we can discuss ideas.' And he put out an arm towards Beatrice, ushering her indoors.

$\sim$ *Theo* $\sim$

Theo surveyed the dinner table that evening with wry amusement. Halfway down the table, John Forbes sat quietly in his tweeds listening to the gentlemen's accounts of the afternoon's exploits, exaggerated for the ladies' benefit, looking like a man who expected to enjoy his dinner rather more than his company. Theo offered him a silent apology, but he had to include John if he was to invite Cameron, and he had wanted Cameron here tonight.

It had been an appalling trip back in the boat the previous evening—heavy seas and a treacherous wind made worse by the heavy rain. But Cameron had command of the situation, hauling on the tiller, shouting instructions to his brother, tightening ropes and shortening sail, and the gentlemen had responded meekly to his authority. Theo suppressed a smile, thinking that perhaps only he and Donald would have recognised that a slightly different point of sailing would have spared the gentlemen the worst of the drenching spray. But he did not begrudge Cameron his cool revenge, and inviting him tonight would, perhaps, belatedly signal to the guests that Cameron's status was not that of a lackey they could order about and insult.

He looked across at Cameron now, his dark head bent towards Baird, politely attentive to some interminable tale, occasionally interjecting a remark, his lean outdoor face contrasting sharply with that of his florid neighbour. Entirely at his ease, Theo mused, playing with the stem of his wine glass. He had sent across a set of evening clothes for him, old-fashioned but of good quality, from a time when his own girth was somewhat less, and Cameron wore them with a casual indifference, appearing as much the gentleman as the others, despite the worn cuffs.

Theo signalled to one of the girls to replenish a butter dish and continued to watch Cameron as the young man nodded and smiled, exhibiting faultless manners, apparently unaware that he was attracting concupiscent looks from the ladies across the table. But Theo knew only too well how much Cameron despised his company. He'd seen the sudden shuttering of his face when he'd invited him to join them, giving him little choice but to accept—he could hardly plead another engagement.

He turned at a tap on his arm from Diana Baird beside him and gave her a semblance of attention. Cameron might not thank him for the invitation but perhaps would see it as a continuing benign interest in his affairs and set it against the abrasion of their escalating disagreements.

Mrs. Baird required only a fraction of Theo's attention, and he let his mind wander back over the afternoon. He had only agreed to take the men out shooting following Beatrice's entreaties that he find something for them to do, as he disapproved of pointless carnage. With the exception of Farquarson, they were hopeless shots anyway, and Farquarson at least had the decency to take only the plentiful mallards. He mused grimly that he had been well-served when Baird had managed to hit the phalarope, a personal favourite, and the look of contempt Cameron had flung him as the bird was picked off the water had compounded his regret.

Diana Baird finally despaired of engaging his attention and raised her voice to address Cameron. 'We were talking of sea bathing, Cameron. Do you swim in the sea here?'

'Rarely, madam. It's not for the faint-hearted.'

Mrs. Campbell's eyes dwelt languidly on him as she leant across the table. 'If the weather is fine tomorrow, we could take a picnic to the sea, and you could swim then, perhaps,' she drawled. 'Your brother too. I'd like to see you two braving those great waves.' Theo looked dryly across at Cameron. 'Could it be arranged, Beatrice, do you think?' Diana asked her. 'The gentlemen have neglected us dreadfully.'

Damn the woman. He saw Beatrice look across at him,

searching for a reason to refuse, but it was Cameron who calmly squashed the idea. 'My thanks, madam, but I have no wish to swim tomorrow, and I believe my father has work for me to do.' John Forbes agreed that that was so, and the two ladies exchanged coquettish pouts.

The conversation moved on. 'I understand now why you come up here, Blake,' said Charles Farquarson. 'One forgets all about Asquith, the horseplay in Parliament, and the confounded Kaiser. Most enjoyable.'

Robert Campbell lifted his glass in agreement, adding grimly, 'Aye, and next week I'll be back confronting the rabble on the docks.' Theo saw John Forbes send a warning look to Cameron. 'There're paid agitators behind the unrest, you know, it's all orchestrated, the whole accursed business.' Campbell grumbled on in the same vein for some time, the others nodding and agreeing while Cameron regarded him steadily. 'And half the ministers of the cloth are socialists these days, preaching dissent.' He signalled for his glass to be refilled, leaning forward, getting into his stride. 'You've the same problem up here, of course, with the land raiders. Pure provocation.' Theo saw Beatrice glance sharply towards Cameron, and his face darkened. Had Cameron been entertaining her with his radical views, enlisting her support? That he would not countenance. 'If they preached the glories of Nova Scotia instead of stirring up trouble,' Campbell was continuing, 'I'd give 'em one of my ships and pack 'em off. And I gather the Reverend Nichol will be gracing these parts again, advocating civil disobedience. Tell them to clear the cells in readiness, Blake.' Campbell looked around for approval, heavy-jawed and belligerent, and took another swig of wine. 'Or get the gunboats back up here, that'd dampen enthusiasm for revolution.' And Theo watched helplessly as Cameron laid his knife and fork together on his half-empty plate and slowly pushed his glass away, his eyes never leaving Campbell's face. *Damn him*. Damn the pair of them!

Ernest Baird, meanwhile, was endorsing the sentiments. 'It's everywhere you turn. Unrest. Dissent. Even the women, God bless them.' He raised a glass towards Beatrice, then to his wife. 'No longer content with your fine plumage, eh?'

'Oh, those women. Mad. Quite mad.' Diana waved them aside with a twist of her hand and turned to Beatrice. 'Aren't they, my dear?' Theo saw that Beatrice had been caught off guard as all eyes turned towards her, and it was his turn to send a warning look. For God's sake, no! Not down that route too. Beatrice and her mother had both surprised him with their vehemence on the subject of female emancipation. A reaction to the profligate father, no doubt, playing fast and loose with his family's security. Understandable, perhaps, but even so.

And sure enough, he saw Beatrice's colour rise and her chin lift. 'Some of their tactics are extreme, of course,' she replied, looking steadily across at him, resenting the warning, 'but their desire to be heard is only reasonable.'

'If they'd anything sensible to say, perhaps so,' grunted Campbell, and Baird guffawed. Theo felt a stab of sympathetic anger as Beatrice flushed.

'What a goose you are, darling,' Gertrude chided. 'They only want to see their names in the newspapers.'

'Many are from good families, you know,' spluttered Baird, his mouth half-full. 'Well-to-do. They could stay at home and be quite comfortable! If you ask me, they've run out of ways to fill their time.'

Theo watched Beatrice survey the table coolly, her annoyance betrayed only by patches of pink on her cheeks. 'Surely the fact that they *could* stay at home but choose to put their freedom at risk shows how passionate they feel.' Silence followed, and Theo groaned inwardly as looks were exchanged around the table.

'Plucky too.'

Cameron's even tones broke the silence, and Theo found himself torn between cursing and cheering. 'Misguided nonetheless,' he said, stepping in hastily, determined to close the topic. 'No matter how much individual acts of misplaced heroism are reported in the press.' He gave Beatrice another quelling look.

'That phalarope of yours, Blake,' said Charles Farquarson, and Theo turned to him gratefully. 'The only other bird I know of where it is the male which rears the young is the dotterel. I saw them once in Norway. Quite devoted, I'm told.'

∼ *Beatrice* ∼

Throughout the meal, Beatrice had been aware of Cameron, darkly handsome in Theo's old suit, and watched him making polite conversation with amused indignation. If only they could have heard him yesterday! But the fact that Theo had asked him to dinner disturbed her, compounded by the matter of the suit, and she had watched the two of them throughout the meal, conscious again of an undercurrent of tension, conscious too of the signals the factor was sending to his son, and of Theo's watchfulness. But Cameron had kept himself well in hand, and no one had noticed his quiet refusal to continue to break bread with Campbell. Except Theo, perhaps. And then he had come to her defence in that surprising way. Plucky too.

She looked up and saw that Theo was signalling to her, and she rose, inviting the ladies to join her. John Forbes and Cameron got to their feet too, making their excuses. Cameron held the door as the ladies swept through, smiling over their shoulders at him. His father turned back to answer a question and Cameron stood waiting for Beatrice, and then he leant forward slightly as she passed him. 'Some women, mind you, would be better strangled at birth.' It was no more than a murmur and he was gone, disappearing down the servants' passage while she looked after him in astonishment.

Chapter 19

'Thank God that's over,' said Theo, throwing himself into an armchair with a groan. The guests and their conveyances were now mere specks on the far side of the strand, disappearing fast. 'I hope Charles manages to fleece the pair of them—then I'll feel it was worth the effort.' He rose to fetch himself a drink. 'I'd no idea they had such ghastly wives. I apologise for inflicting them on you, my dear. I'd have cheerfully drowned all three of them.'

They were sitting in the morning room, as the piano tuner had arrived during the chaos of departure and was now hard at work in the drawing room. 'Better strangled at birth,' murmured Beatrice, recalled from a daydream which had been distracting her from her letter.

'What? Oh, I see. Yes, much better.'

'But they'll have a lovely journey home pitying us for our remoteness,' she said, pulling herself together, 'and our primitive plumbing.'

'Won't they just!' He took a long drink and put his head back. 'Thank God for a bit of peace before the next visitors. Is that Emily you're writing to? Don't encourage them to stay too long, will you.'

'We've got almost two weeks before they come,' she said, and he smiled briefly, picking up a newspaper left by one of the guests, one she knew he had already read. 'Perhaps you can show me more of the island before then. I never got out to the seals, if you remember.'

'Yes, we must do that,' he said from behind the paper. But a moment later he tossed it aside and took his glass to the window and stood looking out, one hand thrust deep into his pocket.

In the background, the piano tuner plunked away doggedly, coaxing the keys back to tunefulness. Would she be able to coax Theo back in the same way, she wondered, looking at his stiff back, or would these bewildering tensions bring further discord?

Theo swallowed the rest of his drink and set aside his glass. 'The man makes an infernal noise,' he said. 'I'll go over to the estate office, I think, until he's finished.' A moment later the front door banged behind him, and through the glass of the morning room window, she watched him go.

But that night he came to her. There was a tap on her door as she was undressing, and he stood there, hesitant, as if unsure of his welcome, then wordlessly he stepped forward and took her in his arms, moving her towards the bed, and it had been almost as before between them. It was too fragile a connection to burden with questions, so she had said nothing, banishing her confusion, trusting to the honesty of his attentions, and responded without constraint, as far as she was able. And he had slept all night beside her, his back warm against hers, and she felt the knot of hurt more profoundly even as it began to ease.

But he slipped away before she stirred next morning. She rose, pushing disappointment aside, noting instead how the sun shafted onto her dressing table, making arrow darts of light on the mirror as she willed herself back into optimism. The shadows under her eyes were less marked today, she decided, as she raised a hand to tie her hair in a simple knot. She looked about for her hat, thinking that perhaps they could spend the day together, as last night he had half promised that they would. Maybe they could go along the shore where the terns had lifted their blockade, or just walk together, as they used to when they first arrived. Or perhaps he would sketch? But she wouldn't suggest it. Since the episode at the rock pool, he had never brought a sketchbook with him but preferred his field glasses or his camera.

As she went downstairs she could hear him in the study, opening and closing the drawers of his specimen cabinets. If the tides were right, perhaps there would be time to go out to the seals. She tossed her hat onto a chair in the hall and swept into the room. 'Theo, do we have time to get as far—' But she stopped at the threshold.

Cameron. Not Theo.

He was bent over the cabinets but straightened as she appeared. 'Good morning, madam. Mr. Blake has gone over to the estate office.'

'Will he be long?'

'There was a message from the manse. He spoke of riding over there, to talk to the minister.' She stared at him, optimism crumbling. 'Shall I fetch him for you?' Cameron put aside the ledger, his eyes on her face.

'No, no.' She shook her head. 'I only thought we might walk. No matter.' She turned to go but paused at the door, looking back over her shoulder. 'How does the catalogue progress, Cameron?'

'It's going well, but it's a slow business,' he replied, 'preparing each illustration.'

'What is it *you* are doing?'

He came out from behind the desk. 'I'm sorting through the material old Mr. Blake collected years ago to see what we can use. Some of it's too far gone.' He pointed to the open drawers. 'But I'm recording the rest while Mr. Blake writes and prepares the illustrations.'

She came slowly back into the room and began leafing through the paintings on Theo's desk. All neatly labelled and numbered, each specimen set against a miniature backdrop of landscape or coast. A ringed plover at the edge of the rocky shore, a tern hovering above the sea's surface, a lapwing guarding a chick. Realistic and convincing. Exquisite. And yet... She lifted her head to look at the same ringed plover, frozen on the shelf, the tern beside it with raised wings, impaled on a pedestal, the faded lapwing and chick. The life in the paintings was illusory. Convincing... but counterfeit.

Cameron watched her as she turned the sheets of paper. 'He's a very talented man,' he said after a moment.

'Yes.' She walked over to the cabinets and stood looking at the dried skins laid out in the open drawers, suppressing a shudder. 'There must be every sort of bird on the island here.'

'Almost, but not quite.'

She looked back at him, pulling aside her skirts as she picked her way through the dusty bookcases and cabinets towards the window, drawn by the view. 'What's missing?'

'The wanderers, the vagrants, the unusual—'

'Like a nesting diver?'

'Just so.' He gave her a wry smile but was not to be provoked into further indiscretion, and she turned back to the window.

'If it were up to me, the whole collection could go to Edinburgh to gather dust in some fusty museum, and our visitors could see the wild birds outdoors where they belong.' Her exasperation bubbled to the surface. 'I'd like to clear them all away, give the house a thorough spring clean and... and paint every room yellow.' She looked out across the bay, swallowing hard and biting her lip, not caring what Cameron thought. But after a moment she cleared her throat. 'Just ignore me, Cameron. I'll wait here awhile and see if my husband returns.'

She sensed him still contemplating her, then he returned to his desk and carried on writing in the ledgers in a silence broken only by the scratching of his pen. She glanced at him and then turned back to the window. There was no real urgency to this book of Theo's, no compulsion. It was an excuse—this room had become his fortress, and he had enlisted these dried creatures as his bodyguards, charged with keeping her at arm's length. But what part did Cameron play?

She felt the tension stretch across her head again and raised a hand to rub her brow.

'Why yellow?'

Cameron's quiet voice interrupted her thoughts, and she looked swiftly across at him. He was still bent to his task, still writing. She turned back to the view and considered her answer. 'Because it's joyful and bright… And it reflects the sunlight. The house is too dark and brooding. It needs light.'

Cameron's pen continued to scratch. 'But you've made such a difference,' he said, still not lifting his head.

'To the house? No! I've hardly touched it.'

'Not to the structure, but to its… its aura. Mr. Blake was too much alone before.'

She studied the back of his head where his dark hair grew long over his collar and felt a sudden rush of relief. Had her suspicions simply misunderstood what was, despite the arguments, a real sympathy, a bond between the two men, forged only by long association? Cameron's words had been spoken with an almost filial understanding, but as she cast about for a reply, she heard footsteps crossing the hall and raised her head hopefully.

But it was Donald, and he paused at the door when he saw her. 'Excuse me, madam, but my father has sent for Cameron, to help mend fences, while the weather holds.'

'Is Mr. Blake still at the estate office, Donald?' she asked him.

'He went to the stables.' And even as he spoke, she saw Theo, on horseback, crossing the foreshore down onto the sand. Cameron began packing away the skins, giving Beatrice a thoughtful look.

'You'll not get your walk, madam. Shall I ask Ephie to give you some company?'

She shook her head. 'It is of no matter. Ephie has enough to do.' Mrs. Henderson then appeared to confirm what Donald had said, adding that Mr. Blake had told her not to delay lunch for him. Cameron gave Beatrice another searching look, made his excuses, and followed Donald.

When Beatrice returned from her solitary walk later that day, she went into the morning room and found primroses, marsh marigolds, and yellow bog iris buds trailed through with strands of bright yellow vetch arranged in a bowl on a windowsill. She paused, enchanted, touching the tip of the emerging iris buds with her fingers and turned to thank Mrs. Henderson as she came in bearing tea. But the housekeeper smiled and shook her head. 'Cameron Forbes said you'd expressed a desire for the brightness of yellow and brought them in earlier. I told him wild flowers never do well indoors, but he said to put them in a bowl and see. And anyway, they'll make a lovely splash of colour while they last.'

Chapter 20

∼ 2010, Hetty ∼

Hetty drove back to the cottage through the labyrinth of peat cuttings and lochans, slowing at the high point to watch the ferry pull away from the harbour, heading for Skye. Soon she would be on board, on her way back to the real world, with a fistful of problems.

She was reluctant to leave. The place had got to her, and she could feel the threads which had drawn her here coiling around her, binding her close; the complex legacy of the past. Her original plans for the house now seemed astonishingly naïve, and James Cameron's assessment of the amount of money needed was plain scary. Thick end of a million! If so, that signalled the end of the project and of her dreams of starting afresh. And that thought, at the moment, was unbearable.

But need it be the end? Giles had already told her that it might be possible to raise capital if a sound business plan was put together, telling her that investors liked that sort of project. But large investors with an eye to profit were unlikely to be impressed by the likes of Diighall and the effect on his 'business', or by schoolchildren gluing shells on matchboxes. *Big money brings big problems*, James had said.

But James himself was something of an enigma, and she wondered again what his real objections to the project might be. Was he just resisting change, or was there more to it? She drove on down the slope towards her cottage, then slowed, seeing someone standing on her doorstep. A man, with a suitcase, but there was no car— She drove on, then drew to a halt and sat staring through the windscreen in disbelief as the figure strolled towards her.

Giles. As if summoned by her thoughts.

'Hello, darling,' he said as she opened the car door and stepped out. 'I thought I'd surprise you.'

Inside the cottage, he explained.

'Emma heard about the bones being found, and she rang me. There was an item on the local radio and it referred to you being here.' He paused and gave her a rueful look. 'I sort of thought you might be.' Hetty said nothing, and he gave a small shrug. 'Anyway, she wondered why you'd not been in touch?' She got up and busied herself tidying away the breakfast dishes left from the morning. 'And I must admit I felt the same...'

He used that injured tone in situations like this, and it annoyed her. 'Giles, I—'

'Anyway, I spoke to the police in Inverness,' he continued hastily, 'who put me in touch with a community police officer here. Forbes, a nice chap. Once I'd convinced him I wasn't the press, he told me where you were.'

Thinking he was being helpful, no doubt. 'Giles—'

He came over and laid his hands on her shoulders. 'Look, I'm sorry if you think I'm intruding, darling, but I thought that dealing with the police might be unpleasant, and that you could use some support.'

And that was always the problem—he genuinely meant well.

She let it ride until, over a scratch dinner of omelette and frozen peas, he dropped the next bombshell. 'Emma was disappointed that you *hadn't* been in touch, you know,' he said, filling her glass from a bottle of wine he'd produced as a peace offering. 'They've had a very downbeat report from the local builder.'

'I know. I've met him.'

'What did you make of him?' He sampled the wine, studying the label. 'Emma thinks she picked a wrong 'un.'

'We went through his report together. It seemed very thorough.'

'She thinks the job's beyond him. We need to find—'

'No. There are real problems.'

Giles flicked at the rim of Diighall's cracked wine glass. It gave a flat, dull ring. 'Sure, but… Now, don't be angry, darling, but you see, I flew up to Glasgow, and then got the train and stayed last night with Emma and Andrew, and we talked things over.' She looked at him, wondering how he *could* be so obtuse. 'And, long story short, they came across with me this morning and checked into the hotel—'

She put down her knife and fork, and stared. '*Giles!*'

'So now we can all go across to the island tomorrow and take a look. Andrew's the man to know what needs doing. Bags of experience.'

'You shouldn't have done this.'

'Whyever not? That's what agents are for! Let them do their job, for God's sake. They're professionals.'

'So why didn't they send me the report?'

'They'd only got it themselves a couple of days ago, and they wanted to look through it first, evaluate it, and then explain the key points.' He made it all sound so reasonable. 'But what I don't understand, Hetty, is why you just took off like that, without a word?'

The sudden shift caught her off guard, and they looked at each other across the table. She'd known she'd have to try and explain this to him somehow, but she was unprepared. There'd been no time to work things through in her own mind, no space in her head for Giles these last few days. They'd reached this point too quickly, and she retreated from it. 'I needed space, Giles. To think.'

'I hated you going like that. I thought you'd left me.'

His expression sought reassurance, but it was not so simple.

'No. I didn't leave because—'

'Thank God for that!' He didn't wait for the rest, but his relief was a further reproach. 'Look, I'm sorry, love, but frankly, I wanted an excuse to come up and find you, and so Emma's call was a godsend. But I shouldn't have brought them, I see that now. Clumsy of me. But believe me, Hetty, it was well-intentioned, and as they're here now, just down the road... ?'

~

The evening ended on an uneasy truce, but she lay sleepless beside Giles through the night, listening to his snores and thinking how incongruous it was that he was here. And he seemed to think he had arrived in some remote colonial outpost. 'What! No mobile signal *at all*? I thought you were just not replying. How do the natives cope?' It was almost funny, especially when she found herself defending the shortcomings of Diiughall's dreadful cottage.

Next morning, however, indifferent to Giles's protests regarding salt water and shoe leather, she refused to wait to be collected by her uninvited agents and said that she would walk across. 'You wait, by all means,' she said as she pulled on her jacket, but Giles seemed disinclined to quarrel again, and so they left a note pinned to the cottage door and left together.

'Great Scott! What a place,' he said, as they squelched up the track from the foreshore. 'Stuck out here in the middle of nowhere.' And as he strode up the drive, she felt her resentment reignite. He was trespassing.

Then she looked back across the strand and saw a Land Rover leaving the far shore. Not a battered workhorse but a shiny black model. It drove slowly across the strand and halted at the bottom of the track, unwilling to tackle the mud. Giles went down to meet them while Hetty waited at the front door, keys in hand, and watched the three of them stepping carefully to avoid the worst of the mire as they came up the old drive.

'*So* nice to meet you at last.' Emma's red lipstick framed perfect teeth, and she kissed the air beside Hetty's cheek. 'I feel I know you already.' Hetty smiled briefly and turned to shake Andrew Dalbeattie's hand. But you don't, she thought, as Dalbeattie beamed at her, well-polished and confident in wax jacket and

Galway boots.

Then, to her astonishment, she saw that another Land Rover was crossing the strand, a familiar, battered one. Emma had seen it too. 'Good, this must be Mr. Cameron. I phoned him earlier this morning and luckily he was free to join us. Seemed sensible.'

This was too much, and Hetty felt her cheeks flame with annoyance. 'I think you should have—' But Emma had already set off down the drive.

Giles glanced uneasily at her as the muddy vehicle pulled up the track, passing the other Land Rover, passing Emma, and parked beside the house. 'I *honestly* didn't know,' he said.

Emma doubled back to greet James. 'So good of you to turn out at short notice,' Hetty heard her say as she introduced herself. 'But an opportunity not to miss, us all being here together.' James shook her hand briefly and was introduced to the others, and his eyes lingered on Giles's face a moment, then he looked across at her and gave a curt nod.

'So, let's get started, then, shall we?' Dalbeattie was clutching a copy of the report, and he took James aside.

'He's not quite what I expected,' murmured Emma, but Hetty ignored her and followed them.

'…Buttressing and ties would hold things together while the underpinning was done,' Dalbeattie was saying.

'Of course. But with that wall fundamentally weakened, it'll be—'

'I've seen worse.' Dalbeattie turned to beam at Hetty. She looked at James, but his expression was unreadable.

'What were you going to say?' she asked him.

'What I've already said.' He looked steadily back at her. 'The cost to—'

'But cost isn't your problem, is it?' Emma had joined them, and she placed an admonishing hand on his arm. 'That's our bit.' James looked down at her hand until she withdrew it.

While Dalbeattie took up the discussion with James again, Giles scanned the pasture behind them. 'What about the land?

How far does the estate stretch?'

Emma took out a large-scale map, which rattled noisily in the breeze, and gave him a corner to hold. Red highlighter described a large irregular tract of land, larger than Hetty had imagined, which Emma now traced with a glossy fingernail. 'And it includes that stretch of land further to the west.' She recognised it as where she had walked and saw a rectangle marked with the word *ruin* in brackets, beside a small cove. Not a ruin now, she thought, and glanced across at James.

'And that's the bit you see joining up with the links?' Giles asked. 'Making it an eighteen-holer?'

Emma smiled back. 'World-class.' James abandoned Dalbeattie mid-flow at that point and, taking hold of part of the map, he studied it intently, his brow furrowed.

'What's the shooting like up here, Mr. Cameron?' Giles asked him, but James didn't look up. 'What is there? Snipe, duck, plover?'

'All of those.' James's face was expressionless as he turned to Hetty. 'You're aware that the bird reserve abuts the land over that way?'

'We know all about the reserve, Mr. Cameron,' said Emma. 'And the links will provide something of a buffer, a sort of green belt for the birds.'

James looked blankly at her, then he turned back to Hetty. 'They oppose the development, as you know, they could hardly do otherwise. An expensive shoot next door to one of the country's most important bird reserves? What'll that do for—'

'I'll tell you what it'll do,' Emma said, her lips a thin line. 'It'll put the place on the map.' And she gave him a twinkling smile.

'New jobs, new money,' Dalbeattie added.

James looked from one to the other, and then directly at Hetty, but Emma moved quickly, before he could speak again. 'Let's go inside while the weather holds good, shall we?' She gestured to a cloud bank building on the horizon.

James remained where he was. 'And the patch of land you have in mind for extending the golf course is not estate farmland.

It's croft land—'

'These plans were drawn up from the land registry.'

'—And the tenant is John MacPhail,' he continued. 'He grows his potatoes there.'

Andrew Dalbeattie gave a short laugh. 'Then I'm afraid he'll have to grow them somewhere else.'

Hetty saw a glint again in James Cameron's eye. 'I'll leave you to tell him that,' he said, and he went to retrieve two hard hats from the Land Rover. He put one on himself and gave the other to her. 'I only have two,' he said to Emma.

'We should have thought,' she replied with another, more brittle, smile.

Hetty pulled out the keys as they went up to the front door, then cursed to herself as she struggled with the unfamiliar lock.

'Shall I?' said James, behind her. It opened for him, of course, and he stood back, gesturing them into the house and followed her in. 'This was a surprise,' he murmured.

'I didn't know—'

'No?' The others were already eulogising the hall, flashing the beams of their torches around the walls, and Dalbeattie called to James and took him off into the morning room. Hetty hung back, and scraps of conversation reached her from Giles and Emma in the dining room.

'…pity about the fireplaces…'

'…easily replaced, and it's got *such* potential…'

She stood alone in the hall and looked up the wrecked staircase to the broken landing. Things were moving too quickly. *Stay in control*, James Cameron had warned. Easy to say. She went and stood at the door of the drawing room, now half lit by daylight from the front door, and saw before her those muted images: a grand piano, draped with a lacy cloth; the chairs pulled up to the fire; and the woman, a pale ghost, seated alone at the window— but much harder to know where her allegiances should lie.

'Oh God. The body! I'd forgotten. It was found *here*.' Emma's strident tones reached her across the hall, and Hetty heard her telling Giles what the local media had said; they'd clearly milked the scant facts for all they were worth, bulking them out with conjecture. 'Who do *you* think it is, Mr. Cameron?' James gave a curt response as he led them back into the hall, and Emma flashed a smile at Hetty. 'It'll add interest, whoever it is. A real live murder mystery!'

James's face was set hard. 'If there's nothing else—'

'What a place!' Giles said as he joined her, squeezing her arm. '…in a pretty poor state, alright,' Dalbeattie was saying, 'but the right contractors can work miracles.'

'Shh,' hissed Emma. 'We'll talk tonight, over dinner.'

James passed her without a glance and stood at the door while they filed out. He banged the door shut behind them and fixed the lock while the visitors stood together, still talking. He looked down at the keys for a moment, then slipped them into his pocket, glancing up at Hetty as he did. 'I'll be off, then,' he said. 'But you know where to find me.' And he was in the Land Rover before she could protest. The vehicle bounced down the track towards the gateposts and swung out of them, spraying mud along the side of the shiny black Land Rover as it went.

Chapter 21

∽ 2010, Hetty ∽

Next morning, Giles offered to go to the shop to fetch fire-lighters. Neither of them had been able to get the peat to light, and the storage heaters were again refusing to cooperate. Giles had gone off with a readiness which seemed to acknowledge the coolness there was between them. The chill had deepened over dinner last night with Emma and Andrew, where there had been plenty of talk of partnerships, finance packages, and shared risk. They had all talked across her, and while much of this was unfamiliar to her, Giles had compounded her annoyance by telling her, in kindly tones, that he would explain things to her later. She was only just able to remain civil. Later she had tried to explain to him how she felt, but had been rewarded again with an injured look and an assurance that he had only come up to help.

She glanced in consternation at the plans behind her on the table, left there after Emma and Andrew's departure. They had brought some artist's impressions, done from old photographs, they told her, showing how the house might appear when restored. It looked fabulous but could be achieved only at a cost. That much she had learned.

At least she could try again to light the fire, so she went and knelt by the hearth. Giles had left her just a handful of sticks, as well as a litter of failed matches, and it was pretty pointless anyway, as they'd have to go for the ferry straight after lunch. But it was cold and wet outdoors, and she was childishly determined to get it lit before he returned. Then she heard him banging on the door. Too late.

'It's open, just push hard. It jams,' she called and struck

another match. Footsteps crossed the kitchen and stopped.

'You've used *all* of those sticks in a week!' She looked round and there was James, not Giles, leaning against the doorframe, arms folded, in characteristic pose. 'But then Diighall's given you poor peat, the old miser.' He straightened and stepped forward, holding out the keys to Muirlan House. 'I forgot to give you these.'

She looked at them, then up at him. 'No, you didn't.'

He gave a faint smile and dropped them onto the table. 'No? I just drove past your... Giles, isn't it? Which is good, as I want to talk to you on your own.'

'Do you.' She rose, but his eye had been caught by the plans, and he stopped, then pulled out a chair and sat, elbows on the table, studying them with the same intensity he had shown yesterday. After a moment he glanced up at her, pointing to the red highlighter line on the estate plan. 'This is what you believe to be the boundary?'

'Yes.'

He said nothing more, but his finger traced the line, his lips moving as if committing it to memory.

'You wanted to talk to me,' she said sharply, and he sat back, looping his arm around the chair back, and looked at her.

'Are you sure you want to go along with all of this?' he said at last.

'Meaning?'

'Are you really committed to what's being proposed?' He gestured to the artist's drawings. 'This lot will cost millions. Much more than I suggested. You know that, don't you?' He didn't wait for a reply. 'I'm assuming you don't have millions, so you'll have to borrow them or go into partnership, which means either huge debts or huge compromises. You do realise all this?'

'You imagine that I don't?' He was as bad as Giles.

His eyes flashed a smile, quickly gone. 'You do. Then good. But make sure you understand what you're getting into before you're in too deep.' She remained silent. 'And believe me, it goes deep.' He looked back at the map. 'Besides, your man's wrong,' he said, tapping the sheet. 'This shows the estate at the time of Blake's death, before Emily Armstrong made a number of settlements to existing tenants.'

'How can it be wrong?'

'God knows.' He bent over it again. 'It shows the reserve, alright, but not the Forbeses' land or the land made over to the crofters. It even seems to claim the old farmhouse is still part of the estate.' He sat back and contemplated her. 'But land ownership is only part of it; the machair is a rare and valuable habitat. The reserve will fight you tooth and nail—'

'With your support?'

'—and you'll find yourself in dispute with tenants who can claim—'

'They can claim what they like, but facts are facts.' Giles had stepped unnoticed through the open back door and now stood, firelighters in one hand and a bottle of malt whisky in the other. 'Otherwise why bother to come and warn her off?'

James rose slowly while Giles slipped off his jacket and hung it on the back of the chair where James had been sitting. Marking his territory.

'Drink?' asked Giles, proffering the bottle with an affable smile. James began to refuse and then seemed to change his mind and sat again. Hetty went to get glasses. 'What did you mean, Forbeses' land?' she heard Giles ask. When she returned, he had pulled up a chair opposite James. She sat too, at the head of the table, in neutral territory.

James pointed to the map. 'That land belongs to Aonghas Forbes, the man who owns the old factor's house.'

'Really?' Giles slid a glass towards him. 'I imagine the agents will have done their homework.'

James looked across at Hetty. 'Blake created new crofts at the far end of the island a few years before his death, and they're still worked even if not inhabited.' And she thought of the socks on the washing line… 'Emily Blake formed a trust with her brother's remaining money to be used for the benefit of the islanders, but she made the farmland over to Donald Forbes, along with the farmhouse.' Setting things right after her brother's death?

'But if that was so—' she began.

'Then Mr. Forbes will have the deeds.' Giles stretched out his legs with another genial smile, his hand cupping his glass. 'And it'll be officially recorded in the normal way.' He took a drink, raising an eyebrow at James. 'Don't you think?'

James nodded grimly. 'There's documentation. Aonghas has it.' He sat forward, tapping the plans again. 'And that patch of land has an existing tenant.'

'Ah, yes. The potato man.'

James glanced towards Hetty, that odd look in his eye again. 'I strongly advise you not to challenge John MacPhail over his rights—'

'But all this can be sorted out through the official channels, Mr. Cameron,' Giles interrupted, 'and Hetty has lots of support, you know. My own firm has represented her family's interests for several years. And, let's face it, the property *is* hers.' He turned to smile at her. 'Besides, the house is of national importance, *Scottish* national importance, Mr. Cameron.'

'It's a rich man's conceit.'

Giles's jaw dropped. 'Theodore Blake—' he began.

'Blake was a gifted painter and it's his paintings which are his legacy, not his father's house. Those paintings captured the spirit of this place, the same spirit which bound the islanders to the land. That's his legacy. And the island has preserved its special quality because of his reclusive years, so we can thank him for that too.'

'But the house—'

James ignored him. 'Did you find the place in your painting, Hetty? *Was* it Torrann Bay?'

'Yes.' Had he used her name before?

'And what did you see there?'

She paused, considering. 'Why, nothing...' His eyes held

hers. 'Only the sand, and the sea.'

'What else?'

He spoke quietly, encouraging her, and the scene rose again before her: the light shafting across the wet sand, the tang of salt on the soft air, wind rustling through the silvery grasses, and the gulls' cries blown back from the sea. Emptiness— 'Rocks, and waves breaking along the beach. Shore birds—' she said, addressing the expression in his eyes and Giles looked from one to the other, uncertain.

James held her gaze for a moment longer, then nodded and gave her a smile as he got to his feet. 'Just so.' It was a smile of approval. Then he glanced again at the plans. 'I said what I came to say to you, and returned your keys.' He picked them up and took her hand, pressing them into it. 'You heard what the man said. It *is* all yours. And that includes Torrann Bay, you see. That's uncontested land. Unprotected, to do with as you think right.' He closed her fingers over the keys, and they dug into her palm. 'And you know where to find me. Ruairidh too. When you need us.' He left his drink barely touched, nodded briefly at Giles, and was gone.

She heard the back door bang behind him, and a moment later the sound of the Land Rover starting up and driving off, and then fading as it headed along the road skirting the wide bay.

Chapter 22

~ 1910, Beatrice ~

Beatrice leant against the folded shutters at the drawing room window, watching the shadows racing across the strand towards her. Fair-weather clouds. Then shapes on the far side began to resolve themselves into a pony and trap, followed by a cart, and she sat forward. 'I think they're here!'

Theo came and stood beside her. 'Looks like them,' he agreed, and then returned to his book. She flung him an exasperated look as she went to the door. 'They'll require entertainment,' he had complained when they had received Emily's last correspondence detailing their plans. 'Especially if Emily's bringing the major with her.' He had glanced balefully at his sister's letter. 'And Kit's coming along as *chaperone*. Ha! But I suppose it spares us their mother's company.'

She went out onto the terrace alone and stood waiting, the wind snatching at her hair. The trap rocked over the stony fore-shore towards her, a cartload of luggage behind it, but as she started down the drive, the front door opened behind her and Theo caught her up, taking her arm. Emily Blake half rose in the trap, waving vigorously, only to be pulled down smartly by the tall figure beside her. The pony had hardly halted before she pulled her elegant skirt aside and stepped down, embracing Beatrice eagerly. 'Bea, darling! We've made it!' She spoke in the breathless, gasping way Beatrice remembered as she hugged her. '*What* a journey. Such hideous roads, Rupert was in *agonies* over his precious automobile. We left it on the mainland, of course.' She offered a cheek to her older brother. 'How are you, Theo? You look well. And oh! The *house*—' She clasped her gloved hands together, and sunlight reflected back a welcome from the high walls.

Her brother strolled over to give Beatrice a casual peck on each cheek and shook hands with Theo. 'Good to see you both. Married life suits you, Theo. I—'

'And here's Rupert,' Emily interrupted, pulling forward the tall man who had stepped down to join them. He clasped Theo's hand and bent to kiss Beatrice, his eyes twinkling a greeting as Emily continued to chatter. Beatrice had approved of Major Ballantyre when they had met in Edinburgh, seeing that beneath the military bearing there was a shrewd eye and a sense of humour. Then Emily squeaked again. 'Look, Kit. It's Donald!' And she rushed forward, elegance forgotten, to greet Donald and the factor, who were approaching from the stables.

'But where's Cameron?' Kit demanded, clasping Donald's hand and turning to Rupert. 'I told you about Cameron, didn't I? Boon companion. I'd have followed him into the jaws of hell, if he'd let me. You said he'd come back?' And even as he spoke, Cameron appeared on the crest of the rise beside the house, shouldering a gun, Bess running at his heels. He raised a hand in greeting and came down swiftly to join them. Kit sprang forward. 'Cameron! Are you well?' Urban nonchalance fell away as he pumped Cameron's hand.

'Very well, Mr. Kit.' Cameron gave a slight bow by way of greeting to the other arrivals, before propping his gun against the wall, laying two rabbits beside it, and went to unbuckle the leather straps which held the luggage in place.

'*Mr.* Kit?' Kit's astonished words were lost as John Forbes took charge of the unloading. Emily tucked her hand into Beatrice's arm and Theo led the family towards the house. Kit paused a moment, distracted, looking back to see Cameron jump up on the cart, voicing his scorn at the number of boxes. Donald's laugh was swiftly silenced by a word from John Forbes, and Cameron looked up to give Kit an ironic salute.

Beatrice took Emily upstairs, where she tossed aside her hat and travelling coat, throwing open her bedroom window and leaning out. 'Oh, Beatrice. I had forgotten—' She took great gulping breaths of air. 'How *could* I have done so?' And she stood a moment watching the seabirds swoop and dip over the empty sands. 'I'm so *glad* we came,' she said, then turned back to Beatrice, her eyes sparkling. 'Even *I* was getting tired of wedding plans.' She dropped onto the bed and began peeling off her gloves. 'So I've left it all to Mama to fuss over and now I have Rupert to myself. Kit doesn't count. Oh, Bea! I am so happy. I can't begin to tell you.' Her eyes rested a moment on a bowl of primroses that Beatrice had picked that morning. 'How lovely! Did Theo tell you this was my old room?' And Beatrice smiled, letting her believe it to be so. 'Where will Rupert sleep?'

The house seemed to rouse from its lethargy to greet the return of the two younger Blakes, and Beatrice felt her own spirits reviving. Voices and laughter lit the rooms like shafts of sunlight, breakfasts were no longer solitary affairs, nor were dinners oppressed by long silences. They had even brought gramophone records, and Kit wound up the Monarch every day until Theo protested. But he too became more sociable, taking Kit and Rupert on fishing or shooting excursions by day, and joining conversations or card games in the evenings. And it seemed to Beatrice that he smiled at her more.

On fine days, bereft of their men, she and Emily would stroll along the foreshore or tramp across the machair to the western shore, and Beatrice found that she was hungry for this easy companionship. In Edinburgh, after Theo and Beatrice's wedding, Emily had declared, with uncomplicated enthusiasm, that she had always longed for a sister and had proceeded to regale her with confidences, never tiring of extolling Rupert's manifold virtues. She did the same now, but Beatrice felt unable to reciprocate. 'Should I *worry* about you, Bea? Do you get lonely up here with no other company?' Emily's puckish face showed kindly concern as she guilelessly hit the mark. 'I suppose you've had visitors, which helped. But do you manage alright?'

Beatrice hesitated, then answered obliquely. 'I quite like the quiet. Theo's visitors tend to be local landowners, apart from the group from Edinburgh whose wives found it all rather primitive. I actually prefer it when we haven't visitors, apart from you, of course.' Emily flashed a smile and squeezed her arm. 'I'm glad you came.'

'And Theo looks so well. You must be good for him.' Beatrice smiled slightly. 'Though, in fact, I don't really know *what* pleases Theo—' and the words found an echo in Beatrice's confusion as Emily stopped to empty sand from her shoe. 'We've spent so little time together. Mama is quite terrified of him, you know, for all that she boasts about him to her cronies. He was grown and gone when we were little, and the Forbes boys were more like brothers, especially for Kit. He was quite devastated when Mama dragged him away, you know, though he'd have had to leave for boarding school anyway. Theo did invite him back here in the holidays, but somehow Kit was never able to come. Mama's doing, I expect.' She paused again, looking back into the past, and then tucked her arm in Beatrice's and they walked on, stopping occasionally to admire the shells which lay tumbled in the seaweed. 'Cameron and Donald have both grown into such *handsome* men, and little Ephie is quite the young woman,' she continued after a moment. 'They used to be the centre of our lives, you know, we spent all our time together, running wild.' Beatrice smiled, imagining a childhood very different from her own, constrained as it had been by finance and etiquette. 'Yet I hear that Cameron is planning to leave again?'

'Yes,' replied Beatrice, 'in the spring, I think.' Or at least he had been— A gull gave a harsh cry above them, and she paused, looking up at it.

'Theo wanted him to stay on at one time, I remember, as some sort of secretary.' Emily's words seemed devoid of deeper significance, and she turned, waiting for Beatrice to catch up.

'He'd still like him to,' she said, and screwed up her face to follow the bird's flight across the bay.

Since the day the wild flowers had appeared in the morning

room, Beatrice had felt both befriended and further confused, drawn to Cameron by curiosity as well as suspicion, lingering if she came across him alone in the study. He would break off and rise, but sit when she did and lean back in his chair, and they would talk quite easily about all manner of things, and now if they met out-of-doors, he would stop and converse, or walk with her awhile. And her response to his presence only confused her more—for whatever Theo might feel towards Cameron, the irony was that it was now she who sought the company of the factor's son.

'I gather he's proved something of a disappointment to Theo.' Emily interrupted her thoughts. A disappointment? Perhaps so. There had been another argument in the study a day or so before Emily's arrival, and she had overheard the name MacPhail again. Cameron had not appeared since, but she had watched him come and go from the window. 'It's a wasted opportunity for him, don't you think?'

'Maybe Cameron wants to make his own way in the world,' she replied, falling into step again. 'And he and Theo don't always see eye to eye.'

'I can imagine!' Emily laughed. 'Theo can be a dreadful autocrat, and I don't suppose Cameron likes to knuckle under.' She gestured to the grassy bank at the top of the beach where a patch of bog cotton shook in the breeze, and they sat on the edge, dangling their feet above the overhang of turf. 'He was always rebellious, even as a boy.' She leant back, plucking at the cotton tufts and teasing the fibres apart. 'Rupert says he has reckless eyes... But Theo has always been very good to him.'

On fine afternoons they would have basket chairs set out in front of the house, where they would chat or read their books and have tea brought out to them. 'How is your garden coming along?' Emily asked one day. 'Mama tried to grow things year after year. I remember her wailing that the storms would tear the house from the land, which used to terrify me, but it was always the garden which got the worst of it.' She sat back, surveying

Beatrice's efforts, sipping her tea. 'Try the things that grow here anyway, the wild iris, or the primroses, or even gorse and broom. Native things do so much better.'

Cameron had said the same to her when he had come across her planting a climbing rose designed to spread across the trellis-work of the bower. He had taken the spade from her and dug a deep hole, and then returned with horse manure to bed it in, but he had leant on the spade and shaken his head when the job was done. 'It'll be a hardy rose that survives up here, Mrs. Blake.'

'The catalogue said it was particularly strong and resilient—'

'It'll need to be.'

'—with creamy yellow flowers,' she finished, lifting her chin.

'Yellow, eh?' He had smiled back at her.

But perhaps he had been right, she thought, looking at tight buds already blighted and brown. 'No doubt I'll learn the hard way.'

Emily, it seemed, was determined to extract every ounce of pleasure from their visit. No one was to rest while the weather held, and one evening when Beatrice mentioned her thwarted trip to see the seal pups, Emily had sat forward with sudden enthusiasm. 'Then we must all go and see them. Why not tomorrow, Theo?'

'It's a very long walk,' he replied, 'and the tides are all wrong.'

But Emily was not to be put off, ambushing John Forbes outside the stables for his opinion, delighted when he suggested that if Cameron and Donald took them in the boats, there were some good mackerel spots on the way. Emily had clasped her hands together. 'Fishing! That's it—I haven't been fishing since I was fourteen. It will be splendid.'

∾ *Theo* ∾

Theo strolled down to the foreshore to see the party off, half regretting his decision not to join them. But it would have been too much: Emily's incessant chatter and Beatrice's reproachful looks. And Cameron— He watched him now as he helped Beatrice into the larger boat, laughing as he pushed it off the shingle and leapt aboard, a single movement executed with his customary skill and grace. Oblivious, it would seem, to Theo's growing exasperation. Or indifferent, more like.

And this land crusade of his was becoming tiresome. He simply refused to leave the matter alone! Like last week: 'There's enough for three or four workable crofts beyond the lochan, sir. And you don't use that land for anything.'

They had been working together in the study, companionably, until that point. 'Snipe and curlew nest over that way, as well as other species,' Theo said, and continued to paint in the detail of a shelduck's plumage. 'Farming would reduce numbers.'

'*Shooting* reduces numbers.'

He had returned Cameron a dry look, and they had worked on in silence. Then Cameron had tried a different tack. 'You could make it part of the tenancy agreement that crofters must protect the nests and nestlings,' he began. 'You'd still get the rents, they'd get a livelihood, and the birds would thrive. It would be ideal.'

He turned to clean his brush. 'You don't give up, do you?'

'How can I? These people are desperate.'

Theo had sat back and considered him, tapping the end of the paintbrush against his teeth, thinking what a fine-looking young man he was, his mother's grace transformed into a lithe strength, her dark colouring defining regular features. And Màili's eyes... He had bent again to his painting.

'Sir?' Cameron's voice had recalled him to the present. 'All they want is a patch of land to plant—'

'Potatoes?' He had raised his eyebrows in mock interest. 'Or turnips? Keep a cow, perhaps?' Couldn't he even *try* to understand? 'It's not too much to ask.'

'It's too *little*, Cameron. Far too little.' Cameron had continued to scowl at him. 'Stop for a moment and look beyond your own indignation, and you might understand a little better.' He dipped his brush in the rinsing water. 'There's not enough here now to sustain people. I'd be condemning them to poverty.'

'Their families were living well enough until your father cleared them off.'

'Were they?' He had kept a grip on his temper. 'And what about the decades before then, after the kelp price collapsed? You don't think maybe myth has clouded the truth over the years?' Cameron had said nothing, containing a tight-lipped anger. 'Besides, I refuse to live in perpetual guilt for what my father did. It made *sense*, Cameron, even if there were individual cases of hardship.'

'*Hardship!* If having your roof burned from over—'

'Face facts, man.' His patience had snapped, and he had taken up the brush again, adding dark umber tones to the colour of the sea. 'By the time this house was built, a generation had already lived in poverty. Reducing numbers made sense. My father did them a favour.' Cameron began another angry retort, but Theo stuck the brush back in the jar and raised a hand. 'Enough. You do no good with your persistence.' They had faced each other across the desk. 'Vilify me by all means, Cameron, but the tenants on this estate are treated well. Your father sees to that.' The words had choked him, and since that day they had hardly spoken.

He turned back to the group at the water's edge, where the boats had been made ready and Cameron had assumed command. A natural leader, with no outlet for his talents, thwarted by his circumstances. Theo wondered how much Kit's presence must irk him, reminding him of the very different courses their lives had taken since boyhood. And yet Cameron still rejected his offers of advancement! Frustration boiled in him again, and he shut his eyes, powerless to resolve the matter, defeated.

And when he opened them, the boats were pulling away. Perhaps he should have gone with them after all—Beatrice had tried to persuade him, but was that out of courtesy, or pity? Had she really wanted him? The sight of her, happy now, brought a guilty pain.

She looked so lovely! Windswept and carefree as she turned to laugh at Kit's antics, and yet he sensed a change in her. In Edinburgh she had had a serenity, a poise; her cool eyes had offered calm, a balm to his spirits, but those same eyes were restless now, evincing thoughts he could only imagine. Her hair, no longer swept back and elegant, had become bleached by the sun, and twisted tendrils escaped from under a carelessly tied hat. Her skin had a new glow, a luminance that would once have had him reaching for his palette but now, too late, caused only anxiety and regret.

He shifted his attention to the others, remembering their idyllic childhood world which he had glimpsed through his own obsession. They had been inseparable companions then, indifferent to him, a grown man, grim-faced, no doubt, as he wrestled with his demons. He remembered coming back, several years after leaving the island, summoned home by his father's sudden illness. Riding across the strand, he had seen figures down by the foreshore. John Forbes, a young man then, was repairing one of the boats, assisted by two small boys who stopped their play to watch as Theo approached. He'd ridden on, steeling himself for the encounter he'd been dreading.

And the young factor had been faultlessly respectful as Theo dismounted and held out his hand, forcing a tight smile. 'John. Are you well?'

'Very well, sir.' He had gripped Theo's hand briefly. 'Mr. Blake will be glad you've come.' Then they had stood awkwardly, Màili an invisible presence between them, and Theo had looked at the two small boys. She had borne John two sons and a daughter since he left, and the knowledge twisted his guts.

'Fine boys, John.'

'Aye, they are, sir. Though I can't lay claim to both.' He held out his other hand to the smaller of the two boys. 'Greet your brother, Kit, he's come all the way from Glasgow to see your father,' he said, and the child had looked at Theo with a puzzled expression. He had been a baby when Theo had left.

'This one is mine.' John had put an arm around the other boy. 'His brother is inside with his sister, and their mother.'

And next day he had seen her, surrounded by a gaggle of children, the older ones running, criss-crossing the sun-dappled sand, erratic as a flock of dunlin, splashing through shallow pools, and there was Màili herself, leading a smaller child by the hand. And he had watched her approach, leaden with resentment, compelled to watch her, compelled to drink in her appearance as a desperate mariner gulps seawater, knowing it will only intensify the thirst. The years had left her unchanged, her hair caught up in the familiar loose knot in the nape of her neck, and sunlight still caught glints in the brown. Her feet and ankles were bare below her dark skirt, and she had radiated such idyllic contentment that it had been an affront. Their eyes had met and blood had pounded in his temples, and only then had he seen her thickened shape, camouflaged by the shawl which crossed over her stomach.

It had been the last time he had seen her—

~

Laughter from across the water broke through his thoughts, and he stood a moment, looking out across the same stretch of sand where he saw her shade still, then he turned to watch the two boats pulling away from him, and Beatrice waved, as if in farewell.

Chapter 23

≈ 1910, Beatrice ≈

Beatrice sat on the thwart and lifted her arms to pin back her cascading hair, watching Theo from under her elbow, and considered whether to ask Cameron to turn back and insist that he come. She really ought to. He looked such a lonely figure standing there on the shore, but he had resisted all her attempts at persuasion and now she was reluctant. Somehow he would cause a restraint on the party.

She waved, but perhaps he didn't see.

When she looked back again, he was walking towards the house, and his departure seemed to trigger a release. Oars were shipped in both boats and sails raised. Beatrice watched as Cameron set about tightening and loosening the rigging, moving with agility, whistling tunelessly, then laughing over his shoulder, pouring scorn on Kit's attempts to bring the other boat up to wind. Donald called something back in their own tongue and Cameron laughed again. He was dressed like any of the island men, wearing his dark woollens and loose trousers with the same careless disregard as he had worn Theo's cast-off suit, at ease with himself. He offered Rupert the helm, and Beatrice trailed her hand over the side, watching Theo disappear into the house. Cameron, now satisfied with the sail, sat on the gunwale opposite her while Emily moved to the bow and sat like a figurehead, shaking her hair loose and lifting her face to the sun.

And Beatrice forgot about Theo.

Being at sea in a small boat was a new experience, and at first she found the broken motion unsettling. She gripped the side of the boat to steady herself and watched tresses of dark weed flowing out from submerged reefs, wafted by the current, disappearing as the water deepened and grew darker.

'Come on, my love. Take the helm,' Rupert called to Emily. 'Show your brother how it's done.'

'But I can't.' She turned to him, smiling her elfin smile.

'Give it a shot. You won't do worse.'

Cameron moved forward and Emily made her way to the stern where, with Rupert's guiding hand on hers, she managed to hold a steady course. They left the shelter of the headland, where the pull of tide and current competed with the wind, and then a rogue wave lifted the bow and Emily gave a little shriek. 'Take it, Cameron! Before I sink us all.'

He took the tiller with a laugh, glanced astern, and then changed course. 'We'll get just beyond that far point and then drift back with the tide. Try our luck.' The wind tightened the sails as the boat settled onto the new course, water bubbling under the bow, but it was smoother now, and Beatrice loosened her grip on the side.

'What about Beatrice, Cameron?' Emily called over her shoulder. 'She ought to have a chance to steer. Bea, you really *must*.'

'Will you try your hand, madam?' There was a glint of challenge in his eyes, so she laughed and edged back to sit beside him in the stern. He clasped his hand over hers as Rupert had done with Emily, demonstrating the boat's responses, then sat back to watch her.

He had set her a course on a silver path laid down by the sun, heading for islands on the far horizon, but the trick that sunlight plays over water seemed to bring the islands close, almost reachable. She fixed her eyes on them, still feeling the imprint of his dry palm on the back of her hand, her senses strangely alive as the water creamed beneath the hull, slapping against the bow as it rode the larger waves. She was filled with a heady joy and felt herself relax, becoming one with the vessel, in tune with its motion and rhythm, acutely conscious of Cameron close by, his eye flicking between the sails, the horizon, and the helm.

Rupert had moved forward with Emily, and they were engrossed with each other in the bow, pointing out seabirds which flew splay-legged low across the waves, wings beating fast. A fulmar accompanied the boat, riding the wind, dipping its straight wing tips down to the waves before wheeling and rising high above the mast, revelling in the mastery of its skill. Beatrice's eyes followed it, forgetful of her course, until she felt Cameron's hand on hers as he reached over to correct the helm. 'You're straying, madam.' He smiled, and the boat's progress stalled a moment in a trough between two waves. And, for a moment, her eyes held his.

Cameron was the first to look away. 'We'll drop sail now and get the rods out, I think,' he said. 'Can you keep her on course?'

Beatrice nodded quickly, and Cameron moved forward, calling out to the other boat. Rupert helped him bring down the sail and yard, glancing shrewdly at Beatrice as he took the helm. 'And for bait, Cameron?' he asked.

Cameron lifted the lid from a small creel of fish heads and began to prepare the rods while Beatrice moved quickly forward to be beside Emily, making inconsequential remarks, and then took a rod that Rupert passed to her.

The boat rocked gently on the swell, and almost immediately she felt a tug at the end of her line, but then nothing. Emily's rod bent next, and Cameron came across to assist, laughing at her glee as an iridescent fish was pulled from the water, scattering silver droplets. He deftly removed the hook and replaced the bait. 'You've got one hooked too, Mrs. Blake,' he said, and nodded at her rod.

After an hour of drifting, several mackerel, lings, and a small cod lay gasping in the basket at their feet, and by then they were only a short distance to the seal island. The men rowed the last few yards and pulled the boats up onto the sand. Rupert lifted the women clear of the shallow waves while Donald placed the fish in a shadowed rock pool, where one or two of them revived and began splashing, desperate to escape.

Emily stood looking down at them. 'Poor things. Wouldn't it be kinder to let them go?'

'Rubbish. That's lunch.' Kit started up the beach. 'Where are these seals, Donald?'

They followed Donald up over the rocks, scrambling to the top from where they could see the seals were hauled out, basking in the sun, keening and moaning softly while others played in the waves nearby, watching with whiskered curiosity as the visitors settled themselves on the rounded summit.

'Do you remember the stories your mother used to tell us, Donald?' said Emily. 'How seals would come ashore at midsummer and take human form.'

'Oh, she was full of such stories, that's a fact.'

'How did it go? They'd shed their skins and dance on the beaches—'

'And the fishermen would steal the skins to stop them returning.'

'That's it. And the seal women would search until they found them again, then take their human children back to the sea, leaving the fishermen tormented by their siren songs.' She gave a long theatrical sigh.

'My mother's family are all a bit fey,' Cameron remarked to Rupert.

'She was *lovely*.'

'Aye, and she swore the stories were true. Her cousin was born with webbed fingers, which she said proved the point.'

Emily pouted. 'She and I always felt sorry for the poor fishermen.'

'Speaking for myself,' said Kit, passing the field glasses to Beatrice and rolling onto his back, 'I can't see the allure.'

'Philistine,' said his sister. 'Seal women are lithe and sensuous, very beautiful and wild. They've a special name… ?' She turned to Cameron in enquiry.

'Selkies,' he supplied.

'That's it. Selkies. Seal women.'

'And men. Selkies are male too. And as it's midsummer tonight, Major,' he added, 'you'd better lock up your woman in case a lusty male down there has taken a fancy to her.'

'Ha! Poor devil. He'll get more than he bargained for.'

Emily laughed and they stayed a little longer, until the seals slipped from the rocks, their heads bobbing in the sea, and hunger drove the party back to the beach. 'Why did we ever leave these islands, Kit?' She sighed as Rupert assisted her over the rocks.

'No shops, no theatre, no concert halls, no dances, no parties, no dressmakers, no milliners…' Rupert murmured as he waited for Beatrice and landed her safely beside Emily.

Emily pulled a face. 'That'll all keep for the winter, but we *must* spend the summers up here. Bea will be pleased of the company, won't you? Then our children and theirs can run wild like children *should*, like we did, and hear the old stories.' She threw herself down on the sand, kicked off her shoes, and tossed her hat to one side. 'Cameron and Donald can teach them to swim and to fish and to sail just like John Forbes did with us, and they'll grow up nut brown and healthy out of the city smoke.' Rupert stretched out his long legs on the sand and slipped an arm behind her.

'Of course, my love.'

Donald had begun collecting driftwood and dry seaweed while Cameron crouched beside the rocks, cleaning the fish and tossing the entrails to a group of waiting gulls who contested them noisily a few yards away. 'That'll have to be Donald's job,' he said.

Emily sat forward, clasping her knees. 'Gosh, yes. I keep forgetting. The island won't seem the same without you.' And Beatrice found the words chimed painfully with her own thoughts as she watched his long fingers filleting the fish; the island without Cameron was suddenly unimaginable.

'We'll all wish we lived up here in a year or two.' Rupert joined Donald at the high-tide line, calling over his shoulder, 'Either the

Kaiser will take us into war or the discontented masses will bring the country to its knees.'

'No politics today, Rupert,' Emily commanded as he dragged a bleached plank towards them. Cameron glanced up and caught Beatrice watching him. She looked quickly away and began smoothing the sand beside her.

'You soldiers are always spoiling for a fight.' Kit had stretched out on his back and was making no effort to do anything useful. 'And it's too hot for the proletariat to turn savage.' Donald dumped an armful of driftwood beside him and began gathering stones to make a fireplace. Cameron raised his head as if to respond, then caught his brother's expression and shrugged, returning to his task.

Rupert's sharp eyes missed little. 'What about you, Cameron? What do you think?'

'Don't ask him, sir, for pity's sake.'

Beatrice silently echoed Donald's plea. Politics, where Cameron was concerned, were best avoided. He spoke freely to her now and was passionate about the running sore of land hunger, nursing a deep resentment for injustices past and present. But he merely grinned at his brother and continued to cut open the fish, pulling out the guts and scraping them clean.

'I have an agreement with my family, sir, not to offend guests with my opinions.'

'*Guests?*' retorted Kit.

'Hardly guests, but nonetheless, *no* politics, Rupert.' Emily frowned at her fiancé, who returned her a bland smile.

'But I'm interested to hear these opinions, my love.'

Cameron kept his attention on the fish. After a moment he said, 'Let's just say that if our titled politicians lived as dock -hands for a month, they'd soon be joining the reformers they're so afraid of.'

Rupert pulled out a packet of cigarettes and patted his pocket for matches. 'Joining the rabble-rousers, eh?' He struck a match and held it. 'Who—having forced the issue in '89—are now back for more. Inevitably.' The wind blew out the flame and he took a second match.

'*Perhaps* they need more, sir. Perhaps they haven't enough.' Cameron reached for another mackerel, and Beatrice prayed that they would leave it there.

But Rupert had cupped his hand to shield a new flame. 'Socialist, are you, Cameron?' he asked, narrowing his eyes to draw on the cigarette, proffering the packet, which Cameron ignored. 'And I had you down as a man of sense.' Beatrice saw Cameron's face darken and felt a flutter of alarm. 'If there *is* a general strike, it'll be the poor who go hungry, you know. What would you say to the strike leaders then?' He blew smoke into the air above them.

'I'd say more strength to their arm. *Sir.*' His reply was calmly spoken, but the appellation was added with deliberate insolence and their eyes met, stags locking antlers, testing the other's intent.

'*Stad an sin,*' hissed Donald.

'Stop picking a fight, Rupert.' Emily's voice was sharp with the sudden tension, and Kit sat up, much entertained. He shook a cigarette from Rupert's discarded packet, stuck it in the corner of his mouth, and looked about for a light.

'Does old Theo *know* he's harbouring a dangerous radical, Bea?' Cameron took a glowing stick from the fire and held it out for Kit to light his cigarette, and as his dark head bent close to Kit's fair one, Beatrice glimpsed the boyhood companions they had been before their different worlds divided them. 'Hardly dangerous, madam,' Cameron said, addressing her directly, his eyes alive and unsettling. Then he began placing pieces of fish on the hot stones, where they sizzled as the heat brought the oil to the surface, and he flashed a look towards Rupert. 'I'm better suited to the colonies, you see.'

Rupert grunted agreement and smoked on, watching him.

'But'—Cameron scanned their faces with some amusement— 'I do know what to do with a piece of mackerel. Fetch the basket from the boat, will you, Donald? I raided Mrs. Henderson's pantry this morning.' He glanced towards Beatrice with an ironic expression which seemed to ask for recognition of his restraint, and she dropped her eyes to hide a smile.

The cries of circling gulls added to the din as bottles of wine and beer were unpacked from the basket and Cameron was congratulated on his raid. And tensions evaporated amidst laughter as fingers and razor shells lifted flaky pieces of fish from the greasy stones, and Emily wiped her chin with the back of her hand, declaring that she had never tasted finer food.

'What will you have, Miss Emily?' asked Donald, proffering two bottles.

'For goodness' sake, stop *Miss*-ing me, Donald. Surely we can be Emily and Kit as we used to be—and Rupert too, for that matter, if military regulations allow,' she mocked with a gruff voice. 'At least for today.' And she held out a glass for wine.

'So what is it to be, Rupert?' Cameron asked cheerfully, and the major returned a dry smile.

'Beer. But damn it, man.' He stubbed his cigarette out and flicked the butt into the fire. 'Have you actually *thought* what a major strike would mean? It'll be working families who'll suffer, you know, the very people your self-serving radicals claim to champion.'

'Rupert, for goodness' sake!' Emily pushed at him, but he imprisoned her hands, ignoring her protest. ·

'And how will they be heard otherwise?' Cameron took a swig of beer, his eyes grown hard again.

'You ask that after all the reforms this accursed government has made? And the changes that are being—'

'Being what? Considered? Debated? *Promised?*' Cameron sat up and thrust a stick into the fire, sending up a small whirlwind of sparks. Beatrice saw the muscles in his face tighten and grew anxious again. 'A man's life can pass before such promises are honoured, while his family live like animals. It's damnable. Shameful.' The flames leapt high as the breeze swung round. 'And how will it ever change?'

'Cameron—'

He swept on, ignoring her. 'The men who run this country will go to any lengths to shore up the institutions which give them power. You know that, and yet you talk of *self-interest*! Good God! Tell me, *Rupert*, what options have working people got, other than bringing down those institutions?'

'Cameron, for goodness' sake!' Donald got to his feet.

Rupert released Emily's hands to reach up and pull him down again. 'Don't worry, Donald. Your brother has a right to speak his mind, just as I have to disagree.' He glanced towards Beatrice with raised eyebrows and took a slow drink. 'But such a radical, up here of all places,' he drawled, watching Cameron narrowly. 'And so very well-informed.'

Cameron went to fetch more fuel, and Beatrice watched him struggling for self-control as he threw it on the fire, the dried wood crackling in the heat. 'You forget. I've been in Canada, which is full of exiled Scots with tales of injustice, and I saw for myself how people live in Glasgow. Island families, some of them.' He looked across at Beatrice, and her eyes fell, remembering what he had told her of the overcrowded tenement where Duncan MacPhail's wife had fallen ill.

Donald rose abruptly. 'I'm off for a swim. Cameron, *cùm do bheul dùinte. Lean thus' ort a' ròstadh èisg.*' He gave his brother a despairing look over his shoulder as he set off up the beach.

Cameron watched him go, then looked back at the fire. 'He says I should shut up and stick to frying fish.'

'What about old Theo, Bea?' said Kit, pulling on his cigarette and grinning at Cameron, seemingly oblivious to the words' underlying bitterness. 'Does he *really* not know there's an enemy in the camp?'

'Not an enemy, Kit, never that.' There was a weariness to Cameron's tone as he took another drink from the bottle, and then his expression changed. 'Besides, he has another radical much closer to him than me'—he leant back on his elbow, the tension leaving him—'and one who is much more effective, working hard to improve the lives of her tenants…'

Beatrice flushed. 'It's little enough that I do.'

'… and I have reason to believe she's a suffragist too.' His expression was unfathomable.

'Oh, splendid, Beatrice!' Emily clapped her hands and Rupert groaned. 'When you come to Edinburgh, we'll go and join the marches. What fun!'

'Wife-beating remains fashionable in military circles, my love,' her future husband remarked, lowering his head to light another cigarette, then winding an arm about her as she leant back against him, smiling and unrepentant.

'Be warned. The Kaiser will give you less trouble than Emily, old man.' Kit got to his feet, brushing the sand from his clothes. 'But you've only yourself to blame, of course, encouraging her wanton ways.' He grinned at his sister's outraged face. 'I'm off to join Donald,' he announced and sauntered up the beach, hands thrust into his pockets, whistling, while Rupert chuckled softly and Emily went pink with indignation.

'He's drunk too much, as usual,' she said, appealing to Beatrice, who simply smiled in return, remembering the stealthy opening and closing of doors she had heard in the night, and soft footfalls across the landing.

'The perfect chaperone, is young Kit.' Rupert stood up, stretched, and then pulled Emily to her feet. 'Come on, up with you. Do you mind if we leave you awhile, Beatrice, to soothe the outraged feelings?' He nodded to Cameron, and they set off up the beach, leaving Cameron and Beatrice alone.

The fire crackled, a spark shot out, and there was silence between them. Beatrice dug her toes into the sand, feeling exposed without the others, unsettled as when the boat had stalled between two waves, and occupied herself by making a circle of shells. A thin blue smoke rose from the embers and the shoreline shimmered.

The silence stretched out, and she covertly studied Cameron's profile. He lay on his side, his head propped with his elbow, staring into the fire, tossing pebbles towards it and sending up little puffs of ash. His face was grave, pensive, as if still considering the debate. Small waves, ripples from turbulence far out at sea, broke on the shingle, and he lifted his head to watch them, a lock of dark hair falling over his brow. How little she really knew of what went on in his head. And yet— He turned to look at her, and she felt the need to break the silence.

'They're well suited, I believe.'

'They are.'

'Emily will shake him up.'

'She'll do him good.'

'And he'll keep her enthusiasms in check.' She tucked a strand of hair behind her ear and looked out to sea.

'He'll try, anyway.' A pebble hit the fire. He sat up, cross-legged, and another silence fell.

'You were very outspoken,' said Beatrice after a moment.

'Did I cause offence?'

'You outraged the major.'

Another pebble bounced off a smouldering plank. 'I don't mind that, but I wouldn't want to offend you again. I get carried away.'

'I know.' She looked at him, and after a moment he smiled, his old uncomplicated smile, and she began to feel comfortable again. 'Besides, how could I take offence, when there's truth in what you say?'

He stared into the fire. 'As Beatrice, here and now, you can say that. Tonight, back at the house, Mrs. Blake has a different role to play.'

Her hand paused over her neat pattern of shells. A role? Cameron was too perceptive. Did he see that that was what it had become? Mistress of Muirlan House, contented wife. It was a role she played unsteadily in the face of Theo's indifference. But indifference borne of what? She avoided Cameron's eyes, swallowing hard, and swept her hand across her circle of shells, then began creating other, random patterns in the sand, her cheek resting on her knees. After a moment she leant back, supporting herself on straightened arms, feeling a languor creeping over her, and looked down the beach. 'Perhaps,' she said, 'I like being Beatrice better.'

He said nothing, and then: 'Mrs. Blake is easy to deal with. But Beatrice? I think she'd be a different matter.' To *deal* with? What did he mean by that? But his head was turned away from her, and she was still considering her response when Rupert and Emily reappeared over the rocks.

Emily flung herself down next to Beatrice, pressing her shoulder companionably against her. 'If it wasn't so dreadfully cold I'd join Kit and Donald. I'd like to swim straight out into the sun as far as I could see. There's something about the air up here, don't you think? Gives you new energy and... fizz.' Beatrice laughed, relieved that they had returned.

'Try it in November.' Cameron sat up and began gathering further pebbles towards him, making a cache of them.

'Oh, I know. I haven't forgotten. You will mock'—she frowned severely at Rupert—'but there *is* something magical up here. Don't you think, Beatrice?'

Beatrice looked out over the sparkling water to where sky fused with ocean. 'It's the big skies and wide horizons.'

'And the sea—' Emily searched for her wine glass and found it empty. Rupert leant across her to refill it.

Cameron sat cross-legged, listening to them, unsmiling, still tossing his pebbles.

'Although it can feel quite intimidating,' continued Beatrice, trying to ignore him. 'Like this morning in the boat, we were just a tiny speck at the mercy of the elements.' She wrapped her arms around her bent knees, pinning her light cotton skirt in place, and rocked gently, looking out at a seal playing in the waves just offshore. 'But there's a sort of restlessness everywhere, and always the wind, shaking the grasses, birds endlessly circling. It's never still! It gets inside you.' She felt Cameron's eyes on her as he paused in his pebble throwing.

Rupert flicked a glance between them.

'It's like being a castaway in one of Stevenson's novels,' said Emily, and Cameron snorted, resuming his game. 'It's true, Cameron! Life is so much simpler here, there are no codes or conventions to offend. We're governed only by the tides and the sun.' She shook out her hair in a gesture of abandon. 'And if we want food, we just catch it and cook it on a driftwood fire, like Ben Gunn.'

Rupert laughed. 'Washed down with a jolly fine hock that floated in on the tide.'

'I knew you'd mock, but *you* understand, don't you, Beatrice?' Beatrice smiled back, loving Emily for her folly. 'Yes. I think I do.' But was it that which had brought Theo back here? *No codes or conventions to offend.* She watched the lacy edges of the waves as they crept up the beach, getting ever closer to the barrier of dead seaweed and broken shells which measured the high-water mark. The seal had vanished.

Emily was continuing with enthusiasm. 'All that time we spend worrying about politics, wars, gossip, scandal, clothes, hats—'

Rupert strolled down to the rock pool where the beer and wine were keeping cool. 'All that time.'

She called after him. 'I really would like to spend the summers up here, Rupert. I think it would be very... very revitalising.' They heard him laugh as he bent to the pool, and then he returned, tossing a bottle of beer to Cameron and filling the glasses with wine.

He handed one to Beatrice. 'And the reality, Beatrice? Do you find it revitalising?' He gave a slanting look at Cameron, who returned it levelly.

Beatrice sipped slowly. 'Revitalising... is that the word?' For Theo, a place to shed pretence, perhaps. But for herself? Liberating, yes, but now, without structure, a bewildering vortex, spinning her certainties into disarray. She saw that Rupert was watching her, awaiting her answer. 'Perhaps so. But whatever else, for today at least, Emily's right—rules and conventions are irrelevant.' She took another sip and placed her glass carefully on a flat rock beside her. 'Best ignored.'

'There, you see, Rupert. What do you say now, Cameron?'

Cameron had stretched out on his back, his hands locked behind his head, and was staring up at the clouds. He had rolled up his sleeves and trouser legs, exposing lean forearms and calves covered with dark hair. 'Absolute rubbish. Both of you. Heads in the clouds—or in the sand. I'm not sure which.' He rolled over suddenly and jabbed a finger at Emily. 'No rules, eh, Miss Emily Blake? Ask the islanders about that, if you will, and you'll hear another story. Your sort just see estates like this as playgrounds for sport and idling, where you can behave as you like, ignoring how others live to support you.'

Beatrice looked back at him in dismay. *Your sort.* A personal swipe. And there was real anger behind the words. She sensed Rupert's eyes on her again, incredulous this time. But how *could* she challenge Cameron? A reprimand might well be in order, but it was unthinkable; she willed him desperately to go no further.

Emily rallied. 'Honestly, Cameron, you're as bad as Rupert. Spoiling—'

'Spoiling the fun, am I?' He lay back on the sand again, his eyes following the glide of a fulmar. 'This game of equality you wanted to play? Play-acting costs nothing, I suppose, but one day it'll stop being a game. Not today, though, not yet.' He had closed his eyes again. 'Today's a midsummer mirage which will vanish at nightfall, won't it, Mrs. Blake.' He rolled his head to look at Beatrice.

'Good God, the man's an anarchist,' Rupert drawled, and Cameron gave a tight laugh, his hand patting the sand beside him until he found his beer bottle, and then drained it.

Emily frowned. 'You've turned very savage, Cameron.' Then her expression became thoughtful. 'Though I do understand *something* of what you say.' She began gathering Beatrice's discarded shells, rearranging them in patterns. 'Seeing Muirlan

House again after all these years, it struck me as rather out of place, as if it got blown here by mistake from some leafy estate in the Borders. You know, elegant shooting parties, kedgeree, and tea on the lawn.' She put her head to one side, addressing Rupert. 'Am I making sense?'

'Not a lot,' he admitted, 'but you've finished off the wine.'

Cameron sat up abruptly and looked down the beach at the tide. 'And we should pack up.'

'Come on, then, Girl Friday, let's go and find the swimmers.' Rupert dusted the sand off himself and set off with Emily along the beach. Cameron began collecting the scattered remains of the picnic while Beatrice sat with her chin resting on her drawn-up knees, staring out to sea. *Blown here by mistake.* It was suddenly hard to breathe. Was that what had happened to her? And was the mistake hers or Theo's? The day had been spoiled, and she felt an ache deep inside as she watched the seal dive, imagining its sleek body twisting below the surface in unfettered freedom, and tears scalded just behind her eyes.

'That time I *did* offend.' Cameron was watching her face as he packed the basket with empty bottles.

'Perhaps you intended to.' She looked away, blaming him for the spoilation.

'No.' He closed the lid. 'My apologies, Mrs. Blake.'

'Mrs. Blake? Not Beatrice?'

He kicked at the fire, scattering the charred wood, and the white ash glowed briefly red. 'Mrs. Blake,' he said firmly. 'Beatrice is too… too dangerous.'

She turned back, shading her eyes with a hand. '*Dangerous?*'

He continued to kick sand over the smouldering embers, saying nothing. Then: 'Beatrice claimed that rules were irrelevant. Just imagine where that sort of thinking would lead.' He stooped to pick up her forgotten glass, glancing up at her as he did. 'You're the anarchist, madam, not me.'

The sea had crept higher, and in just a little while the tide would turn, carrying this extraordinary day with it. She raised her hands to twist her hair back into some sort of order. 'You should not have spoken as you did in front of the major,' she said sharply, pulling herself together. 'He wondered why I let you continue in that manner.' Cameron raised an eyebrow. 'You took advantage of an old friendship with Kit and Emily, and you wouldn't have dared to say those things if Mr. Blake had been here.'

'He knows my views.'

Of course he did, only too well. 'But he wouldn't expect you to express them quite so freely in front of his guests.' She heard her own primness with disgust, and frowned at him. 'And you didn't attempt for a moment to understand what *I* was trying to say. Just dismissed it, as you did us all, with contempt. *Your sort.* Spoiled. Self-indulgent.' She stared out to sea, to where the seal now hung in the water, looking back at her. 'But by coming here I was able to leave the stifling life I had in Edinburgh, to step outside it, like shedding an old skin which had grown too tight. While you'—she looked across at him, cool yet angry—'*you* see things only in terms of class, or politics, and then pour your scorn over us.' Dried sea-wrack at the edge of the fire crackled as a charred plank split and fell in two, filling the silence.

'I'm rebuked, madam.'

'And you call me *madam* in that sneering manner as you did once before.'

'So what should I call you?' He looked back at her, half -mocking, half-serious.

Something twisted inside her at his expression, and she felt suddenly reckless. 'Beatrice. You allowed that the fantasy could last until nightfall.' She looked up at him, then quickly dropped her chin at his expression and began tracing the faded pattern of daisies on the knee of her skirt. *Dangerous.*

Donald and Kit appeared over the rocks, running to warm up, with Rupert and Emily not far behind, and Cameron called them over to help him with the boats. 'Sharpish, if you will. The tide's already turned.' He looked back at her once more and seemed about to speak, but kicked the fire again instead and strode down towards the boats.

And as he reached the edge of the beach, the seal reared back in the water, startled, and slid silently beneath the waves.

Chapter 24

∼ 1910, Beatrice ∼

Two days later, Beatrice came downstairs for breakfast to hear a shout of laughter from Rupert in the dining room. 'Straight over the side,' Kit was saying as she crossed the hall. 'Head-first into six foot of icy black water. Shark bait.' She hated to think of them leaving, but in just two days they would be gone. 'Then they half killed me getting me back on board. I'll show you the bruises if you like.' The house would feel so empty, filled only by Theo's silences, left prey to a creeping belief that something was fundamentally wrong.

'Utter madness,' Rupert was remarking as she entered the dining room, 'and nothing to show for it.'

'Except pneumonia and chilblains.' Emily smiled as Beatrice pulled out a chair beside her. 'Have you heard about this silly caper, Bea? *Night* fishing with Donald and Cameron.' Beatrice shook her head and half listened as Kit repeated his story. And prey now to another sort of danger; these past few nights she had slept badly.

'I'd have thought Cameron Forbes had more sense,' said Rupert, pushing the marmalade towards Beatrice.

'Cameron?' Kit scoffed. 'Reckless to a fault.'

Was he? Beatrice had not seen him since the picnic. Theo had not recalled him to the study, so he had not come to the house, but she found she was looking out for him. Yet surely the danger he spoke of was just a frisson, a temptation to be resisted, spawned by a sunlit day, a fine wine, and a shimmering heat haze rising from the sand—and a look that had been held between them.

'Got to make the most of the last few days,' said Kit, attacking a pair of kippers with gusto. Various schemes were suggested until Emily proposed that they invite the whole Forbes family for a meal before their visit came to an end, and she shot off to put the plan to Theo before Beatrice could express her half-formed reservations. She returned triumphant.

'He said no at first but finally agreed as long as it was a midday meal. So I'll fix it with Mrs. Henderson for Sunday, the day before we go? That's alright, isn't it, Bea?'

Despite Theo's instructions that the meal be informal, Emily had taken matters into her own hands and insisted that the table be set as if for a party. 'It's hideous, I know, but we always used it,' she said, tweaking the yellow iris she had placed in an old-fashioned silver epergne. 'Goodness only knows when we will all be together again, so the occasion must be marked.'

Beatrice wondered anxiously what Rupert had told Theo of the day on the seal island as she checked the table settings. Cameron had overstepped the mark with careless bravado, and if Theo learned even half of it— She paused and straightened a serviette, acknowledging that another boundary had been approached that day, approached but retreated from, not crossed.

Theo ushered the guests into the dining room, and Cameron greeted her quietly before turning to study the elaborate arrangements. She saw him exchange a grimace with Kit and regretted again that Theo had given in to Emily's entreaties. The sentiment was compounded as she watched Theo's eyes following Cameron as he took his seat at the far side of the table; she felt her face flush and a prickle of heat in her armpits, and sent one of the girls to open a window.

The younger Blakes' store of reminiscences, however, provided easy conversation. 'Your thrashings were always worse than my father's,' Kit remarked, glancing affectionately at the benign face of the factor. 'And I'd have put up with a daily dose if it meant I could have stayed here. I loathed Edinburgh, school was purgatory, and I spent hours planning how I would run off and come back.' He grinned at Ephie. 'It was the lure of your mother's kitchen, you know. Food and warmth, the essentials of life. And she always made us welcome.'

At the end of the table, Theo signalled for more wine, cutting across Emily's next remark. He had been silent during these reminiscences but now turned to Rupert. 'I read the army could be put on standby. Will that affect your plans, Major?'

'I very much hope not.'

'Oh, Rupert, *no*! Not a war. Not now!'

'If there's a *strike*, my love. The troops will have to make sure the country can keep functioning.'

'If the situation worsens, Asquith will have no choice.'

'I'd far rather confront the Hun.'

'The folly of it all is quite breathtaking, given the situation.' Theo cut vigorously at his meat, glancing briefly down the table at Cameron, and Beatrice sensed a deliberate intention to provoke. She saw Kit raise his eyebrows challengingly at Cameron, who ignored the invitation and continued chewing.

'We can only hope that things settle.' Rupert reached for the water jug. 'Theo, I've been meaning to ask, do you intend to exhibit next year, in Glasgow?' He leant over to replenish Beatrice's glass before filling his own, and smiled across at her, and she knew then that Cameron's indiscretions had not been discussed.

'Exhibit what?' Theo scowled, studying his plate. 'I've done nothing new. And from what I hear, Fry's exhibition at the Grafton is setting London on its heels. It won't be long before I'm a quaint footnote to posterity.' He took up his knife and fork again. 'Not before time, I daresay.'

'No!' said Emily. 'Your paintings are as popular as ever, and I read that the prices are rising steadily.'

Theo sat back, wiping his lips with his napkin, and gave her a sardonic look. 'Financially sound, am I? Ever your father's daughter, my dear.' He overrode Emily's indignant protest. 'If I'm becoming a good investment, you'd better have that one in the hall you go on about, call it part of your wedding present.' *Torrann Bay*, thought Beatrice, suppressing a pang, but she smiled at Emily's obvious delight.

'You *know* I didn't mean it like that,' she said, after Theo had held up his hand to stem her thanks. 'And you should start painting landscapes again, Theo, now you're back here. No one else comes close. When the bird book's finished, you really should. Don't you think so, Beatrice?'

'Of course.' Beatrice looked across at Theo, who grunted dismissively.

Kit speared another roast potato and rolled it in gravy. 'But surely your days *are* numbered, Theo, like all your cronies. Isn't that why painters have gone all strange and avant-garde? They just can't compete. Who'll buy landscape paintings if you can have photographs at a fraction of the cost?'

Theo gave him a sour look. 'And there speaks a *mother's* son.'

Kit and Emily exchanged amused glances, but Kit was not to be silenced. 'No, quite seriously. Colour photography will soon do a better job at the close of a shutter. And anyone can do it.'

'Dear God.' Theo rolled his eyes and proceeded to refute Kit's challenge. Beatrice, anxious that their guests were being ignored, urged them to second helpings while Rupert, taking her cue, began discussing likely stock prices at the forthcoming cattle fair, consulting Donald's views in a frank man-to-man tone. She herself chatted to Ephie Forbes, who had sat quietly in her own calm little world, unmoved by the shifting tensions around her. Seeing her sitting beside Cameron, Beatrice was aware of their physical similarities, both darker and more gracile than their brother and father, favouring their mother, Mrs. Henderson had told her.

At the other end of the table, Emily was still defending Theo against her brother's mischief. 'But a photograph couldn't capture Torrann Bay as Theo's painting does—'

'It's only a matter of being lucky with timing and light. Catching a wave or two.'

'Idiot. There's no movement or depth or texture to a photograph. It could never catch the mood, the subtleties, the play of light on the water… There'd be nothing of the passion of Theo's—'

'So eloquent in my defence, Emily! I must make you gifts more often,' Theo remarked, signalling for another slice of roast duck. 'But some painters do use photographs instead of a sketchbook these days, if only to help them with the tonal quality of—'

'Worse and worse, brother!' Kit was enjoying himself. 'Are you saying that painters now just *copy* photographs?'

'Certainly not.'

'And why would they bother? Photographs are so much more realistic.'

'Perhaps that's the reason.' Cameron suddenly joined the discussion, and his father looked up, breaking off from his description of swimming cattle across from off-shore summer pasture to listen.

'Meaning what?' asked Theo in the ensuing silence.

'In a painting, the artist can select from a scene to suit his ideas, choosing what mood to convey, while a photograph must show what's really there. Unless the photographer has tidied it up first, of course.'

'And that's what you imagine painters do, is it? Tidy things up?' Theo asked, and Beatrice grew tense again.

'No, but in a painting there's scope to interpret. A photograph of the kelp harvest, for example, would show hard-pressed people wrestling with the filthy wet tangle, while an artist could romanticise the scene, depicting the nobility of labour, the honest peasantry, and so forth. Realism doesn't mean *reality*.'

Theo contemplated him dryly. 'How slow of me, Cameron. For a moment I thought you were talking about art.'

'I was.' John Forbes cleared his throat and Cameron frowned. 'And I simply make the point that photography is perhaps more… more truthful.'

Mrs. Henderson put her head around the door to ask if more

potatoes would be required. 'No, we do very well, thank you.' Theo waved a hand in dismissal, and Rupert stepped suavely into the brittle silence.

'I suppose photographing birds must be difficult, though, getting the blighters to stay still.'

'Quite. And photographs don't always capture the texture and colour of plumage, which is why I still need the models in front of me, despite Cameron's misgivings and the outright disapproval of my wife.' He raised his glass towards Beatrice, and she gave a slight smile.

'But painting stuffed dummies hardly counts as painting from *life*, Theo.' Kit was unstoppable. 'They're corpses.'

'Well, it's the best I can manage.' The edge to Theo's tone gave warning that his brother's goading had gone too far, and Beatrice seized the moment to signal for the plates to be removed. When the dessert and fruit had been brought through, she released the serving girls from their duties and bid them close the door, glancing uneasily at the French ormolu clock on the mantelpiece, calculating when she might rise.

Rupert came to her rescue again. 'I was leafing through one of your journals, Theo. *The Ibis*?' Theo nodded briefly. 'There was an article about new work on bird migrations and the distances some species travel. Fascinating stuff.' And he described what he had read about ringing migrating birds to learn about their routes.

'They're doing the same now on Fair Isle,' added Theo, 'where they get a lot of migrants, as well as unusual wanderers blown off course.'

'Trophy hunters flock there for the same reason, to add to their private collections,' Cameron remarked, and Beatrice's hope for peace evaporated as Theo turned his attention back to him, eyeing him sourly. They were like two terriers growling at each other, offering provocation but no direct attack, and she wondered again if they would make it through the meal without a row.

'Private collections provide the backbone of current research.'

'But deliberately going there to catch rare species is surely not acceptable, Theo,' Emily protested, and Beatrice signalled to Kit, hoping to occupy him filling empty glasses.

'There'll always be a place for scientific collecting, and besides, the word "rare" can be misleading.' Theo gestured above the fireplace. 'Take that diver, for example, ten a penny in Iceland or Canada, but unusual here, so it hardly threatens the species to take the odd wanderer for study. You saw a great many in Canada, I believe, Cameron.'

'They're common in the northern lakes but—'

'Thank you. You make my point for me,' said Theo smoothly before turning back to Rupert. 'It's my great hope that one day they'll stay here and breed.'

'But there's an irony there, don't you think, sir?' Cameron remarked, twisting the stem of his glass. 'While Canadian *birds* are welcome to settle here and breed'—too late, Beatrice saw where he was heading—'you give the islanders and their families little option but to do the opposite.'

The meal had finished abruptly. Beatrice learned later from Emily via Ephie that the factor had been furious, and that a tightlipped apology had been offered and accepted—with ill grace on both sides—but she doubted that would be the end of it.

Next day the same party assembled uneasily at the front door to set the visitors on their journey. Donald and Cameron loaded the cart with trunks while Theo took photographs, thrusting the camera at Cameron and instructing him to take one of the family group, and then it was time to go.

'The place won't seem the same without you, Cameron,' she heard Kit say. 'We'll hear of your doings, I expect, but I'll always think of you here.'

'Safe journey, Kit.' Cameron gripped his hand, and held on to it a moment.

As Kit turned to say farewell to the factor, she saw Rupert hold out a hand to Cameron, first checking that Theo's attention was elsewhere. 'Good luck, Cameron. I detest your politics, but I daresay you'll thrive in Canada where there's more elbow space. But allow me to recommend that you learn restraint, my friend, or you'll land yourself in trouble.' He raised a quizzical eyebrow and released his hand.

Emily, meanwhile, was embracing everyone with equal gusto. 'Goodbye, Donald. Ephie, darling. Goodbye, Cameron. I shall always remember this visit, especially the trip out to the selkies. The most *perfect* day of my life.'

'I thought that had yet to come, my girl,' objected her fiancé, hoisting her onto the trap. 'Up you get. We'll be back next summer and all the summers to come, I promise.'

Chapter 25

∼ *2010, Hetty* ∼

Hetty looked out over the ferry's broken wake as the islands receded and melted away into the blue-grey seascape. She had left the observation lounge and come up on deck to escape the brittle politeness of a conversation that was going nowhere, and Giles had watched her go, his expression a mixture of exasperation and remorse.

She was leaving the islands with her thoughts in disarray, plagued by conflicting emotions—a decaying house, a cracked skull, and broken lives. Images of gulls sweeping in on the tide, a flock of children running wild, and a man in worn jeans whose eyes had held hers.

A pair of puffins flew low over the water, wing beats fast and furious. It still seemed incredible that the discovery of the bones had found no resonance amongst the people she had met. Could families simply bury secrets? And then forget them— Surely there would be something, some hint of wrongness, of something off-key. The Forbes family had always been on the island, absorbing the changes, adapting to the shifting sands of passing decades, carrying forward an understanding of the past. Surely they knew *something*!

It was different for her own family, in which Theo Blake had been no more than a name. For them the connection with the island had long been broken, and continuity between generations fragmented, no stories had been passed down. But such a connection had once existed, and now some of the past figures had faces and substance. Emily, in particular, had become very real—a vitality had burned through the muted sepia in the old photograph, a bright captivating joy. *Same smile...* And there were those sketches on James's cottage wall too, of an island girl with a provocative smile. A young Theo Blake's soft pencil had caressed her form with a familiarity that was surely borne of knowledge—and desire. Was she an early love about whom history had recorded nothing? But had that love persisted, and had it intruded into the life of the pale woman who sat at the window and stared out over Muirlan Strand?

She had stumbled into so many lives, past and present. Not least among them the descendant of a defiant-looking young man who covered his cottage walls with images of the island and its past. And now, because of her, feared for its future.

~

This kaleidoscope of emotion spun around her brain all the way home, excluding Giles, who sat beside her, staring out of the train window, saying little. She had yet to find the words to explain. And always at the core was the youthful face of her great-grandmother. 'Aonghas remembers his father standing with his arm around her as they watched the bonfire after the auction,' Ruairidh had told her, 'and he said she looked like a young girl, though she must have been almost sixty by then.' And he had described how Emily had spent her last night in the old farmhouse 'sitting with her elbows on the big old kitchen table, drinking tea and reminiscing with him about childhood days. A lovely woman, Granddad said.'

It was Emily's gift of land to the factor's family, and other islanders, that was now under contention. And Emily was remembered kindly. 'We'll check again, of course, but I'm quite *sure* about estate boundaries,' Emma Dawson had said as they parted. And yet James had been equally certain it was otherwise, and so how could that be? And if Dalbeattie and Dawson *were* right and James wrong, that would have major implications for Ruairidh and his family. Unlike Emily's, her own visit to the islands would be remembered with anything but fondness.

And then there were the bones. That matter was now in police hands, although Ruairidh had been unable to say when they might hear back, beyond remarking that it was unlikely to be a priority. There was nothing she could do there, but the ownership of the land did need resolving, one way or another.

When she got back home that first evening, having separated from Giles at the station, she went straightaway to find the box that had been sent back from the nursing home following her grandmother's death. It was hardly more than a shoe box, the pitiful residue of a spent life, but she remembered seeing a notebook there, the first pages of a journal. She had flipped through it once before and found little of interest, but there had been something— It had begun in 1946, at the beginning of a sea voyage to South Africa and, in the way of most journals, that entry was followed by only skimpy notes, which had soon died away. After a description of the wartime devastation at Southampton docks, she found what she had been looking for. *We sail tomorrow, weather permitting. Heading for what? And leaving so much. The only way to deal with loss, Mother always told me, is by accepting it, however painful, and looking to the future and taking only the best of the past with you. I never saw her cry, except that once, when she came back from the auction and told me about the stones.* The reference to the auction she now understood. But what stones? *Don't ever let despair consume you, she said, that way lies the abyss. So I must be strong, but some days it's so hard.* Hetty sat back on her heels. *Loss.* That word again, but this too she shared with Emily. And was she right? Could you move through loss to a future and not lose the people held dear? It was a compelling thought, but it required strength to believe it.

Had there been strength written on Emily's bright young face on those fading photographs? Perhaps not. Perhaps strength in the face of adversity had to be learned.

She had packed the mementos away again, remembering as she did that her grandmother had been born to Emily's second husband, Edward Armstrong, and wondered again what had become of the tall, handsome man she had leant against in front of Muirlan House. But perhaps there was no mystery there, for a man who was young in 1910 had only uncertain chances of growing old.

Over the next few days, with the help of the Internet and a few emails, she set herself the task of finding out, following every lead that might bring her to Emily, and from there, perhaps back to the island. Eventually her work began to pay off: she found a marriage entry for the 10th of October 1911 for Miss Emily Blake and Major Rupert Ballantyre, and a year later a birth certificate for a daughter, followed with painful swiftness by the registration of the baby's death. Kit Blake had married in 1914, just weeks before war was declared, and although he had survived it, injured and gassed, Rupert Ballantyre had not. Twice decorated for outstanding bravery, he had been blown to pieces amidst the chaos of Passchendaele. Kit had died the year the second war was declared, the year that Theo Blake gave away half the island as a bird sanctuary. And by dying then, he had been spared the knowledge that his own son, a spitfire pilot, was declared missing over the Channel in 1940.

She sat back, almost wishing she had never started. It was ghastly! No less so as it must have been repeated in so many families during those years—the lost generations—and she saw again those images taken in front of Muirlan House in that summer of 1910. Carefree, youthful faces, looking to the future, captured in a moment in time before their world convulsed, exploded, and vanished, cheating men of life and women of their dreams.

She got up and went to the window, looking out at the darkening street. And what of Theo Blake, learning of these tragedies alone on the island, deserted by his wife, bereft of family, growing old and senile? What must it have been like for him? And all the time buried under the floorboards of his house there was a tragedy of another sort. He *must* have known about it; it seemed impossible that he did not.

She had seen little of Giles since they had returned from Scotland, and preoccupied as she was, she had hardly noticed. Relations between them had been patched up, but not fully repaired, and by unspoken agreement they avoided the subject of the house. But he had phoned the previous evening to tell her that three of Blake's works were coming up for auction that Saturday, and a friend of his from a local gallery was going along to bid for them. Did she want to come?

She did, of course, and so Giles was now in the kitchen making coffee until it was time to go, while she was, once again, glued to her laptop.

'*Theo Blake reached his peak very early but did not sustain his initial excellence,*' one source told her. '*He embraced the aspirations of the Glasgow School, working "en plein air", exploring ways of combining realism with landscape painting, evoking emotion from everyday scenes while avoiding cloying sentimentality.*' And there was an illustration of an unfinished sketch of a lithe young boy hauling himself out of a deep rock pool, the water trickling down his spine towards naked buttocks. She skipped over pages of comparison with contemporary painters, then paused and reread the next bit. '*Like his contemporaries, Blake peopled his compositions with local characters. His technique, however, offered something more, an intimacy with his subject. . .*' And she thought again of the sketches in James Cameron's cottage, and of *The Rock Pool.* She was seeing the same girl in his other work too, sometimes close, often in the distance, but read no speculation about her identity.

And then she came across a link to Blake's role in bird conservation in Scotland, and switched to that. If she was going to find herself in dispute with the reserve, the more she knew, the better. '*Established in 1939 with a generous land grant from the landowner, the painter Theodore Blake, it was one of the earliest of its kind. Using his collection of Hebridean birds begun by his father, Blake published an early catalogue, together with his own exquisite illustrations. Some of these specimens, including what must be one of the last native sea eagles, still survive…*' And there was a photograph of the faded sea eagle that James Cameron had pointed out to her in the museum, with a caption: *Sea eagle shot in August 1910, by Theodore Blake.* And there was that date again—1910. The date of the photograph of the family in front of the house, the date after which the conservatory was built, the date after which a body had been hastily buried.

She read on. '*Other surviving specimen include a red-necked phalarope and what has recently been identified as an isabelline shrike, but tragically much of the collection was put on a bonfire and destroyed after Blake's death in 1944.*' And then the next lines had her sitting bolt upright. '*The establishment of the reserve coincided with other land claim settlements, leading some writers to speculate that Blake, who was by then a recluse, was troubled by a guilty conscience and that these gifts were in atonement for the damage his Edwardian shooting parties had done to the local wildlife, as well as resolving other long-running disputes over land…*'

'Giles! Come and look at this.' He came through carrying two cups of coffee.

'Guilty conscience, eh?' he said, reading over her shoulder. 'But about birds—'

'And land.'

'Yeah, maybe. But it's what happened after his death that matters. Those alleged gifts of his sister's are in the forties, and that, like it or not, is what we need to unravel.'

She stood up and took her mug to the window. *Understand what you're getting into,* James had said. *It goes deep.*

Giles took her place at the computer. 'Hmm. Girls *and* boys?' he said after a minute, and she came back to see that he had flipped back to the previous link of the sketch of the young boy heaving himself out of the rock pool. 'No wonder his wife left him.' She flicked the laptop off and closed it. 'Sorry, darling!' He laughed. 'But Blake's past redemption, you know. Drink up. I said we'd collect Matt at eleven.'

An hour later they pulled up outside the auction house and

got the last parking place. 'The Blakes are his weird later stuff,' Matt told them. 'More William Blake than Theodore, with a healthy dose of Munch for good measure. Rather an acquired taste, I imagine, so I'm hoping we might get at least one of them.'

Matt was right. Two of the paintings were dark-toned and sinister, with broad brush-strokes emphasising strong patterns, and in one a caricature of a man in evening dress stood beside surf breaking on the shore, with a scarf knotted into a noose blown back behind him. He was staring intently out to sea just beyond the waves, at a face masked by a wild tangle of seaweed hair which floated back towards the curve of a finned tail. Half-woman, half-seal, the creature held up her palm in greeting—or was she forbidding an approach? Behind her, riding the swell, was a young seal. An oversized moon rose from the horizon to cast an unnatural, green light over the surface of the ocean, illuminating the anguished face of the man on the shore, his mouth wide open, calling. The whole composition had been executed with heavy swirls of charcoal, viridian, and indigo, in the manner of a woodcut, to disturbing effect.

'They're weird, but feel the tension between those two figures.' Matt and Giles had come to stand behind her. 'What d'you reckon he was on?'

Hetty moved to the second painting, and stopped, finding it oddly familiar. And then she remembered the sketch of the boy they had been looking at just that morning. This painting depicted the same scene except that this time it was not a young boy emerging from the pool, but a seal. No, not emerging, slipping back; she could see trails of water on the rocks where the fins had lost their grip. Except... She leant closer. They weren't fins but long webbed human fingers splayed across the rock surface, and the head was half-human. Two figures, far distant, were running towards the scene from opposite directions, and Blake had conveyed a sharp sense of urgency across a madly undulating landscape.

'Wild!' said a man beside her, lifting a tattooed arm to beckon a friend.

She moved on again. This last work was much smaller, clearly unfinished, and in it Blake had contorted perspective to depict a series of images on overlapping, vertical planes. On the first was a figure, a woman, but as the planes receded, the figure was deconstructed, Escher-like, until by the last planes it had resolved itself into a graceful wing, a gull's wing. Then the wing became a wing tip, and the final plane was empty.

But it was the first image which had grabbed Hetty's attention. In it the woman was looking obliquely at the artist, her hands raised to her hair, smiling, and Hetty recognised her.

It was Beatrice. Without a doubt.

Giles tugged at her sleeve, pointing to the seating, and a moment later the bidding began. She sat, but couldn't tear her eyes away from the painting where it now stood on an easel beside the others. She was barely aware that Matt had dropped out early, relentlessly outbid by the man with the tattoos, who paid considerable sums for the first two paintings, exchanging looks of satisfaction with his black-clad, elaborately pierced companion. Giles whistled softly beside her. 'Never even considered the Goth market for Blake. Must tell Emma.'

Matt leant across him. 'It's Jasper Banks! Wacky, but worth a fortune,' he whispered, and Hetty saw the auctioneer step towards the last, unfinished, work.

Again the tattooed man kept early bidding lively, and she clenched her fists, gripped suddenly by a desperate anger. The Goth market. Was that to be Beatrice's fate? No one would know it was her. She'd be lost and the work would become just another example of a once great painter's mad phase, fuelling idle speculation as to who she might be. Almost without thinking, she raised her own hand as the auctioneer reached two thousand pounds. 'Whoa!' Giles looked at her in astonishment, but she stuck with it until the bidding reached two and a half thousand, and then she began to feel panicked; only the tattooed man was still with her. Two and a half thousand! What was she doing?—

She glanced over her shoulder at her adversary as he raised his hand again, but he seemed to catch her eye, stopped, stared at her a moment, and then shook his head at the auctioneer, folding his hands on his lap. The hammer fell and the painting was hers.

Matt raised his eyebrows. 'Might be a good investment. Who knows?' he said, but Giles looked at her as if she were mad.

As the room began to clear, the tattooed man came up to her and proffered a card. 'If you change your mind, I'll give you what you paid.' She looked at the card and then back at him. He gave her an odd smile and put a hand on her shoulder. 'Sorry I bid you up.' Hetty watched his retreating figure as he passed the clerk for the auction house coming towards her, carrying Blake's deconstructed painting of his wife.

Chapter 26

≈ 1910, Beatrice ≈

Beatrice sat again on the window seat in the drawing room, looking out over the dull surface of the bay, her chin cupped in her hand. It seemed that Emily and Kit had taken the brightness of summer with them, and skies were now low and heavy, the winds fretful, and a thin persistent fog hung over the island. The horizon had disappeared, the world turned in on itself, and Theo, keeping to his study, did not send for Cameron.

The picnic at the seal island lingered in Beatrice's mind like a lovely dream, unfocussed and insubstantial, but persistent. What was it that had passed between them that day? Surely nothing, something more imagined than real, brought on by the warmth of the sun and the wine, truly a mirage. Since the disastrous luncheon party, she had only glimpsed him as he came and went around the buildings or set off across the strand with Bess at his heels, but she was conscious of watching for him.

Then Theo appeared abruptly at the door, interrupting her daydream, clutching an account. 'Beatrice, did you request that Dr. Johnson visit Duncan MacPhail's child?' It was his Edinburgh face, and she felt herself flush like a negligent housemaid. He had stonewalled her concerns following her visit to Mrs. McLeod's croft, telling her firmly to leave matters relating to the tenants to himself and John Forbes. But she had pursued her intentions to help nonetheless, guided to where there was need by Mrs. Henderson, uncertain how much Theo knew of her activities.

'They had no money for the doctor.' She met his eyes with determination. The account should have been sent to her, not the estate. 'But the child is better now.'

He contemplated her a moment. 'We agreed, my dear, that you would leave such matters to me.'

'The child was suffering, Theo, and her mother was desperate. She herself is unwell.' After all, what were a few shillings to the estate? Pin money.

'I'm not necessarily disputing the need, Beatrice, but I'm wondering why you said nothing.' He came further into the room. 'I particularly asked you not to get involved, especially in matters relating to the MacPhails.'

But their need was the greatest. The hostility between Duncan MacPhail and the estate had been brought home to her during the last few days of Emily's visit, when their walks had taken them down to a small cove in the south-west of the island, and Emily had stopped in surprise. 'Oh, look! Someone's repairing the old croft house. We used to play there as children.'

At the sound of their voices, a thin, drab woman had appeared at the doorway and Beatrice started down the rough path towards her. 'Eilidh! It's you! Good morning. Do you know Mr. Blake's sister, Miss Emily Blake?' The woman gave a bob, her eyes warily bright in their dark hollows. 'Is Morag quite better now?'

'Aye, madam, she's—' A man appeared from behind the house, carrying a spade and an old tin bucket, his sleeves neatly rolled above the elbow. He halted abruptly when he saw the women together.

'Mr. MacPhail,' said Beatrice, and she heard Emily repeat the name in surprise. 'Good morning.' The man's eyes slid from one to the other. 'I'm glad to hear your daughter is better.'

'We're very grateful, aren't we, Donnchadh?' The woman looked beseechingly at her husband's rigid face, and he gave a perfunctory nod.

While they stood there, Emily examined the house, where an old sail had been spread across part of the rotted roof and bunches of heather plugged gaps in the stone walls, and her scrutiny became too much for the man. 'I'd ask you in for a cup of tea, Miss Blake, then you could have a good look round.' He propped the spade against the wall. 'But we weren't expecting guests.' His wife gave Beatrice an agonised look, and Emily bristled. 'And we've no tea.' He came closer and dumped the bucket down with such force that potatoes jumped from the top. 'You can have these, but I suppose they're your brother's anyway.'

'*Donnchadh*—' The woman had bent in a spasm of coughing, and Beatrice put her hand on her arm to calm her, bid a cool good day to her husband, and pulled Emily along with her.

'What an appalling man!' Emily had begun, as she stumbled back up the path, the man watching them go with hard eyes. 'Wait until we tell Theo.'

'No. Don't, Emily. Please. It'll make more trouble for Eilidh. I don't think they're supposed to be there.'

Theo was standing over her now, his face stern. 'Mark my words, they'll start to play you off against me, and then where will we be? I know you meant well, Beatrice, but you're interfering in something you don't understand.'

There was much she didn't understand, she thought, swallowing her indignation, but it didn't include a needy child in a comfortless home. 'Surely we can show generosity in this regard at least, even if we cannot in other matters.'

His frown deepened. '*Other* matters? Has Cameron been lobbying you too?' She made no reply. 'Causing trouble seems to have earned that family legendary status, and Duncan MacPhail is cast in the same mould as his grandfather.'

'For which his child must suffer?'

Theo glared at her. 'I insist on being allowed to run the estate as I see fit.' His words were clipped and angry.

'So what is *my* role here, Theo? Am I to make no contribution?' Exasperation replaced anger. 'My dear girl! You're my *wife*.' She bit back a sharp retort. How long was it since he had come to her bed, preferring to continue his late vigil, then sleeping in his dressing room?

'You run the house,' he continued quickly, his eyes flickering away from her.

'Mrs. Henderson runs the house.'

He sat down heavily, and when she held his look, his eyes slid to one side, the veil descended, and once again he eluded her. 'You're my wife,' he repeated quietly, 'and, God willing, in time you'll be mother to our children. Then you'll have little time or inclination to go running around the estate offering inappropriate charity.' He placed the bill on a side table and smiled thinly at her. 'Oblige me, my dear, and leave well alone? I prefer instead to discuss Sanders's visit at the end of the week. His patronage is important and his comfort *is* your concern, so I'm rather counting on you.'

$\sim$ *Theo* $\sim$

He put aside the offending bill, watching moodily from the drawing room window as Beatrice flung out of the house and set off down the track, her hat in her hand, her shawl slipping from her shoulders. Perhaps he had spoken too harshly, but surely she must see that there had to be a *consistent* approach to dealing with the tenants. Especially the accursed MacPhails with their persistent demands and outraged attitude. Or had she, like Cameron, cast him as a villain?

He dropped into a chair, scowling up at the painting which had brought him and Beatrice together. What on earth had possessed him to give it to her? Madness! *A mirage...* she had said, and on that one percipient phrase, he had constructed a future. He should sell the damn thing. And yet, painting it all those years ago had soothed the pain of loss. On the day he had received news of Màili's death, he had stood at the window of his Glasgow studio, stunned and disbelieving, the letter from his father loose in his hands. A mass of starlings filled the air, sweeping back to their roosts, but he had seen instead a cloud of shore waders lifting off the sands. In a frenzy he had sought out his old sketchbooks, turning their yellowing pages imbued with salt air, heavy with promise, and he had seen Màili again, silhouetted against the darkening sky, or lying with her hair entwined with sea-wrack, or seated beside the rock pool, smiling at him, a seal-wife. Unreachable, even then.

A mirage.

And he had been drawn back to the island then, seeking her spirit in the places they had once frequented, sitting for hours with his back resting against the wall near the rock pool, a place cushioned by grassy tussocks, hidden from sight, tormented by memories. And it was there that it came to him what he must do, as a tribute, privately, to numb the pain. It was all he had left to offer her.

So he had risen early over successive mornings, set his easel on the lower foreshore, and begun painting, his hands guided by some force other than his brain, and gradually the painting had taken shape. He had felt oddly detached from the task— driven, not driving—and somehow two figures had emerged, crossing the strand in the early morning haze. Two figures, illusory, barely hinted at, disappearing into the soft grey mist. Two figures walking side by side and yet apart, drawn to each other by an unseen force but never quite meeting.

He stood in front of that painting now and was transported back. It was the last good thing he had done, the last time he had painted from the heart. And you were wrong, Beatrice, my dear. It was painted not to prove that I was still alive but in acknowledgement that the soul of me had died.

Chapter 27

∼ *1910, Beatrice* ∼

'Damn it, Blake, you didn't tell me you'd caught a beauty. What the devil does she see in you?' The round-faced, glistening man placed a lingering kiss upon Beatrice's hand and his small eyes sparkled up at her. 'We shall become great friends, my dear.'

More guests, all sportsmen. They had arrived with their guns and their rods and their noisy male bravado, and Beatrice felt squeezed to the margins of her home. The round-faced Glaswegian, George Sanders, was Theo's special guest and a patron of the forthcoming Glasgow exhibition, and he followed her with hot eyes, never missing an opportunity to touch or caress, leaning close to engage her in conversation, placing a hand on her arm or in her lap. But when she looked indignantly to Theo for support, he seemed quite unaware.

Sanders's bulk precluded him from many of the party's expeditions and, despite pleading with Theo not to leave her alone with him, Beatrice frequently found herself in his company and had to devise ways of avoiding him. She would watch him from her turret window, tottering along the foreshore with his shotgun, and only then deem it safe to leave the sanctuary of her bedroom. But one day she misjudged matters and went out onto the front steps only to encounter Sanders crunching up the drive towards her, his gun in one hand, the other holding up, in the manner of a great hunter, the dripping carcass of an otter. 'I bring an offering, Beatrice, my love!' he bellowed. 'I shall have him turned into a smart little collar for you. Should you like that? I know just the man for the job.' She stared at the creature in horror, remembering the one she and Cameron had seen coming in on the tide that time, and felt suddenly sick. In a fury, she turned and went back inside, fleeing down the servants' passage and out of the back entrance, past an astonished housemaid taking in washing, and into the pasture beyond, indifferent to a damp grey mist which was swirling around the low-lying land.

Her anger fuelled her over some distance, and she was oblivious to where her feet took her until she stopped and looked around in consternation at the thickening mist, regretting the shawl left behind, and felt a sudden fear. The house had vanished, even the chimneys were no longer visible, and low cloud had flattened the landscape, rendering it unfamiliar and strange. By now her flimsy shoes were in tatters, and her next step brought peaty water welling up around her ankles. Which way took her back?

And then, from nowhere, came a wild, wailing cry, echoing strangely through the still air, amplified by the mist. *Dear God!* She froze and looked round, pulse racing, seeking a refuge, and saw a rocky knoll ahead of her beside a small narrow inlet from the sea. Stepping swiftly, searching out the firmer ground, she set off towards it, and had crossed only half the distance when she looked up again.

A grey shape rose from near the water's edge and she stifled a cry, turning back to flee.

'Mrs. Blake?' she heard herself addressed in astonished tones. 'What on earth—!' She stared into the mist and saw it was Cameron. He came quickly to her, looking over the undulating land she had just crossed. 'Are you alone?'

Her breath came out in a gasp, and relief made her sharp. 'I'm not a child! I can go out alone and come to no harm. You simply startled me.'

'Never mind.' He continued to scan the landscape behind her, his manner distracted, his tone urgent. 'Are Mr. Blake and his guests behind you? I thought they'd gone over towards the west, looking for snipe.'

'They did,' she answered slowly, struck now by his odd

manner. 'Why? Are you up to no good?' The strange cry came again, and her eyes flew to his face. '*What is it?*'

He looked back at her and gave her a half-smile. 'Just a bird, madam,' he said, 'a bird who'd do well to keep quiet,' and it was only then that he seemed to take in her dishevelled appearance, and he frowned again. 'But whatever brings you all the way out here?'

'I had to get away.'

He searched her face, saying nothing. Then: 'Perhaps so. But this presents me with a problem.' He glanced over his shoulder at the inlet, then turned back, his eyes narrowing. 'You once told me you could keep your tongue between your teeth, Mrs. Blake. I wonder if you will.' And without further explanation, he took her arm and helped her over the wet rocks to the loch side, gesturing to her to crouch low behind them, and handed her his field glasses. Ragged veils of mist drifted over the surface, grey and ethereal. 'Just keep watching fifty yards or so out towards that little island.' He spoke softly, pointing to where the mist had thinned. 'There! Just came up.' She trained the glasses on the neck and body of a large black-and-white bird.

'Oh!' she whispered. 'You beauty.' The bird turned its head towards her, then dived.

'And he's been calling as if to a mate.'

She had not been alone with Cameron since the day of the picnic and was suddenly very aware of him beside her, his dark woollen jacket dewed by the mist, a grey scarf knotted at his throat, his hair flattened by the damp air.

Then the bird resurfaced, and he touched her arm, gesturing her to raise the glasses again.

'When did you find it?' she asked.

'I heard its call when I was out with Kit one day, and went looking.'

She lowered them again to stare at him. 'All that time ago? Since Kit and Emily were here?' He looked steadily back at her, saying nothing. 'Will you tell my husband?' she asked, after a moment.

'No.' He took the glasses from her. 'Will you?'

'No.'

His expression did not change. 'He would want to know, of course. And his guests would be interested too.'

'Would they?' she asked in a bitter tone, and told him about the otter.

He listened gravely. Then the diver surfaced again and let out a series of low, plaintive calls. 'This must not make trouble between you,' he said.

Trouble? She lifted her chin. 'And by which of us would he feel most betrayed, Cameron, for keeping the news from him?'

Cameron hesitated, frowning slightly. 'He's used to me arguing with him about the collection,' he said, 'but from you—'

'He is owed compliance?' She brushed the heather twigs from her skirts, picking fragments off her sleeve, glancing sharply at him. 'In this, as in all matters.'

'Mrs. Blake—'

'Beatrice. Today I'm not disposed to play the role. But why do *you* care about this bird, Cameron? Or do you simply delight in thwarting my husband?'

He leant back against the rock and folded his arms, looking at her, and took time to consider his response. 'I want it to have a chance,' he said at last.

'But they are plentiful in Canada, you said so yourself. Why not let him have it?'

'Because it's chosen to come here, all those miles,' he said softly, and she looked at the bird again, at its glossy black-and-white plumage and sharp, intelligent head. 'But it is different for you, Mrs. Blake.'

'Beatrice.'

He gave a wry smile. 'Beatrice the anarchist. I had forgotten.'

'And anarchists behave badly to bring attention to themselves, do they not? So if Theo learns that I knew of the diver and is angry, what then—' It would make a change from silence and indifference. Tears scalded her eyes and she turned away.

Cameron was silent, still leaning against the rock, and looking at her. 'You know,' he began, then faltered. 'You must understand. Mr. Blake lived alone for a long time—'

'And why was that?' she snapped, dashing an arm across her face, angry at her tears. 'He broods, heavy-eyed and grim, Cameron. Tell me why that is?'

Cameron looked disconcerted. 'He's been a changed man since you came, I told you before.'

'Changed?' She gave a short laugh. 'Is he, Cameron? You know him better than anyone, I think.'

He sat looking at her for so long that she thought he would never reply, and she felt her colour rising, anxious now for what he might say. 'I don't understand him, any more than you do,' he said eventually. 'The contradictions in him, when he has so much.'

'But not, I think, what he wants.' It was as close as she dared to tread. Out on the loch, the diver gave another haunting cry, and Beatrice turned aside, closing her eyes to halt the tears. Cameron made no response, and when she turned back he was replacing the field glasses in their case, his head bent forward, his expression hidden, saying nothing. When he straightened, his face was rigid, as it had been once before when he had kicked at the embers of their fire.

'So, Mrs. Blake. As conspirators, perhaps we'd better return to the house separately.'

She looked about her, biting her lip in consternation. 'Except that I'm already lost—'

His laugh broke the tension. 'So that was just bravado a moment ago, was it?' His eyes glinted at her as he reached down and pulled her to her feet, taking in her brown-stained stockings, her skirt streaked with dirt from a stumble, and shook his head. 'What a mess you're in, *madam*'—he used the word with gentle deliberation—'and all on a dead otter's account. No coat or shawl'— he looked down at her feet—'and your shoes. Can you walk in them?'

'I'll have to.'

'How long have you been away?'

'Some hours, I think.'

He looked back across the way she had come and frowned. 'Then they'll have started a search for you. Come on, I'll not leave you.' He took off his jacket, brushing aside her protests, insisting she put it on. It felt warm and comforting, and she clasped it to her, conscious of the pressure of his hands on her shoulders as he turned her to face him, his grip tightening. 'I can't ask you to keep secrets from your husband, Mrs. Blake.'

She dropped her eyes to rest on the scarf knotted just below his Adam's apple. 'But you don't ask it.' Neither spoke. Then his grip slackened and his arms fell to his sides. 'And now, you must take me home.'

Gradually, familiar landmarks emerged from the mist and, as the world became recognisable again, she remembered her place in it and walked with her face averted, shaken by what had passed between them, by words spoken and those left unsaid. 'Do you think he'll find out?' she asked abruptly.

'If he hears it, he'll not rest until he finds it.'

Guilt found its way to the surface. 'If I believed he'd leave it in peace, then I *would* tell him, for it might bring him joy.'

Cameron made no reply, and they walked on in silence until the house suddenly loomed up ahead of them, solid and forbidding. And through the thinning mist they saw the figure of John Forbes striding purposefully down the ridge towards them.

～ *Theo* ～

Theo saw the gentlemen settled with brandy and cigars, and then excused himself, closing the door and crossing the hall to the stairs. Dinner had been delayed until Beatrice had been found, and then eaten without her, but he had been distracted during the meal, scarcely conscious of the ebb and flow of conversation.

What a state she had been in! Hair wet and bedraggled, skirts streaked with mud, clasping Cameron's jacket round her like an overlarge skin. But it was her face, lifted to him with such defiance, which had unsettled him.

He mounted the stairs swiftly. Thank God Cameron had come across her. But what had possessed her to bolt like that? Sanders said she had shrieked at him and fled. 'Didn't know she would be squeamish, old boy. Don't apologise, I must have upset her. Women can be skittish creatures, y' know, 'specially if they're… Well, hrmph, but I'm a family man myself.' Theo crossed the landing and paused outside the door. Perhaps that explained her recent strangeness, but why had she said nothing? He knocked and went in, pausing just inside the door.

She was standing motionless at the turret window, staring out across the dark bay, her hair cascading down her back in crinkled curls. A Rossetti painting, *Fazio's Mistress*. A single oil lamp burned on the dressing table, raising a sheen on her hair. The sight of her arrested him, but she looked over her shoulder at him and regarded him coolly, saying nothing. 'Are you warm again?' he asked, disconcerted. 'Did they bring you something on a tray?'

'I had tea and toast. I wasn't hungry.' Shadows shifted across the room as she moved from the window, and his eyes strayed to her midriff, but beneath her silk dressing gown she was as shapely as before, and when he lifted his eyes he saw that she was watching him. 'Sanders told me that you took exception to him shooting an otter and fled.' He paused. 'What really happened?'

'Just that.' She pulled the dressing gown closer and met his eye steadily. Flying insects caused the oil lamp to flicker. 'He offered to have the corpse made into a collar for me.'

He looked at her in disbelief. 'Is that all? Could you not have simply said something gracious?' He spoke sharply, and she raised a hand to the wall as if to steady herself. 'You need never have worn the damned thing.' Still she said nothing, and he felt anger stir. 'I would rather you had not offended him.'

She shrugged, walked over to her dressing table, and began pulling the remaining pins from her hair. 'I told you before, Theo, I don't want to be left alone with that odious man. You take no notice.'

He went past her to stand by the window, staring out across the bay. This was a Beatrice he did not know, assured and defiant. Yet if she was pregnant— He half turned and saw she was watching him through the mirror, her eyes shadowed and confusing. 'That's all very well, Beatrice, but he's our guest.'

'*Your* guest.'

He looked at her in astonishment. 'Mine. Ours. It makes no difference. He's a guest in this house and can expect to be treated as such.'

'And how should your wife expect to be treated, Theo? Your guest behaves offensively and you do nothing.' Her reflection returned his look boldly. 'He's quite repellent.'

He felt a prick of self-reproach. *Had* Sanders been offensive?

She'd said he was overfamiliar, but the remark seemed consistent with her tetchy humour since Kit and Emily had left, and he'd thought nothing of it. He'd been preoccupied. But her haughty stare reflected through the mirror now stirred him to anger. 'You flatter yourself, Beatrice. He's a married man with grown children.' He decided to take the plunge. 'In fact, he hinted that your odd behaviour might be because you were—'

'Because I was what?' She froze, hairbrush in hand.

'Oh, for God's sake, Beatrice.' Too late he saw his mistake, but she was nettling him. 'With child, pregnant, breeding—whatever term you *don't* find repellent!'

She put down the brush. 'So you discuss such matters with your cronies, do you?'

'Of course not!' His temper rose to match hers. 'We were alone when he suggested it, and it seemed to offer *some* reason for your strange conduct these last days.'

'So you said I was?' Her reflection, framed by wild curls, was that of a fey stranger.

'It might excuse your abominable manners if you were.'

'Well, I'm not.' She picked up her brush again. 'It would be little short of a miracle if I was. Shall I make an announcement at breakfast tomorrow to settle the matter?'

Static flew from the bristles as she brushed, and he stood staring at her, feeling his face suffuse with colour. 'What the devil has come over you, Beatrice? You seem quite, quite… crazed!' She shook out her hair and continued brushing, her head averted, refusing to meet his eyes. The accusation of conjugal neglect was deserved, but it shook him that she had made it. He was at a loss and went slowly towards the door, then turned back, struggling to find words to explain, and saw her reflection staring back across the room at him, repeated infinitely in the angled side mirror, and he remembered an earlier time—as if in another life.

Chapter 28

∼ 2010, Hetty ∼

Hetty sat at the window of her flat watching for the postman, while her mind reran the telephone conversation she just had with Ruairidh. He had rung to tell her there had been another roof fall at the house, and she felt oppressed again by her responsibilities. 'We'd terrible gales up here at the weekend. Westerlies.' She had been so engrossed with tracking down Emily and the other figures in the photograph that the question of the house itself had been sidelined, but Ruairidh's call had brought it back to centre stage. And then he had gone on to tell her about a dreadful road accident on the mainland—a coach full of German tourists had come off the road when the driver misjudged a narrow bend, and there had been a horrific fire. 'The lab will be tied up with that for the next wee while, so they'll not be getting back to us about the bones anytime soon.'

'Of course.'

There was a slight pause. 'Úna said you were getting someone else to look at the house? Another survey?' Ruairidh tried hard to mask it, but she could hear the constraint in his voice.

'I think perhaps I should. Just to be sure.' She wanted to talk to him about the disputed ownership, but it was all so awkward, so she had let the conversation slide off the subject, and she told him instead about the extraordinary discovery of Blake's letters, promising to get back to him once she had seen them.

Knowledge of these letters' existence had come to her via the tattooed Jasper Banks, who had recognised Matt at a gallery opening and asked if his friend was enjoying Blake's painting. Matt had lost no time in telling him about Hetty's connection to Blake, and two days later a packet of letters had been delivered to Matt's gallery with instructions to hand them on, if they were of interest, and Matt had phoned to say that they were on their way, registered post.

She looked up then and saw the Royal Mail van turning the corner and went quickly to the door, signed for the package with a hasty scrawl, and returned to the sitting room, turning the package over in her hands.

She slit it open and spread the contents on the table. Letters, photocopies to be sure, but written in Blake's own elegantly sloping hand, addressed to a Charles Farquarson, who Matt had said had been a notable patron of the arts in Edwardian Edinburgh. There were twelve of them, and she arranged them carefully in date order.

Her mouth was dry as she took up the first, July 1909, and began to read, but it was disappointing, dealing only with mundane matters relating to the shipping of paintings from France in advance of Blake's return. The second one had been written from Charlotte Street, Edinburgh, and was dated March 1910, and it set her pulse racing.

My dear fellow, what a characteristically generous gesture! I know Beatrice has written, but allow me to add my thanks to hers. It is a beautiful piece, which we shall always treasure. I'm sorry you missed the wedding, but you must make up for it by visiting us this summer, I absolutely insist. You see, I've persuaded Beatrice to leave Venice and Rome for another time and go to the island. She sat back, overwhelmed by the sudden direct connection with the man. *I'm pinning my hope on her falling under the spell of its spring loveliness, so that we can return each year. And I shall paint again, my friend. From the heart! I can abandon the counterfeit passion for foreign lands and return to sacred soil. The old compulsion is thrumming deep within me already. See what acquiring a charming wife has done for me! Yours, Blake.* Hetty breathed deep with satisfaction. There it was, in just a few lines his love of the island, his passion for his work, and for Beatrice. She reread and smiled at the final line: *acquiring* a wife? He wouldn't get away with that now.

She took up the next letter. It was dated June 1910 and dealt briskly with an imminent visit. *A larger party will not discommode us. You are all welcome, I assure you. I'll do what I can to persuade Baird and Campbell to open their coffers, though I don't know them well. You ask about my work, but I confess I've little to show you. By all means put some of the old ones forward for selection, but there is younger talent about, and things have moved on. I've been spending what free time I have on illustrations for the catalogue. The factor's son assists me intermittently, when he isn't preaching socialism to me. (Galling when you consider I supported the blighter's education!) Oh, for the idealism of youth... He seems to think we can roll back time and make the world a better place. But I stand my ground. It's all I can do. Beatrice is looking forward to your visit, as is your friend, Blake.*

The factor's son? She remembered the self-conscious youth, a mirror of the burly factor, and knew that it was not he to whom Blake referred. It must be the other one, who had stared out of the past with a defiant intensity. A socialist, was he? She'd seen the same expression on the face of his descendant when he had dismissed Muirlan House as *a rich man's conceit.* A consistency of view captured in the DNA.

Entirely hooked now, she picked up the next letter, dated August 1910, and found that the tone had changed. The romantic jubilation of the spring had vanished. It began with another reference to the selection of paintings, apparently for some large exhibition. *By all means have them, as Sanders seems to think there's a shortage of appropriate Art to offset Industry, so at least they'll serve as wallpaper. I only wish I had something else to offer you. Strictly speaking, 'Muirlan Strand' belongs to Beatrice, but I daresay she will loan it for the exhibition. I'd cheerfully sell it, but that, apparently, is out of the question. I've promised the other to my sister as a wedding present, since she reckons I'm becoming a good investment, but she'll loan it too if it is selected, and if Reed will let you have 'The Rock Pool', then all well and good. Though I feel they belong to a different era, the work of another man.*

Anyway, I'm considering returning to Edinburgh earlier than originally planned. I don't flatter myself that my stepmother requires my presence, but Beatrice might enjoy the bustle of my sister's wedding preparation. She's been restless since Emily and Kit left. Feeling the isolation, I imagine. Perhaps we will consider Venice another year. I suppose it was asking too much that she would feel the same as I do about the island, and I always was a selfish creature. She says the house is cold and dark, so I'm considering building a conservatory where she can sit on poor days. She enjoys plants and flowers, so I think it would help her.

And there it was, in black and white: a conservatory. Hetty sat back. A chill ran through her, and she felt an absurd desire to put aside the remaining letters, to stop things where there was still evidence of affection, of concern, of kindness. She read it again. Beatrice was restless, he said, so were the cracks already beginning to show? Whatever else, this was crucial information, the date of the letter confirming the evidence of the early photographs quite precisely. Ruairidh ought to be told, but as she turned to the phone, it rang.

'Morning. Ruairidh said you were at home and that he told you about the roof.' James Cameron. Direct and to the point.

'Yes.'

'The damage is round at the back, above the old scullery. A chimney stack fell, crashed through the roof, and made a proper mess, slates all over.' He paused. 'Have you got your second opinion lined up to come?'

'The agents are dealing with it.' That wasn't quite true. Giles had got her to agree to phone Emma and arrange it, but she hadn't yet done so.

'Well, give 'em a prod. The place is dangerous, and it's up to you to make it safe. I've put stakes around the fall area and taped it off, but if anyone gets injured, even trespassers, you'll have all sorts of hassle you could do without.'

She felt her stomach turn over. 'Perhaps the schoolchildren—'

'We moved them into one of the barns at the farmhouse.

Seemed a good idea anyway.' There was another pause. 'Ruairidh said you had some letters?'

'Yes, I was going to ring you.'

'Where did they spring from?'

She told him about the auction, about meeting Jasper Banks, and how the letters had subsequently arrived. 'And those sketches of yours must be worth a fortune—'

'They're not for sale.'

'—but Matt says you shouldn't take any more out of the book because of the signatures.'

'Does he.' His tone dismissed Matt's opinion, and he scoffed at the sums she told him were paid for the paintings. 'Silly money. Tell me about the letters.'

'I'm still working through them, but in August 1910 Blake was thinking of building a conservatory for Beatrice.'

'Was he now?' That *had* taken his interest.

'And there were obviously problems between them, not spelt out, but there—although he still seemed fond of her, concerned to make her happy.'

'Perhaps he still was—in August 1910.'

'He said she was restless, implied she was lonely.' James was silent. 'There was a painting of her at the auction. It was very strange, disconnected and rather sad, although somehow very tender too.' Giles had believed her mad when she'd tried to explain why she'd bought it, but she had a feeling that James Cameron might understand.

'Did the same chap buy it?'

'No. I did.'

'Good God! How much did you part with?'

'I couldn't just leave her there.'

He snorted. 'That much, eh? This business is going to your head, woman. Get a grip on yourself.' She smiled, finding his bluntness strangely reassuring. 'And, by the way, the girl in *The Rock Pool* is Màili Forbes. Aonghas said I ought to know that, but if I did, I'd forgotten. She was Aonghas's grandmother.'

'Oh.'

'And she's up there in the burial ground with a stillborn child, so the bones aren't hers.'

'Were she and Blake lovers?' she asked, without thinking. He laughed. 'Aonghas didn't say.'

'No, of course— But you can see it in the sketches, and in the painting too. He was in love with her.'

She could almost hear the shrug. 'Painters often had favourite models.'

'It's more than that.' The touch of brush and pencil was so sure, subtle enough to be a caress.

'Maybe.' There was silence, and then they both spoke at once. 'You first,' he said.

'I was wondering about the land question—'

'So was I.'

'Emma Dawson's looking into it again, but she hasn't got back to me yet.' He grunted. 'Have you... has Aonghas found anything, any papers?'

'Aonghas remembers your great-grandmother giving his father the land and the house.' The bluntness had developed an edge. 'He was there. He heard them discussing it.'

'And the deeds?'

'Must be somewhere.'

She paused. 'It needs resolving.'

'It does.'

A stand-off. James Cameron didn't make things easy. 'Look,' she said, 'if Emily gave that land away, then I've no intention of trying to claim it back.'

'Good. It's Ruairidh's livelihood, and others'.'

No pressure, then. His tone piqued her. 'But I gather it's only one of the problems I've inherited. Tell me about this tenant.'

There was a longer pause. 'He's an old codger who grows potatoes over there.'

Her bloke. 'But there's more to it than that, isn't there?'

'Is there?'

'Something you aren't telling me?'

He laughed briefly. 'He's another part of the Blake legacy, but he'll help you resolve the matter himself.'

She heard a key in the front door. 'Why can't you—'

Giles called a greeting from the door.

'Sounds like you've got company. I'll let you get on.' And he rang off.

Chapter 29

≈ 1910, Beatrice ≈

At Sanders's leave-taking, his eyes had slid down to Beatrice's waist, and he'd smiled in a manner which made her half-formed excuse for the previous day dry on her lips, and she held out a cold hand in farewell. Theo eyed her sourly, and the moment the trap reached the gatepost he went back into the house, instructing one of the girls to go and find Cameron and send him to the study.

On hearing this, she retired to her bedroom, pleading a very real headache, refusing tea or a tonic, and stretched out on her bed, listening to the rising wind, staring up at the crack which had spread across the ceiling in the course of the summer, and anxiously reran the events of the previous day. It was as if the mist had swirled off the machair and into her head, dizzying her senses, and the weird cry of the diver echoed from another world. What exactly had she said to Cameron? And what an absurd situation to have got herself into, a conspiracy of silence about a wretched bird, a conspiracy, moreover, shadowed by an aura of betrayal. She rose, fretful, and went over to the turret window, drawing back as she saw Cameron walking up the drive, buffeted by the gales. When he glanced up at her window, she stepped back, out of view, but he knew she was there.

Next day she met him crossing the hall on his way to the study, and he gave her a conspirator's smile. 'There's two. I heard them calling to each other, quite clearly.'

'What can we do?'

'Not a thing.' He smiled briefly and knocked on the study door.

But the following day, while Theo went with John Forbes to

view the damage to the stable roof wrought by the wind, she found herself compelled to seek him out again. She could not help it. 'Have you seen them?' she asked, hesitating at the study door.

He lifted his head. 'No. I heard them, though, out towards Oronsy Beagh, some distance away. But I'll find them.' He paused, taking in her drawn appearance. 'You're pale, Mrs. Blake.'

She came into the room. 'A little tired, perhaps.'

He continued to look at her, then went over to one of the bookcases, selected a large volume, and took it to the light of the window. 'There's our fellow,' he said, finding the page. 'It says they choose freshwater lochs for their nests, preferring islands or promontory sites. The lochan on Oronsy Beagh is a bit small but might suit their purpose.' She joined him at the window, and he lowered the book to show her. As she bent over it, she sensed him grow still beside her, and the study's silent witnesses went on guard. Then the front door banged and heavy steps crossed the hall to the study. They turned from the window to find John Forbes halted in the doorway, staring across at them.

'Is Cameron still in there, John?' Theo's voice came from behind him in the hall.

Cameron replaced the book on the shelf and returned to his desk; Beatrice moved to the fireplace.

'Aye,' replied the factor, stone-hard. 'But I'll take him back with me, and we'll start to put matters right.' He moved aside to let Theo pass.

'If you must. Did you find the missing ledger, Cameron?' Theo barely acknowledged Beatrice's presence, and she took the opportunity to withdraw, feeling John Forbes's eyes following her retreat.

For days after that Cameron did not reappear in the study, and Theo complained that he was never available to assist him. His father was keeping him busy on the estate, repairing storm damage, he said. Beatrice was torn between relief and a quite different emotion, stifled and kept indoors by the weather.

Eventually, it began to clear and the sun filtered through the thin clouds. Beatrice escaped down to the foreshore, gulping at the fresh sweet air, seeking the clarity of mind she found more easily outdoors. Distress at Theo's neglect she had grown used to, but she was now in the grip of a much more powerful emotion, carried forward and shaken by the strength of it.

The sand steamed slightly as the re-emergent sun turned the shallow pools into ripples of quicksilver, and some sixth sense told her that Cameron was approaching. She looked up to see him rounding the cove, Bess trotting behind him. He seemed to break step when he saw her, then he came on, greeting her with a constrained smile. 'The weather's clearing, Mrs. Blake,' he said.

'Yes.'

'It's often fickle like this in the later summer.' He gazed across the sands and up at the sky, clicking his fingers at the dog.

'Is it?'

'Sun and storm.' They stood awkwardly, like players on a wide stage, uncertain of their next lines, then he turned to her. 'Did Mr. Blake tell you—' he began, then broke off, his attention caught by something behind her, and she turned to see John Forbes and Donald emerging from the stables. The factor had stopped and lifted his head to watch them. 'Excuse me, madam.' He nodded and left her, whistling sharply to Bess to follow.

She mounted the front steps and placed her hat on the hall table, then went slowly into the drawing room. What else could she do? Theo lowered his book as she entered and gestured to the tea tray. 'Been for a breath of air, my dear? I saw you down on the foreshore.'

The fire had burned low and the room was dark, as it always was at this time of day when the sun swung behind the house, but she sensed he was making an effort and smiled. 'Everything smelled so fresh after the storm.' She poured herself a cup of tea. 'The air was very clear.'

'If the weather settles, shall we give it a week or so before we return? Though you'll want to be in Edinburgh in good time to prepare for Emily's wedding, I'm sure. New gowns and the like.' He smiled wistfully across at her, an echo of his old countenance. 'Will you be glad of a change, Beatrice?'

She sipped at her tea. 'I'd rather be here if the weather is good; the city can be so oppressive in August.'

'We'll see what it does.' He paused. 'There are things I want to complete here, but I can finish the writing in Edinburgh.' He hesitated, then glanced across at her. 'I've asked Cameron to return with us and lend me a hand over the winter,' he said, and she looked up in astonishment. 'One last attempt to get him to see sense and stay. I've offered him a decent salary.' He reached for his cup and raised it to his lips, watching her. 'What do you think?'

She put her own cup down to stop her hand from shaking. What *should* she think? 'But you get so annoyed with him, Theo.'

'Oh, we rub along. He needs to widen his horizons. See sense. And when his mind's on the job, he's very useful. Would you mind if he came?'

She turned away to refill her cup. 'Of course not, if it's what you want.'

'John's being difficult about it, but I think I can persuade him. He'll still have Donald, after all.' And if he came, would she and Theo then be in competition for Cameron's attentions? The absurdity, and the perils, of the situation expanded in her brain like giant bubbles and smothered rational thought. 'Although Cameron's behaving rather oddly,' Theo continued. 'Keeps disappearing. Particularly since the guests left. God knows where he goes in this weather. His father doesn't always know either.' He paused again and laughed self-consciously. 'I begin to wonder if he's courting.'

Courting? One of the bubbles popped. *Courting?* She looked across at Theo, but he was staring into the fire. She swallowed hard, now entirely bewildered, and tried for a light tone. 'Well, he's a personable young man, though it's hardly something you can ask him about.'

Theo leant forward and filled his cup. 'No. And I'm probably wrong. I can't imagine who would take his interest among the local maidens. He should aim higher.' He stirred his tea thoughtfully. 'And if John decides he needs him here, there's not much I can do.'

Beatrice played with the cuff of her sleeve, struggling for composure. 'Well, if he *is* courting, he may not wish to go with us anyway,' she said. 'And I'm sure there are all sorts of lovely local girls you know nothing about. I understand that Cameron's mother was an island girl and very beautiful.'

Theo replaced his cup with a clatter. 'Servants' gossip, Beatrice?' he remarked coldly, picking up a book. 'I thought you had more dignity.'

~

'It must be a woman,' Theo complained again the next day. 'I can't get a firm decision from him. He's clearly distracted, in a daydream if I don't keep on at him. God, what fools love can make of us.'

Fools indeed, she thought, stung by his words. Last night Theo had come to her room, tapping softly on the door. When she opened it, he had stood there, as he had once before, and looked at her. 'May I come in?' And she had stepped aside, saying nothing. He had blown out the lamp almost at once, and in the darkness she had allowed him to undress her, his touch uncertain, and he had kissed her, tentatively at first, and then with a growing desperation, turning her to the bed, as if determined to persuade them both that all was well between them.

But it was not enough! Words had become impossible, so her fears remained unexpressed, and her suspicions could never be voiced. But she *needed* words; she needed an explanation and to understand what had happened since they came there. Why things had gone so wrong. And she had lain awake beside him, dry-eyed, until almost dawn, then slept deeply, and woke to find him gone.

She stayed abed until mid-morning, staring up at the ceiling, her thoughts wildly adrift. For if Cameron came to Edinburgh… What then? She rose at last and went to the little turret from where she could see Theo and the factor heading down the drive together, and dressed quickly. Perhaps Cameron was alone in the study again, and she could speak to him, ask him what he intended to do. She went rapidly down the stairs, hearing him sliding the cabinet drawers in and out, then hesitated outside the door, digging her nails into her palms, struggling to find the words to express what she needed to say.

Cameron looked up as she entered, then straightened, his eyes guarded. 'Theo's been noticing your absences,' she said in a rush. 'Says no one can find you.'

He gave a slight smile and shrugged. 'No matter. I can't find a nest. And I haven't heard them again, so I think they've gone.'

'Have they?' She came slowly into the room, stopping to examine a small dunlin on a shelf. 'Prudent, perhaps.' Her finger smoothed the dry, faded feathers, her hand barely trembling. 'I understand Theo has asked you to come to Edinburgh?'

'Yes.'

'But he thinks you won't come'—she straightened and finished on a gasping laugh—'because you're courting.'

'*Courting!*' He stared at her, then turned abruptly away and went over to the window from where Theo and John Forbes could be seen talking to two men she recognised as tenants, gesturing at the wall. She studied his back as he stood there watching them, then he came and sat on the edge of the desk. 'Perceptive of him, don't you think?' he said, looking directly at her now. 'Only slightly wide of the mark.' The room was still and silent, and the sentinels grew watchful again, while the hammering in Beatrice's chest became a physical force. 'Hardly courtship—but I'll not come to Edinburgh. I'll stay here and help my father over the winter, then leave. Before you return.' His eyes held hers, knowing that she understood. 'My father might have misjudged what he saw the other day, but not by very much. In Edinburgh, it would happen.'

'Cameron—' She reached out a hand to him, but he shook his head, almost angrily.

'No. Say nothing. Though God knows—' He broke off as they heard the front door open, voices and footsteps crossing the hall. He straightened and stood, his face dark and strained as Theo entered, followed by John Forbes, who stood stock-still and stared.

'So, my dear,' said Theo, oblivious to the ricocheting of tensions. 'They'll start early next year, so you can have the fun of planning your conservatory over the winter.' He turned to Cameron, eyeing him coldly. 'And I gather you'll not be joining us in Edinburgh.'

'I'm grateful to you for the offer, sir.'

Theo considered him for a few moments, a muscle twitching in his cheek. 'No matter.' And as he turned away, Beatrice saw the pain behind his eyes.

～

Life became intolerable after that. Theo set a date for their departure, and Beatrice packed and repacked, discussed camphor and dust sheets with Mrs. Henderson, cut back brambles in the garden, and nurtured her rose. Anything to keep herself occupied.

The brief spell of late summer sunshine was gone, the skies were pewter grey, and the gales had started again, hostile and vindictive, whipping the shallow waters of the bay into angry wave-crests over which the gulls dipped and rose, their cries blown back by the gusts. There was little incentive to go out, but Beatrice was desperate to escape from the house and from her sense of impending loss, so she grabbed a shawl and went out onto the drive, battling the wind, determined to get at least as far as the ruined chapel, seeking the solace she had often found there. But the elements were relentless and she soon turned back, rain stinging her face.

As she approached the farm buildings, she heard raised voices coming from the old McLeod croft house where Theo's specimens were cleaned and prepared, and drew closer to stand beside the tiny window. It was Theo's voice she could hear, sharp with anger, and then Cameron's responding in kind, combative and impassioned.

'Cameron. You've said enough.' It was John Forbes. Thank goodness he was there.

But Cameron's voice came again, shaking with fury. 'It's just another bloody trophy.' The divers, she thought, he's found them! The factor spoke sharply again, but Cameron ignored him. 'How could you? When there are so few.'

'Rubbish. In Scandinavia they are—'

'But not *here*, where they belong. Maybe *you* have forgotten standing on the Bràigh years ago, watching them, but I haven't.'

The gulls fell silent as she strained to hear Theo's clipped response. 'I have not forgotten, Cameron. But it's of no concern of yours except to do as I ask.'

'What? Skin the wretched creature so that you can preserve it? What mad logic is that?'

'Be very careful—'

'Can you *never* see the harm you do? You disregard your tenants, you neglect your—'

'*Bi sàmhach!*' the factor thundered, and Beatrice put a hand to the wall to steady herself, her legs suddenly weak.

'It's a wicked waste. A crime.' Cameron's anger had carried him beyond restraint, but his next words stunned her. 'Maybe I'll bring a prosecution against you, Mr. Blake. I could, you know. For this.'

There was silence in the old croft house. Then Theo's awed tones: 'Do you *threaten* me, Cameron?' Beatrice closed her eyes.

'*Tha sin gu leòr!*' the factor commanded.

'Too late, John.' Beatrice felt sick, she knew that tone.

So did the factor, and he now took control. 'Enough. Cameron, go.' Beatrice shrank against the wall as she heard Theo protest, but John Forbes responded with authority. 'Tempers must cool, sir. *Go*, I said.'

Cameron flung out of the hut, not seeing Beatrice pressed against the wall, and she watched him charge up the slope, his jacket thrown over his shoulder, careless of the biting wind, his fury still upon him. Through the window she heard John Forbes's deliberately measured tones. 'I will deal with the bird, sir, and have it ready for you to take when you go. There will be no more talk of prosecutions, and Cameron will apologise.' The silence deepened as she awaited Theo's response.

'I don't give a *damn* for an apology.' A longer silence. 'I won't have it. He leaves the estate, John. This can't go on.'

Beatrice stopped breathing. Theo sounded so strange. There was another silence, then John Forbes spoke again. 'Whatever the rights and wrongs of the business, he should not have spoken as he did.' He paused, and it seemed for once that even the factor was at the limits of his abilities. 'But I ask you to wait, sir, and consider.'

'After all these years of—'

'Let me keep him here this winter,' the factor cut him off. 'You needn't see him again, and he'll be gone when you return.'

The wind that was blowing across the pasture seemed to hold back, as if awaiting Theo's verdict. 'Perhaps I owe you that much.' He spoke in a strange, tight voice, then his tone hardened. 'But that's it. I've done with him. No more.' His voiced faded as he moved away from the window. 'Come to the house later. Both of you.' And she drew back as he left, striding towards the house, his gait echoing that of Cameron's a few moments earlier, and then she heard John Forbes's boots on the cobbles heading for the stables.

Cautiously, she edged around to the door of the building and stooped to enter. On the table before her lay not the black-and-white diver as she had expected, but a great eagle, its mottled wings folded against its body, yellow talons curled above a fan of white tail feathers. Its eyes, closed as if in contempt, gave it a haughty, patrician air. A small bloodied disturbance just below the hooked beak was all there was to show where Theo's expert shot had found its mark. As she looked down at it, all the heartache of the summer rose like a sob in her, and she felt a sharp stab of fear, a deep foreboding. Of consequences unforeseen.

'*Iolairesuilnagreinel.*' A low voice spoke from the doorway, and she turned to see John Forbes standing in the entrance, a small saw and a knife in his hands. 'The eagle with the sunlit eye,' he said quietly and stepped forward. 'You heard the row. You were outside.' Statements, not questions, and she nodded. 'Harsh words, on both sides.' Deep, sad eyes looked at her from under his bushy eyebrows, and she found she could not meet them. 'But there must be no more damage.' His meaning was very clear, and she felt a sudden compulsion to confide in him.

'Mr. Forbes, whatever you think—' But he cut her off as sharply as he had done with Theo.

'Leave it. This runs deep.' He shook his head at her and held up the saw. 'What I'm about to do will not be pretty so I suggest you leave me, Mrs. Blake.' She moved towards the door, wondering where Cameron would have gone. 'Go back to the house, Mrs. Blake,' he said, as if reading her thoughts, and the command in his eyes was unmistakable.

Theo did not appear in the drawing room for afternoon tea. News of the row had spread through the house, and wary servants went silently about their tasks, avoiding her eye. Just before dinner, Theo came and joined her, taking up a journal to forestall her questions, and they sat in a tense silence until Mrs. Henderson tapped quietly on the door and announced that John Forbes and Cameron were in the kitchen. Theo shut the journal and got to his feet. 'Ask John to step into the study, if you will.

Cameron can wait in the morning room until I send for him.' He excused himself to Beatrice and withdrew, leaving the drawing room door ajar.

Without stopping to think, she slipped out of the room, hesitated a moment, and then went across the hall to the morning room. Cameron was standing with his back to her looking out of the window, but he spun round as she spoke his name.

'He can't send you away like this—'

He stepped towards her. 'Beatrice! Go back. You mustn't get involved.'

'It's your *home*. Let me speak to him.'

'God, no!'

'Then make it right, somehow. A dead bird isn't worth—'

'Was it only that, do you think?' he said with a bleak smile. 'But, go, Beatrice—' She made no move, she couldn't. 'You must—' Then he stepped forward abruptly and took her face in his hands. 'No?' He bent swiftly and kissed her, and as he pulled away she glimpsed his old unruly smile. 'Then at least I've that much of you if he sends me away.' His smile vanished as they heard John Forbes call him to the study, and he brushed her cheek with his fingers, then went across the hall.

She stood where he had left her, barely breathing, his touch still on her. *If he sends me away*— And go he would, for she had seen Theo's face.

A breaking point had been reached, and boundaries crossed. She lifted her fingers to touch her lips.

—And so where did that leave them, the three of them, the loving and the unloved?

Beyond the boundaries.

She came to her senses then and slipped back across to the drawing room just as she heard the study door open. Theo joined her almost immediately and headed straight to the side table, oblivious to her standing beside the window, and took up the decanter, spilling whisky on the polished surface.

He said nothing.

'Theo. Tell me what's happening.'

His eyes slid towards her, then he looked down into his glass and took a long drink. He went over to the fireplace, where he stood, staring into the fire. 'Cameron Forbes is on notice to leave the estate,' he said at last. She gripped the back of the chaise longue and waited for more. 'He would leave today were it not for the respect I have for… for John. But for that, he would be gone already.' He stopped again, and through her own blinding mist, she glimpsed his pain again. 'All summer he's been trying my patience, deliberately defying me.' He spoke almost as if to himself, then his eyes refocussed on Beatrice, and he scowled. 'Pushing at the limits of my tolerance. But today he went too far and threatened me with prosecution for shooting a blasted sea eagle.' He took another long drink, shaking his head like a wounded animal, and Beatrice watched him with a thudding heart.

'I'm *sure* he wouldn't have done so.'

'*So* sure?' She flinched as Theo looked up and searched her face. 'Well, he can go to the law or to the devil himself. I've done with him.' He stared out across the strand, to the place where she knew she could not reach him, and as he dropped his head, she saw the depths of hurt and rejection beneath his anger, and even as she wondered at it, she felt pity for him.

But his devils lay too deep for her.

As he stood looking down into the empty fireplace, lost in those dark reaches, she turned back to the window. Only a few short months ago, the soft clouds had seemed to draw her towards the island. But clouds cast shadows, she had learned that much— And as she watched, a gull flew slowly along the ridge in front of her, carrying the last of the sun's rays on its wings before it turned away from the house, dropped down to the darkening foreshore, and disappeared against the empty stretches of the strand.

Chapter 30

The entrance to Matt's gallery was brightly lit, and there was a red carpet laid at the threshold. Matt himself was hovering by the door, and he came forward with a smile when he saw her. 'Aha! The VIP. I was told to wait there and not budge 'til you came. No Giles?'

'He's at a client's drinks party, but he'll try and come later.' Actually, Giles had offered to cancel and come with her, but she had said no, and this was the compromise they had reached.

'Not to worry, it's you Jasper wants. And he's got a surprise for you.'

Matt had prospered since he had made the acquaintance of Jasper Banks, and when the eccentric patron had selected the gallery Matt worked for as the venue for a new exhibition, Matt's prestige, and salary, had shot up. His boss, the gallery owner, was now weak with gratitude and still reeling from the budget Banks had given her for the opening. Hetty saw her now in the corner, together with Jasper Banks and a clutch of smartly-dressed guests.

'Come on,' said Matt. 'I was told to take you straight over.'

Blake's letters, Matt had explained when he'd brought round the invitation a week ago, were not the only things that had been found during the sorting out of Farquarson's estate. They had uncovered a treasure trove of paintings: two lost Guthries; an unknown Nairn, painted at Brodick; and Hornel sketches which had long been thought destroyed. 'As you can imagine, it's giving Scottish art dealers a seismic attack of the vapours,' he had said, 'but Jasper's managed to persuade the family to exhibit them before they go on the market. Here first, then Edinburgh.

He says you *have* to come to the opening and won't take no for an answer.'

As Matt brought her over, Jasper Banks ruthlessly abandoned his companions. 'Haven't you got a drink?' he asked, and sent Matt scuttling away. He was dressed in trendy art-school black, which probably cost a fortune, and somehow managed to look like a student, although he must be fifty. This, of course, was the intention, and she smiled at him as Matt returned with two drinks on a tray.

'Has Matt spilled the beans?' he asked, his eyes whipping from one to the other.

'Not a word,' Matt assured him.

'Good man. So! Come on, then, and be amazed.' He put a hand under her elbow and led her to the far end of the gallery, where a dozen or so paintings had been hung slightly apart from the others, separated by well-positioned screens and sophisticated lighting. She recognised the two paintings he had bought at the auction. 'What do you think?'

'They look good.' She smiled. Was this the surprise?

'Now look at the others.' He was as smug as a Cheshire cat.

She turned to look more closely at the other paintings, strange abstract works. Then she saw one of a fallen cross. 'No. Surely… ?' Wordlessly, he pointed to the signature in the lower corner, shaky but unmistakable. She put her glass down and left him then, going slowly from one to the other, in disbelief. And as she did, she began to recognise the underlying scenes or themes— the house itself, the ruined chapel, seabirds in flight, shore waders with their long legs reflected in a tide pool. And yet, had it not been for the unmistakable signature in the corner of each, she would never have believed they were Blake's. Nothing could be further removed from his earlier works, from the romantic realism of *The Rock Pool*, or her own *Torrann Bay*. Some of the paintings were clearly related to the heavy disturbed images Banks had bought at the auction, but others were quite different. Free-flowing, fractured, or abstract in composition, more like the one he had begun of Beatrice that she had been unable to leave behind. In one, a vortex of ice-white swirls pulled the eye into its core, where the tone rapidly darkened into clouds corkscrewing around the centre where, in the still heart of the painting, there was a tiny image of the two houses. An ethereal sheen lit the factor's house, while Muirlan House loomed behind it, overbearing and dark.

Jasper Banks leant against the wall and watched her. 'From Farquarson's attic,' he said. 'In a portfolio, marked *Muirlan House auction*—'

'Oh!'

'—where they've been for decades. Not many are dated, but most seem to be late thirties or forties, just before he died. One or two are earlier. The old inventories suggest Farquarson sent someone to the house auction with instructions to buy anything he could. Sentimental reasons, probably, as he was old himself by then and died soon after. The ones I bought the other day set me on their trail—and so I went a-sleuthing.'

'It's incredible.'

'Yep. Look at this one.' He pulled her over to the painting of the shore waders. 'When you think of the precise, almost photographic paintings in the bird catalogue, and then look at this, pared down to basics…' The birds had been reduced to a pair of legs, doubled in length by their reflection with only a hint of body and beak, and yet this conveyed all that was needed. 'Or this…' A pair of seabirds in flight had become mere wisps, Blake's brushstrokes unerringly depicting wings which flew off into their own dimension, into a grey-white oblivion. Jasper's eyes were alive with excitement. 'These two are the earliest of them and show that he was developing a style which was so advanced, so innovative…' She bent closer to read the date: 1911. 'It's as if his talent had lain dormant and then went off in an entirely new direction, out on a limb, a complete break with what he'd done before. A *conscious* break.'

He signalled for his glass to be replenished and gestured to hers. 'Top up? I always thought there was an unfulfilled genius to the man, and these paintings prove it. There's only one other work I know of where this new style is hinted at—its conception, if you like. And it's much, much earlier. I'd hoped it might have been amongst them, but it wasn't.' He narrowed his eyes as he contemplated her over his glass. 'And that's where you come in.'

'Me?'

He reached behind one of the screens and drew out a folder from which he took a worn, dog-eared catalogue. *Exhibits in the Palace of Art. Scottish Exhibition of National History, Art and Industry. Kelvingrove Park. 3 May–4 November 1911.*

'Check out numbers 370 to 372.'

She took it, and it fell open at a marked page. Each entry had a small photographic reproduction beside it. Number 370 was, inevitably, *The Rock Pool. Loaned by A. Reed,* and it was with a stab of delight that she recognised her own painting, number 371, *Torrann Bay. Loaned by Major and Mrs. Rupert Ballantyre.* Only for a brief time had Emily been Mrs. Rupert Ballantyre, but Banks was pointing to the next entry, number 372: *Muirlan Strand. Private collection.*

It was a poor reproduction but good enough to show that the missing painting depicted a view across the strand, of low sun shafting through a veil of mist, and two faint figures walking close, but separately, across the sand. 'He refers to the painting in one of his letters as belonging to his wife, you might have noticed, and I think it's this one, and it's the most important thing he ever did. And to me, "private collection" means family.'

She wrenched her eyes away from the catalogue and shook her head. 'I'm sorry. I've never seen it before.'

'Any ideas?' James flittered into her head. She would have to ask him. 'It's important,' Jasper continued, *'because* it's so early. The date's too small to read but that's an eighteen not a nineteen. He was trying something new way back then, but he gives up, goes abroad, and then chugs on with his bird catalogue instead, denying his talent. Then maybe ten, fifteen years later, around 1911, he releases it in his last great burst of creativity, experimenting with light and abstract concepts, and the result is brilliant! But it takes him nowhere, and then there's a gap of what, two *decades*? And when he starts up again, in the twenties or thirties, his work is hard-edged and heavy, and by the forties he's lost it, gone certifiably weird, deconstructing everything around him into jagged fragments. But back in 1911, he was trying to put something together. He was inspired! But it was short-lived. Something happened, and whatever it was, it was catastrophic and it stopped him in his tracks.'

Chapter 31

≈ 1911, Beatrice ≈

Steam blew back down the station platform, enveloping Beatrice as she stood in her dark travelling clothes, waiting where Theo had left her. He had gone to find the guard, and now she saw him coming back towards her. 'It's this one, my dear,' he said, taking her arm. 'The mistake's on the ticket.' He hustled her into their compartment, tipping the porter as he closed the door behind them and the whistle blew. 'Alright?' he asked.

She nodded like a fairground automaton as the train pulled out of the station, then leant her head against the window, overcome with weariness again, watching as the grey city receded. 'Sure?' he asked a moment later. She gave him a tight smile, and he lifted his newspaper and was soon absorbed. As grey gave way to green, the train took up a regular rhythm, and she looked dully across at him, wondering if the chasm between them was now quite unbridgeable. For what if she answered him truthfully? That she felt entirely broken, not just in body, but also in spirit. What then?

When they had returned to the city six months ago, wedding preparations had been in full swing. She had tried to rouse herself to share in Emily's excitement but had struggled under an overwhelming melancholy.

Theo's antipathy towards his stepmother was palpable, and old Mrs. Blake treated Beatrice with a gracious condescension. 'Beatrice looks pale, Theodore. Why did you submit the poor girl to that outlandish place?' she said one night over dinner at her house.

'She tells me she's never been to Rome, or even Paris. Surely you won't go back up there next year? There's no company for her, other than the natives.'

'Savages,' agreed Kit, grinning across the table at her.

'Really, I—'

'Poor child. It's too cruel of you, Theo.'

He had remained coldly silent, and as they returned to Charlotte Street through the dark city, she had watched the wind spinning withered leaves on wet pavements, heartsick and silent, remembering how Cameron had described the swirling colours of the northern lights over the sea in winter.

As a rule, she had tried not to think of Cameron, keeping herself occupied by day, but waking or dreaming, he invaded her nights, giving rise to feelings of such *hopelessness*. And when the day came for Emily and Rupert to exchange their vows, she stood beside Theo in a packed St. Giles, feeling oddly detached from the celebrations, dizzy, and prey to a persistent headache.

The next morning she had rushed to the washbasin and retched, shaking uncontrollably, and then the dizziness had a reason, the volatility and the lethargy an explanation. Despondency was replaced by astonishment, for Theo's appearances in her bedroom had remained infrequent and his lovemaking perfunctory, but somehow from this distant coupling a child had been conceived.

Theo too had seemed taken aback but expressed himself delighted. Emily, returning a few days later from a honeymoon cut short by national concerns, went into raptures when she was told. 'So I've become a wife and an auntie all at the same time. So *very* grown-up.'

Theo had overheard and stopped in the doorway, giving her a wry smile. 'Grown-up? You'll always be a hoyden, Emily, while Beatrice will become a serene and lovely Madonna.' And she had dropped her eyes at his expression, flooded suddenly with hope, ashamed then of her wayward dreaming, and after that she had tried to focus on the baby. Theo's baby. Their salvation. And inch by inch in the passing weeks she had felt the breach between them begin to close.

And then they received Cameron's letter. It had arrived in February, following a spell of bitterly cold weather, and Beatrice had come downstairs, trailing her loose gown behind her and giving a great yawn; city life and her pregnancy seemed to drain her of energy. She had entered the morning room to find Theo standing quite still beside the table, a letter in his hand.

He had looked up as she entered. 'From Cameron Forbes,' he said, handing it to her, and he had gone to stand by the window, his hands clasped behind his back.

The letter told of an accident. The factor had fallen, breaking a leg, while working alone at the far side of the island and had not been found until morning. He had survived only by some miracle, but now pneumonia had him in its deadly grip. She skimmed rapidly through the pages, Cameron's closely-written words jumping before her eyes. Surely nothing could threaten the life of that formidable island man! *Dr. Johnson remains deeply concerned. We can only pray that the crisis comes soon and that he survives it.* Cameron went on to describe the steps he had taken regarding the estate, finishing on a constrained note. *You will, of course, have expected me to be preparing for my departure, but I beg you to permit me to delay until my father is out of danger, as I cannot leave my family so hard-pressed. Be assured, sir, that Donald and I will do everything necessary until I hear from you.* She had lowered the letter and looked across to where Theo still stood at the window, his back to her, his reactions hidden, and wondered what it had cost Cameron to beg.

The train jolted suddenly on an uneven stretch of track, bringing her back to the present, and Theo looked up. 'Comfortable, my dear?' He searched her face for a moment, then returned to his paper. If she told him how she felt, the profound emptiness, the despair which had replaced the hope, would he then confront the matter, talk about their loss, or would he slide away from her again? And even as she watched him, he lifted his head and looked out of the carriage window, his eyes distant, fixed on a dark place in the shadows of his own mind, oblivious to her needs. Huddled in her own grief, she no longer even tried to guess where that place might be.

~

A day later, after a rough sea crossing, she sat beside him in the trap as they started out across Muirlan Strand, as they had done a year ago almost to the day. But spring had not yet awoken the colours from the landscape, and shifting showers drenched the sky, while out at sea dark-fringed curtains of grey showed where heavier rain had yet to make landfall. She pulled her cape close against the cutting edge of the wind and wondered if there could be a greater contrast. Last year she had looked across at the island with eager anticipation, and Theo had smiled at her as he sprang onto the trap and taken her hand.

But even as she watched, a strong rainbow, like a flash of hope, arched briefly across the strand, vivid against the darkening clouds. And she remembered her last sight of Cameron all those months ago, as he walked away from Muirlan House across the sand, Bess at his heels. The dull ache of it had stayed with her all the way to Edinburgh.

There were figures on the drive as they approached, and she steeled herself for the encounter. But as they drew close, she saw it was only Donald and Mrs. Henderson who waited outside the front door, while two of the tenants stood at the gate to assist with the luggage.

'Welcome home, sir.' Donald stepped forward to take the reins. He seemed to have grown in stature and presence. 'We wondered if the weather would have held up the crossing.' Then Cameron appeared on the top of the steps, and she felt something twist inside her.

'We were not much delayed,' Theo replied. He had seen him too. 'How's your father, Donald?'

'Improving, sir, but weak. The fever comes and goes.'

Behind them, Cameron descended the steps, signalling to the

men to begin unloading the trunks, and Beatrice gripped the sides of the trap watching his approach. But his attention was fixed on Theo. 'Welcome home, sir.' He spoke in even tones, holding out his hand.

Theo hesitated for a moment, then grasped it, searching his face, agreeing to the truce. 'You and Donald have done well, keeping my house in order,' he said. 'I'm grateful.' Cameron gave a slight bow and, half turning, gave a quiet, impersonal greeting to Beatrice and offered a hand to help her down, and they all stood a moment in uneasy silence. Then Theo gestured to a ladder leaning against the front of the house. 'Trouble?'

'Fallen slates, sir. After the last storm.' Beatrice had seen a man on the roof above her bedroom as the trap pulled up the drive, but he must have slid down the other side, out of view. 'The roof's fixed, but we still need to repair the damage indoors.' He looked leaner and older. Sterner. And there was a careworn look to his countenance, lines on either side of his mouth that she did not remember, a groove between his brows.

Theo nodded again, and as they moved towards the front door, Cameron stood aside for Beatrice to pass, his eyes resting briefly on hers, but there was no message there, no comfort. Just a distant, shuttered look, like the one Theo gave her when he wanted to keep her at bay.

Chapter 32

Two days later, Theo sat at his desk, sharpening his pencils with a pocket knife. It had been easier to forgive Cameron than he had imagined, and the lad had risen to the occasion commendably, as if born to it. The blade slipped, nicking his finger, and he swore softly.

When Cameron had taken him to see John Forbes the first day back, Theo had been shocked by the factor's appearance. He seemed to have aged by a decade, his beard grown long and grey, and he had struggled to sit up when he saw who it was, but Theo laid a hand on his shoulder. 'No, John, rest easy,' and between them he and Cameron had eased the sick man back down onto the bleached pillows.

'You'll stay for a while?' he had asked as Cameron led him back down the farmhouse stairs.

'Of course.'

It had been a painful, distressing visit, the room too weighted by the past. Cameron would have been born in that bed, his siblings conceived there. And Màili—she must have died there. He stared out of the window, where a gull hung, motionless, over the drive. And what if *John* were to die? Ashamed, he pushed the thought aside and picked up the account books, studying them intently as Cameron appeared at the door in answer to his summons.

'Come in and sit down. I won't keep you long.' Cameron pulled out a chair opposite him and sat, saying nothing. Treading carefully, thought Theo, as he tapped one entry in the account books and frowned. 'Putting a roof back on an outbuilding doesn't constitute an *improvement*, you know. I'd as well penalise him for allowing the dilapidation than give him compensation.' A quick glance at the estate books last night had shown that little had gone amiss since John's accident, but it did no harm to re-establish authority.

'He's not asking for compensation, sir,' Cameron replied with studied calm. 'Just for lenience regarding the arrears.'

'Get something from him on account, and the arrears are to be reduced by quarter day.' Theo strove to keep his tone light, giving ground occasionally, remaining firm in other cases, and Cameron responded carefully, 'Yes, I hear you.' Theo cut short his explanation a moment later, 'But the matter cannot rest there. You must tell him so.' And they went on to discuss expenditure and predicted stock prices, slipping into the old understanding, the old camaraderie, and Theo felt the same pull, that strong familiar bond.

Then he picked up the rent books again and began running his finger down the columns, stopping halfway down the page. 'I see Aonghas MacPhail is falling into arrears.'

'He's a little behind, sir. No worse than—'

'Why would that be?' Theo interrupted. 'Is his brother's family still living off him?' Would Cameron explain what he had seen when he had ridden out earlier? He wondered—the washing spread on the rocks, blue smoke rising from the roof, a potato crop pushing through.

He watched Cameron hesitate. 'They're still here, sir.'

'Still sharing Aonghas's house?'

Another hesitation. 'No, sir.'

'No.' Theo let the silence deepen. 'I wondered if you'd see fit to tell me.' Cameron said nothing but looked vexed. 'I gave permission last year for the old ruin to be roofed for use as a byre. But either you or your father seems to have given Duncan MacPhail permission to move his family in.' He paused, one eyebrow raised. 'And I imagine that was you?'

Cameron's face took on a more mutinous look. 'I intended to discuss—'

'There's nothing to discuss. My position hasn't changed.'

'It was a hard winter, sir. One of the children grew sick again. It seemed better that they were not so crowded.' Theo heard him struggle to maintain an even tone. 'Duncan's been very useful around the estate. It was him on the roof when you arrived, fixing the slates.'

'Was it, by God!' Duncan MacPhail repairing the roof his grandfather had threatened to raze. Had the irony not struck him? 'He'd pay you rent for the house.'

'And so legitimise his claim? No, Cameron.'

There was a longer silence. 'Are you saying he must quit the house?' Cameron asked quietly. 'His wife is ill, sir. She too... She lost a baby last winter.'

So Cameron knew, did he? It had been given out that Beatrice had been unwell, thus delaying their return, but these things always got out. Theo pushed back his chair and went over to the window, seeing Beatrice asleep in one of the basket chairs, wrapped in a shawl like a spent child. Remorse still tormented him, but he found himself unable to reach out to her, knowing that she held him in part responsible. Perhaps he was, but a fury had gripped him that evening, as it had the day that Cameron had threatened him, and that moment's blindness had cost them dear.

He came back to the present, aware that Cameron was expecting a response. He had no stomach to continue fighting with him, but he would not have his hand forced. 'Tell Duncan he has the summer to find another place for his family, and some other means to support them. He can stay for the summer, until quarter day.'

At dinner that evening, he referred to the incident and Cameron's handling of it. 'A newly-thatched roof and a patch of potatoes. All with Cameron Forbes's blessing! After what happened last year, you'd think he'd exercise a little judgement.'

'Hadn't we intended to plant potatoes there ourselves?' Beatrice asked, reaching for the butter.

Theo looked up sharply. 'You know damned well it's the principle of the matter. I'd sooner help MacPhail take himself off to Canada, where he could make something of himself.'

'And yet last year you argued the opposite, in your bid to persuade Cameron to stay.'

Theo sat back and stared at her but recovered quickly. 'Cameron Forbes is not without prospects here. I saw to that when he was younger. And the offer I made him is still open, if he wants to change his mind.'

Beatrice's eyes fell to her plate, and she said no more.

Chapter 33

~ 1911, Beatrice ~

Beatrice went early to bed and lay there looking up at an ugly damp stain where rain had seeped through broken slates to find the crack in the ceiling. Already she felt the strain of the same shifting tensions which had blighted last summer— And how different this homecoming should have been! They would have brought their child back with them, a tiny emissary who might have brokered peace, and Cameron would have been long gone.

And they could have begun to rebuild.

But on a single, fatal decision to accompany Theo that night, she had hung all their futures. She had gone along only to please him, regretting it as soon as they entered the packed assembly rooms where Edinburgh's patrons and leaders had gathered for the annual Society dinner. There was a dreadful crush of people, all greeting each other, taking note of who had come and who had stayed away, and it had been unbearably hot.

Charles Farquarson had soon spotted them and guided them to his table with such exaggerated consideration that she wondered if perhaps Theo had dropped a hint of her condition. She had endured the meal with teeth gritted, playing with the rich, unwanted food, uncomfortable in her constricting clothes, responding with effort to the conversation around her.

Lectures followed dinner, and the last speaker's voice would be etched forever in her brain. '*Ladies and Gentlemen, you have your heads in the sand,*' he had begun. '*Why debate nomenclature when every year more species disappear from our shores...*' She had allowed her attention to wander, aching to be gone. '*... relentlessly poisoned, shot, or their nests destroyed by keepers at the command of landlords concerned only with their game birds and* *their sport.*' Around her she sensed rustling and discordant murmurings and began to pay attention. A red-haired young man was addressing them in the manner of a firebrand minister ranting over his errant flock. '*Even among our own members this slaughter continues, adding to collections which grace—or rather shame—their country houses.*' Mutterings grew louder, and she saw that Theo was eyeing him sourly. '*The osprey is now extinct here, and will soon be followed by the white-tailed sea eagle, whose survival hangs in the balance.*' Beatrice's head had begun to pound as the charged scene in the old croft house returned to her. '*Consider them doomed, gentlemen! Gone within the decade.*' And she heard John Forbes's deep, sad voice, and saw again the majestic corpse laid before her. The eagle with the sunlit eye— The next words were lost to her in a haze of despair, and she had felt again Cameron Forbes's swift kiss, the pressure of his hands on her shoulders. '*… lawless arrogance, even in the western islands, their last refuge.*' The speaker paused and looked over his audience. '*Only today I heard that one of the last, a male in the prime of its life, has just left the hands of an Edinburgh taxidermist.*' Theo stiffened as the speaker's gaze flickered towards them. '*But doubtless that crime too will go unpunished even as it tips the balance towards disaster.*' And then faintness threatened to overcome her.

Amidst a thin spattering of applause, Theo had helped her to her feet. 'Damnable. Outrageous!' he had muttered as he propelled her, stumbling, to the door, his face dark with fury. She was still dazed when they reached the three small steps which led to the main gallery, and she had stepped onto the first one, turning as someone called Theo's name.

It had happened so quickly, a heel caught in a hem, a stumble, and then that sickening sense of falling. Blackness, and then an all-consuming pain. Theo had carried her to the carriage, rushed her home, ordering the doctor to be sent for, blankets, a tonic, something, anything! But by the time the doctor arrived, there was nothing to be done.

She woke to birdsong next morning, but unrefreshed, having

lain awake much of the night. Somehow she must bestir herself. At least she should rise and go and assess the damage the winter gales had wrought on her infant garden. And so, after breakfast, she went out and stood looking in dismay at where the trelliswork of the bower had come away, and at the shrubs sheltering under the wall, which showed no signs of life at all, blighted by the elements. She lifted her hand to smooth her hair and then went back indoors, donned boots and an old drab coat, and returned with a hand fork. Perhaps here, at least, there was something she could mend.

Keeping busy, in fact, seemed to be her only option, and being outdoors was better than being inside the house, falling prey to despair. Since they had arrived back, Theo had maintained a chilly distance, never speaking of their loss nor venturing close. Was this how it would always be? She found a little clutch of buttery primroses nestling under the wall and took heart, but discovered that her yellow climbing rose had been reduced to a single wiry thread clinging to the wrecked trelliswork.

But still it felt good to be outdoors, the wind fresh on her cheeks, and gardening was better than walking, for she could not outpace her thoughts. She'd gone a few times to the ruined chapel and sat with her arms locked around bent knees, thinking of St. Ultan's tiny orphans and grieving for her lost child while watching the seals coming in on the tide. One of them, darker than the others, seemed always to be there, lying on the half-submerged reef, looking back at her as the tide rose around it.

She tugged ineffectually at the briar. In Edinburgh, Theo had been devastated by the loss of the child, apparently too distraught to wonder why she sat tight-lipped and silent, with tears unshed in his presence, not seeing that her grief was augmented by the corroding bitterness of blame. Perhaps blame was unwarranted, but if he had not brought down the eagle... *Lawless arrogance*, the young man had called it, echoing Cameron's fury and contempt. She straightened, brushed an arm across her eyes, and stared out beyond the boundary wall to where primroses and daisies were dotted amongst the bog cotton, and where nesting birds flew sentinels, guarding eggs from thieving gulls, then bent to her task again. Even a small display of regret, of remorse, or at least a recognition of shared sadness would be enough to begin the healing. But he neither sought her comfort, nor offered her his, and it was as if the whole tragic incident must be put aside, not spoken of. He passed the evenings reading or staring into the hearth, oblivious to the dark thoughts which consumed her, while the days he seemed to spend poring over estate books in the study. With Cameron.

She crouched down, coat-tails dragging in the soil, and examined the stem of the rose more closely and found that in fact there *were* tiny buds of green along its length. She straightened and began wrestling again with the broken trelliswork, disentangling it from the encroaching brambles, fired with a new determination. Then, from the corner of her eye, she saw Cameron standing at the study window, watching her. They both turned away. He was avoiding her, she knew he was— His shuttered expression conveyed a clear message to stay away, and yesterday, when she was out walking, Bess had appeared from nowhere, her tail thumping a greeting, only to disappear as rapidly in obedience to a sharp whistle from the adjacent field. She had turned just in time to see the top of Cameron's head disappear behind a rise in the land.

Then she heard the front door close and looked up to see that he was coming down the steps towards her. 'If you tell me what you want doing, madam, I'll see to it.' His eyes held her at a distance. 'It's too much for you, on your own.'

'The rose.' She gestured to the collapsed trellis and tangled briars. 'It's still alive.'

He crouched to examine it, then glanced up at her, and she glimpsed his old warm smile. 'Aye, it is. One moment.' And he disappeared, returning with tools and a bucket of stable straw, and rolled up his sleeves. She stood back as he cut away the remaining briars, digging in the straw, hammering the trelliswork back onto the upright posts, holding the nails between his teeth. He said nothing more, working with the same concentration and neatness she had seen him use to rig a boat or fillet a silver mackerel… and she felt a hard lump rise up in her throat. How absurd it was that she and her husband both loved this same young man.

'There, let's hope—' He broke off when he saw the twisted expression on her face. He stood, resting his elbow on the handle of his garden fork, and gave her a long, grave look. 'I'm very sorry, Mrs. Blake, about the babe,' he said at last.

'You know?'

'Servants' gossip, madam,' he said, with something of his old irony.

Slowly, carefully, she threaded the stem of the rose back through the trelliswork, not looking at him. 'Perhaps the spring will mark a change,' she said, when she found she could speak. Then: 'Does your father continue to improve?'

'Aye, but slowly.' Cameron glanced towards the factor's house. 'He's a strong man, but he's not young.'

Now that he was here beside her, she wanted him to stay. 'Tell me?'

He seemed to hesitate, then went and leant against the wall a little way from her. 'There's not much to tell,' he said, scraping the soil off his boot with a prong of the garden fork. 'We didn't think to look for him until after dark.' And he described how they had searched through the night using storm lanterns, their calls snatched away by the wind. A hopeless task, and by dawn they feared the worst. 'In the end Bess found him, a little south of the Bràigh, unconscious in one of the drainage dykes. Half in and half out of the icy water. Half dead.' His face grew strained as he told her about the weeks of uncertainty that followed, the night when they were sure he would die. 'If he had, and I'd been gone, I wouldn't have known, not for months.' The muscles in his face tightened. 'God knows what Donald and Ephie would have done.'

'My husband would have taken care of them.'

He gave her a crooked smile. 'Aye, he'd no quarrel with them.' He stamped the soil firm around the rose again before gathering up his tools. 'And, as you say, perhaps the spring will mark a change.' He gestured to the rose. 'You, at least, remain hopeful.' He gave her a slanting smile, then his eyes came suddenly alive. 'And you aren't the only one. The divers are back. Out on Oronsy Beagh.'

'The divers!' He nodded, watching her face. 'Are they nesting?'

'They're thinking about it.' He smiled into her eyes at last just as the drumming of hooves sounded on the track, and they turned to see Theo riding up the drive towards them. Cameron set aside his tools and went to take the reins.

Chapter 34

◇ 1911, Beatrice ◇

Spring brought the island fully to life, and the doctor declared John Forbes to be out of danger although not fit yet to leave his bed. Ephie Forbes's footfall was lighter as she went about her work, and Beatrice heard Donald whistling as he passed in front of her window, and the darkness of foreboding seemed to lift from the house.

Between Theo and Cameron, the management of the estate continued without evidence of further discord. In unspoken defiance of Theo, Beatrice resumed the philanthropic work she had begun the year before and sent food to those tenants in need after the hard winter, and extra things for Duncan MacPhail's family. She ordered books for one of the older boys who was keen to pursue his studies and gave sewing materials to the girls, instructing Mrs. Henderson to send household linen to Eilidh MacPhail for repair. The woman had learned to do neat work in Glasgow, and Beatrice paid her generously. If Theo knew of these activities, he made no remark. And she doubted that he noticed, for he was painting again— He had not spoken of it, keeping this, like everything else, clutched close to himself. She knew of this renewed activity only because she saw him leave the house early, sometimes mounted, often on foot, with his bag and easel slung over his shoulder, and his paints were spread about in the study. And he became even more distant, distracted, barely speaking when they were alone, and yet she sensed in him a suppressed excitement, a new zeal. How fine it must be, she thought as she watched him go, to be able to lose oneself in that way, to become absorbed in some private world and so escape. With no thought to those left on the outside.

She saw little of Cameron either, except once when she was emerging from the repaired croft house after visiting Eilidh, when she came across him on the track locked in animated discussion with the MacPhail brothers. Aonghas pulled off his cap, greeting her respectfully, but Duncan had stood his ground, scowling until Cameron spoke curtly to him, and then he too had bared his head. 'A fine morning, Mrs. Blake,' Cameron had said, glancing towards Eilidh, who stood at the doorway clutching the basket Beatrice had brought, and she read approval in his eyes.

But this spell of calm was not to last.

Next day a letter came from George Sanders with an invitation to come and stay with him for the opening of the Exhibition in Glasgow. Theo brought it across to the morning room, his face animated for once.

'It's to be a grand affair. You'll enjoy it, my dear. The Duke and Duchess of Connaught will be there to open it. And there's nothing to stop us going now, so I'll write straight back and accept. You know this letter's taken over a week to reach us!' He dropped into one of the chairs by the fire, skimming the pages again.

Nothing to stop us going now. The words stung, and the proposal horrified her. 'But we'd agreed to attend the closing ceremonies in October.'

'Cameron will see to matters here; the responsibility has done him good. And John's well enough to advise if necessary.' He continued reading the letter, quite unaware. 'And it's time I showed my face to the world again.'

'But we've only just arrived.' She lifted a hand to her head. A stifling city full of people!

He looked up at her tone and smiled encouragingly. 'We can make the journey in easy stages, my dear, and you can rest in the Sanders house when we get there.'

'But I'm just starting to feel well again. I want to stay here.' She swallowed to stop her voice from cracking. 'You go, Theo. I feel sure that George Sanders doesn't want to see me any more than I do him.'

He looked at her in astonishment. 'For goodness' sake, Beatrice, just because you were upset over some damned otter.'

'Can't you just tell him that I'm unwell? It needn't stop *you* going.'

'And I'm to say I left you here alone? Unwell?' He scowled at her and then rose and went to the fireplace, staring for a while into the empty hearth before turning back to her. 'Life goes on, Beatrice,' he said at last.

Would they now speak of it? Was this their chance, and would he respond if she reached out to him? 'It does, Theo, but perhaps we need—'

'This'll take you out of yourself.'

'We need time together, quietly, to come to terms with—' She broke off, discouraged by his expression. 'I prefer to be here.'

'And play the invalid?'

'*Play!*' she gasped. He might as well have struck her.

He dropped into the chair and tried a more conciliatory tone. 'You were well enough to make the journey up here, my dear, and since then you've had nothing to do. You look so much better.'

'Because I'm *here*. Where I can please myself.'

'And now I'm asking you to please me,' he said. And then added, 'Is that unreasonable, do you think? On this occasion?'

'Theo, you make no effort to understand.'

He gave her a long, hooded look, and his tone hardened. 'The child was mine too, or have you forgotten that?' Then he threw back his head against the chair and closed his eyes. 'Learn *acceptance*, Beatrice,' he said heavily. '*Try* a little. You've done nothing since we got back but begin again your fey wandering. It's unhealthy, brooding like this.'

'Can you not see—?'

But he shook his head, refusing to listen. 'It's self-indulgent, Beatrice.'

'To want a little peace?'

He made a dismissive sound and got to his feet. 'You need to be amongst people, Beatrice. And so do I. There's no stimulation here, no discourse, and this mawkish clinging to what is lost is no good, you know, no good at all. Believe me.'

'Theo—'

'I begin to think we should leave altogether once John is up and about. So we *will* go to Glasgow, my dear, because a change will do us both good. I will write tonight and accept.' He left the room abruptly. A few moments later she heard the front door bang, and from the window she watched him walking rapidly down to the foreshore, his painting bag over his shoulder, and she knew he would now be gone for hours.

She sat back, defeated by the row, and stretched out the toe of her shoe to cover the place where a rogue spark had landed on the hearth rug, leaving a blackened hole. So that was it, was it? She must bend to his will. In Glasgow she would be on show, touring the exhibition halls on his arm, the envy of other women whose husbands were less lauded, less rich. And she would nod and smile, suffering Sanders's advances, playing the role in a world from which last year Theo too had sought escape. He had come to the island to rediscover inspiration, but it was she who had fallen under its spell.

And now he spoke of leaving.

She heard a sound and looked up to see Cameron standing just inside the doorway. He was looking across the room at her, his face rigid. 'You heard us?' He must have been working in the study and they had forgotten. 'You should not have done.' The expression in his eyes alarmed her, and he took a step forward, but she turned her head. 'Cameron, it's no concern of yours. Go. Please, just go.' And when she looked back, he was gone.

Next day, just before lunch, she passed the study door and saw that Theo was on the library ladder, replacing a book. 'I understand you've enlisted the support of Dr. Johnson,' his voice followed her.

She halted and then took a step back. She had spent the

morning stretched out on her bed, watching the weak sun making patterns on her crumpled bedclothes, and had been on the point of getting up when one of the girls had come to tell her that Dr. Johnson was below, asking to see her.

Theo looked across at her, awaiting a response. 'I only told him what I told you,' she replied. 'That I wish to stay here and get well.'

She had found herself confiding her misgivings to Dr. Johnson, an elderly, kindly man, and he had listened sympathetically, then agreed that rest and calm were what was needed. 'I will talk to your husband,' he had said, snapping the buckle of his bag into place. 'Cameron Forbes said you were looking poorly when I visited his father just now. I'm glad he mentioned it.'

'You seem to have convinced him of your frailty.' Theo's expression was chilling as he descended the ladder. 'But then, he hasn't seen you traipsing all over the island.'

She clasped her wrist behind her back and lifted her chin. 'He said fresh air and exercise will do me good. I will get neither in Glasgow.'

Theo made a derisive sound and went over to his desk, where he took up another letter and handed it to her. 'You need not have troubled yourself. This arrived this morning.' She skimmed the pages quickly. It too was from George Sanders, and he now wrote of unrest in Glasgow following the dismissal of striking workers. *By all means come, my dear fellow, but I thought I should warn you. They are advising people to keep off the streets and there's a feeling that anything might happen. What is the country coming to!* 'But for this letter, I would insist that you join me.' Theo's face remained forbidding. 'As it is, you shall remain here and have your rest and your quiet. Dr. Johnson will visit you regularly, so stay close to the house. And when I get back, we will close up the house again and spend the rest of the summer in Europe.'

Chapter 35

≈ 2010, Hetty ≈

Hetty sat on the floor of her sitting room with Blake's letters spread about her and nursed a cup of coffee. So that was it. She had read and reread them, and there wasn't another drop to be squeezed from them. But what had she really learned? She picked up the handful of early ones, written in the critical years of 1910 and 1911, and thumbed through them. Some useful insights gained but few concrete facts, and there had followed a long gap of almost two decades before the next ones. And there had been no further mention of Beatrice.

Jasper Banks had come round earlier that afternoon, keen to see her painting of Torrann Bay, and had stood in front of it for a long time. 'So much talent in one so young, and he'd the world at his feet then, you know.' He went over to the picture of the deconstructed Beatrice, then turned back, looking speculatively at her, and said, 'There was a desperate look in your eye that day at the auction, which is why I let that one go. I recognise obsession when I see it. Now, about these bones—'

Matt, it transpired, had told him the essentials. And she found herself explaining not only the bones but also the conflict over the land, her dilemma regarding the hotel, and her concerns about the island itself. 'I was looking to start afresh, you see, to build on my family's connection with the island, but I've been told the house is past saving and that the hotel scheme would not be welcome, even if I could get the money together. The last thing I want is to get into conflict with the people there.'

'And be cast as a despoiler!' He smiled, then shook his head. 'You know, I've never been up there, and I can't think why not. But your project sounds interesting, and I'd like to hear more.'

Then his phone had gone off and he'd glanced at it. 'Must go. But let's talk again.' She'd felt a flicker of apprehension as he left, thinking that another heavyweight putting his oar in was the last thing she needed. 'And keep asking about that other painting, won't you? We've got to track it down.'

So she had felt honour-bound to send an email to Ruairidh asking if he knew anything about it, and took the opportunity to fill him in with what she had gleaned from the letters. It also gave her an excuse to tell him that a second survey of the house had now been commissioned, and after a moment's hesitation she copied the email to James. It was cowardly not to phone, of course, but the situation was so awkward.

She took her empty cup through to the kitchen. Head versus heart. Was it actually as simple as that? But for the dispute over land ownership, surely some compromise could be reached. A more modest project, perhaps, which balanced everyone's needs and allowed her to realise something of her own dream. Maybe it *would* be worth talking further to Jasper Banks.

She made another cup of coffee and took it back to the sitting room, and checked her emails. No reply from Ruairidh, who was probably at work, but as she sat there, James's response crashed into her inbox. *I don't know about a lost painting, but I do know about the survey. I almost threw them off the island yesterday, very indignant they were. I don't know what you expect them to tell you that's different—you have the facts already. Trust me on this. You have the choice of pulling the place down or shackling yourself to the Dalbeattie and Dawson bandwagon and accepting the consequences. Do you really want that great morgue of a place hanging around your neck? I could build you a fabulous cottage on the site. Go the other route and you'll be in for a whole heap of trouble. I needn't elaborate, you're an intelligent woman, just trust your instincts, but don't take too long about it.*

That's all I'm going to say. Must go. But it's make-your-mind-up time, and I haven't quite given up on you yet.

Given up on her! Indignantly, she clicked the reply button,

then hesitated, her fingers poised over the keyboard. Emails could be dangerous, dashed off in haste and then regretted. She took a breath before typing, more calmly. *It's good of you to keep an eye on the place, but you must see that I have to wait for their report before I can decide. This is a big decision, and I've got to get it right.* She reread it and, satisfied that it struck the right tone, pressed send. The response was swift.

You will.

Indignation evaporated, and she indulged a moment in the thought of having a cottage there, with that incomparable view across the strand. A place of refuge, with none of the hassle.

The thought sustained her through the day and grew on her as she clung to the overhead strap in the underground, and as she stopped to pick up some groceries from the corner shop and walked home. There would be time there for all those things, she promised herself—walks, reading, photography, time to think, and she could still work from home.

But she couldn't see Giles there.

As she unpacked her bag, she heard his key in the front door and looked up in enquiry. Had he said he was coming round? She must have forgotten.

'I was in the area,' he explained, and put a bottle of wine on the counter. 'Thought I'd drop by.'

Something in his tone rang false. 'Great. Are we celebrating?'

'In a manner of speaking.' He pulled the cork. 'Let it breathe for a bit.'

She waited for more. 'Are you staying to eat?'

Then the phone rang, and it was Emma Dawson. 'We wanted you to know immediately,' she said, 'but your Mr. Cameron is trouble.' Hetty sat down. 'We don't know *exactly* what he's planning—' Hetty listened with a growing disbelief. In telling her story, Emma managed to combine professional concern with good old-fashioned spite, and when she had finished, Hetty put the phone down and sat staring at the table. Giles was watching her from the kitchen door, and she now knew why he had come round, clutching the bottle of wine: he'd already been told. She kept her eyes fixed on the table, because lifting them would mean encountering his inevitable smugness. 'I can help you with the figures, darling, but I'm not a property guru,' he had told her when he had first pressed her to engage Dalbeattie and Dawson. 'So take them on. Property development is a shark-infested business.'

And it appeared that Emma had unmasked a great white.

She picked up a pen and spun it compulsively on the table, rerunning the telephone conversation in her mind. 'He and a man called Andrew Haggerty, who styled himself principal development officer, had a scheme to restore Muirlan House three years ago, before you came on the scene.' Hetty said she knew. James had told her. 'But now he's up to something else.' Emma insisted; she had a mole in the planning office. 'But he's not working with Haggerty this time but with a woman, Agnes McNeil, and six months ago they were enquiring about restoring the farmhouse and outbuildings for public and commercial use. It's only an initial enquiry, but it must be for a hotel, what else? And so *that* explains why he was so keen to condemn Muirlan House. Sabotaging the competition! Don't you see? And apparently he's got some very big backers behind him. American money.' Emma had paused to draw breath. 'There was *something* about James Cameron.'

Hetty had begun to think so too.

But this news stunned her, beggaring belief, and she sat there as her daydreams crumbled to dust around her. *Could* it be true? She could still feel the imprint of the keys he had pressed into her palm and see the warm approval in his eyes, and just now that two-word vote of confidence in response to her email. Had she so *completely* misread him? And what about Ruairidh? He, surely, was genuine, the embodiment of integrity, but if the farmhouse was his grandfather's and James was planning to develop it, then he must be involved too. She felt quite gutted by the thought.

Giles strolled over, carrying two glasses. 'I know, don't tell me. Andrew rang me at work this morning.' Of course he had. 'But what a facer, eh? Cameron's a cool operator, I'll give him that.' He handed her a glass and sat down opposite, leaning back in the chair, watching her. 'Although he seems to have rather overplayed his hand—'

'I don't believe it.'

'No? Well, rumour has it that he's shipped out. Uncontactable. Ask Emma. She's been trying all afternoon. And your policeman friend's gone on holiday with his family somewhere.'

'James emailed me this morning.'

Giles sat forward. 'He *did*? What did he want?'

'Just the roof fall. And other stuff.'

'Pressuring you to decide?'

Yes, pressuring her to decide. 'But he *encouraged* me to get a second opinion.'

'Like I said, he's a sharp operator. But look, sweetheart, it doesn't matter.' He leant forward, cupping his glass between two hands, demanding eye contact. 'His ship has sunk before it sailed, holed below the water line. Andrew's had confirmation that the factor's house, and associated land, *does* still belong to the estate. To *you*.' She looked dully back at him. 'The Forbes family have been tenants for generations and, as such, will have rights, even though no rents have been collected for decades. But in the eyes of the law, the house, the farm, and all the contested land belong to the estate. That's what I came to tell you.' He raised his glass in a toast. 'So Cameron's high and dry, my dear. Game, set, and match.'

She stared back at him. 'But he said there *was* documentation.'

'He also *said* that land to the west was croft land still worked by some old geezer, but as the last record of a tenant there was 1956, with an address in Toronto, he can only be a squatter. Some local derelict, I expect.'

The wine suddenly tasted sour. She put down her glass and went over to the window. Darkness was falling, and she watched the daily trudge back from work pick up momentum. Grey figures shuffling along the grey pavements back to grey homes. That neatly kept croft belonged to no derelict.

And who, in all this, was Agnes McNeil?

~

She tried to phone James and left a message, and two days later she had still failed to get any response. Emma Dawson was right, he'd vanished. She had phoned repeatedly and always got the answerphone, and emails went unanswered. Ruairidh was not replying either, presumably still away. She made one last attempt to reach James from her mobile before leaving a client's office at the end of the working day, then snapped it off, declining the invitation to leave yet another message.

You know where to find me, he had said.

And then, as she stood in the office lobby, she remembered. What a fool! There was no signal at his cottage, and his last email had been sent from his phone, so he could be away too. She rang the mobile number from which it had been sent, but this too went to answerphone, so she typed a rapid text demanding that he ring her. He'd switch it back on sooner or later, and then he'd have to respond; for God's sake, he couldn't hide forever.

She stepped out into the street, dodging the traffic and ignoring an irate taxi driver's horn, and crossed to the bar where she was meeting Giles. He'd become supercharged since this new development, an almost unstoppable force, and so far she'd felt too shaken to rein him in. 'Look, forget it,' he said repeatedly. 'It doesn't matter. They haven't got a leg to stand on and Emma and Andrew are coming up with a range of very promising opportunities. There's a company interested in a franchise for the shoot, and the trout fishing, as well as some eccentric banker who's keen to develop the golf course. He's offered to buy you out completely...' He had paused, letting the last suggestion sink in, then continued hastily at her expression. 'There might be European funding to be had for a wind turbine, you know, out of sight of the house, of course, but the demand for power would be high. Now that it seems we can restore *both* houses, the opportunities are endless. Those old stables would make a wonderful spa.'

We…

She saw him as she entered the pub, buying drinks at the bar. 'More news!' he said, as she joined him. 'Got caught at the last minute, by Andrew.' He raised a hand at her expression. 'Don't bite my head off, he tried to get you first. But look, I can't stay long, I've got to meet a client. Let's grab a seat.' He led her to a table in the corner, then broke his news. 'Andrew's discovered who your tenant is. A John MacPhail.'

'Yes, James Cameron told us.'

'Ah, but what he didn't say was that John MacPhail is Mr. MCP Software Inc., did he? Worth millions. One of the biggest software companies in Canada. And *he* was James Cameron's backer for his previous scheme. He's been over recently, quite a regular, it seems.' And she remembered the craggy-faced, soft-spoken North American, the exchange of looks with James in the café, the narrowing of eyes, and her heart sank.

She had been played for a fool. 'So all that time—'

'Look, it doesn't matter. But if *he* could interest MacPhail, so can we! Don't you see? And you've got Jasper Banks, with his millions, eating out of your hand. And one big investor attracts others, you know they hunt in packs, and Jasper Banks could be a great advocate. With him on board, we can put together something more convincing than some half-baked local scheme.'

'Wait—'

'Andrew wants to contact MacPhail and sound him out—'

'No.'

'Whyever not?'

'Because I've met him.' She heard again that great joyful laugh as the man steered the wild-child duckling back to the flock, and saw the carefully restored croft house with its neat potato patch. There could be little doubt where his sentiments would lie.

Giles stared at her. 'You *did*? How? When?'

'When I was up there. And he's on James's side.' She picked up a cardboard coaster and began bending it in two, her brain whirring.

'Then get Andrew to talk to Banks instead—'

She ignored him. 'I'm going back.' The coaster snapped along the crease. 'It's the only way. Úna'll have to be back for school, so Ruairidh'll be home soon, and I'll just sit on James Cameron's doorstep. He can't stay away forever.'

'You're not going on your own—'

'Yes, I am.'

'I could try and rearrange my appointments.'

'No, really, don't—'

'Then get some backup from Emma and Andrew, at least.'

'I will if I need to, but I'd rather deal with it on my own.'

He gave her an exasperated look, then reached back to pick up his jacket, ushering her out of the bar, hailing a passing taxi. 'Don't just leave like you did last time, with no warning,' he said as she got in. 'Let me know—'

The taxi left him standing there and sped through the puddles, sending up an arc of spray, and for a moment she was transported back to that first evening when she had seen James's Land Rover racing the tide across the strand. That first evening, when it had all seemed so easy.

Chapter 36

~ 1911, Beatrice ~

There was a light morning mist on the foreshore on the day that Theo left, and the tide was well in. Cameron and Donald loaded his travelling trunk into the boat, and Theo paused on the sand to look back at Beatrice where she stood with her shawl clasped around her, shivering in the damp air. 'Go indoors, Beatrice, the mist is chilling.'

'I will, in a moment. Safe journey, Theo.'

He nodded briefly before stepping aboard. 'I'll send word when to expect me back.' She saw a look, almost of grief, cross his face and felt an instant of remorse.

And she knew then that this separation would mark a watershed, that things could never be the same again, and she moved forward, uncertain, as if to halt the moment and go back. Too late—Theo lifted his head and bid her a curt farewell as Donald took up the oars and Cameron pushed the boat out into deeper water and then stood back. Cameron walked past her as she watched it pull away, waiting to see if Theo would look back and wave, and when he did not, she walked slowly back up the track.

Cameron was leaning against the boundary wall shredding the leaves from one of the yellow iris buds, watching her as she approached. 'I believe I have you to thank for my reprieve,' she said as she reached him. 'You, and the Glasgow trade unionists.' He gave her a questioning look. 'You dropped a hint to Dr. Johnson that I was unwell.'

'I did,' he said, his attention on the iris. 'But the trade unionists?'

'It seems they threaten riot and disorder, and so it was safer if my husband went alone.'

He gave a short laugh. 'God bless the working classes,' he said, then looked shrewdly at her. 'But your reprieve came at a price, I think.'

The torn iris lay at her feet. 'He thinks I'm half-crazed by the loss of the baby.' She looked back at the departing boat. 'Perhaps I am.'

Cameron contemplated her a moment longer, then straightened, tossing the remains of the iris over the wall. 'He impressed on me that I should not disturb you, madam, and left me a good long list of tasks. So, if you'll excuse me, I'll be about my work.' He too glanced at the boat now midway across the strand, gave her a curt nod, and strolled off up the track.

～

The breeze blew fitfully as Beatrice mounted the top of the dunes next day, and she looked down on the white sands stretched out before her. It was deserted but for seabirds balancing on the wind. The sun had woken her early, and she had seen it glinting on the waters of the bay and felt an echo of last year's joy. She had pulled out an old dress and grabbed a shawl, swallowed some breakfast to satisfy Mrs. Henderson, and set off. There was only one place she wanted to be today—Torrann Bay, with its limitless horizons and the pounding surf.

She stood now on top of the dunes, at the place where Theo told her he had set up his easel, on the one occasion they came here together. And he should be here now, she thought in despair, where the cries of the gulls were blown back from the waves, not miles away, displaying the place's likeness in a crowded exhibition hall.

How had they so comprehensively failed each other?

Dropping down to the beach, she disturbed the shore waders, which rose in a cloud as they had done a year ago, when she had come here with Cameron, when they had seen the divers offshore, exploring the coastline seeking mates and congenial nesting places. Cameron Forbes had been entangled in that failure from the beginning, absorbing Theo's attention and taking it away from her—and then, as last summer progressed, he had begun absorbing her own. She stooped to take off her stockings and shoes, and walked along the edge of the tide, gasping as the icy water covered her feet, and let the wild sounds and the emptiness wash over her.

Eventually she tired and turned back, picking her way slowly up the beach across the high-water mark of seaweed and driftwood. From somewhere a rank odour assailed her, and she stopped, looking about for the source, to find it lay almost at her feet, and she recoiled, stepping quickly back. An empty eye socket stared back at her, lips fallen away from bared teeth, a face half covered by the dried-out tangle of seaweed. It was a seal, a young one, its glossy pelt matted with sand and reduced to the texture of old felt. The creature had been dead for some time, its ribs visible under decayed flesh. Boring insects had left tiny holes in the taut skin, and the eye had been picked clean. A doomed selkie, she thought, looking down at it, or a selkie's child stranded between two elements. Another child lost.

She walked rapidly away from the unsettling stench and climbed into the dunes to find a sheltered hollow, away from the wind. After a while she dozed, her legs tucked up under her, lulled by the breeze rattling softly through the marram grasses, the sand warm beneath her. But her half-dreaming mind took her back to the dark days in Edinburgh, to where she had forged a connection between Theo's shooting of the sea eagle and the disasters which had followed. *Doubtless that crime will go unpunished...* the man had predicted, but in her dream the words were spoken by Cameron... *even as it tips the balance towards disaster.* And disaster had struck, taking their child, their hope—and in her dreaming despair she reached out to Cameron for consolation. He gave an odd shout and came to her, drawing close, his breath warm on her face.

She woke abruptly, her mouth dry and her head throbbing,

to look into the limpid eyes of Bess as she nuzzled close, blowing into her face, before barking again. Groggy and disorientated, she was trying to pull herself together when Cameron appeared on the top of the dunes, silhouetted against the sky, his jacket blown open by the breeze.

He stood there looking down at her. 'I thought I might find you here,' he said at last, 'when you weren't at the old chapel.'

She squinted up at him, still caught in her dreaming world, still reaching out to him. Wanting him. 'You came looking for me?'

'Mrs. Henderson sent me to find you.' His tone was brusque. 'She was anxious.'

'She had no need to be.'

'Mr. Blake had told her you'd be staying close to the house.'

She straightened her legs, stiff from her cramped position, and pushed her hair from her face. 'House arrest, in fact,' she said, running her tongue over dried lips.

He came down a few steps from the top of the dunes, his face still in shadow. 'This was a long way for you to walk, more than you should have attempted.' She looked up at him again, the wanting becoming a need, but he refused to meet her eyes. 'Let me take you home. The trap's at the edge of the fields.'

She gazed out across the bay, saying nothing while he stood watching her. 'Sit with me a moment?' she asked softly, feeling the need in her growing, but he did not move. 'Please, Cameron.'

He came only a little closer and sat on one of the grassy hummocks, resting his elbows on bent knees, gazing out to sea. 'Put your hat on, Mrs. Blake. Your face is fiery from the sun.' His tone held her at a distance.

She made a sound somewhere between a laugh and a sob as she reached for her hat. 'Are you still looking after me, Cameron?' Her need became a pain, but he said nothing, and they sat in silence. 'I was remembering the day you brought me here to see the divers,' she said at last. 'I thought I'd never seen a place more beautiful.' Still he said nothing. 'And now there's a seal pup down there, rotting away in the seaweed. Stinking of death—' Her voice shook, and the shoreline became blurred and indistinct.

'Let me take you home, Mrs. Blake.'

She wet her lips again, dragging her fingers through her hair. 'And I was remembering the day at the seal island, when you damned us all to hell, pulled the edifice down around us.'

The wind blew his hair across his eyes. 'I damned the edifice, not you,' he said. 'It was you, I recall, who was for anarchy.'

'No. You damned *us*. Your sort, you called us. Self-indulgent despots. Living a fantasy.'

He made no reply, then stretched out his legs and reached a hand to fondle Bess's ears. 'That whole day was a fantasy,' he said at last. 'A silly pretence of equality.' Bess arched her neck, revelling in the attention. 'And from that moment, I dropped my guard and let myself think you were someone I could be in love with.' Beatrice's heart lurched and she turned to him, to find his eyes focussed on the horizon. 'But you aren't, are you, Beatrice? You're someone else's wife. The man who rules here, my one-time patron.' Patron? She watched him closely as he pulled at a handful of dune grasses, letting it score through his hand. 'So all I can do is watch him finish what he began last summer. Destroying you.' He turned his palm over and examined the thin red cuts, the tiny beads of blood, before wiping them away on his knee, and looked directly at her at last. 'And so you must take note of what your husband tells you. Pull yourself together, madam. Learn acceptance.' He hurled a stick out to sea, and Bess sat up, uncertain. The gesture was friendly but the tone was not. 'It's not a bad situation, after all. You'll want for very little.'

She looked back at him. 'And that must be enough?'

His eyes narrowed as he followed a string of gannets gliding down to the surface of the sea before disappearing against the waves. 'Most people settle for much less.'

'But I want more.'

'I know.' The two words fell into the space between them and, like pebbles dropped into a rock pool, their ripples disturbed the surface of calm.

She watched the gannets rise up again amidst the spray blown back from the waves. *But I want more*. The silence lengthened until she spoke again, taking her courage in her hands. 'Both Theo and I have, in our different ways, disappointed each other.' She became transfixed by the sharp angles of the sunlight where they struck the waves far out to sea. 'I don't understand why.' She caught at her blowing hair, the uncertain breeze of the morning now a strengthening force. 'Except—except that I believe it's you he wants, not me.' Cameron looked up.

'Such a tangle.' She felt faint again, the thrumming in her head growing louder. 'I had thought that this summer we might repair the damage. There was to be a child, and you... *you* would not be here. For either of us.' She paused again. 'You see, he cannot love me because of you.'

He stared at her.

Clouds of dry sand spiralled along the beach towards them, and the grains stung her face, blinding her. 'It's absurd, of course. We *both* want you, and while you reject him, he rejects me.'

He slid quickly down the side of the dune and was there, beside her, his hands on her shoulders. 'You *can't* believe that.' And he took her head between his hands as he had done before. 'You *can't*—'

'But it's true.'

'No!' He pressed her back against the grassy hummock, holding her close, and she felt the strength of him. There was salt on his lips as his mouth sought hers, and her fingers found sand matted in the texture of his hair as she raised her hands to him.

Then Bess lifted her head, her ears flattened back by the wind, and gave a sharp bark. Cameron looked up. They heard a shout, and he rose, cautious now, and looked out towards the edge of the fields. 'Donald,' he said, 'probably sent on the same mission,' and he stood, raising a hand to signal. 'He'll have seen the trap.'

By the time Donald reached them, Beatrice had put her hat back on, pulling it low across her eyes, and Cameron had moved away. 'Mrs. Blake fell asleep and has a touch of the sun. Bess found her.' He spoke quickly, then turned back to her. 'Are you alright to go now, madam?' She nodded dumbly, and he offered his hand, crushing her fingers briefly as he helped her to her feet, avoiding his brother's eyes. 'Take Mrs. Blake home, Donald, but stop by the spring first; some water will help. Drink plenty, madam.' Then, to Donald, 'I'll go back by the Bràigh and check on the calves.' He gave them a quick, distracted nod and made off down the dunes.

~

Beatrice slept better that night than she had since she lost the baby. She slept long and deep, and her dreams took her to sweet forbidden places where Cameron's arms still held her, his face close to hers. And as she woke and lay there, grasping at the fading dream, a new resolve grew within her.

Each day she had watched him set off early to tour the lambing fields, usually returning mid-morning astride a sturdy island pony, before heading off for other tasks. It was a pattern he seldom varied, and she rose, dressing quickly, planning to meet him on his return, and she left, reassuring Mrs. Henderson that she would not go far.

Yesterday's wind still blew in ragged bursts as she followed the winding field track. She gave up on her hat and let it fall on her back, feeling the breeze through her hair and savouring the warmth of the sun on her neck. Halfway along the track she saw him, and this time he did not try to avoid her but came steadily on. 'You don't learn, do you,' he called out as he approached. 'You'll get freckles and sunburn. Put your hat on, Mrs. Blake.' He slid off the pony and walked over to her, his eyes sharply alive. 'What brings you out this way?'

'I came to find you.' His look held hers. 'I want you to take me to see the divers.'

His eyes narrowed and he looked away, back over the pasture, and was silent for a long time. 'No.' The word held finality. He locked his fingers into the pony's coarse mane and stared across towards Oronsy Mhor. 'It can't be done. The tide has to be right, and even then you have to wade across one bit.'

'I can wade.'

'It's too far.' He turned away, his face set and unyielding. 'Mrs. Henderson would have them combing the island for you.' The pony lowered its head to crop at the grass, and he stared out across the fields, his hand on the animal's neck, not speaking.

'They might be nesting by now.'

'Oh, they're nesting alright. I went to see.' The pony raised its head, blowing softly at him.

'Then you *must* show me.'

'It can't be done, Mrs. Blake,' he repeated, turning back to her. The pony nuzzled his pocket hopefully. 'Give over, damn you,' he said, pushing its head away.

'Last night as I lay in bed—' She broke off, daunted by his expression, then dropped the charade. 'Cameron, these few days are all we have before Theo returns. Can we not allow ourselves that much?' He stared at her, and his eyes grew a shade darker, but he stayed silent. 'Cameron?'

'You'd tear up the rule book, would you?'

'Yes.'

'And let the devil take the consequences?' She made no response. 'Have you actually *considered* the consequences?'

'Of course.'

He looked at her, unbelieving. 'And you think you're prepared to take that risk?' She watched his face harden. 'And I'm to be as reckless with *other* people's lives, am I?' He took up the halter and flung himself across the pony's back, looking down at her. 'If you stay out in this sun, you'll grow faint again. Turn back and go home.' And he rode off rapidly, leaving her alone on the track.

Beatrice picked at her meal that evening, eating little, gently scolded by Mrs. Henderson for overdoing things. Later she sat on the window seat in the drawing room and watched the light fade across the bay. It felt as if the ebbing tide was draining the last bit of spirit from her, for if Cameron too rejected her—what was there left? Then she heard a crunch on the gravel and looked up to see him approaching from round the side of the house, his face intent and unsmiling. He thrust a paper through the open window at her and was gone as swiftly as he had appeared.

A single sheet. The scrawled words jumped before her eyes. *So be it. Don't go to church tomorrow. Give Mrs. H leave to visit her daughter after the service. Wear old clothes and be at the old chapel when everyone has left. I'll bring the boat. Don't be seen. But think what you're about. There'll be no time later for regrets.*

She stood up, fearful suddenly, and looked across the bay to where the last of the sun's rays lit the peaks of Bheinn Mhor, setting it alight like the flames of a fire that was yet to burn there. A moment's chill premonition quivered through her, and she clasped her arms across her chest, then turned, crushing the page in her hand, and threw it on the fire. A brief spurt of coloured flame consumed the words, and as she closed the door behind her, the paper, scorched by the heat, fell as ash into the hearth.

Chapter 37

It was easy to tell Mrs. Henderson that she would not go across to the church the next day, harder to persuade her not to remain as well. 'Stay with your daughter for the day, Mrs. Henderson. She needs you, so near her time. I'm not unwell. I just crave a little quiet. Really, I insist.'

She consented to breakfast on a tray in her room, and from her window she could see Cameron helping Mrs. Henderson and Ephie into the larger of the two boats. Then he and Donald rowed them across the tide-filled bay towards the main island. When they were safely away, she rose and dressed, her hands trembling as she did. Quite how Cameron intended to make the rendezvous she had no idea, but she followed his instructions, encountering no one as she walked to the old chapel and sat, crouched in her usual place, screened from the land, biting her lip, unbelieving of what she was about. Off-shore, the seals played in the sea, and the dark one lifted its head, as if in greeting, then dived sideways and was gone.

Fifteen minutes later, when Cameron had not appeared, her courage began to fail and she scanned the bay one last time. She should go back—this was folly! *Madness.* Then she saw him, in the smaller boat, pulling hard towards her, and a moment later the bow scraped on the rocks.

'You came,' he said as he moved forward. 'I didn't think you would, in the end.' He glanced at her as he helped her aboard. 'Stay low. Sit on the bottom boards and keep your head well down.' And he pushed off again, rowing strongly away from the shore. 'Alright?' he panted, smiling down at her. 'Only for a little while. Just until we get round the headland.'

From the bottom of the boat she watched him, turning his head, scanning the shoreline as he strained at the oars. His feet were bare, and he had changed from his Sunday clothes into an old woollen jersey and loose dark trousers, rolled to just below the knees—and she thought of that other time, when the boat had stalled between two waves. They made swift progress with the tide, and he soon told her it was safe to sit up. She rose, stretching cramped muscles, and looked around, trying to get her bearings, and discovered that they had swung around the northern tip of the island. But even at this distance she could see the chimneys of Muirlan House rising above a fold in the land.

'Should be alright now. Most people will be at the kirk, but it would be thought odd enough that I'm out here on a Sunday, without seeing two figures in the boat.' He had left his family with the excuse of feeling unwell, he told her, and then hidden his Sunday clothes in the rocks. The boat he had concealed earlier. He began shipping the oars, glancing over his shoulder as he prepared the sail. 'Take the helm?' He smiled at her, and she did her best, watching him intent upon his task until he was satisfied that the tan sail was filling. Then he stepped over the oars and came to sit beside her. He took the helm and lay his arm along the gunwale behind her, and pulled her shoulders back to rest against his chest, kissing her temple. 'I wanted to kiss you that other time,' he said, glancing up at the sail, tightening the sheet, 'but resisted. And besides, we had the sharp-eyed major in the bow.'

'Rupert?' She turned to him. 'What do you mean?'

'He's no one's fool, isn't Emily's man.' She dropped her head as anxiety clutched at her. He reached out and turned her chin to face him. 'I told you you were reckless, Beatrice, and it's not too late to turn back.'

But just then they left the shelter of the land and the wind caught the sail, blowing her hair across her face. The boat plunged and bucked in the broken water, and she tasted the salty spray on her lips. 'You also said there would be no time for regrets.' He watched her for a moment longer, then laughed, kissing her swiftly before shifting his position and turning the boat towards the rocky shore.

They did not speak again. His attention became focussed on keeping his course through the contrary waves, and occasionally glancing back over his shoulder. But they were on the wild, uninhabited side of the island, and they saw no one, and she glimpsed a fringe of white sand in the distance. 'Torrann Bay,' he said, following her gaze, then went forward to take down the sail and retrieve the oars.

A few moments later, the bow scraped softly on the sandy beach, and he helped her step ashore, then led her across the turf to a patch of slightly higher ground. From there she could see a long finger of water, once an inlet from the sea cut off centuries ago by a violent storm. Gradually it had become a freshwater lochan, fed by a spring, bordered on its margins by rushes and iris. A small promontory reached out into it, and at the end was an untidy pile of sticks and seaweed heaped together, apparently haphazardly. And sitting atop was a large black-and-white bird, its neck settled back, relaxed and unconcerned. Silently he passed her the field glasses.

'Oh!' Then, 'She looks so large out of the water.'

'It could be him,' he replied. 'One fishes and the other sits, then they swap.' A tremolo came from across the loch, and the nesting bird went on the alert, rising from the nest. Cameron bent close and spoke softly. 'Watch as the other one comes ashore.' The two birds met briefly on the water and then the second bird laboured in an ungainly manner up to the nest. 'I think this is the female. But see how she drags a leg? I believe she's injured.' The bird settled herself onto the pile of twigs while the male bird dived. 'It's perhaps why she stayed.'

'And he stayed with her.'

They looked at each other. 'Aye.' Then he reached over and pulled her to her feet. The fishing bird surfaced close by and gave a shrill warning cry to its mate, who rose and staggered down to the water's edge, where it too dived.

'The eggs! They've abandoned them—'

'They'll be back.' He took her hand again, leading her away from the lochan, then he stopped. 'Wait.' He disappeared around the boulder, reappearing a moment later crouched low along the promontory. She watched him reach into the nest and then retreat rapidly as the birds surfaced, only to dive again. 'Two eggs, big speckled ones,' he said as he rejoined her and the birds came up again, some way distant, very low in the water and silent now. 'Let's leave them to settle.'

Nearby, a grassy knoll was screened from the loch by reeds and iris, and he led her there, spreading out his jacket, and pulled her down beside him. He held out his hand, fist clenched, and then turned it, uncurling his fingers to reveal a soft black feather tipped with white. 'A memento.' She took it, held it, and stroked it slowly along the line of her chin, her eyes on his, and then she pulled a gold chain and locket from the neck of her blouse. His hand closed over hers. 'Let me.' And his fingers brushed her neck as he took it, still warm from her skin, opening it to reveal a small blank picture frame. 'Empty?' he asked, his face close to hers.

'Empty.'

He nodded, then curled the feather into it, closed it, and touched it to his lips. 'A keepsake,' he said, letting it fall back between her breasts, and she reached up to pull him down with her.

And all the while, above them, unseeing and uncaring, the gulls gave their wild cries, swooping and wheeling on the strengthening breeze.

That night Beatrice lay in her bed in Muirlan House, her hands locked behind her head, staring up at the ceiling, eyes wide, aghast at what had taken place, yet glad with every fibre of her being that it had. She could still feel his hands discovering her, the lovely warmth of him, his skin next to hers.

And somehow the rightness of it outweighing the wrong.

They had lain, spent and wordless, on the flattened grasses until at last he had raised himself up to look out over the reedy curtain to the water. 'You see, all well again,' he said, and she had rolled over, brushing aside her cascading hair, lifting her head to see. One bird was on the nest, the other fishing calmly nearby, and she smiled, sinking back to gaze up at the sky while he lay beside her, his head propped on one elbow, watching her, stroking away an errant strand of hair from her lips. 'And on the Sabbath too. Every rule broken, Beatrice.' A bleak expression had crossed his face, quickly gone, as he bent to kiss her.

Eventually they had drawn apart again, and a thin haze had begun to form over the sky, a prelude to the next change in the ever-changing weather. He looked up, sensing the wind shift, then turned back to her and began pulling together the lacy edges of her blouse, twisting the buttons, straightening her tumbled skirts. 'We must go.' His face was sober for a moment, then he had reached out and plucked the head from a yellow iris and tucked it between the roundness of her breasts. 'Yellow, madam. For joy.' And out on the headland, the divers exchanged low sounds of reassurance as they met at the edge of the loch, then the male disappeared beneath the surface and the female returned to her vigil.

But now, in her bed, Beatrice rolled onto her side, drawing her knees up under the sheets, clasping her arms around them, screwing her eyes shut as the image of Theo hammered into her mind. Fear and remorse swamped the joy, and she lay flat again, her eyes fixed on the ceiling, where the crack had been filled and where fresh paint now covered the rainwater stain.

Theo must never know.

Chapter 38

'How could you ever think it?'

'I see it every day, in his eyes, in his manner whenever you're around. And everything I learn confirms it.'

'*No.*' Cameron had cleared a space for them inside one of the ruined crofts to the west, on estate land where few ventured, well hidden, down by the shore with clear views in both directions. He had filled hay bags for them and they lay there now, under the rotting thatch, passion spent for the moment, reflective. 'What there is between us goes back a long way, but it was never *that*. Not ever.'

'Not on your part, perhaps, but I'm certain he feels otherwise.'

Cameron sat up, frowning down at her. 'No,' he repeated, and reached out, turning her face to him. '*No!* He enjoyed showing me things, explaining things. We shared the same interests, and I—I admired him hugely.' Beatrice saw that same bleak expression cross his face, and he told her how, when he was a boy, he had been sent with a message and was told to wait in the study. Theo had come back to find him sitting at his desk, engrossed in one of his books, struggling with the unfamiliar words and, far from punishing him, he had spent the rest of the afternoon with Cameron studying the stuffed birds and animals, discussing their habits. Cameron had described his own observations, and Theo had listened, encouraging him. From there it had grown. 'I was so pleased to be given the run of the study I never questioned why, and then, bit by bit, I began assisting him and learning more. When the suggestion of an education came up, I suppose I just took it all for granted.' He dropped his eyes back to her. 'But he never laid a finger on me.

No hint of it. Then he began travelling again and was hardly ever here. Restless. And lonely, I believe. And whenever he came back, he sought my assistance.'

'Why only you and not Donald?'

'Donald reads the land, not books, and he was always my father's shadow.'

She lay back, staring up at the dense mass of cobwebs which hung like a tangled mist from the roof above them, remembering how Theo's eyes seemed to follow Cameron, unsettled by his presence. Despite Cameron's denials, those looks held longing.

'But he's changed.' Cameron's tone was grim, and Beatrice turned back to him. 'There's a hardness to him now. A bitterness. Since he returned here last year.'

'With me.'

'But not *because* of you.' Cameron pulled her to him. 'That I cannot understand.' He held her tight. 'But he'd stayed away too long, visited too briefly, and over the years he has lost touch. All he wants now is for time to stand still or, better still, wind it back. He can't see beyond himself, can't see that there's a new restlessness up here, a refusal to conform.'

After a long silence, Beatrice spoke again. 'Are we so very wicked, Cameron, to steal these few days for ourselves?'

His head lay close to hers. 'Do anarchists acknowledge right and wrong?' He smiled, and after a moment added, 'But I wonder if, in the end, we'll regret it.' And he pulled her to him again, smothering her question.

Later she remembered. 'You meant if we get found out?'

He shook his head. 'That mustn't happen. But do you expect just to walk away from this unscathed?' He had brought a blanket from the house, and she pulled it close, chilled suddenly.

They became artful in their deception, meeting in different places, at different times to allay suspicion. Beatrice was already a familiar figure out on the estate, known for her long walks, and they would arrange to meet as if by accident so then they could stay and talk together in the open. Reality was put aside as they lost themselves in the delight of each other. It seemed to Beatrice that everyone must know, must sense the joy radiating from her. Perversely, she chose to believe that that same joy was also a shield, protecting them. 'These are stolen days, Cameron,' she said. 'Ours alone. And then you will go and build a life for yourself, remembering, perhaps… And Theo and I will learn to rub the sharp edges away.' But they were careful, avoiding risks, knowing that the consequences of discovery would reach beyond themselves—the position of Cameron's father would become untenable, the family cast adrift. And as the days passed, the future began to loom more darkly until one afternoon, as they lay together in the old croft house, Cameron raised his head and looked down at her, his face set and serious.

'If I had gone this spring as planned, if ₁ny father hadn't fallen, I'd have left and not come back. Feeling as I did about you.' He threaded his fingers between hers. 'But not now. It's all changed now. You must come with me when I go.'

She had been plucking straw from her skirts, and stayed her hand. Go with him? Her breath caught in her throat. 'You know I cannot.' He rose and went to stand at the threshold, his back to her, and said no more.

Sometimes she watched him from her bedroom window, remembering how she had once mistaken him for Theo crossing the strand towards her. And when she saw him now, Bess running beside him, her heart would lift and she would find some excuse to leave the house to encounter him as he came up from the foreshore. Through Mrs. Henderson she asked if he would complete the repairs to the bower, and she worked beside him, delighting in his close company. Mrs. Henderson brought them tea each day, and they spun the job out for as long as they could, and he smiled, conceding defeat, when her first rose opened tentative yellow petals in the sunshine.

There followed a progression of glorious days, and it seemed to Beatrice that the elements conspired in her celebration of this stolen time. For surely the machair had never before blazed with wild flowers in such profusion, reckless and abandoned, and the air was clearer, sharper, the breeze more caressing, while the cries of the wild birds found an echo within her. Only at night, when she lay in bed, did the sense of betrayal return to overwhelm her. She fought it, argued against it, for Theo was guilty too in his betrayal of *her*. He had brought her here to his dreamworld, and she had been enchanted, eager to share it with him, but his passion had turned aside, turned inward, excluding her, darkening to something she could not understand, and she had become lost. But no longer! She felt willful, as unrestrained as the elements themselves, for a different sort of morality operated here, where the skies were wide and open, and the island recognised only rules of its own devising. And she refused to consider the future.

Yet, through the maelstrom of delight, she would glimpse a strained look on Cameron's face, troubled shadows in his eyes. But her questions brought no answers, only an increase in the intensity and urgency of his love, and at night she would banish her unquiet thoughts, and the guilt. For in these few precious days, there was room only for joy. So pure and profound a feeling that none other could survive beside it.

But wispy clouds, mares' tails, crept unnoticed across the skies, and one day she woke to clouds and a strengthening wind. Defiantly, she pulled a shawl around her and set off to walk across the island. She looked back and saw that Mrs. Henderson was standing at the morning room window, watching her go.

They had agreed to meet that morning at Torrann Bay, where the tenants were once again bringing the tangle ashore, and she stood beside him watching from the top of the dunes. 'Last year we met here and you reproved me for bemoaning my lot,' she said. 'Called it a benign slavery.'

'Last year you were a whey-faced doll in city clothes.' He turned and glinted at her in the way she had grown to love. 'Eyes as wide as dinner plates, as if you'd landed among the heathen of Africa. Donald and I laid bets on how soon you'd demand to be taken home.'

'But you were wrong.'

'So very wrong.' He spoke slowly and then gave her an odd, angry look as she gazed out over the ocean, remembering the feeling that had welled up in her last year. Limitless horizons. But now the horizon was blurred, grey and undefined. Beside her he spoke again, his tone hard. 'And now you tell *me* to go, and leave you.'

'Cameron—'

'Steal a few days, you said. Fool that I was. And that's to be the end to it? We just walk away?' He half turned to hide his face from the shore. 'You *must* leave with me, Beatrice.'

'You know I cannot. Theo—'

'He had his chance. He held a precious thing in his hand and was crushing it.'

'Your father, your family—'

He was still. Silenced again. 'Then we should stop now,' he said. 'Better that we had never begun.' And he strode off towards the kelp workers, calling sharply to one of them.

She waited until it was clear that he would not return, then walked back to the house, and she was almost at the top of the rise when she heard the sound of hooves on the grass behind her.

He slid from the pony in front of her. 'Sometimes it's too much to bear.' Her eyes filled and she dropped her chin. 'I'll be at the old house as soon as I have toured the lambing in the morning. Will you come?' She nodded and he remounted, riding off towards the strand.

As she walked up the drive, past the veronica and escallonia bushes, alive with the chattering of buntings and sparrows, she felt the house looking down at her, grave and reproachful, and felt the chill as she entered the hall. For it *was* a betrayal, when all was said and done. *You can always take a lover in a year or two*, the pert young woman had told her when her engagement to Theo had been announced, and she had been affronted. But this was not the ritual adultery of her own class where infidelity was a game, the rules clear and known to all, tolerated provided that care was taken to avoid a scandal. This was something different, more primitive, more honest. More dangerous— And for all that she drew confidence from the wild landscape, she knew that the consequences of discovery would go far beyond mere scandal. And she knew that it was this which brought the shadows into Cameron's eyes. This, and thoughts of the future.

Next day at the cottage, those shadows were darker. 'Give me a little time out there, just enough to get established. Then I'll come back for you.' He had been waiting at the doorway, looking out for her, and had grabbed her two hands, pulling her to him. 'Leave him. When you're in Edinburgh. Next winter. Leave him then. Before you return in the spring. And I'll come back for you, and then we'll return to Canada together. No one need ever know you left with me.' He gripped her hands, crushing them.

'Disappear into Canada?'

'I see no other way.' She looked aside as the image of Theo on the shore came back to her, that look of anguish, of grief, and she felt a rush of remorse. Cameron released her hands and his eyes narrowed at her silence. 'What is it?'

'Last winter I lost Theo's baby. By next year there might be another. What then?'

His fist smote the doorframe. 'Then leave with me now and *damn* the consequences. I won't leave without you.' He reached for her, but she pulled back, suddenly fearful.

'Perhaps you're right, my love. We should stop.'

But he gripped her by the shoulders and kissed her fiercely. 'Too late,' he said, and she felt the pressure of his legs against hers as he forced her backwards, pulling her down onto the hay bags, tugging aside her skirts to reach her. 'No time for regrets, Beatrice. I warned you.'

Chapter 39

∼ 1911, Beatrice ∼

Beatrice stood at the door of the cottage next day, watching the gulls blown on the wind, waiting for him, the morning already shattered. The weather was changing, and far out at sea a dark smudge spread along the horizon, widening and darkening as it approached land, blowing a chilling wind before it. She had been unable to stay in the house once she had read the letter, but waiting here was worse, bringing forward the moment when she must tell him, and she almost willed him to stay away. Then she saw him, striding out, his head swivelling from side to side, half raising a hand in greeting as he approached.

He stopped when he saw her face. 'What is it?'

'He's on his way back. A letter came.'

And her trials that morning were far from over, for later, as she walked back along the shore, the emotion of the past hour still churning within her, she saw the gaunt figure of John Forbes sitting on the stone bench in front of the old farmhouse.

He looked down at her like an Old Testament prophet and raised a hand, and she was compelled to go to him. 'Mr. Forbes, how good to see you out-of-doors!' she said. His beard had grown long and grey, and his clothes hung from his diminished frame, but he was still a formidable figure, and she approached him with apprehension.

'Will ye sit with me a moment, Mrs. Blake?' he said, calling to Ephie to bring a chair, rearranging his splinted leg on an old fish box and moving his crutch aside to make room. She could hardly refuse, so she smiled her acceptance and fell back on social convention.

'You've had a terrible time of it this winter, Mr. Forbes, and we're all so thankful you're now out of danger.'

A slight nod acknowledged her words, but his eyes searched her face, essaying her defences. 'I need to get my strength back. And you've had troubles of your own, Mrs. Blake,' he added, his expression softening. 'For which I'm deeply sorry. For you both.' He paused, searching again, more guarded. 'But you're looking well now.'

She smiled in return, and a silence fell between them. 'I'm sure my husband has told you how grateful we are to—' she began.

'When does your husband return, Mrs. Blake?' And she knew then why he had summoned her.

'I've had a letter just today telling me he'll be back in two days, as long as he can make the crossing.'

'Good.' He breathed his satisfaction and looked away at last.

'He says that the opening went well.' And she described what Theo had told her, but the factor's face conveyed his opinion that these were not good reasons for abandoning an ailing wife. Then his attention was caught by something over her shoulder, and she turned to see that Cameron was on the path, having swung round the back of the house to approach from the opposite direction.

He called out as he approached, 'Are you downstairs, then! However did you manage?' He turned and made a small bow to Beatrice. 'Good morning, Mrs. Blake.'

'I can't stay laid up forever.' The factor's eyes now explored Cameron's face, flickering briefly between him and Beatrice, his forehead furrowed. 'What news then, son?' And Cameron described the calving which was taking place in the fields beyond the ridge where he had been earlier that morning, and his father nodded. 'Mrs. Blake tells me that her husband will be returning in a day or two.'

'Is that so, madam?' Cameron looked calmly at Beatrice, then back to his father. 'He'll be glad to find you up and about.'

The factor returned him a long and hard look. 'It's time now that I was.'

~

Theo had ordered fires to be lit as soon as he returned, and when Beatrice entered the stifling drawing room, she went to open a window. 'No, don't. There's a chill, you must feel it.' She sat down, pushing her chair back from the fire, smiling tightly, and asked him to tell her about the exhibition. 'Were your paintings much admired?'

'As one might admire a fossil, I suppose—' He broke off, contemplating her in a puzzled way. 'You look well, Beatrice, remarkably well. Perhaps you were right to stay.' Guilt swamped her as she agreed she was much better, then she knew a flutter of alarm. If he came to her bedroom later, she could hardly deny him.

His description of the lavish opening had provided them with conversation over dinner. 'You would have enjoyed it,' he said, as he picked at his food, pushing his plate away, refilling his glass with claret. And now, back in the drawing room, he seemed agitated, rising to poke at the fire, adding more peat.

'Are you feeling unwell, Theo?'

'Of course not. What makes you ask?'

He did not come to her room that night, nor any night that followed, but kept to his study, working late, and she was puzzled. Once such neglect would have wounded her, but now she felt only relief, and this relief muted her senses. It was only gradually over the next few days that she noticed a difference in him and realised that he was drinking heavily. She found empty whisky glasses in the study and in his dressing room, and the levels in the decanter dropped alarmingly, to be quickly refilled. He looked unwell, prone to flushing and sudden sweats, and she found a sleeping potion on his shaving table.

Conscience pricked her, and she grew fearful. It seemed his eyes followed her whenever they were in a room together, sliding away in their customary manner when they met hers. Had they been discovered? The thought terrified her. Or had he somehow heard a rumour? Impossible, surely—Yet he watched her with a strange expression and his face seemed heavier, pouched under the eyes, his expression unfocussed and distant, but her solicitous enquiries were brushed impatiently aside, and she watched with alarm as his drinking increased.

Cameron now came in for censure. 'What about the sheep? Those tupps and hoggs should have gone by now, surely. Why the delay?' she overheard him in the hall.

'The ship had to put into port for repairs, sir, so the sale has been postponed. It'll be a day or two, but they'll send word.'

'I see nothing gathered ready in the fank. They're still out in the fields!'

'They'll be ready, sir. I promise you.'

'And I understand the rye was only planted last week. What the devil's been going on?'

Cameron fielded the barrage as best he could, tight-lipped, his own temper held in check, and life became insupportable. Opportunities to meet became far fewer as the factor resumed control from the estate office, bringing Cameron's stewardship of the estate abruptly to an end. And Theo's strange anger simmered, molten, just below the surface, his eyes bloodshot, the pupils pinprick bright, his hand trembling as he filled his whisky glass. And still his brooding eyes watched her, considering her, looking away when she returned his gaze. She grew restless and fretful, alternating between frustration and fear, rebellion and remorse. Guilt made her wretched, and the separation from Cameron was unbearable.

In snatched conversation, she learned that Theo had threatened Duncan MacPhail's family with immediate eviction when he had discovered the man had driven in stakes marking out a croft. He had told Cameron to pull them up and then burn the roof off the house, goading him that he would do it himself when he refused. It took the factor's warning to stop him—such action would light the touchpaper of dissent in the region, he said, playing straight into the hands of the most radical land agitators. Duncan MacPhail, after all, would have nothing to lose in widely publicising his treatment. Backing down did nothing to improve Theo's temper.

The factor pushed himself to recover, as if sensing a renewed crisis, using Donald as a go-between from the estate office to Muirlan House, sending Cameron far out onto the estate to work. And Beatrice could only watch him come and go, not daring even to signal to him.

The balmy weather had vanished completely, as if the fickle elements, having indulged her for so long, now abandoned her, and she was confined to the house overshadowed by Theo's moods. She had a fire lit daily in the morning room and spent her days there, writing letters or attempting to read.

Or watching from the window for a glimpse of Cameron.

It was two evenings later when she went to bid Theo good night that she found him slumped over his desk in the study, his head on a pile of drawings, an inkwell overturned, a dark stain spreading. Drunk or sedated—or both? She set the ink bottle aright, moving aside some of his paintings laid out on the desk, studying them as she did. They made no sense to her, strange whirling patterns, wisps which were birds' wings, shore waders reduced to exaggerated stilt-like legs joined to their own reflections. Quite unlike his previous work.

Gently she lifted his hand away from the spill, and he stirred. 'Theo,' she said softly, leaning close to mop his fingers with her handkerchief, but he yanked his hand away and flung out his arm.

His elbow caught her hard just below her eye. She cried out, stumbling backwards, slipping on the ink, and fell, catching one of the domed displays, and lay there, stunned, amongst the shattered glass beside a tiny skylark, its beak open in mimicry of her shock. Theo staggered to his feet and looked down at her and spoke her name. Then he reached out to her, his hand trembling, and she watched with alarm as his eyes rolled back in his head, and he too fell, his face amongst the broken glass, the weight of him across her.

The noise brought one of the girls rushing to the door, and she gawped in horror and then vanished, to reappear a moment later with Mrs. Henderson. 'Oh, *madam*,' she cried.

The women hurried to help Beatrice as she struggled to extricate herself. She rose, panting and shocked, conscious of the girl's eyes on her swelling face. 'He fell. He didn't— Mr. Blake's unwell.' She was shaking, mortified, and looked down at Theo lying with his head hard up against the fireplace, the ink dripping black onto the cuff of his shirt. '*Help* him. Fetch someone—'

Half an hour later she followed dumbly behind Cameron and Donald, Theo's feet dragging on the stair carpet as they half carried him up the stairs, his arms slung across their shoulders, his chin sunk on his chest. Mrs. Henderson had gone on ahead to turn back the covers of the spare room bed, where they laid him down and Donald began removing his shoes.

Cameron turned abruptly to where Beatrice stood, uncertain, at the door. 'Are you alright, Mrs. Blake?' He took a step towards her, but Mrs. Henderson put a hand on his arm.

'Look to the master, Cameron. I'll take care of Mrs. Blake.'

'He woke suddenly,' insisted Beatrice, as the housekeeper steered her towards her bedroom, sending a girl for warm water. 'Flung his arm out. He didn't mean—he's unwell.'

'I know, madam, I know,' she soothed. 'But you must take care.' Her hands were gentle and her eyes bright with understanding. 'Rest now, madam, I'll bring some tea.' She left Beatrice sitting at her dressing table, the ink-stained handkerchief balled in her fist, staring at her reflection, and she raised a hand to her bruised face. It *had* been an accident.

She heard movement in the adjacent dressing room, drawers opening and closing, footsteps retreating, then the connecting door opened a crack.

'What happened?' Cameron hissed savagely.

'He's been taking an opiate of some sort, I found a bottle.' She paused. 'Is he alright?'

'He'll do.'

'He didn't mean to—'

'No?'

'No! Is he asleep?'

His face had an odd expression, and he looked aside. 'He roused briefly, but he's asleep now.' They heard Mrs. Henderson tapping on the bedroom door, and Cameron drew back. 'Lock your door tonight, Beatrice.'

~

'A fever, Mrs. Blake. A bad one, but it will pass. Something he picked up in Glasgow, I expect.' Dr. Johnson had come early, alarmed by what he heard. 'No reason for concern.' He patted her hand as his eyes strayed over her bruised cheek. 'I'll come again tomorrow.' Theo had refused to be examined, the doctor told her, beyond permitting confirmation that he had a fever and agreeing that his eyes were bloodshot and his face cut about with small scratches, red and blotchy. 'I've given him a mild sedation. Not like the other bottle. I'll take that away. Perhaps he will explain—?' Beatrice nodded quickly. 'Water down the whisky, my dear'—he pulled a wry face, tugging at the strap of his bag—'and persuade him to be *moderate*.'

Did Dr. Johnson think him merely drunk? How shaming! But she was certain it was more. She went back to find Theo sleeping, the curtains half drawn, and sat quietly in the corner of the room watching him. He looked peaceful now, but how much he had changed! These were not the urbane features of the man she had watched across the room in Edinburgh, watched and felt drawn to. The skin around his eyes was puffy, the lines exaggerated by the redness of his face.

Guilt flooded her again. Had he guessed? Was that why the whisky decanter was no sooner full than empty again? But surely

Theo was not the sort of man to tolerate infidelity in silence. She turned her face to the window, pressing the back of her hand to her mouth. But what if he suspected, and had no proof? She shut her eyes and leant her head against the wall. And if he was ill, seriously ill, she couldn't leave him. Cameron had become ever more persistent in his demands that she must go with him, but leaving Theo ill and alone was much more reprehensible than leaving Theo angry, and so she was caught, snared by her own treachery.

Gradually, she sensed that he was watching her, but when she turned to him, his eyelids fluttered shut. She spoke his name, softly, and again, a little louder. 'Theo?' No response. But he was too still, too tense. Feigning sleep. And then he stirred and turned his back to her. She stayed a few minutes longer, then left.

$\sim$ *Theo* $\sim$

Beatrice. When he was sure she had gone, he turned onto his back and opened his eyes. He moved his head slightly, looking around at the unfamiliar room. Why was he here? Slowly the confused memory took shape—the sound of breaking glass and Beatrice's shocked face looking up at him from the floor. Had *he* done that?

He raised a hand to his brow and awoke little pinpricks of pain, and he lay still as his brain began to piece it together. An ugly scene.

And yet he had dreamed of Màili. So clearly, as if she were there. He had opened his eyes to find her dark ones looking down at him, her cool fingers on his face, and had felt a profound but fleeting joy. And he had spoken to her, an endearment: *God bless.* But she had gone, and then there was Cameron. Or was it Cameron all along? Not Màili.

And then it had been Beatrice. He'd watched her through slit eyes as she sat there beside the window, her hand pressed to her mouth and speculated, in a detached way, what she might be thinking. But he could no longer guess— She was different, changed in some incomprehensible way, slipping away from him. He was losing her, as he had lost Màili— And again it was his own fault; he was driving her away. He had left her pale and thin, nervous and fretful, but returned to find her restored, shining with health and beauty, and with an enigmatic glow. Dear God, how he had wanted to go to her that first evening, a supplicant, begging forgiveness. And he could have gone to her, but for— He screwed his eyes shut and clenched his teeth, wincing with pain from his scarred face.

If only she had come with him to Glasgow, the whole wretched business would never have happened. Shame welled up in him again, and he groaned as his mind replayed the wild excesses of that night. Sanders and his cronies drinking madly, not permitting him to be moderate, that vile show, and then the overblown women. Good God, *how* did he let it happen? And next day, the humiliation, and the appalled, fragmented recollection.

In Glasgow, he had managed to put the episode behind him, kept busy by the events of the opening, but towards the end of the visit there had been cause for concern. He had slipped away and found a discreet doctor who had done little to allay his fears. 'Earlydays, my dear sir, early days. It will probably clear up in no time.' The doctor had handed him a bottle. 'This might be beneficial and will help you sleep. Married man, sir? You must stay away from your wife, you know. Until you're sure.'

And now Beatrice's eyes sent him the same clear message. *Stay away, stay away…*

Chapter 40

∼ 1911, Beatrice ∼

'Make an excuse, any excuse, and meet me. In an hour.' Cameron spoke in a low voice from the door of the morning room the next day, fetching rent books from the study as an excuse to come across.

He was waiting at the threshold of the croft house, tense and furious, when she arrived. 'So this is the man I must leave you with?' he demanded, pulling her in. '*Now* he offers you violence!' He gripped her shoulders, deaf to her protests. 'Leave it now, and listen. Yesterday, before all this happened, he and my father discussed my leaving.' She tried to pull away to look at him, but he held her tight. '*Listen.* They've agreed on the day after the celebration for the King's coronation, midsummer day. I've no reason to stay, and my father smells trouble.'

'He can't know!'

'He suspects. He's said nothing, but he wants me away.' Beatrice's face crumpled as he released her, but he shook his head, and his grip tightened on her shoulders. '*Listen.*' And he outlined a plan. He would work the summer on the docks in Halifax or Montreal, hard work but good money, then return in the autumn, not to the island but to Glasgow, in secret, and send word to her in Edinburgh. He paused, drawing in breath. 'And if you come to me there, we will head out back to Canada on the first ship next spring.'

Behind him a spider dropped down from the old rafters, spinning a long thread behind it as it fell. He caressed her bruised cheek with his thumb. 'The decision is yours, *ghraidh mo chridhe.* It won't be easy living, but no one will find us there.' He moved back, fracturing the silken thread as he pulled her down beside him.

~

Later that day she tried hard to listen as Theo discussed the arrangements for the midsummer celebrations, but her mind was in tatters, unable to focus. He had insisted on getting up and seemed much recovered, back in control, the fever almost gone, his eyes less manic but his temper only slightly less volatile. 'More tea, Mr. Forbes?' she asked, inadvertently cutting across him.

'Beatrice, I—' Theo frowned at her. 'Perhaps I will leave the matter to you, Mrs. Henderson, after all.'

The factor and the housekeeper both refused more tea, and Beatrice tried again to pay attention. There had long been plans for a party to celebrate both midsummer and the coronation, which would involve a gathering across the strand on the main island, and a huge bonfire would be lit on the top of Bheinn Mhor, a beacon for the surrounding islands. And they would have music, fiddlers and accordions, dancing and pipes. The estate would provide food and drink.

And by the end of it, Cameron would be gone

Theo became exasperated. 'I want you to make sure there is ample food, Beatrice,' he said, after the others had left the morning room and it was clear that she had paid scant attention. 'Mrs. Henderson has done all the planning so far, so it's now your turn to take a little responsibility. I'll have enough to do overseeing the rest, as well as the workmen.'

Theo's fever might have left him, and he was drinking less, but over the next days he was restless, pushing everyone hard, abruptly giving and withdrawing instructions, calmed only by the steady hand of John Forbes and the tolerance of Mrs. Henderson, who adeptly covered Beatrice's frequent oversights. Work on the extension to the morning room had hardly started but was now accelerated. Theo wanted it completed, finished before the summer was gone, and he drove the men hard. Beatrice stood and watched as the men wrestled with a large frost-damaged boulder, leaving one end embedded deep in the foundations, filling the remaining hollow with quantities of bone-white sand to level the uneven ground.

Chapter 41

≈ Midsummer Day 1911, Beatrice ≈

In the end, it was Beatrice herself who betrayed them.

There had been activity since daybreak. Provisions had been ferried across by boat while the bay was full, and by cart as soon as the water was below the axles. The morning was fine and Beatrice had wandered down to the foreshore, desperate to get away from the house, watching the comings and goings and hoping for a glimpse of Cameron. But she knew there was little chance, as he had been sent across early to oversee the arrangements on Bheinn Mhor. From there he would leave directly once the celebrations were over, catching a lift across to the mainland with one of the returning fishermen.

They had contrived one last meeting at the croft house. 'I went to see the divers again,' he had told her as he lay beside her, his face next to hers. 'I thought perhaps the eggs would have hatched, but they hadn't. It seemed important to know.' He gave her a twisted smile, his eyes gleaming as he bent to kiss the locket where it lay on her breast.

She watched as one of the larger carts set out across the strand, carrying the carcasses of two calves which had been slaughtered for the feast, their feet already bound around poles, ready for roasting. John Forbes had positioned himself in one of the basket chairs on the drive, with his crutches beside him, calmly overseeing the frenzy and either confirming or modifying Theo's orders. The men had been taken away from the building work to help, stacking trestle tables and benches from the schoolhouse in readiness for transport. Boys were used as runners, conveying messages, and in the midst of the chaos Beatrice saw Theo lean down to listen to one lad, gripping his shoulder as the boy nodded vigorously. And as she walked back up the track, she saw him striding towards the stables, the boy at his heels, but had thought nothing of it. It was only when Mrs. Henderson met her at the front door and delivered the message that Beatrice should wait for Mr. Blake there, and that they would go across together, did she wonder where he might have gone.

Too weary to be much concerned, she had nodded and gone upstairs to escape the bustle of the frenzied household. The trap would be sent to take them across that evening, and until then there was nothing to occupy her. From her window, she watched small groups setting off across the strand, women with creels on their backs, holding small children by the hand while older children, giddy with excitement, ran beside them. The day dragged on, hot now, and sultry, and slowly the island emptied of its inhabitants. She turned away from the window and stretched out on her bed, her head aching wretchedly. But for seeing Cameron one last time, she would have cried off. There would be little joy in seeing him—to be close but not able to approach him, to see him but not to touch him. She turned over and buried her face in her pillow.

Gradually, the house grew silent. And as the sun began to sink, Beatrice rose and trailed downstairs to where Mrs. Henderson hovered anxiously, giving last-minute instructions to the departing girls.

She glanced up with relief as Beatrice descended. 'I've put a cold meal in the dining room, madam, so you and the master can have something when he gets back. But I'll stay, if you like.'

Beatrice gently pushed her to the door. 'Go with the others, Mrs. Henderson. Calum will bring us once Mr. Blake is ready.' Still, the housekeeper hesitated, her face anxious. 'Why not come with us now, madam? Mr. Blake will understand.' Beatrice was tempted. Cameron would be there, but defying Theo's explicit instructions was too great a risk. She shook her head and watched as Mrs. Henderson took her place on the last cart, looking back at her mistress until the cart dropped down to the foreshore.

It was impossible to settle.

She stood at the drawing room window, twisting her handkerchief. Where could Theo have gone? Across the strand, perhaps. But why? Guilt gave wings to her imagination, and she grew fearful as the light faded and the room grew cold. And still she waited.

When at last Theo returned, he came from the side of the house and she did not hear him until he was at the front door, shouting to someone, his voice exultant. 'Off you go now, and enjoy yourself! I won't forget what I said. No, no, it'll keep until tomorrow. Off with you.' She leant forward and caught sight of Tam, Calum's brother, running down the drive towards the foreshore. Had Theo simply been out shooting? He often took Tam with him when he did. But today of all days! She waited and listened, and heard him cross the hall to the study.

Ten minutes passed, and then fifteen, and Theo did not come to find her. Unable to wait any longer, she went into the hall. She could see him through the study door, still in his outdoor clothes, with his back towards her and attending to something on his desk. He turned as she approached, and in so doing he revealed what his body had hidden.

'No!'

He looked up in astonishment.

It was the smaller of the two divers, its head lolling grotesquely over the edge of the desk, its large feet splayed apart. A basket lined with fleece lay beside it. '*And* the eggs!' Tears filled her eyes. 'Oh, Theo, *what* have you done?' He stared back at her, his hand poised over the dead bird. And then, sickeningly, she realised what her words had revealed.

And there was no way to unsay them.

The silence lasted for an eternity, then Theo straightened. 'You knew,' he said slowly. 'You *knew* about them.' They stood looking across at each other, motionless as waxworks, then Theo opened the drawer to put away the measuring rule. Closed it and turned back. 'All the way out on Oronsy Mhor—and yet you *knew.*' He sank down into the chair behind the desk, his eyes never leaving her face. Seconds ticked by. 'How could that be, my dear?'

Alarm rang through her like static, but it was too late. She dug her nails into her palms as Theo continued looking at her, a strange expression on his face, his eyes stripping through her defences. Words would not come. Beads of sweat appeared on his brow, and his face drained to an ashy grey. Then from below a bank of dark cloud, the low sun briefly illuminated his easel with its brushes and paints, and he looked away. 'Cameron found them, eh?' She said nothing, numbed by her fear. 'And how long have *you* known, Beatrice?' He turned back to her, fixing his eyes on her face as she struggled to find words which would not condemn her, but like a rabbit caught in the poacher's lantern, her senses were stunned. 'Decided not to tell me, did you?' He paused. 'A little secret between the two of you, eh?'

Her heart began to pound. She had to make an effort, but her mouth was guilt-dry. 'He told me—' she began, and faltered. 'I told him not to. I was afraid that—that you would do this.' She gestured despairingly towards the carcass and the eggs, but he was no longer interested in them. He sat back with his elbows crooked against his chest, his fingertips lightly bouncing off each other as he watched her, and the silence stretched out between them. She tried again. 'It seemed such a shame—'

'*Shame?*' He sat forward abruptly, and the blood rushed to his face. 'You talk of *shame*, Beatrice?'

Her pulse leapt, and she knew then that her own face betrayed her. 'I don't know what you mean.'

'Oh, I think you do.' He sat back again, still watching her, and she felt a wild impulse to flee. Desperately, she thought he must not be allowed to accuse her, but it was too late. 'In fact,' he continued slowly, 'I'm certain of it.' He leant forward, his eyes not releasing hers. 'Because it explains so much.'

She was defenceless.

He rose to his feet, and she stepped back instinctively. His hand trembled as he gripped the side of the desk, white-knuckled, his mouth working, but before either of them could speak, there was a knock at the door of the study. He swung round like an island bull sensing a challenger, but it was Calum McNeil who stood there, oblivious to the dark vibrations in the room.

'The trap's at the door, sir.'

Theo looked blankly at him. Everything outside the moment had been forgotten. Then he looked down, distracted, and paused a moment before sitting again. 'Thank you, Calum, but plans have changed. Saddle the mare for me again, then come back and collect Mrs. Blake. She'll go across with you now and I'll follow.'

The man left.

Beatrice turned desperately to Theo. 'Theo, I don't want—'

'You'll do as I say, Beatrice, and make no complaint.' His face was expressionless, closed to reason, and his calmness terrified her. 'We're expected at the celebrations, and we will be there.' He stood up again, clutching the side of the desk. 'I need... to consider.' Even through her fear she was struck by how ill he looked. It was imperative that she try to reason with him now while she had the chance.

'Theo, you must hear—'

But he pulled himself upright, his face ash-grey. 'Fetch whatever you need and be ready for Calum when he returns.'

'Theo, listen to me.'

A dangerous glint appeared in his eye.

'I beg you to—'

'*Damn you, Beatrice.*' The words exploded from him. '*Go.*' He wiped the spittle from his mouth with his sleeve and turned back to the window, shaking, and she knew then that she must get to the bonfire. Find Cameron, and warn him, before Theo got there. But what then? She ran upstairs, rifling through her clothes to find her shawl, desperate and trembling. Out of the window she saw Calum returning, while beyond the shore the last stragglers were strung out across the strand, some on foot, others on the small island horses. There would be safety there, amongst them. For her? For Cameron?

She started as she heard Theo call her name from the hall and left the bedroom, descending to the half-landing, pressing her hand to her pounding heart, knowing that Theo was watching her from the study door. 'Take Mrs. Blake up to the old shieling, Calum. You'll find Mrs. Henderson there, with the others. I'll not keep you long.' And he went back into the study.

∼

A large crowd had gathered on the hillside, and excitement buzzed through them at this rare treat. Beatrice struggled to appear as if she shared in their enjoyment. It was the hardest thing she had ever done— Tenants she knew greeted her respectfully, introducing her to others she did not know, giving her their thanks and good wishes. She smiled woodenly while scanning the crowds for a glimpse of Cameron. Families had been arriving all day from off-shore islands and had come together with the crofters from Muirlan Island and now sat crammed onto benches at makeshift tables laden with food and drink, circled by excited children. The roof of the old shieling had been covered with torn and faded sails, which would provide some shelter should the weather turn bad, for the cloud bank was still gathering on the distant horizon. She scanned the hillside again. Where *was* he?

'It's almost sunset, madam.' She turned to find Donald gesturing towards the bonfire. Fiddle music was growing ever more intense as competing musicians showed off their skills, drowned occasionally by the drone of pipes. Everyone was waiting for the moment when the fire would be lit. She felt curious eyes turning to her, and Donald still stood there awaiting an answer. She looked out through fading light and shadow across the strand but saw no sign of a rider.

'I think you should light it,' she said quickly. 'Mr. Blake wouldn't want you to wait.' And delay would only draw further attention to his absence. Donald passed the word back, and the waiting men wasted no more time. Excitement reached a crescendo and then burst into a great cheer at the mighty paraffin-induced roar, and flames leapt high to greet the darkening sky. The musicians threw themselves into their task, dancing began, and the fire made wild silhouettes of the leaping revellers. *Lucifer's henchmen at the gateway to hell.* Cameron's teasing words came back to her. Where *was* he?

With attention now diverted elsewhere, she was able to keep to the margins of the firelight, searching ever more desperately. Bess appeared from somewhere, a co-conspirator with her tail wagging, and Beatrice's heart leapt. 'Where is he, Bess?' she whispered, bending to fondle the dog's ears, but saw the question reflected back in her puzzled eyes. Nearby, another fire had been lit to roast the two calves, and the smell of cooking meat sickened her as she scanned the gathering again. There was John Forbes, seated against the old shieling, his crutches beside him, in conversation with an endless stream of well-wishers who had not seen him since the winter. Several times she looked over, to find him watching her. And there was Donald. And Ephie. And Mrs. Henderson, organising the distribution of food. She heard one man asking Donald where his brother was, but Donald had simply shrugged. Her eyes raked the shadows again, but she dared not ask, and fielded deferential enquiries about Theo's whereabouts, smiling brightly, repeating the same story, that he was slightly delayed but would be joining them soon. Soon, but not, dear *God*, not before she found Cameron. Dizzy now with apprehension, she took another turn around the bonfire, her cheeks burning from the heat. She felt faint and stepped back exhausted out of the ring of light away from the watching eyes, to hide there.

But even as she turned away, she sensed a movement beside her. A hand grasped her elbow, and a firm grip drew her back away from the arc of firelight into the darkness.

Chapter 42

A man stepped out from the shadows and she froze. 'Here. Give me something. Relax, I shan't mug you. Your groceries or something.'

Hetty had staggered up the short path to her flat, juggling briefcase, groceries, and a take-away, cursing the persistent bass from the flat above. Not *another* party. And as she struggled to get at her keys, the plastic bag had split, and a tin rolled down the path.

As the man bent to retrieve it, the accent clicked into place. 'You!' She gaped in astonishment. 'What—why are you here?'

'You wanted to talk to me.'

'I did. I *do*.'

'Then open the door and ask me in.' He took the shopping bag from her, and she fumbled with her keys again. She managed to unlock the door and they jostled a moment in the tiny hallway as she took back the shopping.

She gestured him to the sitting room, avoiding his eyes. 'Go through,' she said, but he paused at the door and looked across the room at Blake's paintings on her wall. 'I'll be there in a minute.'

The kitchen offered refuge, a moment to recover and steady her pulse. She began unpacking the groceries. He was *here*, in person! But why now, so suddenly, after the long silence? Should she phone Giles and ask him to come over? No!— She was struggling to remember exactly what she'd said in her last text when he appeared, filling the kitchen doorway, saying nothing but leaning on the doorframe, arms folded in a now familiar pose.

'Have you been in London long?' she asked, busying herself getting mugs out. Should she offer him tea?

'I just arrived.'

What *had* she said in that text? She dived down to the fridge to hide her flaming cheeks; she'd forgotten how tall he was. 'Would you like a drink or something?'

'I don't want a drink. I want to talk to you.'

She risked another glance. He looked tired and drawn, and he also looked very angry. 'I've been trying to talk to *you* for almost two weeks,' she said, closing the fridge door firmly. 'But you ignored all my phone messages and emails. I'd got tickets to fly up on Friday, you know, to come and find you.'

He raised an eyebrow. 'Did you imagine I was hiding?'

'What was I supposed to think?'

'I only read your emails and texts yesterday. At the hotel. In Mombasa.'

'*Mombasa?*' She put a hand to her head.

'I flew back this afternoon. Thought I'd break my journey to come and salvage my reputation.' He gestured at her take-away. 'Do you intend to eat that muck, or can we go somewhere for a decent meal—and talk. Where's nearest?'

She noticed for the first time that he was tanned. Not the wind tanning gained on northern shores but a deep, dark tan from hot sun. Africa? It made his eyes seem even darker, and his crumpled linen jacket and lightweight trousers were hardly English weather clothes, not given this year's June. A restaurant offered the safety of a public place. 'There's an Italian round the corner.'

'That'll do.'

They left the curry congealing in the kitchen and went back down the path. He glanced up at the open window of the flat above, where the volume of noise had increased. 'How do you bear it?' His foot caught an empty beer can and it clattered across the road.

The restaurant was reassuringly clichéd with red gingham

tablecloths, a candle in a Chianti bottle, and faded prints of Roman landmarks. He led her to a quiet corner at the back and ordered a bottle of wine. The waiter left them studying menus. James said nothing more until they had ordered their meal and the bottle had arrived; he waved aside an offer to taste it and filled their glasses. Then he raised his own and took a drink, looking at her in that direct way she remembered.

His eyes were still hard and angry. 'I haven't got the full list of my offences as spelt out in your emails and texts, but the bottom line, as they say, is that I'm a charlatan, a cheat, and basically a shit.'

She reddened and put her napkin back on the table, preparing to leave. 'If you're going to be offensive—'

He sat forward and gripped her wrist. 'I've had twenty-four hours to feel angry about this, and besides, you're the one who's been offensive.' He released her, sitting back, and gestured to her glass. 'So have a drink and make a start.'

Slowly she replaced the napkin. Where *should* she start? There'd been no time to prepare. 'You've got some scheme of your own, at the farmhouse, and you want to sabotage my project. The agents found out.' The last words were ill-judged.

He leant forward again, his elbows on the table, his eyes like jet. '*Found out*, did they? How very clever.' She took up her glass and wondered again if she should text Giles.

'They heard about your application to restore Muirlan House—'

'I told you myself.'

'But now they said you're planning to make the old farmhouse into a hotel.'

'They're wrong.'

'It's no good, you know,' she said, her voice sharpening with remembered anger. 'They know about the other man, the property developer, Haggerty, was it?' He looked up, astonishment written on his face. 'And now you're working with some woman, with Canadian money behind you.' He sat back and stared at her, his jaw set hard and his lips a thin line of anger. He needed a shave and the overall impression was unnerving. She maintained eye contact for as long as she could, then reached again for her glass. Thank God they were in a public place.

'Who's feeding you this crap?'

'You've been applying for grants, talking to the planning office—'

'It's the divine Emma, isn't it?'

'You've done everything you can to discourage me. Throwing up obstacles. The condition of the house, local opposition, the bird reserve, contested land—'

'I stand by every word.'

'Giles said—'

'Oh yes. I want to hear what Giles said.'

He was looking dangerous again. Perhaps best not to tell him what Giles had called him, but she couldn't resist playing her trump card. 'Amongst other things, he said there's no record of any gift of the factor's house from Emily Blake to the Forbes family. Legally that house and all the land belong to the estate. To me.'

To her astonishment, she saw his eyes cloud over and he sat back. 'I know.'

'You know?'

Two steaming plates of pasta arrived. James shook his head in answer to the waiter's solicitous enquiries, and the man withdrew. 'Eat your dinner,' he said as he refilled her glass, 'while I see if I can unravel this mess.'

He began tearing a roll apart, his eyes fixed on the tablecloth. 'Three years ago I bought a cottage across the strand, opposite Muirlan House. I'd been abroad for years, but the island has always been home, even if only during school holidays.' He paused. 'The big house fascinated me. It always has. Despite what it once stood for, it was part of my life, it was in my blood.' He lifted his glass, watching her over the rim. 'And I *told* you I'd looked into saving it.' He paused again, demanding confirmation, and she nodded. 'I was hatching a plan with Andy Haggerty who, at the time, was principal development officer at the bird reserve, a man of great integrity and vision.' His mouth twisted. '*Not* a property developer.'

He told her how they had put together a proposal to restore the house, make it a centre for the reserve and the ecology of the island. Experimental farming. Rare breeds. 'And we would encourage artists and writers to come. The restoration itself would be done slowly and carefully, training young people as apprentices, developing their building and conservation skills while getting the job done, and island people would run the centre. We approached the Blake Trust and got a favourable response. They were looking to wind up the trust anyway, and this seemed the perfect solution. Put the remainder of Blake's legacy into Blake's old house to support his various interests.' He glanced up at her. 'It ticked every box they could think of, and we would make as little impact as possible and so preserve the special quality of the place.' He stopped and chewed for a moment. 'My one offence, if you like, was that of trespass. I went in and out of the house, trying to establish what needed to be done, and got more and more disillusioned.'

He sat back, aggression fading, and began running his finger around the rim of his glass as he had done with the museum's teacup, staring down at the chequered tablecloth. She felt the tension go out of him as she listened. 'But it never seemed like trespass. Ruairidh had keys. His dad had had keys. And his granddad too, I expect. They'd been looking after the place for generations. Faithful retainers for some phantom master—' He looked up at her again. 'But we didn't know who was master anymore. It was only when the fireplaces were all stolen that Ruairidh tracked down your grandmother's solicitors. It was quite a job.' Now that he had begun to shed his anger, he looked simply tired. 'And then everything went pear-shaped. It became clear that the project was beyond our reach, Andy was diagnosed with cancer, and the ownership issue, well, it became fogged too.' He looked away.

'Meaning?'

He hesitated, giving her an odd, faintly anxious look. 'It was three years ago. I'd asked the solicitors who I might approach to buy the house'—he paused—'and chose a bad time to ask.' She dropped her eyes. Three years ago, when her world had fallen apart. His eyes, when she looked back, were deeply sympathetic. 'I'm sorry. I read about the crash. A bird strike, wasn't it?'

She nodded. 'Shortly after take-off.'

'An awful irony, somehow.' He poured her some more wine and gave her time to recover. 'So we didn't pursue it, and as Andy sickened, we had to drop the whole idea.' They ate in silence for a while and the waiter came over, solicitous again, but James waved him away and sat forward. 'By then the idea had taken root in my head, it wouldn't go away, and the obvious solution struck me. The factor's house. Of course—I talked to Ruairidh, and the family, and everyone was in favour. Aonghas won't live forever, Ruairidh's dad doesn't want it, nor do Ruairidh and Ùna. So we went back to the Blake Trust, got some heavyweights interested, and things were progressing well.' He sat back, his face hardening again. 'And then the rumours started flying. The old lady had died and the new owner of Muirlan House had big plans.' She felt her colour rise under his steady scrutiny. 'Plans which would transform the island forever.' He picked up his fork and began eating, his eyes on his plate.

'My plans aren't so very dreadful,' she said after a moment. Naïve, perhaps, but only half-formed.

He ate doggedly on, not looking up. 'They're expanding, I hear. Shooting parties, yes, and the golf course I knew about, but a helipad? A wind turbine to power a spa?' He spoke between mouthfuls. 'I even hear talk of a causeway.'

'Not from me!' She was outraged. Was this Emma again?

'And now some *bloody* banker wants to buy you out!' She stared at him in amazement. How had he got wind of *that* in Mombasa? More emails? But someone had an ear close to the ground. Agnes McNeil, perhaps, although *she* had not been mentioned again. 'So things have cranked up a notch or two since I left.' Hetty made no reply, and he continued to glare at her. 'Will you sell?'

'No.'

He considered her for a moment longer, then went back to eating. 'But you're pressing on?'

'Giles says—' He raised his head, and she frowned at him. 'Giles says the scheme will bring prosperity to the area. Sustainable development.'

A savage look crossed his face. 'Aye. He's right, and that's why you'll probably get all the planning permissions you need.'

It made no sense. 'I don't understand.'

'Don't you?' His face was set very hard. 'I thought perhaps you might.' He remained silent for a long moment. 'As far as I'm concerned, "sustainable development" means whatever you can get away with this time. Then wait and push a little more, and then more again, until there's no going back. I've seen it happen all over the world where there are financial interests at stake. A lovely little two-word excuse to screw things up, as long as it returns a profit.' He offered her the last of the wine, then took it himself when she refused, and lifted his glass. 'I asked you once before if you thought that sort of development was appropriate to the island.' His knuckles whitened as he gripped the glass, and she waited for it to crack. 'To my mind the island's done its time as a rich man's playground, with money calling the shots and the islanders dancing a tune at the beck and call of incomers. It's now a precious place, wild and unspoiled, a sanctuary for more than just the birds.' He set the glass down. 'Blake saw that, for all his other shortcomings.' Then he reached out and took hold of her hand across the table, as he had done before, but gentler now, almost in an appeal, and she did not pull away. 'Something went terribly wrong for Theo Blake, but in the end the reserve he founded safeguarded a great swathe of the island. His neglect did the same for the rest, so time has stood still, and that special quality of the island has survived.' He released her hand and sat back again. 'I asked you once about Torrann Bay because I thought, perhaps, you could see it too. For God's sake, woman, you look at his painting of it every day.' Then he began rubbing his forehead with the heel of his hand. 'Sorry. I'm dog-tired.'

She drew her hand slowly back from where he had left it and felt relief spreading through her. She *hadn't* been wrong about him, and after a moment she asked quietly, 'You believe your own plans would safeguard it?'

His eyes were red-rimmed with exhaustion. 'That intention underpinned everything.' He took some time arranging the pasta on his fork, but it seemed too heavy to raise to his lips. 'But it looks like we've hit the buffers again.'

'Why?'

'You said it yourself. There's no record of the factor's house, or the land, being given away. Aonghas told us he had all the necessary papers, but it turned out to be just a letter from Emily Armstrong to his father, Donald Forbes, stating her intention. *Intention*, mind, not commitment. He has no deeds, no legal record. Nothing. It's a right old mess.'

'When did you find out?'

'Your... *Giles* alerted me to the potential problem that last time I saw you, and I went straight round to see Aonghas. The letter on its own is worthless. The family has been hunting for something more while I've been in Africa and found nothing. So technically they're still tenants, your tenants, and we can't do anything without your permission.' He tossed back the remainder of his wine. 'Which, in the circumstances, *mo charaid*, seems unlikely.' He looked at her for an endless moment. 'So you hold all the cards, madam. Emily Blake never followed through.'

~

Two days later, Hetty was on the underground on her way to Heathrow, replaying in her head James's parting words as he dismissed her offer to pay half the bill. 'I'm happy to stand you a meal, but understand this: if you press on, I'm going to do everything I can to stop you.' He had searched her face again. 'I thought that the state of the house would be enough, but I hadn't reckoned on the scale of the scheme, or known you had other interests pushing you on.' He paused. 'You're coming up at the weekend, you said?'

'Emma has the report from the second survey, and I arranged to meet her and Andrew. It was all sorted before you turned up again.' It seemed like an insult now, and he listened, poker-faced, then hailed a taxi and opened the door for her.

'Then next time we meet, Hetty, my dear, it'll be gloves off, in opposite corners of the ring. A pity, really.' She had got into the taxi, searching for something to say, but he just nodded briefly and closed the door behind her.

The underground reached Terminal 1, from where she would fly to Glasgow for her connection. Giles had been determined to come, but a big deal he was involved with had begun unravelling and he was going to be tied up in meetings. Just as well, as it would have precipitated a showdown to stop him, and she didn't need that just now. 'If we get it sorted, I'll come up on the afternoon flight, there's space, I checked.'

'Look, Giles, why not—'

'I just don't trust that lot up there, love. Not after Cameron turned up on your doorstep like that. Bloody nerve! You shouldn't have let him in, you know. Tantamount to harassment.' He had been deaf to her account of what James had told her that evening. 'You should have called me.'

No, Giles, much better not.

So now she was flying up alone, trusting that his meetings would run well into the afternoon. They usually did. And now she could deal with whatever confronted her on the island without the distraction of Giles.

One thing at a time.

She pulled out Blake's letters as she waited in the departure lounge, although she almost knew them by heart now. *I've been abroad for another spell of treatment,* he had written in July 1937. *Much good it has done me, though, and God knows when I will get back there. Germany is very worrying these days.* And she thought of him, bent over his desk, perhaps lifting his head to gaze through the window where she had first made her entry. Elderly now, ill and alone, turning visitors away. *I couldn't make you comfortable, my dear friend. Not like in the old days.* And there were fewer and fewer references to his paintings. *You are persistent, Charles. I will send you some if only to keep you quiet. You won't like them, I fear. I hardly do myself. I start with an idea but lose it somewhere in the execution.*

She gathered the letters up as her flight was called but pulled them out again once she had boarded. By 1940, the handwriting was spindly, and there was a weariness, a loss of confidence. *There is agitation again, you know,* one letter read, *and I am still being pestered to divide up the farmland. For what? Impoverished lives on an unforgiving soil. God knows I've tried to explain my position. Will they never leave me alone? I burn the letters now, or let Donald deal with them.* And in each successive letter evidence of belt-tightening and reduced circumstances. *Prices are bad again. It's hard to sell at all, sometimes. The hoggs fetch next to nothing, and even the bull brought three pounds less than we expected. But at least we can feed ourselves. I set a line for flounders in the sea pool, they make a tasty meal.* Was he reduced to catching fish in order to eat? Surely not! Or was this the eccentricity of a recluse? And always, between the lines, that heaviness, that deep sadness. *The land makes the people poor, Charles. Beauty might sustain the spirit, but it won't fill their bellies. The men work until they drop, their women grow old before their time, their children ill-nourished and ignorant.* So you were wrong, James Cameron—he did care, and that thought brought pleasure. And then, in a letter dated 1942, *Three pairs of red-necked phalaropes are nesting on the loch behind the house. Do you remember the one Baird took? Curse him. They hadn't nested there since. But they're back! I leave my gun at home these days, and I've resolved to give land over to be a reserve for the birds. They at least thrive here, and planning it gives me some solace. Perhaps some small absolution.* And as she stared out of the plane window, she thought of the painting of the desperate man calling out across the waves, the running figures on the other canvas, that sense of urgency, of things slipping from his grasp, of loss. *It's only when the fever is on me that I burn to paint again, but then a dark force takes hold of my brain, and it gives me no pleasure. My sister Emily persists in trying to persuade me back to Edinburgh. But I shan't go, you know. I'm bound to this place forever now, and I claim sanctuary here.*

As the plane came down to meet the tarmac of the runway, Blake's words mingled with what James had said: '... *a precious place, wild and unspoiled, a sanctuary for more than just the birds.*'

Chapter 43

'Lovely to see you again, darling.' Emma came out to the car park to greet her, having watched for her in reception, and eyed the battered hire car with astonishment. 'Good journey? It's a shame Giles got held up. Do you think he'll make it?' She opened the hotel door and ushered Hetty in. 'I spoke to the banker's representatives again this morning. They're *very* keen, you know.' And she prattled on, undaunted by Hetty's silence. '*Lots* to chew over. Plenty of options. And I understand you've been making some pretty powerful connections yourself. Jasper Banks, of all people! *Well done.*' She waited beside her while Hetty registered at reception and said that they would have tea. 'You being Blake's relative is worth a great deal, you know, and his work is making something of a comeback. That rock pool painting is so romantic; we can use it in all the advertising. It's perfect! And Giles tells me you've bought another original yourself. Is it a good one? Either way, there's *loads* for any good marketing team to get their teeth into. I'll order tea.'

'Thank you, but no.' Emma looked surprised, but Hetty was firm. 'There's something I didn't finish last time I was here, so please forgive me, and I'll see you later.' She went to her room to leave her bag.

The woman in the library recognised her at once and fussed kindly as she showed her how to load the images, explaining that the room they were in had once been the manse's parlour, knocked through into the original dining room. When she had gone, Hetty sat back, soothed by the stillness that is peculiar to old houses, and began. The timeless quiet added to the sense of unreality as she began to scroll once more through the collection of images, and she was left suspended between two worlds. The knowledge that wild birds now flew unhindered through the rooms before her on the screen was forgotten as she stepped again into that other time.

She lingered over the picture of Emily leaning against the man who would so briefly be her husband, oblivious then to what lay ahead, joyfully unaware that too soon she would have to learn acceptance, learn how to endure and move on. As Hetty herself was learning— The zoom brought her face closer. Perhaps there *was* a strength there behind that bright youthfulness, lying dormant until it was needed. She moved the zoom to Theo Blake's face, then back to Emily's, convincing herself she could trace the resemblance between them. Both faces had the same directness, the same assurance. It was more softly defined in Emily, but it was there. She moved back to Blake and focussed on his eyes, hooded and dark, and believed that she saw the artist there.

And then with a jolt she realised that for all the other photographs, she was, quite literally, seeing through Theo Blake's eyes, seeing what he had seen, captured by his camera's shutter. These fading images linked him directly to her, and she was as close to him as if she were inside his head.

Suddenly he was very real. Gripped by the thought, she went back to the beginning. And now as she scrolled through the images, she felt an intimate connection to him and began to appreciate his skill with composition, his painter's eye for drama. A slash of sunlight cut across the dark hall from the open front door, a curlew posed on his desk mirrored a half-finished sketch beside it, a rainbow's arc was captured through the dining room window and framed by the window itself. And gradually she realised that there was a sequence to the photographs, as if they had been taken on the same occasion, and that they followed a route inside the house.

She leant forward towards the screen, gripped now, and followed him down the hall into the drawing room, across to the dining room, the morning room, and then the study, lingering for a moment in each. Then he began to mount the stairs, and she went with him—past the stag which kept its gaze aloof and distant, a clever camera angle followed the curve of the banisters to the tiled floor of the hall, and a shot taken through the round window on the half-landing was over-exposed and fuzzy, exploiting the contrast between the dark of the stairwell and the ethereal brightness of the outside world. A dream world... She imagined him framing the image, then pausing a moment to look out across the pasture to the dramatic skies above the western dunes. Then came a series of images which she had not seen before, taken on the decaying upper floor. Doors opened from the intact landing, and she had glimpses of a linen press, a bookcase, a polished table, an oval mirror, a painting on the wall. And suddenly she was in the room that should have been hers, and she could see the rounded niche of the turret in one corner. The edge of a brass bedstead protruded into the image, slippers lay askew on a rug beside it, clothes discarded on the counterpane, a washstand with jug and bowl. And she saw, reflected in the mirror, two figures.

Her hand stayed. The manse's parlour vanished, and she was right there in the room in Muirlan House, an interloper. Beatrice was sitting at her dressing table, her hands raised to her hair, looking back at her through the mirror, laughing. No, looking back at *him*, for he too was reflected in the mirror, bent to the camera with only the top of his head and one arm visible. He was raising his hand, palm uppermost, in encouragement. In the photograph he had contrived a layering of images, the vertical planes of the angled mirror wings reflecting back through the central mirror an infinite number of Beatrices. Tears burned behind Hetty's eyes as she realised what she had stumbled upon. For this was it! Before her was the inspiration behind the painting she had been unable to leave behind. A moment of intimacy that he had remembered years later and had painted—not with the playfulness of the photographic image but as a hard-edged record of a marriage that had fractured and fallen apart. For that joyful moment before her now had been a fleeting one, soon gone, the sentiments soured and vanished, together with every rug from the floor, every stick of furniture, every stuffed bird, every breath and every heartbeat—gone with the auctioneer's hammer or on a gull's wing to oblivion. She had come too late.

~

She left the museum in a daze. She had reached through the years and experienced a past emotional charge, a charge that Blake's photograph and, later, his painting had captured in ways that were poles apart, depicting the joyful beginning and the broken end. And Beatrice's sepia phantom had seared herself onto her mind's eye. She walked slowly back to the hotel, past the lochan fringed with yellow iris, thinking how, over these last weeks, through his paintings and letters, the jagged, ill-fitting pieces of Theo Blake's life had begun to come together. And it had been a tragic life, almost operatic in its drama.

She remembered her first reaction to the house, when she had seen it as an abandoned film set. And that's what it was, simply the setting for lives that were now played out. Past help. Past saving

But the island wasn't.

And suddenly the house itself no longer mattered. It could go. It was more important that there would always be lapwings swooping low across the machair, waves coming ashore on the empty stretch of Torrann Bay, below wide skies which reached to clear horizons. It was that which mattered.

And somewhere there would be a battered Land Rover crossing the strand and guarding the marches.

Rain blew fitfully as she hastened towards the hotel. The wind was strengthening, and as she crossed the car park she overheard a man say that an unseasonably large storm was on its way. 'We'll not see the ferry back for a day or two,' he remarked, 'and the airfield's closed.' Closed! So Giles would not have made it anyway. Just as well, as explaining to Emma and Andrew how she now saw matters was going to be awkward enough as it was.

But Giles had made it. As she pushed open the door, she saw him, having a drink with Andrew and Emma in the reception lounge. He got to his feet. 'There you are! We were wondering where you'd got to.' He gave her a hug and she smelt alcohol on him, more than a glassful. 'God, what a flight. Caught it by the skin of my teeth and then—whew! Bounced all over the place. Titchy little plane too. Got in just before the airport shut.'

It had always surprised her that a man of Giles's self-assurance should be afraid of flying, but he was. In airport lounges she had got used to watching him sweat and fidget, drinking more than he should, becoming agitated and short-tempered. It was never easy. To be fair, this probably had been a rough flight, but how much *had* he drunk? 'The guy next to me spewed, which didn't help.' With a sinking heart, she recognised that he was now in the next phase, where relief brought out bluster and aggression to cover any suggestion of weakness.

But he had recovered enough to change into well-creased trousers and a sharp sports jacket, and was looking decidedly metropolitan amongst the locals. 'Let's go through and get you a drink, shall we?' he said. 'We've booked an early table, so lead on, Em.'

'Giles, we need to talk—' Hetty tried to hold him back, but he patted her arm and propelled her forward in Emma's wake.

'Plenty of time.'

The Island Inn catered to everyone from serious fishermen and bird-watchers to tourists passing through, but the locals were the mainstay of business. Being Friday night, the bar was already doing a brisk trade, and they were met by a warm beery smell and the sound of laughter. Emma looked around and gestured to an empty table just beyond the bar, while Dalbeattie went to get drinks. And, as the group at the bar parted to let him through, it seemed inevitable that Hetty would find herself looking across a sea of customers to James Cameron, leaning on the bar, Ruairidh Forbes beside him, deep in conversation.

He looked up, straightening slowly when he saw her.

Then Giles caught sight of him. 'Well, well,' he muttered, too loudly. 'The man himself.'

Ruairidh Forbes turned at his words and saw Hetty. He stepped forward with a warm smile and a hand outstretched. 'Good to see you again.'

She clutched his hand gratefully and felt obliged to introduce him to the others. 'Forbes, did you say?' Giles's voice seemed to boom out. 'Ah... Yes. How d'ye do?' Then to her dismay he turned back to James. 'Sorry to have missed you last week, Mr. Cameron,' he drawled. 'Just a flying visit, I gather.' James fixed his eyes on Giles, saying nothing. 'Took Hetty by surprise. On her own. You quite unsettled her, you know.'

'Did I?' James transferred his gaze to Hetty, raising an eyebrow. He had, but not in the way Giles meant.

'Last-ditch attempt, was it?' Giles continued. If he hadn't drunk so much he might have noticed that James had become very still. This had to be stopped. She stepped forward, but Giles moved in front of her and continued. 'I can see, from your point of view, why you were keeping your cards close to your chest, but under the circumstances, don't you think, some sort of declaration of interest, eh?'

'Giles!' She watched, mortified, as James's face darkened, and she saw Ruairidh mutter something and lift a hand as if to calm things. But Giles was unstoppable.

'At least we now know where we stand,' he continued relentlessly. 'And once the dubious ownership claims have been cleared up—'

'Giles!'

Ruairidh clamped his hand on his cousin's arm and turned towards Hetty, blocking James's path to Giles. 'Bit of a surprise, that was,' he said, and gave her a reassuring smile. 'But your visit's well-timed. Una rang just now to say there's an official-looking envelope waiting at home. Inverness postmark. Probably the lab.' He lifted his half-full glass. 'I'm away home to see when I've finished this.'

'Oh, golly. The bones!' exclaimed Emma. 'I keep forgetting. A *real* challenge for the marketing team.' James transferred his stony gaze from Giles to her, then muttered something inaudible and presented a contemptuous shoulder. Ruairidh addressed Hetty again. 'If there's news, shall I find you here in the morning?'

'Yes.'

'Best not make any commitments as to time, darling,' said Giles, slipping an arm round her waist. 'We've got to get to the island and back, remember, negotiating the tides. Perhaps Mr. Forbes could leave the report or something at reception.' He smiled briefly at Ruairidh and turned back to Emma. 'Let's eat, shall we?' Hetty stayed rooted to the spot, wanting to explain, wanting to make things right, but was now daunted by James's uncompromising back. And besides, a public bar was hardly the place for what needed to be said. 'I'll be in touch,' she said, but he appeared not to hear, and then Giles steered her away.

Chapter 44

∼ 2010, Hetty ∼

The restaurant was already busy and their table was right in the centre. They took their seats, and Dalbeattie began at once to explain the findings of the new surveyor.

Hetty tried to stop him. 'Wait, there's something—'

But he was as unstoppable as a juggernaut. 'Let me just run quickly through the main points, m'dear. It's in a bad state but not hopeless. The principal cost will be— Ah, yes, let's order.' He paused while the waiter hovered and they considered the menu. Hetty looked at the door to the bar, wanting to go back and talk to Ruairidh and James, but she owed it to Giles, and his friends, to explain first how everything had changed. The waiter was doubtless a local man, though, so she must wait until he had gone. It wouldn't be easy, but at least it would be done. There'd be the legal matters to sort, of course, but for the rest, it was over.

She looked across at Giles. His face was glistening and his eyes were bright, and he was talking too loudly. Drinking didn't suit him; it made him into a caricature of himself. But that too was over, and she found herself sad at the thought. Would he mind so very much? He had been good to her at a time when she had most needed help, when she had felt so very alone. He had seen her through the worst times, but he had begun to consume her, absorbing her into a world which she knew now was not for her.

She became aware that the others had fallen silent. This was her moment. But then she saw a look pass between Giles and Andrew, and Andrew leant across and poured wine into her glass. 'I believe Giles has told you about the other interest there has been?'

'The banker, my love,' said Giles. 'Apparently he's keen—'

'There's a terrific deal to be struck, you know—'

'No. Look—'

But still they didn't listen. 'We'll help steer you through it, of course, we'll still be on board.' And through his genial smile she realised that Dalbeattie and Dawson were already nurturing this potential new client.

Giles looked nervously at her. 'I'm not sure Hetty has quite decided—'

'Oh, I have. I won't sell. In fact—'

'Bravo!' Emma raised her glass, swinging back in line. 'I'm so pleased, it's a brave decision. There's a lot of hard work ahead but—'

'Are you sure?' Giles interrupted. 'It's a *lot* of money. We haven't really talked it—'

'I'm sure. You see—'

'Just one big celebrity wedding and we'll be on the map.' Emma was smiling and beaming at her, certain of her interest now, her complicity. 'Sorting out the ownership question will take a little time, and might be awkward, but—'

'It won't be.' Her tone finally got through. 'That land is theirs. Emily Blake gave it to them. I'll not take it back.'

The expressions on their faces were almost comical. Giles spoke first. 'But we've never even *seen* this famous letter, and they said it expressed *intention*. The old girl changed her mind!'

Hetty shook her head, sure of herself now. 'She didn't. I know she didn't. She gave the factor's house and the land to the Forbeses, and then she closed up Muirlan House, turned her back on it, and walked away.'

They looked at her in astonishment, and Giles laughed awkwardly. 'What's this, darling? Second sight?'

'No. But I'm certain nevertheless.'

And suddenly she had to get out of there, while her resolve held firm. There was, after all, no point in staying. She pushed back her chair, scraping it on the floor, and the other diners fell silent, hopeful of a drama.

Giles leant forward urgently, his hand on her arm. 'But, darling, surely you must see—'

'No. I do see, but differently to you. Though I didn't at first—I don't really expect you to understand, but I'm pulling out. Saving Muirlan House would be too costly—and I don't mean the money. It belongs to the past and should stay there. It's the island that matters, you see. And where we were heading, there'd be no return. We need places like that, we really do, but they're fragile and vulnerable, and we were all set to destroy something irreplaceable. And that mustn't happen.' She stood up and addressed Emma and Andrew. 'So I'm sorry, but this stops here. No legal action, no bankers, no finance packages, no franchises. I shouldn't have let it go so far, and I've wasted your time. I'm sorry… No, Giles. Stay where you are. Let me go.'

Somehow she managed to escape from the dining room, leaving behind a ripple of conjecture from the other diners. The waiter bringing their starters stopped to stare as she walked swiftly out of the room and into the bar. But as the door closed behind her, her legs felt suddenly weak.

Where on earth did she go now?

The locals around the bar had dispersed to their houses, leaving only two figures, James Cameron and the bartender, in conversation across the bar. She paused in the middle of the room and then walked towards him. He turned and straightened as she approached.

'Tell Ruairidh Forbes it's alright. About the house and the land.' She heard her voice becoming unsteady. 'It was Emily's gift.'

James looked back at her, his expression unreadable. 'So you can do what you want with it, what you'd planned.' She was flooded suddenly by an all too familiar sense of loss. 'And Muirlan House must go. I see that now.' He took a step forward, but she had had enough of all of them. 'No—' She turned and left the bar quickly, crossing the reception area, through the outer door, and into the darkening evening.

Chapter 45

∼ 2010, Hetty ∼

There was only one road around the main island, so it wasn't difficult to find the spot where the track led down to the strand. Even in the fading light, Hetty recognised it, and she turned down it, still driven by that surge of energy that had propelled her through the door and out into the car park, and by a compelling need to go once more to the island, and to Muirlan House.

She cringed as the car rocked over the stony ruts and down onto the wet sand, hearing a sickening scrape as she dragged the underside over the uneven surface. The car was not designed for this! There was another bad moment as she lurched through the deep channel and it almost stalled, but she managed to keep going and then sped across the strand. God, what a night! She had to lean forward with the windscreen wipers on full and noted fleetingly how the dark clouds had lowered the sky. The tide still looked well out, but how long could she spend on the island? Fifteen minutes? Not long, but it would be enough. Then she wouldn't come back again, not while the house still stood. But she had to come back this last time, alone, as she had first seen it just a few short weeks before. Once she had given the word, its fate was sealed and it would be gone.

It took longer than she remembered to drive across, and she felt the car being buffeted by the rising gale. The wind was being funnelled through a gap between land and island, blown in from the ocean. What was it that Ruairidh had said about westerlies?

But fifteen minutes would be enough, and then she would return to the hotel and face the music. She almost panicked at the midway point when low cloud masked both shorelines and she was left without landmarks, but she pressed on, teeth gritted.

Then she saw the chimneys of the house in front of her. She headed straight for them and was soon pulling up the foreshore and onto the old drive, and the light from the headlights bounced off the high walls. Leaving the car where Ruairidh had left the Saab that first day, she got out and ran, head bent against the driving wind, tripping over the uneven surface awash with mud, and regretted her thin clothing. The walls of the house were streaked with wide damp patches from fallen gutters, and the gaunt ribs of roof timbers moved in the wind. Intruders had torn away the front window boarding again and got in through the porch, where the makeshift door swung loose on its hinges, flying open and banging shut as the gusts caught it.

She reached the porch's shelter breathless and soaked. Above her was the room with the little turret, where that intimate scene had been played out, that brief moment of laughter. And as she stood there, the rhythm of the swinging door became hypnotic. It flung back two or three times, then banged, flung open again, and banged shut. She found herself timing it, repeating the rhythm and, as it flung wide, she grabbed the handle and held, and next moment she was in the hall, dripping rainwater onto the dung-cushioned floor. Ten minutes.

Darkness and deep shadows hid the dereliction, and in the fading half-light she saw the century-old images of the past clearly before her. In the drawing room, a pale light filtered through the liberated windows, and she went to stand where she had seen Beatrice and looked out on an unchanged scene, watching the storm clouds blackening the strand. Beatrice— she felt conscious of her presence, and of her absence, as one might feel in an ancient tomb, sensing an emptiness, filled only by sorrow and loss. If the bones were hers, would she rest more easily having been recognised and reclaimed? *There's damp in the drawing room,* Blake had written in 1942, *so I closed it up. I never use it now.* Her throat tightened and she withdrew, pausing at the door of Blake's study. *It's easier to heat the study, and everything I want is there.* Then her feet took her to the morning room, where

Aonghas could only remember lumber being stored, next to a conservatory that had never been finished. Numbly, she went back into the hall.

Was that it? Could she go now? She hesitated, then looked up, feeling a sudden compulsion to follow the rest of Theo Blake's photographic route through the remnants of his house. It would be her last chance. If she went as far as the half-landing, she might be able to see inside the room she had hoped to make her own, where she had witnessed that sweet moment through Blake's camera lens. If she kept close to the wall where the staircase was firmly attached, she would be safe, and a glimpse would be enough. Five minutes more?

A rumble of thunder seemed to sound a warning as she stepped onto the lower treads. They were splintered in some parts but firm beneath her feet, and she reached the small half-landing safely, pausing to look through the round window. For a moment the broken rooflight was clear of storm clouds and lit the stairs with an unnatural light, while the scene through the round window was dark and threatening. It was the negative image of the photograph Theo Blake had taken there, and for a moment she felt his unsettled spirit around her. Gulls, like lost souls, swept past the jagged hole in the roof.

Mustn't linger. Three more steps above the half-landing looked sound, and she went cautiously upward until her eyes became level with the landing. She stood on tiptoe, and from there she could just see through the doorway and into the room with the small turret.

It was a wreck. Of course it was. The roof was gone, and the floor was littered with broken beams and fallen slates. But what on earth had she expected? And then as surely as she had needed to come, she needed to leave. The house would go, and this room would go, but the photograph would survive, and that moment would outlive the house and endure. Then another thunder clap sounded overhead and rain began to fall steadily. She stepped backwards, catching her leg on a jagged splinter of wood, and she bent to look, feeling the wetness of blood on her skin.

'*For Christ's sake*, woman!' a furious voice roared from below. 'Are you *mad*?' Only now, she realised that the rhythm of the banging door had been interrupted, and she peered down to see James Cameron looking up at her from the bottom of the stairwell, his face pale in the half-light. The last rumble of thunder must have masked the arrival of the Land Rover, which she now saw had drawn up outside. 'Come down, for God's sake. It's not to die for.'

As soon as her foot touched the last stair, he grabbed her arm, propelling her swiftly across the hall, out of the door, and onto the drive before opening the door of the Land Rover and pushing her in, glancing over his shoulder as he did. It was only then that she realised how much the wind had strengthened; the banging of the front door was now echoed by a loud knocking and creaking as loose roof timbers struggled to withstand the gusts.

He drove away fast, bumping over deeply carved channels running with rainwater, and stopped where she had left her hire car. 'Look at you. Soaked to the skin and bloody. *Jesus!*' He leant forward and rested his arms on top of the steering wheel. 'And what now, Hetty? Back over the strand, is it?'

'Yes.'

She dug into her pocket and pulled out the car keys, but he reached across and took them. 'No.'

She stared at him. 'Why not? What are you doing?'

He let out the hand brake and they rolled back down to the main track, pausing where it forked. 'I was ten, maybe fifteen minutes behind you, but that last channel was above the axles when I crossed.' He took the track which led away from the foreshore towards the farmhouse. 'We're stuck here until the wee hours, maybe longer given the storm,' he said as he swung the Land Rover into the courtyard. 'Sit tight.' He ran across, hunched over the padlock on the farmhouse door, and then pushed it open and beckoned. She left the Land Rover and he swept her in, half closed the door, and took an oilskin from a peg behind it. 'There'll be slates flying about soon. I need to move your car.' And he was gone again.

It was calm and still inside the old farmhouse, the thick walls absorbing the noise of the storm, and the fading light shone pearly-grey through cobwebbed windows. She stood dazed and breathless, and looked about her, steadying herself, as her heart rate slowed. They would have to spend the *night* here! But where? In the dim light she could see an old cast-iron range and a wooden dresser beside a row of 1950s wooden cupboards, piled high with plastic fish crates and empty petrol cans. A coil of rope festooned with dried seaweed was stashed in a corner next to coloured net floats, crab pots, old newspapers, and a roll of barbed wire. And in the centre, as if rooted there, stood a large pine table with broken chairs and stools arranged around it, and she remembered what Ruairidh had told her: '...*She sat at the big old kitchen table, drinking tea and reminiscing about childhood days. A lovely woman.*' Hetty went across to the table and ran her hand over the worn surface.

Emily. She had spent her last night on the island here.

James returned, bringing with him a blast of rain-soaked air, and hung the oilskin behind the door, where it dripped steadily and formed a pool on the old flagstones. He rubbed a hand briskly through his damp hair, then pulled off his sweater, throwing it towards her. 'Put that on. I've got this.' And he pushed his head through an old torn fisherman's gansey that lay beside the oilskins. 'You're shivering. Put it on,' he insisted, 'and let's have a look at your leg.' He lifted a hurricane lantern from the windowsill, lit it, and placed it on the table, then from somewhere he produced a first aid kit.

He gestured for her to sit down and sat beside her, raising her leg to rest across his knee, and pulled aside her skirt to examine the cut. His sweater swamped her with a comforting warmth; it smelt of woodsmoke and salt water. 'Bare legs, on a night like this,' he scoffed, bringing the lantern closer.

'I hadn't planned to leave the hotel.'

He made a derisive sound and wiped away blood which had dried in streaks from her knee to her ankle. But his fingers were gentle, and his efforts revealed a small gash along her calf. 'Tetanus up to date?' he asked and dabbed antiseptic liberally on the open wound, adding, 'serves you right,' and not looking up when she gasped, biting her lip. Then he sat back and viewed her gravely. 'Alright?' She nodded and lifted her leg from his knee.

He got up and began rummaging in one of the old cupboards, producing a bottle of whisky and two mugs. 'Medicinal. And then it's a choice between baked beans or tinned pilchards.' From the same cupboard he produced an old primus stove, two tins, and a pan, which he took to the sink, holding it under a hand pump, pumping briskly. She watched, fascinated, and he smiled slightly at her expression. 'We often stay here during lambing,' he said, over his shoulder, 'and besides, old Aonghas never quite finished moving out.' He set the primus going and poured baked beans into the pan, his movements economical and competent, his hair drying in spikes and the old sweater unravelling at both elbows. She tried, and failed, to imagine Giles in such a situation.

After a cursory inspection, he discarded the pilchards and then sat across the table from her. 'So, tell me.'

And haltingly at first, then more fluently, she described what had passed in the dining room, what she had decided. He was a good listener, saying nothing, not even when she finished, but simply nodded and went to crouch in front of the old range and began laying sticks in the fire basket. After a moment, he spoke, his back still to her. 'An old newspaper cutting turned up amongst Aonghas's papers while I was away. He said he didn't know it was there.' He rocked back on his heels and turned to her. 'But it answers one thing. Emily Armstrong and her second husband were both killed in a motor accident in France a few weeks after she came up here.' He began making spills from old newspapers and struck a match. 'Armstrong was South African.

A racing car driver.'

She spread her hands over the surface of the table again, reaching back. 'So that explains why my grandmother was going out there, to her father's family. There was no one left here. And Emily died, leaving trailing threads.' He nodded, watching the fire as it took hold. Then he came and sat down opposite her again, and she found herself telling him about revisiting the museum, about the photographs, her sense of being behind the camera and seeing the house through Theo Blake's eyes, and how she had felt compelled to trace time back to that brief moment of brightness. 'I had to see the place where he and Beatrice had been happy. Just once.' Would he understand?

Perhaps he did, but he shook his head at her. 'Madness. I guessed you'd set off to come here, but I thought you'd have enough sense not to cross over. And then I saw your headlights on the far side as I swung round the bay road.' He got up to stir the baked beans, cursing when he found they had stuck to the pan. 'And then I knew there was every chance you'd be crazy enough to go inside, or try to cross back.' He scraped the beans onto two chipped enamel plates and pushed one towards her. 'But you're alive. So eat.'

They ate in silence. Then: 'So you'll make over the house, legally, to old Aonghas?' he said between mouthfuls, fixing her with his intense look.

'Yes.'

'He was all set to move back over here, you know, thinking occupancy would make a difference, got into a terrible fret.' She began to apologise, but he cut her off. 'And the land?'

James Cameron took no prisoners. 'That too. All of it. And I've no intention of taking on Mr. MCP Software Inc. either.'

He looked up at that and grinned. 'So you worked that one out, did you? Pity, really. I was looking forward to seeing MacPhail versus Blake in the courts. Playing out the last episode in a long feud.'

'Who is he?'

'John MacPhail? Nice guy. Canadian. Son of a post-war emigrant whose forebear was thrown into jail for resisting eviction by Blake's father.' He reached over and poured whisky into the two mugs. 'In one of Blake's later bizarre acts, he granted the family croft land, and their descendants have held on to it like a sacred trust ever since. John repaired the old house himself some years ago and comes over for a week or so every summer. No electricity, no running water, but he says it keeps him sane. If you'd tried to claim it back, he'd have chewed you up, spat you out, and then jumped on the remains, with a legion of MacPhail phantoms cheering him on.' He laughed at her, his teeth white in the lantern light, and she found herself smiling in response. 'He was the ace up my sleeve, you see.' And his laughter was as warming as the amber whisky, but then she saw his face grow thoughtful again. 'Blake gave them croft land about the same time he set up the bird reserve.'

'Bad conscience?'

He shrugged. 'It was years later, but maybe. By now Ruairidh will have opened that package and might have the answer to that little mystery. I was about to go round to him when you made your dramatic exit.' In the poor light she could no longer see his expression, but she sensed him grow tense again.

He spooned more baked beans onto his plate, his eyes in shadow. 'You think it *was* Theo Blake, then?' she asked, shaking her head at his gesture, refusing her share.

'Maybe. But there's a lot we don't know about the man. At the end he wasn't just a recluse, he was tormented. Mad, perhaps, some of the time. The stories which come down tell of him striding out across the machair, talking and gesticulating to invisible companions, odd manic behaviour, short spells of normality followed by periods when he was stoned on morphine. Apparently he went berserk on the day of the old factor's funeral, sobbing and cursing, and then became obsessed about renovating the house. Crazy stuff. And then'—he paused—'and then he took his own life, drowning himself in the strand.'

She stared. 'Drowning *himself*?'

'It was covered up to avoid a scandal.' She sat back, stunned, and looked at him, the light from the lantern glinting in his eye. 'Donald Forbes found him when the tide had receded, his body caught against a reef near the ruined chapel. Aonghas remembers it well, he'd just come home on leave.'

'An accident, surely!'

'He'd filled his pockets with stones.'

She stared at him, struggling to absorb this new twist to the tragedy, and then another piece fitted into place. 'Emily knew,' she said, and told him about the reference to stones in her grandmother's journal. 'It *must* have been a guilty conscience.'

'Maybe.' His face had closed again, discouraging further questioning.

But later, when they had finished eating, their plates scraped clean, he rose and closed the shutters, lighting another storm lantern, and they sat in a small circle of light at the old scrubbed table. And he began to talk.

'These islands, this place, has always been important to me, the only fixed point in my life.' For once he looked almost vulnerable. 'As a boy I used to get parked up here, with the Forbeses, when my father was between jobs. Kenya, Nepal, Belize. Big engineering projects. He was everywhere.' He looked down, running his finger around the top of the tin mug. 'And I began to realise that my being here was part of a pattern, one that goes back a long way'— his face was thoughtful, the angles of his features exaggerated by the shifting shadows—'part of something unresolved.' He looked up at her again. 'You see, it wasn't just *me* who'd spent my childhood up here, almost fostered by Ruairidh's family. My grandfather had been taken in by them, and after *he* was killed in the war, his son— my father—grew up here. All strays, all finding sanctuary here with the Forbeses, generation after generation. Drawn back.' He stared into the fire, disappearing again into a private world.

A question which had long hovered at the edge of her mind suddenly came to her. 'What about the surnames? Why are you

Cameron and not Forbes, like Ruairidh?'

He pulled a wry face. 'I wondered when you'd ask.' He sat back, one arm hooked over the top of his chair, the long fingers of his other hand wrapped around the mug. 'It's part of the mystery, perhaps an important part. I told you before that Cameron Forbes argued with Blake and left the island in 1911.' She nodded. 'Well, my grandfather, Johnnie, was Cameron's son, so we're told, and was always known as Johnnie *Forbes*, as you'd expect. He got married during the war, in London, to an island girl who was nursing down there. Old sweethearts, apparently, and she came back to the island after he was killed, pregnant with my father. When Dad was born, they dug out Johnnie's birth certificate to find it stated that his father was a John *Cameron* and his mother Jane Cameron. Big surprise all round, and no one left to explain. Johnnie hadn't been born on the island, you see. Old John Forbes brought him here as a small child, saying that his mother was dead but that he was Cameron's son.' He waited while she absorbed this, watching her face, then went on. 'If true, it would appear that Cameron Forbes didn't stay in Canada after all, but came back, changed his name, fathered a son, and then disappeared again.' Shadows from the lantern threw half his face into darkness. 'All of which suggests that Cameron Forbes was very keen *not* to be found. It's the only reason to change your name that I know of.'

She nodded slowly, recognising that this was something he had thought through many times. 'And so you think the body is the reason Cameron had to disappear?'

He nodded, his face still tense. 'The letter he sent when he arrived in Canada seems deliberately vague about his plans, gives no address, so maybe he was on the run. And then a few years later John Forbes brings his child here, to wait for Cameron to come for him, he said. The old factor knew something, and *he* expected Cameron to come back.' He tossed down the last of the whisky and got to his feet. 'I just don't get it. Never have. And God knows who Jane Cameron was. I can't trace her at all.'

They cleared away the remains of the meal in silence and

he set the primus alight again for coffee. 'You can understand why they all kept coming back to this house—there's something reassuringly solid and practical about the place. And unlike Muirlan House, it was built to endure. Want to look around? No mysteries here.'

And he was right. There was no place for ghosts amongst the assortment of junk which the years had accumulated. Plastic fertiliser bags, hessian potato sacks, and obscure pieces of machinery filled the front parlour, and a rusty paraffin heater still occupied a blocked space in front of the old stone fireplace. Dark rectangles on the stained wallpaper showed where pictures had once hung, and more potato sacks spilled from the cupboard under the stairs.

The lantern cast moving shadows on the walls as they went upstairs, their footsteps ringing hollow on the bare wood. Under the sloping roofs of the bedrooms there was more junk, a child's cot, a dented tin trunk, a bewildering array of household and farm utensils, and broken pieces of furniture as old as the house itself. Opposite the window in the largest bedroom, the rusty frame of a double bed still stood propped against one wall.

'Like I said, Aonghas never quite moved out.' Hetty went and stood by the window, looking through the broken glass at where white crests now tipped the waves, and the wind blew spray across the dark surface, and she understood the danger James had saved her from.

Then he was there beside her, very close. 'What a way to go, drowning in a rusty Ford Fiesta,' he said. 'I'd never have forgiven myself.'

And even as she willed it, his hands were on her shoulders, turning her towards him, and he kissed her. He drew back after a moment to look at her. 'I've been wanting to do that for a while.' The angles of his face were sharply etched by the light coming through the window, and his eyes glinted a smile. 'Right from the start, in fact'—she raised a hand to his face, and he twisted his head to kiss her palm—'despite the difficulties.'

'Consorting with the enemy?' she said, a little unsteadily.

'Something like that,' he said, drawing her closer, his cheek cool against hers. His old gansey smelt vaguely of creosote and sawdust, nostalgic, familiar smells, and on his lips she could taste the whisky they had shared.

How strange was this feeling, of things falling into place.

A flash of lightning startled them apart, followed by a crash of thunder which shook the house. He glanced up at the ceiling. 'Right overhead.' He bent to pick up the lantern. 'Come on. You're shivering again.' He scooped up a pile of potato sacks, guiding her back down the stairs and into the kitchen, where the kettle on the primus was dancing. 'Sit over by the range and warm up. I'll be back in a minute.'

Cold air filled the room as he left, and the primus flame stuttered. She dragged one of the old chairs close to the fire and tucked her feet up under her, pulling his sweater over her knees, and a deep sense of well-being crept over her. No longer the enemy. How suddenly, and how quickly, matters corrected themselves. The current of connection which she had sought had become live and vital in a way she could not have imagined, separating the before and after. And she sat there, staring into the fire, absorbing the idea of James, and with it a quiet thrum of excitement. No longer the enemy! Then she rose and searched the cupboards, finding a small jar of dried-out Nescafé and a twisted bag of solid sugar.

She had hacked off enough of both for two mugs when the door opened again, and he came in clutching the potato sacks now plump with hay, and glanced at the steaming mugs. 'Good girl,' he said and went back for more, arranging them on the floor in front of the range. 'A couple more should do it,' he said, and disappeared into the narrow hallway where they had seen sacks in the under-stair cupboard.

A few moments later he returned, walking slowly, the sacks tucked under his arm and carrying a large rectangle covered in hessian.

'Maybe now I can show you this.' She looked up at his tone. 'I wasn't going to tell you, things being as they were, but now—' He crouched down beside her, pulling a package from its sacking cover and removing a layer of corrugated cardboard. He held it for her to see.

It was a painting, a watercolour, and in the flickering light she could see it was the foreshore on a misty morning when the light filtered softly through the grey veil. And out on the strand there were two faint figures, disappearing into the mist. The light from the hurricane lamp fell on the corner and lit that confident, well-known signature.

Theodore Blake 1897. Muirlan Strand.

Jasper Banks's catalogue exhibit number 372, the painting that couldn't be traced.

James was watching her face. 'I was so annoyed with you about the second survey that I forgot about the painting, but later I remembered and described what you said to Aonghas. He thought he did remember something like that, hanging here when he was a lad. So I came a-looking.'

She could not peel her eyes away from it. 'Where was it?'

'Under the stairs with a load of old frames and potato sacks. Must have been there for decades, thought to be just another empty frame. Thank God the place is dry.'

'And you left it here? It's worth a fortune.'

'It had been safe there for years. I hadn't told anyone, and I was going away. And frankly, since I got back, I'd forgotten. It belongs to Aonghas anyway, so what happens to it is up to him. Emily gave it to Donald, and that gift at least is documented.'

He turned the picture round, and she saw that a piece of card had been stuck on the back with words written in faded ink: *To Donald. Hang it in the farmhouse, yours now, in memory of our lost beloved ones, and to keep alive a childhood shared, and vanished times. From Emily, with love, 21 June 1945.*

She lifted glistening eyes to him. 'So she *did* mean this house to be his.' James nodded slowly, his eyes still on the painting. The hurricane lantern cast a diffused light, giving the painting a soft sheen, and in the flickering firelight the two figures seemed to come alive. 'Lost beloved ones…' he said softly.

'Those figures, they're almost spiritlike.' And Jasper Banks was right, the painting was extraordinary. *His best, I reckon.* So much was conveyed with a subtle wash and a few brushstrokes, a stillness, a moment held and cherished. They sat in silence, drawn into the painting, and then he went and set it on a chair.

She watched him as he built up the fire again, and the pungent smell of peat filled the room. Outside, the gale raged, hurling rain against the windows, but the old farmhouse felt solid and safe, and she dropped down to the hay sacks, hugging the sweater to her like an overlarge skin and looked across at the painting. The wind blew back down the chimney, causing the fire to glow, and he came and sat close, slipping an arm behind her, his face lit by the low flames. Then she remembered. 'Who's Agnes McNeil?' He pulled away in surprise. 'I thought you got on rather well.' He looked amused and gave her his slow smile. 'Ruairidh's wife? Her name's Agnes but everyone calls her Ùna, and you don't think she'd give up McNeil for Forbes, do you?' He pulled her close again. A mighty crack of thunder told them the storm was still circling overhead, and it was followed by a long low rumble which seemed to go on forever, echoing round the courtyard. He got to his feet. 'I'd better move the Land Rover into the barn, your car too. And I've got some old blankets in the back.'

He was gone a long time. He returned with them tucked under the oilskin and dropped them wordlessly onto the table and then stood looking across at her. 'I think you'd better come.' He reached for another oilskin, draped it round her, and steered her out into the courtyard.

There was a false, theatrical quality to the light as he led her up the ridge, and they could see waves breaking against the headland, sending spouts of spray high into the air, while above them the darkness still hung low and heavy. She followed him, buffeted by the wind, then stopped at the top of the ridge and looked ahead in disbelief. The western wall of Muirlan House had split, torn apart along the crack by the force of the elements and, in falling, it had brought down most of the remaining roof, leaving only one corner with part of the little turret standing tall and jagged reaching out of the rubble. And where once there had been a rich man's mansion, there was now a view beyond to the dunes in the west, to a line of brightness on the horizon, across a war-torn image, the aftermath of conflict.

Chapter 46

∽ 2010, Hetty ∽

They talked long into the night, freely now, without constraint, as if the destruction of Muirlan House had cleared away the last vestiges of discord between them, while outside the storm passed over, its violence spent.

'It's as if the house decided for itself,' she said. 'It didn't need me, after all.'

'No. It'd had enough.'

The hay bags took the coldness off the stone-flagged floor, and they sat resting against each other, sipping whisky, and she could feel her cheeks glowing in the firelight as she told him about her nomadic childhood, the paralysing shock of loss following the air crash, how Giles had helped her.

'And where does Giles figure in your future plans?' he asked softly.

She paused before replying, but there was only one answer. 'He doesn't. It's been clear for a while now, but I lacked the courage to break it off. But don't misjudge him, James, underneath the bluster he's a good man.'

'Of course.' He pulled her to him again, no longer tentative.

Later he told her of the school and hostel he was involved with in Kenya, for a charity begun by his father. It had been that which gave him inspiration for what he planned for the island. 'We're just there to help now, mostly fundraising, but they do the building, with youngsters learning the skills. There was some big funder interested, which was why I shot over there so suddenly.'

'And you would do something similar here?'

'If I could—'

'You can.'

And he bent to kiss her again, his eyes catching the firelight. 'Can I?' he said, asking a different question as his hand slipped under the sweater, exploring the warmth of her. Then he lifted it over her head and pressed her gently back onto the hay bags. She raised her hands to his head, returning his kisses, running her fingers through his hair, finding sand grains in its thickness, and was filled again with that dawning sense of rightness.

Later, he pulled the blankets over them, and eventually they slept, her form curled against his.

When she woke some hours later, stiff and cold, he was crouched in front of the range, reviving the fire. He swivelled on his heels and bid her good morning, smiled at her, then rose to open the shutters. She sat up, quickly slipping into her dress, pulling his sweater over it and stretching it down to cover her knees. 'Still blowing hard, but the rain has stopped,' he said, looking out. 'I'll make some coffee and then we'll go back over. See if my cottage is still standing.' He reached into his back pocket for matches and had just lit the primus when they heard a vehicle in the courtyard and a car door slam. He looked up and grinned across at her. 'The search party, I reckon,' he said as the door was flung open.

'Thank God.' Ruairidh stood in the doorway, tousled and unshaven.

'Close the door, you're blowing out the primus.'

His cousin came in, followed by his dog, and looked around the room, taking in the half-empty whisky bottle and dirty plates, his eyes lingering on the hay bags by the hearth. 'So I needn't have worried,' he said, as the dog settled in front of the fire and began scratching.

When James had not turned up, he explained, he'd phoned his cottage, then the hotel, and the bartender had told him what had happened, how Hetty had left the dining room, how Giles had come looking for her, and how James and Giles had quarrelled. 'Said you were both spoiling for a fight.'

'A *fight*? With Giles?'

'His idea, not mine.' James grinned at her astonished face, and Ruairidh looked from one to another.

'And then Giles mentioned that Hetty had a car—' Ruairidh paused and turned to his cousin. 'Tam says to tell you you've left nasty skid marks on his car park.' James laughed. 'The airport will reopen later this afternoon, the ferry's on its way back, and the tide's low enough to cross now. Back to the hotel,' he added blandly.

'Or you can skulk at my cottage,' said James.

Again Ruairidh looked speculatively from one to the other. 'Things are different this morning,' he remarked to James, and Hetty saw their eyes meet in understanding, but he gestured innocently towards the door. 'Muirlan House.'

'Very different,' James agreed. 'Let's take a look?'

~

There was a sweet rain-drenched smell as they walked up the ridge together. Every blade of grass, every cobweb and wisp of sheep's wool held droplets which sparkled in the low morning sun, shaking in the slackening breeze.

They stood together and looked across at the tumbled ruin. 'I'm sorry,' Ruairidh spoke softly beside her.

Hetty shook her head. 'I think I'm glad. The storm took matters into its own hands, which somehow makes it alright.'

They stood a moment longer, and returned to the kitchen. Then Ruairidh saw the painting propped against the chair in the corner. 'Good gracious. Where did *that* come from?'

'The cupboard under the stairs.' James went and fetched it into the light. 'Wrapped in an old potato sack. I was going to tell you—' Ruairidh gave him an incredulous look as James handed it to him. As he did, the card came off the back and fell to the floor. He bent to retrieve it. 'It's a note from Emily Blake to Donald Forbes.'

Ruairidh read it, glanced at Hetty, and then turned the

painting over. 'But it was stuck over something else,' he said, and read: '"*To the future, Beatrice, and all that it holds for us, Your loving husband, Theo. March 1910.*" Good God. Poor devils.'

James stared at it, and then went back to the sink and poured boiling water into three mugs. 'Was the package from Inverness, then?' he asked abruptly.

'It was.' Ruairidh pulled out a chair and sat.

'And?'

'It takes a bit of telling.' He hooked another chair out with his foot. 'So sit down.' James sat, his eyes fixed on his cousin's face, and Ruairidh looked back at him. 'There can be little doubt, James. Taking the DNA evidence and the bones, there can be only one answer.'

Chapter 47

≈ Midsummer Day 1911, Cameron ≈

Cameron Forbes walked along the path which linked the two houses. The light was fading, that slow creeping change of midsummer as the long, soft evening gave way to a fleeting night. He lifted his head, turning it slightly to feel the breeze on his face, and drank in its sweet familiarity. A day to live for, his mother would have said.

The clouds were piling high on the horizon, but the weather would hold for the bonfire. Good. Everyone had worked hard for the celebration, and they deserved their holiday. Once all was in readiness there, he had crossed back over the strand and waited until he saw from the window of his room that the trap bearing Blake and Beatrice was halfway across the sand. Then he had picked up his travelling bag and gone down into the empty kitchen, giving it a last fond farewell. He had gone up the track to Muirlan House, where he would leave his letter and cross back over the strand to the bonfire. See Beatrice, then go. Morning would find him on his way; he would catch a lift with one of the fishermen, cross on the early mail boat, then to the port of Glasgow and his passage to Halifax. Leaving all this behind.

For now.

He paused on the ridge between the two houses, dropping his hand instinctively to fondle Bess's ear. But she was with Donald on Bheinn Mhor, forging a new alliance, and the thought made him sad. It was so very hard to go, leaving Beatrice here, and he felt again the now familiar stab of pain and anxiety.

Leaving would be very different this time. From the back-woods of Ontario, the island had pulled him back here, tugging at a bond, reeling him back. But this time when he left, it might well be forever. If his plan worked and if Beatrice did find the courage to leave and join him, he knew he'd never come back. He could never sustain the necessary lies to his all-knowing father, nor look Blake in the face. And if Beatrice's courage failed, and she stayed, he couldn't come back to see her still bound to the man, faded and diminished; it would be more than he could bear.

He looked at the letter clutched in his hand and wondered again if it were better not written. There had been several drafts as he struggled with the dreadful hypocrisy of the task. But some form of farewell would be expected, and his father had more or less ordered him to try and make amends before he left. Not knowing what he asked.

He looked up at the walls of the great house in front of him, and it seemed that the house looked back, affronted by what he had done and appalled by what he was planning. Muirlan House and those hours spent beside Blake in the study had made it almost a home to him, and yet he had abused it.

He crossed the drive to the front door. He rarely used this entrance unless he was with Blake or Beatrice, but today it seemed important that he did. It lent a little dignity to the undignified act of slipping in to leave a letter of gratitude and peacemaking to a man he had wronged—and intended to wrong more grievously. A man who had supported and encouraged him, treated him for many years almost as a son. He shook his head, dispelling Beatrice's conviction that it had ever been more.

It was hard to justify his actions, even to himself. Conventional morality would be outraged, his father mortified. Both would damn him unconditionally. But there was another morality that he now believed in, a deeper judgement which would exonerate him, vindicate him for releasing Beatrice from a loveless marriage to a man who was incapable of love.

His footsteps crunched on the gravel of the drive. Blake had changed, and Cameron had watched it happen. Where once he

had been questioning, talented, and creative, he had turned in on himself to the point where he was capable only of grasping and holding, controlling and possessing on terms of his own devising. He had brought Beatrice here, then neglected her shamefully—and he had wanted to control Cameron. He looked down at the letter again, turning it in his hands. There was a time when, as a boy, he had worshipped Blake, grateful for the unexplained attention, the world he had opened up. But now...
To leave Beatrice with Blake would be as great a wrong as taking her from him. And it served no purpose. Blake would be no more content with her there beside him than with her gone, and Beatrice would droop and fade like the rusty brown buds on her yellow rose.

And besides, he thought savagely as he mounted the steps, she wanted him as much as he wanted her. The memory of her as she lay in his arms yesterday brought renewed conviction. From the beginning she had loved without reserve, her cool demeanour cast aside. This was the woman that Blake had rejected! And in so doing he had forfeited both her love and Cameron's remorse, and his own actions became justified by a code more sacred than cold convention. He clamped his jaw tight, opened the door, and entered the hall.

He was met by a great stillness. The stillness of an empty house, vacant of life. Only the longcase clock ticked on, indifferent to the passing hour, and he stood a moment in the hall, looking about him, watched warily by the stag and fox. This house was as familiar as his own, known intimately since childhood. He shook his head. There was no room for sentimentality; he would leave the letter and then go. Cross back over the strand to the bonfire. Then there would be time for only formal farewells, not the wrenching pain of parting yesterday, accompanied as it had been by the exchange of keepsakes and promises. A pain which was compounded by the ache of leaving his family and by the sharp stab of deceit. He crossed the hall to the study, pushed open the door... and froze.

Blake sat at his desk like a stone effigy, staring into the empty hearth. As Cameron halted at the doorway, he lifted his head and looked across at him.

Cameron looked back, thrown off balance, his mind racing. Blake. *Here?* So who had been beside Beatrice in the trap? Had Blake come back across? But why?

And only then did he see what lay between them on the desk, its head fallen to one side beside the basket with its blue-grey plunder.

He came slowly into the room, dropping his bag in front of the fireplace, and went to the desk, running a finger along the black-and-white feathered necklace of the dead bird, turning his wrist to feel the chill of the eggs on his skin. He lifted his eyes to connect with Blake's, and the air between them crackled, charged with something more complicated than anger and much more dangerous. Neither spoke, then Cameron turned abruptly to leave, his letter still in his pocket.

'These *trophies* are no surprise to you, of course.' Blake's words followed him. Cameron's head went up then, and he turned. Slowly. Wary now. What did he mean? Blake regarded him steadily, then gestured to the dead bird. 'Am I not to receive another lecture?' he asked, letting the silence deepen. 'No? Is it, perhaps, that you no longer have the moral high ground?' Cameron held his look, his heart hammering hard, saying nothing, as Blake's face grew darker, beads of sweat erupting on his brow, and the air tightened between them.

He knew. Dear God, he *knew!* Cameron's mind roared. Where was Beatrice? It had been her in the trap for certain, even though he had mistaken Blake. Fear jagged through him, and he turned to leave, knowing he must find her.

'If you go *anywhere* near my wife, I will break you both.' Blake's voice cut the space between them. 'You have my word on it.'

'Where is she?'

'Where do you think?' Blake raised his eyebrows and barked

a laugh. 'Do you imagine I had Calum dispose of her in the sea pool? Settling the matter in the traditional way? My dear Cameron!' Cameron looked back at him, thinking frantically but finding himself incapable of thought. Blake's face was rigid, implacable, but for Cameron there was only one solution, and it hit him hard and sure.

'Let her come away with me. We'll leave tonight.'

Blake's eyes widened in incredulity. 'My God, I believe you're serious.' Cameron clenched his fists by his sides, willing him to see the rightness of it. 'That was the plan, was it? You'd slip off together tonight?'

'I would have gone. Beatrice would have stayed.' He did not add *for now*, Beatrice might need that protection.

Blake sat a moment, digesting this, watching him, and again the silence lengthened. 'So this—this little *affair* was just for sport, was it, to pass the time before you left?'

Cameron kept a tight grip on himself. If it would spare Beatrice, let Blake believe it to be so. He looked away instead, and his eyes fell on the limp form of the bird, the female, judging by its size. As ever, Blake's shot was perfectly placed to do the least obvious damage and so preserve the specimen, and he felt again the stirring of anger. A stranger would not see the wounds on Beatrice either, nor see the emptiness inside. He lifted his head and looked again at Blake, knowing his position was indefensible. 'So what happens now?'

Theo continued to watch him. 'What happens now?' he echoed softly, then rose and walked over to the window, looking out to where the sun had disappeared behind the cloud bank, one hand gripping the other wrist behind his back. 'My God, if you only knew.' The words were hardly more than a murmur, and Cameron raised his head in enquiry, but Blake continued to stare out at the darkening water before abruptly turning back. 'Adultery is a *crime* in the eyes of the law. Did you know that?' He leant across the desk to confront him, his eyes now hot with fury. 'More serious than shooting some wretched bird, I think.'

Cameron watched him, unflinching, and Blake sucked in his breath. 'I could make things very unpleasant, you know—for both of you.' Then he slumped back into his seat behind the desk, his face drained and haggard, his anger spent for the moment, and he looked aside, as if weary with the matter. 'I think you should leave, Cameron. Go now, before I find the thought of seeing you both shamed too tempting to resist.'

But Cameron could not leave, not now. 'Beatrice—'

'Beatrice is nothing to you.'

Wrong! She was everything. Sunlight across the strand. The breeze rippling over the marram grasses. The sweet heart of a yellow rose. How could he possibly make him understand?

Anger had suffused Blake's face again. 'It is as you said. Beatrice stays. You go.'

'That was before tonight. I can't leave her here with you now.'

'You have no choice.'

No choice? At the quiet words, Cameron felt the net tighten and braced himself against it. 'No, but *she* has.' Blake's head snapped up again, but Cameron had nothing left to lose. 'Do you imagine she will stay with you?'

'*Go.*' There was a deeper anger in Blake's voice now—and something else.

'How can I?' Cameron looked down for a moment at the dead bird and the eggs. 'How long is it you've searched for a diver's nest? Twenty years? More? And the very day you find it, you destroy it.' He took up one of the eggs between his thumb and forefinger. 'And now you'll blow these clear of life, to *preserve* them, and add to your collection.' He clamped his jaw tight. 'But you won't do that to Beatrice. She loves me, and so she leaves with me.'

Blake stood slowly and straightened, staring back at Cameron with a new intensity. He was silent for a long moment, then looked down at the dead bird and began to shake his head slowly from side to side. 'I don't think she'll go with you, Cameron,' he said.

'She will.'

Blake's expression held a new, strange intent. 'No. Not when she learns the unpalatable truth.' He made a sound somewhere between a sigh and a groan. 'For so many years I've wanted to tell you, since you were a child. But not like this, Cameron. Not in anger.' Cameron stood still, distracted. What the devil made him look so strange? 'But you see, I think she'll find she can't. It'll be too much for her, learning that she's been bedding her husband's son.' The room held its breath, as the long-held secret was exposed at last, every beady eye focussed on Cameron, awaiting his reaction. 'Incest, of a sort, I suppose. On top of adultery? I think not.'

Cameron stared back at him, his guts absorbing the kick.

'You don't believe me?' Blake raised his brows. 'Ask the man you call Father. Or look in the mirror—'

'No.'

'Ask him how soon after his wedding you were born. *Ask him*, Cameron. Because only a few weeks before, I had lain with your mother and she said she loved me.'

'No!'

'Ask him.'

Cameron's world spun as he stared back at Blake. *I believe it is you he wants, not me*, Beatrice had said. And Blake's fevered *God bless* as he slipped into oblivion the night he had struck her. And as the orbit of Cameron's world spun out of control, other incidents crowded into his mind, pieces fell into place. And made sense.

Blake was speaking again. 'Once she knows that, you see, she'll not go with you.'

The words brought Cameron back to the moment. Beatrice. He must focus on Beatrice. The rest could wait. His eyes locked onto Blake's, and he felt suddenly calm. 'Oh, I think she will, sir. Because I will tell her that if you could leave my mother shamed and in trouble, Beatrice can leave you.'

Blake shook his head from side to side again like an injured beast. 'I didn't leave Màili. I wanted to wed her! I never knew about you; it was years later that I guessed, when I first saw myself in you. And could never claim you—'

But Cameron wasn't listening. 'So *she* left you? And why was that, do you think?' He felt the blood roaring in his head. 'Because she loved my father, perhaps? My *father*, Mr. Blake. Not the laird's son who could take what he pleased and then throw it aside. Possess or destroy'—he gestured to the dead bird—'was it all you could *ever* do?' An almost animal sound came from Blake as he staggered round the edge of the desk, but Cameron had not finished. 'I love Beatrice. *Love* her, in a way I don't think you can begin to imagine. Whatever you tell her, I'll not leave her here with your cold heart for company. She comes with me tonight.'

As he turned to go, Blake moved swiftly. Cameron heard him and swung back, looking into his wild eyes as the older man went for him, and he stepped quickly back to absorb the lunge. Stepped back and stumbled against the bag he had dropped behind him, and as he fell, arms flailing, his hand caught the basket which held the diver's eggs. When they hit the ground, the shells broke apart, revealing two fully formed but lifeless chicks whose eyes would remain closed and whose beaks would never give the wild haunting call which some say is the foretelling of death.

And as Cameron went down, with all Blake's weight and momentum on top of him, the side of his head smashed hard against the corner of the granite hearthstone, and then he too lay still and quiet in the empty house.

Chapter 48

'Cameron?'

The name hung there, stark and exposed.

'But he went to Canada.' Hetty looked from one to the other. 'You said there were letters.'

Ruairidh tore his eyes from James's rigid face. 'Forgeries, it seems.' James looked up sharply. 'I sent them to forensics as well, together with letters from Cameron's earlier trip to Canada. Two different hands, they said, the later ones consciously imitating the others.'

James sat forward, his eyes not leaving Ruairidh's face. 'It was Blake. It had to be.' His cousin nodded, and James got up and went over to the window, his hands thrust deep into his pockets, and stood there a few moments before turning back to them. 'And the locket—'

'BJS—Beatrice Jane Somersgill. It's on the Blakes' marriage certificate.'

'So. The timeless motive—'

'Jane?' said Hetty sharply, glancing at James.

But he was shaking his head and had not heard her. 'And because of the building works, Blake had the opportunity to get rid of the body. It was his house, and then he had a network of contacts to get the letters sent back, and'—he gave a harsh laugh—'and he got away with it!'

Cameron Forbes. That defiant, handsome young man in the photographs. And Beatrice. Hetty watched James's tense figure by the window. What had become of her? She turned back to Ruairidh. 'And no one in your family suspected?'

Ruairidh shook his head, still watching his cousin. 'Far

from it.' James caught his tone and looked back at him. 'You see, there's something else.' Ruairidh reached into his pocket. 'Last night when I asked Alasdair to put the letters back in Granddad's old biscuit tin where he keeps them, he pulled out the old newspaper in the bottom. Something about U-boats up here, contemporary stuff, 1944, which he's doing at school. And underneath it he found these.' He held up two envelopes.

'You're joking. From Cameron as well?'

'No. *To* Cameron. Unopened.'

'Good God.'

Ruairidh placed them on the table. 'From two different people, different handwriting on each.' He pushed them towards James. 'They'd been left for Cameron when he came back, and it seems to me they're yours now.'

James sat looking at the two letters. Then he picked up the nearer and opened it. It was only a couple of sheets, and he read them quickly, his face giving nothing away, then he handed it to Hetty, his voice very quiet. 'From Beatrice. Read it out loud for her.'

The handwriting was faint and spindly, difficult to read in places.

'My darling Cameron,

'It seems that the fates were against us and it was not in the great scheme of things that I should be with you. This illness I suffer would have come upon me whether I was with you or with Theo, whether I was happy or discontented. Perhaps it's divine justice, but I cannot believe that loving you was wrong.' Here the pen seemed to splutter and the ink had run, watery. *'The times spent with you were the defining moments of my life, my true salvation, and I would do the same again. My only regret is the pain we must have caused Theo. Between us we used him badly. I had intended to be a better wife, and I do believe that he loved you too.*

'I also regret the shame we caused your father. He has been my rock and my unfailing comfort these last weeks. His faith that you will return has given me courage, and his many kindnesses have been

the solace of these last weeks. I love him dearly for your sake and for myself. I leave our son with him until you come back, as I believe you will. Had I known I was carrying him, I would have left with you, I promise you, my love. But I didn't know, and when I did, I left Theo to keep Johnnie safe, changed my name to hide from him, and waited for you, unaware then that my own time was running out. When I knew, I turned to your father for help—there was no one else—and he did not fail us. I was so fearful that you would come back and find me gone, and never know you had a son.

'I love to think of Johnnie growing up where you grew yourself, in a place which I came to love so well. And I have no fear of death, Cameron. Your father has promised he will care for me until the end and then take Johnnie home with him. From this I draw my courage. He is everything I grew to love on the island and very dear to me.

'Kiss our boy for me.

'God keep you both, my love

'Beatrice'

Hetty set the letter down, and there was silence in the room. After a moment, James reached for the second letter and opened it. It was much longer, and he flipped to the last page. "'*Your loving father, John Forbes.*" Thought so.' He went back to the beginning, but after the first few paragraphs he grew very still and turned away from them, reading on fixedly. Then he sat with the letter loose in his hand, staring out of the window, and passed it to his cousin. 'Your kin, Ruairidh, not mine.'

Ruairidh took it, giving him a puzzled look, and skimmed the contents, stalled a moment, glancing up at James, read more carefully, and then passed it to Hetty.

It was a long letter, a letter written by a man to whom unburdening himself had not come easily, but its central message leapt out at her. '*She was very young, you see, and had followed a fancy that she was in love with him, but the strength of his passion overwhelmed her, frightened her. When she found she was in trouble, she came to me, asking for help and for my protection, and I would never have denied Màili anything. I would have agreed to any terms,*

Cameron, any price, and I saw you as a sacred trust. You are as much my son as ever Donald was, and every bit as dear to me.'

She looked sharply at James, but he was staring out of the window and did not turn his head. Ruairidh met her eyes and nodded in understanding. She read on. *'Cameron, I had loved your mother since she was a child and I was in terrible dread that I would lose her. And years later, when she was taken, you were my strength and comfort, for you are the image of her.'* Such weighty words, and Hetty thought of the bearded giant who had stood between his two sons, knowing that only one was truly his… *'I will tell Theo Blake, though I fancy that he knows, and I will tell him that Johnnie is your son, and who his mother is. I cannot rest until I do. I know that you loved Beatrice Blake, even though you ought not to have done, but I do not judge you, my son. I had forgotten what it was to love like that.*

'I know too that she has left you a letter, written years ago when her time was close, and kept safe. Believe me, after she came to me with pains growing inside her, I searched for you, sent letters to the places you stayed before, contacted everyone I could. I pray to God the trenches did not claim you. Donald knows nothing of this, other than that Johnnie is your son, and that the boy's mother is dead. Deal with that as you think best.

'I did what I could for them both, Cameron. For your sake, to set it in the balance against other things. I arranged for her to be nursed on Skye and went over every week so that the boy got used to me. And then I brought her body back here, passing her off as kin, and she lies in an unmarked grave beside Màili because they both loved you. I never told her the truth about you, though, as she had enough to bear. I grew very fond of her, and it pains me that her husband could not see what a jewel he had in his hand, hankering still for what we both had lost.

'And now he is sick in mind and body too, hunted and haunted. You must square things with him as best you can. He was ever a difficult man, but I sometimes feel that I have robbed him of Màili, who he once loved, of his son, and even of his grandson, and I had the

burying of his wife. And I pity him, Cameron, but I cannot change these things now. All my life I have wrestled with my conscience, but I had given Màili my word.'

She read his touching final words and looked across to James, still staring out of the window. Ruairidh took the letters, replaced them in their envelopes, and sat back, watching his cousin. 'Alright, Jamie?'

James nodded. 'Just give me a minute.' He squeezed Hetty's shoulder as he went past her, out into the courtyard, and as the door closed behind him, Ruairidh smiled reassuringly at her.

'He'll be fine, it's a lot to take in. But it explains the DNA tangle.' Briefly, he told her what the report had said. 'The results showed a connection between the bones and all three of us, but for different reasons. Some links were common to both you and James, going back to Theo Blake's father, while others were common to James and me, from Màili Cameron. But the hair in the locket only related to James—it must be Beatrice's, you see.'

'She'd given him her locket?'

'Aye.'

She stared at him, following the threads in her mind, and they sat in silence, listening to the muffled sounds of the wind still gusting through the courtyard, then Ruairidh turned to look at the painting again. 'There's a sadness to it,' he said, and bent closer to read the date. 'The year Màili Forbes died, 1897.' He paused. 'Perhaps it is a sort of farewell.'

'And yet he gave it to his wife—'

Ruairidh shook his head and went over to the window. 'I'll go and see if he's alright.' He took a step towards the door, then stopped. 'No, you go.'

James was standing on the ridge between the two houses, looking across at the remains of Muirlan House, his jacket blown open by the wind, his hair across his face. Ruairidh's dog had followed her from the kitchen and went up to him now, snuffling at his boots. Hetty saw him look down briefly, then drop his hand to fondle her ears.

At last he turned and saw her waiting at the bottom of the ridge, uncertain, and he came down to her, drawing her close and holding her. They went back into the kitchen, where he pulled out a chair and sat, looking across at Ruairidh, his face vulnerable, as she had once seen it before. 'The one person who comes out of all this well is old John Forbes, gathering up the fallout from Theo Blake's passions—first Màili and Cameron, and then Beatrice and Johnnie.' He gave his cousin a twisted smile. 'And his descendants have kept up the tradition through the generations.' He reached for the whisky bottle and slopped some into his mug. 'You've done rather better than me in your choice of forebears.' He took a drink and turned sharply to Hetty, his eyes glinting. 'And this makes us cousins of a sort, though not close, thank God. And our bloodline, by contrast, is one of seducers, adulterers, murderers, and fraudsters.'

His face was strained, and she reached out, laying her hand on his sleeve. 'But it's that of lovers too.' He returned her a look, which brought back the warmth of the night.

Ruairidh looked from one to the other. 'Why fraudsters?' he asked, to fill the silence.

'Those letters from Canada. Cold-blooded forgeries.'

'I suppose they were. But by then Blake had to see it through. He must have known the noose was hanging over him.'

James took another drink, more slowly this time. 'And yet I imagine he suffered more living on.'

'The day Blake drowned—' Ruairidh began, then stopped, glancing towards Hetty.

'I told her.'

Ruairidh nodded approval. 'Aonghas had just come back on leave. Remember? Bringing news—'

James caught his thought. '—that Johnnie was dead. Yes! And by then John Forbes would have told Blake about Cameron, and he would have known that Johnnie was *his* grandson and his last link with Cameron and with Màili.'

'And with Beatrice.'

'Christ, the poor bastard,' said James. 'The tidal race across the strand must have been a release from hell.'

Epilogue

Between Beatrice's unmarked grave and the grave of Theodore Blake, there had been a space in the family burial ground, and it was there that they buried Cameron, with his father on one side and Beatrice on the other. Beyond Beatrice lay Màili Cameron Forbes.

'What a mess they made of it all,' James said, standing back to look at the graves. 'A right old tangle.' He and Ruairidh had made a coffin from timbers salvaged from Muirlan House, and the minister had carried out a short ceremony when the bones were buried, together with the lock of hair and the decaying feather James had placed in the empty locket around Hetty's neck. The two men had carried the coffin between them. It weighed little, and James had insisted that the burial be done as soon as the bones were released, to draw a line under the tragedy. Then, he said, building works could start on the factor's house and they would be free to plan for the future.

There was a slight haze and barely the whisper of a breeze as Hetty and James crossed back over Muirlan Strand to James's cottage that evening. The low sun shafted briefly through the clouds, flooding the drained sand with light, turning the pools left by the retreating tide to quicksilver, and their two figures, walking close, hand in hand, became silhouettes etched sharply against the sand.

Acknowledgements

Thanks are due to many people for their support in writing this book.

Firstly I am very grateful to Adrian Searle and all at Freight Books for their belief in the book from the outset and for their continuing commitment to it. I am also indebted to my wonderful agent, Jenny Brown (Jenny Brown Associates), for all her hard work and guidance throughout the book's development, and to Fiona Brownlee (Brownlee Donald Associates) for her enthusiastic support. Jhanteigh Kupihea (Atria/Simon & Schuster) helped me to develop the book and publish in North America.

Early help was given by the writer Kathy Page who sent invaluable and heartening comments on initial drafts from the Pacific west coast of Canada, and author Pamela Hartshorne has been unfailingly supportive and generous with her time as the story developed. Rosemary Ward at The Gaelic Books Council kindly provided the Gaelic phrases and encouragement.

The House Between Tides is a work of fiction, inspired by the beauty, and the history, of the Western Isles. Part of my family's lineage reaches back to Skye and perhaps that, and annual holidays first as a child and then with my own children, helped formed a lasting bond with that very special part of the world. I owe my love of wild places to my father and my love of books to my mother, for which I will always be grateful. The book is dedicated to Richard, my rock, and to A and G, and to memories of glorious times in the Hebrides.

About the author

Sarah Maine was born in England but grew up partly in Canada before returning to the United Kingdom, where she now lives. *The House Between Tides* is her first novel.